THE ROSE GRAVE

THOMAS FINCHAM

The Rose Grave
Thomas Fincham

AUTHOR'S NOTE
This book is a work of fiction. Names, characters, places and incidents are products of the author's imagination or are used fictitiously. Any resemblance to actual events or locales or persons, living or dead, is entirely coincidental.

Visit the author's website:
www.finchambooks.com

Contact:
finchambooks@gmail.com

Join my Facebook page:
https://www.facebook.com/finchambooks/

ECHO ROSE SERIES

1) The Rose Garden
2) The Rose Tattoo
3) The Rose Thorn
4) The Rose Water
5) The Rose Grave

PROLOGUE

Two Years Ago

Suzanne Hyland, days away from turning sixty, was glad to be leaving her fifties.

Her fifth decade was brutal, and perhaps resignedly, she figured things were only going to get worse. After the events that followed, nobody would ever call her pessimism unwarranted. Suzanne was tall for her generation and still thin. Wearing her hair short for the last decade, she'd resorted to a little coloring, but she left it a conservative silvery gray. Mrs. Hyland, mother of three, the *former* wife of a well-respected surgeon, felt she'd earned it.

She'd agreed to allow her three children, professionals with busy lives, to throw her a "surprise" birthday celebration the following week because she rarely saw them once they'd gone off to live their own lives. Knowing their mother hated surprises, her eldest, Mark, proposed they keep her knowledge of the party from invited guests, friends, extended family, and a few enemies that they didn't want to offend. That way, she'd be privy to their plans. And nobody had to know the enthusiasm was fake.

She'd act shocked and appreciative when she walked into the home of her middle child, Lisa, and some aunt or cousin flipped on the light switch. Everyone would yell, "Surprise!" and the smiles and pretending would begin. It was a good plan. However, that was later. Right now, she had something else on her to-do list.

Bernard Hyland, Suzanne's ex-husband, lived on Elm Drive in a six-bedroom Mediterranean-style home. Last summer, after thirty-five years of marriage, Bernard delivered the biggest shock of Suzanne's life: he demanded a divorce. The accomplished surgeon was going to marry a twenty-eight-year-old woman. He'd met her at Bransonite Electronics, a robotic firm that bought an algorithmic surgical program he'd developed.

The two-faced liar!

Suzanne hated visiting Bernard. He'd screwed her out of her share of the fourteen-million-dollar sale to Bransonite by using a series of off-shoring banking tricks. Worse than anything, he was going to change his will.

She'd get nothing.

The kids would get nothing.

Life wasn't fair.

The only reason she'd driven out to his home was that her youngest child, Danny, had insisted that she bring one of the old family picture albums that his father had kept after the divorce. The album had pictures of all the kids and even a few black and whites of their grandparents. And that was why, against her better judgment, she was parking her Honda Accord next to Bernard's bright yellow F-Type Jaguar, on a Tuesday afternoon.

"Hey!" she snapped after closing the Honda's door and seeing Missy and Tulip panting under a bush. "Whatcha doing outside? Come!"

Her ex-husband's mistresses' pair of Shih Tzu purebreds didn't listen.

"You're spoiled rotten, like my children."

After chasing them down—they'd been running free in the street—she said, "You have a bad mommy." The soon-to-be-new-wife was as high maintenance as adulteresses come, and Suzanne hated her with every ounce of her being. But she could never hate a dog, even if its human was evil, conniving, and far too young for her ex. *What does she think? She's going to become a mother to my kids?*

"Come on, girls," she said, pushing open the side gate. The two dogs obediently followed as she walked up the side of the main house towards the backyard, no doubt expecting a treat.

"Backyard" wasn't the best noun to describe Bernard's remodeling efforts. It was more like a five-star resort on an exotic island. He'd built a massive pool along with a guest house, a tennis court, and an outdoor kitchen with stainless steel appliances–enough to fill a commercial kitchen at a medium-sized diner. Suzanne frowned, searching for doggie treats. She knew there must be some beef sticks or pork chews in one of the many kitchen drawers. She became peeved and felt a malicious bitterness forming, so she quit looking after another minute of frustration.

The dogs walked across the Turkish travertine that surrounded the turquoise water. The stone, cut into intricate patterns and intermixed with red, green, and gray marble, shouted pretentiousness. At the far edge of the pool, they halted and barked in unison. They acted like an intruder was breaching the ten-foot-tall security fence that bordered the rear of the grounds and the pines on the neighboring hilltop.

"Stop that!"

The dogs didn't obey.

No surprise. Their owner, Jenny, lived a more spoiled life than her kids. Suzanne took great pleasure in knowing that her ex would become tired of her, and after the thrill vanished like a mist, he'd repeat the cycle.

Some men…

Jenny was a master at scheduling trips to the spa, the mall, shoe stores, jewelry boutiques, and car dealerships. She had a personal trainer, a dietician, a masseuse, and even a local celebrity chef who cooked for Bernard and her once a week. Decadent, frivolous, and disgusting. The Shih Tzu puppies? They'd cost seven grand each. Suzanne's kids complained specifically to their mother regarding that expense, not the second Mercedes Bernard had bought Jenny—she needed a proper sedan for the city and an SUV for the country, apparently. No, the children couldn't forget that their father had denied them a puppy year after year until they gave up asking. The boys sent text messages castigating their father for his purchase of the pets, but Lisa called her mother late on a Wednesday night and screeched for an hour about her father's terrible life choices and how much she hated her soon-to-be stepmother, a title she swore she'd never give that greedy gold-digging cheater.

The dogs continued to bark.

Suzanne walked towards the pool and gasped. Her ex-husband floated face down at the opposite end of the pool, a golden-veined sculptured marble cherub sprinkling him.

With a dissipating cloud of blood surrounding him, she knew Bernard, still clothed, was a corpse.

The suit was Brioni Vanquish II.

Over forty grand.

For a suit.

Made of exotic and rare wool blends. It was undoubtedly ruined.

Suzanne was aware of its cost because Lisa, mad about her student loans, car payment, and mortgage, had shown her mother a picture of Bernard dressed up and about to go to the opera. She'd repeated the price tag to her mother and then cried. The Amedeo Testoni shoes he wore, also ruined, ran over a thousand dollars. These she'd bought back when she believed they might reconcile.

He's got no taste.

She punched 9-1-1 into her cell.

No taste at all.

ONE

Present Day

He walked past an ornate mailbox adorned with Chinese characters along a path bordered by gardenias trimmed perfectly square and straight.

The moment he thought about how pleasant the weather had been, he felt a drop of rain on his face. *Why?* he thought. *Why couldn't it be sunny for once when there's a murder?*

Detective Lew "Skip" Malloy stood out in the neighborhood, not only because he was black, tall, and had the medium build of a wide receiver, but also because the Fairview neighborhood he was in was predominately Chinese and all wealthy.

Trees flanked the residence on both sides and at the rear. They gave the home privacy, but Skip imagined they also allowed the residents to forget they lived on the edge of a bustling city. The houses here had manicured yards, Asian statuary, and more Mercedes than a well-stocked dealership.

Skip loosened his tie and checked his phone for the time. He heard a car door slam and looked back over his shoulder.

Detective Ralph "Bud" Smith, his partner, approached him at a brisk walk.

"We better get inside," he said. "It's about to pour."

Bud adjusted his raincoat over his portly frame and slapped Skip on the back. He had thinning blond hair that he'd tried, unsuccessfully, to give a modern style. His goatee didn't quite fit his round face.

"Why are you wearing a sports coat?" Bud asked. "Haven't you heard of this new thing they call a weather report?"

"Yeah, haven't you heard about this invention called exercise?" Skip asked.

"Funny man," Bud replied. "Let's head up?"

Skip nodded and resumed his walk towards the crime scene.

The front door was tall, wide, and painted a deep red. In Chinese culture, the color red symbolized good fortune and health. A red door protected a home from evil. It was the mouth of the residence, creating–in the belief of some—a welcoming energy. Skip didn't get that sense as he entered the foyer.

"Hey guys. Welcome back, Skip."

Chuck Wainwright was a massive two-hundred and ninety pounds and stood a good six-six in his socks. Muscles threatened to burst out of his uniform. He was an all-star linebacker once, back in his university days, but a shoulder injury had sidelined him, and he left football in his past.

These days he proudly wore a different uniform: Fairview PD.

"How's the shoulder?" he asked.

Skip rubbed the scar on his right shoulder. It was a daily reminder of his near escape from the brutal attack he'd received from the serial killer, Gary Summerhill. He shook his head. "I have good days and bad days. It's worse when the weather's like this."

"If you're surrounded by friends, family, and good vibes," Chuck said, "it's always a good day."

"Still dating the spiritual yoga guide, I see," Skip observed.

"Yoga makes you flexible and relaxed. It allows inner peace."

"Yeah, yeah, *namaste,*" Skip said. "*Allons, cher*, we've got work to do."

"The Cajuns made you multilingual?" Bud laughed and put his hand on Chuck's tree-branch-sized arm. "Do you even know what he said?"

"*Namaste* is a traditional and respectful greeting," Chuck answered. "It's common at the hot yoga place I go to. I don't know about the other stuff. I played linebacker in college, not trivia nerd."

"*Allons, cher* means 'let's go, dear'." Skip pointed toward the crime scene. "We've got work."

"Yes, master," Bud said with a grin.

Skip rubbed his injury again and frowned. Vivian, his wife, and their station sergeant had insisted he take a vacation after the chief resident had released him from the hospital. Summerhill's booby trap had inflicted serious damage. Skip knew he was lucky to be alive. As soon as he could safely travel, they'd gone, along with their twins, to Vivian's sister's place in Louisiana. Skip drank beer, ate a boatload of Cajun food and Southern barbecue, and thought hourly about how much he wanted to get back to work. He loved chasing down bad guys.

The twins, Lew Jr. and Lucy, had been excited at first, but after a few days, the lack of data service for their cell phones made them bored and restless. They bickered and pouted. They missed their friends and routines. Skip wanted them to find things to do in nature, but they were used to living in the city, and they looked at the bayou as if it was a dangerous alien planet.

During Skip's absence, Bud had sent a selfie from Fairview with a background showing sunny skies. No big cases had landed on his desk during his partner's absence. It was as if the criminals had decided it was a suitable time for them to take a needed break as well. Now, Skip was back home and on the job.

Past the foyer was a sitting room with windows that faced the front, towards the street. The view was spectacular because the residence sat on the apex of a hilly section of the neighborhood and was high enough up that the city was visible over the neighbor's roof.

On a couch, with her face in her hands, a young Chinese woman sat crying. Two uniformed officers flanked her.

"That's the daughter," Chuck said. "May Lau. She just turned eighteen yesterday."

"Only child?" Skip asked.

"Yeah, she's it."

"All right," Skip said. "Keep your eyes on her. The last thing we need is for her to contaminate our crime scene. Keep her in that room. Shout if she objects to anything other than sitting tight."

"You got it, boss," Chuck said.

"You'd better take us to the body," Bud said to Chuck.

"This way." Chuck pointed down a hall floored with polished exotic hardwood. Beautiful works of Asian art hung on the walls. Horses. Dragons. Forests. "And it's *bodies*, sadly, a Mr. and Mrs. Lau," Chuck explained.

TWO

She stood alone, staring at two plain gray headstones.

Her lips, often covered in black or purple lipstick, were plain. A week ago, she'd added three minimal streaks of dark red to her hair. Subtle and tasteful. Deep violet polish covered her nails, and after she glanced at them, she curled her fingers into fists.

Then she relaxed and wiped a single tear from her cheek.

She'd cried so many times already. There was little left to give. She placed her finger on her nose and rubbed the spot where she used to wear a nose ring. Phantom itchiness.

Her full legal name was Grace Kelly Sanderson. Everyone except her closest friends and family knew her as Echo Rose. She was lithe and athletic. Strong. Capable. But today, observing the gravesite of her birth parents, she felt empty and weak.

The first time she'd visited was the worst. Conner, her boyfriend, had accompanied her. Afterward, he'd told her that her emotion shocked him. He didn't realize there was so much pain bottled up inside her. Echo had said, "I'm glad you came. I need a friend with me to face this."

Today, she wanted to be by herself.

It was her sixth visit. The pull to come and reflect on what life would have been like under different circumstances had her parents not died when she was a baby remained strong. She knew it wasn't practical or healthy to visit the graveyard daily, or even weekly or monthly. She had to heal. But, for now, she consoled herself by coming.

The first marker read: "John Weston, loving husband." Other than the two inscribed dates—he'd been twenty-eight—there was nothing else.

On the second marker, there was a chiseled rose next to the words "loving wife." Glancing at the name "Clara Weston", Echo pondered the dates of birth and death. She did the math. "Twenty-four," she said. "I wish I'd known you." She sniffled and held back further tears.

Echo's mother, her adoptive one, had broken down one night. She'd been drinking wine, and it led to a confession. Didi, her mother, had suffered a terrible depression after a miscarriage. She and Echo's father, Edward, had adopted a baby girl whose parents had died in a car accident.

The revelation left Echo bewildered and confused.

She went hunting for her birth parent's identities. Her search was like trying to decode a top-secret cipher. She convinced—practically coerced—a private detective named Lee Callaway into helping her. Then she met Officer Figus. He was the one that had pulled her out of the wreck that took her parents away from her forever.

Callaway and others had warned her that taking this path might be painful. But she'd risk that for the truth. Echo's instincts were a significant part of why she was a skilled investigative journalist.

Her gut told her that something was hidden under the surface in this case.

She was going to discover what it was.

THREE

Bud and Skip walked down the hallway, Chuck leading the way towards the bodies. Bud felt good being back on the job with Skip. It didn't mean he was happy about a murder—a double murder in this case—but it felt good to be productive.

"I'll be back at my post," Chuck said. "It's good to see you guys back in business together. Bud was getting depressed by your absence."

"Noted," Skip said. "He's like a brokenhearted teenager."

"More like a spurned woman, I think."

Bud looked over his shoulder. "Everyone's a comedian."

"Some of us *are* funny," Skip said.

"Yeah, haha. I'm already thinking of booking another trip for you."

The Lau residence was even more opulent as they got deeper inside. They passed a formal banquet room with ceilings that had to be sixteen feet tall, a Bechstein grand piano, two massive stone statues, and a dozen smaller ones, both in stone and bronze. More Asian art adorned the walls. Bud wasn't sure, but he thought it was Chinese art, not Japanese or Korean. He made a mental note to follow up with an expert in the field.

In case it was relevant.

Many things at a crime scene weren't important, but until detectives began digging, the differences between important and unimportant weren't always obvious.

"The living room," Skip said. "The first body is there."

Bud smelled the murder before he saw the body of Lee Sum. The scents of death mixed and triggered his adrenaline. It was the most alert he'd been in weeks. He assessed the first location with an eye towards the big picture first. He'd start looking at the little details afterward.

There weren't any obvious signs of a break-in or struggle. The Lau's weren't young, so it would have been easy for an assailant to overpower them. Lee Sum Lau was the husband. He looked about a hundred pounds.

He lay face down. Apparently, he'd been dragged through a short hallway. Blood led to a door that opened to the basement stairs. The steps were wood, painted white, and blood splatter created eerie designs and splotches. Ming Lau's body was in a seated position on the landing.

"Hey, Skip," someone said from the main hallway. "You back from the South?"

The medical examiner and the forensic team had arrived.

"Yeah," he answered. "It is I. Back from voodoo and magic."

"Give us a second here, guys," Bud said. He didn't want his first impressions marred by stories of Skip's trip. "I need to walk around a bit before you guys set up." The sound of equipment being dropped echoed. Someone shouted, "Ten-four!"

Another voice rang out. "I'm going for a cigarette break."

"It's not the spouse or partner this time," Skip said.

"Not unless it's a murder-suicide, but it doesn't seem that way." Bud got down on his haunches and inspected the floor next to Ming's right side. There appeared to be an Asian character written in blood, presumably, Chinese. Written hastily, but it was clearly not random.

Skip took a few more steps down towards the landing. "You read Chinese?" he asked.

"Yes," Bud answered. "Of course, that and Russian, Italian, Japanese—"

"Okay, point taken." Detectives and crime scene techs relied on humor to help relieve the stress that accompanied the job. Seeing the worst of humanity took its toll. "I took two years of Spanish in high school. Does that help?"

"Not really." Bud knew the crime scene techs would take photos. Eventually, someone would interpret the symbol, but maybe it was one of those time-sensitive clues? He opened his phone to see if an image search or a translation program would recognize the mark, but it was too messy and unclear. The symbol would need a human with linguistic skills to interpret. He took a photo and put his phone away.

"She's been tortured," Skip said.

There were three broken fingers on her left hand. Someone had snapped them backward. Bruises and cuts covered her face. Bunched above her knees was a red silk gown, and both her knees were crushed. Something heavy was used to shatter her patella.

"This is ugly," Bud said.

"What kind of monster would do this to a couple of old people?"

"The world has all kinds."

"Sad, but true."

They went back to the husband. It was obvious an intruder had tortured him before death. Like his wife, all of his fingers were broken. His nose was crushed. Knees obliterated.

Bud looked closer. He noticed a pattern of blood on the top of Lee Sum's head. "Look at this." He used a pencil and moved a patch of hair away from an entrance wound.

"A small caliber."

"Done like an execution, but not in the back of the head."

"Straight down. Probably a twenty-two."

"A tall assailant, maybe standing face-to-face?"

"Could be," Skip said. "They must have interrogated him."

Bud nodded. "You ready to let the team in?"

"Yup, let's check out the rest of the property."

"Start in the basement?"

"As good a place as any," Skip replied. He shouted down the hallway to the medical examiner and the tech team, letting them know they could begin processing the bodies. They'd get a report confirming the cause of death and outlining the rest of the injuries in due time. For now, they'd move to the next step:

Searching the residence for clues.

Regardless of how clever criminals acted, they'd always leave something behind, and they'd always pick up something from the scene. *Transfer Evidence.* It was simple physics and sometimes a bit of luck.

FOUR

Skip walked past Ming Lau's body with caution. He scanned the steps as he moved, looking for additional writing or other clues left in blood. Shoe prints, handprints, or even blood from the assailant or assailants were possible. That was often the case when a victim fought back.

The Lau's were elderly. They appeared to have been in good health, but their stature would have prevented them from fighting even an average-sized person. If there had been a group of intruders, even two, they wouldn't have stood a chance.

The ME would bag their hands on-site and check for evidence under their nails once back at the county morgue. It was easier to be precise in the lab, but work in the field was crucial. It could make or break a case.

In the basement was a game room. There were several La-Z-Boy recliners and a red leather sofa facing a white screen. Between them, an ornate gold-leafed wooden table held a projector. It was a striking juxtaposition between modern and vintage. Past the in-home theater was a ping-pong table, and to the left of it, a bar. A neon sign for Tsingtao beer glowed behind it.

On the opposite side of the room, a door splashed with blood stood ajar.

It led to an office.

"Well, well," Skip said. "A clue."

There was a combination safe inset into the wall. They had hidden it behind a brightly colored abstract art piece which was trashed and lying on the floor. There was a slight outline of dust showing where the painting had hung before being ripped off the wall. A picture hanging hook was still in place but bent.

"This explains the torture." Bud wiped the sweat from his forehead. "It's hot in here."

"It doesn't look like this room got much use. Look how dusty and messy it is compared to the rest of the house," Skip said. He approached the safe and peered inside with a penlight. "Empty."

There were papers scattered across the floor. A lone desk sat on the opposite side of the room. It was made of gray metal and wood, not an antique, but not modern. The drawers were out, and the contents scattered.

Bud said, "Look." He pointed at the safe's dial. "More blood."

"Theirs? The perp?"

"Why would our perp make them open the safe? Wouldn't they just demand the combination and do it themselves?"

"Normally, sure," Skip replied. "But I don't think they'd be worried about one of them grabbing a hidden weapon or anything—so maybe, in this case, they made one victim open the safe while they watched."

"So, it's the victim's blood transferred from the torture?"

"Could be. Either way, there's a bloody print here."

"Has to be from a victim, right?" Bud asked. "I mean, unless we're dealing with the world's dumbest robbers, and they weren't wearing gloves."

"Yeah, probably his or hers. We'll know soon enough. I'm heading upstairs. If we don't split up, we'll be here a week."

Bud just nodded his head and went back to searching the office.

Skip headed upstairs.

The kitchen was at the back of the house. There was a window at the double sink that revealed a garden in the back and a secondary garage with space above it. Skip asked the team if anyone had searched the rear building.

Chuck heard him and answered. "It got a quick walk-through by the first officers on the scene, no other vics. That's a guest apartment above a garage. There's a pickup truck with some gardening supplies in the bed—but no signs any of the intruders got inside. The upstairs appears undisturbed."

"Okay, thanks," Skip said. He walked out the rear door, paused, and then asked Chuck if the door had been open when the first responder had arrived.

"Yup. No signs of forced entry, and the door was open."

"Any signs of pets?"

"None, but I can ask the daughter?"

"No. Leave her for now. We'll be back to talk to her soon. We just need a lay of the land and a basic feel for what happened."

"Sure thing."

Skip went to the master bedroom instead of heading to the guest house.

It was relatively undisturbed. Someone had rifled through a few drawers, but there was no sign of violence. He looked under the bed and pulled out a shoebox-sized gun safe. It was one of those types that could be opened quickly in the dark by using your fingers to push any of eight buttons in combination, and it was closed.

He shook the safe and felt movement. The Lau's had a gun, but they didn't have the warning time to get to it.

In the master bath, there were no signs of anything disturbed.

The dual walk-in closets were also untouched.

Skip went down the hall to the other bedrooms, three in total. Two appeared to be unused—except perhaps as guest rooms. Both beds had nightstands and jade lamps. There were also antique dressers, but other than a few miscellaneous toiletries and linens, the bedrooms were empty.

The third room had to be the daughter's.

Her bedroom was neat except for a sweater and a pair of socks in the short hallway between the room and its private bathroom and walk-in closet. There were no pieces of art in the room, Chinese or otherwise. However, there were a couple of posters for rock bands that Skip didn't recognize and another poster that had no images, only proverbs. There was a desk flooded by a bright white LED lamp, which sat next to a large desktop computer. It was pink. A stack of textbooks was neatly arranged, and a notebook sat open.

Skip examined the notes. Biology.

On the wall near the desk hung a daily calendar. May Lau had covered the calendar with notes about class schedules, music lessons, tennis lessons, and other appointments. Each item was in different color ink, and there was little blank space left to write anything else. There was a family portrait on the dresser. May Lau and her parents. She was in a graduation cap and gown. *Not high school*, Skip observed. *Must be junior high.*

He returned to the proverb poster, which was written in Chinese characters, followed by English:

The best time to plant was last season, but the second-best time is now.

If you're going to do something, do it well, or don't bother starting.

Defeat isn't bitter if you don't swallow it.

Skip read the last proverb out loud. "'Patience, persistence, and perspiration is the unbeatable combination for success'."

"The keys to being a good detective," Bud said from the doorway.

Skip jumped. "You trying to give me a heart attack?"

"Nope, just got your back. I think it's time to speak to the daughter and let the techs do their thing."

"Well," Skip said, looking back at the poster, "Pearls don't lie on the sand. If you want one, you must dive for it."

"Ancient wisdom."

"Indeed. Let's go interview our first witness."

FIVE

Skip put out his right hand. "I'm Detective Malloy." He handed May Lau his business card with his left hand. She took the card reluctantly and looked at Bud. "This is my partner, Detective Smith," Skip said.

She looked back and forth. "Am I in trouble?"

"No," Skip said. "Please, take a seat."

"Okay."

Skip sat down across from her. A lacquered black coffee table, on which an architectural magazine lay open next to an ornate bronze ashtray, was between them. May offered Skip a cigarette. He declined.

"I normally don't smoke in the house," she said.

"Understandable."

"Am I in trouble?" she asked again. She inhaled, exhaled, and then covered a childlike cough. "I mean, do I have to do this now?"

"It's the best time," he answered.

"Okay."

May Christine Lau had become a legal adult the day before. She was due to graduate high school in a few months, with honors. A few universities, she told them, had accepted her. But she hadn't decided which to attend.

There was nobody, she insisted, who might have a reason to kill her parents. "Unless it was the Chinese mafia," she added as an afterthought.

"The Chinese mafia?" Bud asked. "They have a syndicate here?"

"I don't know," May replied. "Never mind. I'm just nervous. My parents are dead. I'm sure there must be a triad or gangs. Who else would do something like this?"

"May, were you aware of the contents of the safe in the basement office?" Skip asked.

"Not really," she answered. "I don't know. Probably a lot of paperwork."

Bud coughed. "Excuse me, but that seems *strange*. Don't you think?"

It was Bud's role to shake up an interview anytime it got slow. He could play the "bad cop" if needed.

"Strange?" May asked. She shrugged her shoulders. "I don't think it's strange."

Skip jumped back into the interview. "You're not a child. Your parents are elderly. It seems reasonable to assume you'd have at least a basic knowledge of their affairs. Doesn't it?"

"You're not Chinese," she said matter-of-factly.

"And?"

"If I were male," she said, "you'd be on the right track." She took out another cigarette and placed it in her mouth. May was slender, flat-chested, and had a boyish face. Her hair was black, straight, and cut short. She wore a thin Merino sweater and black slacks. On her feet were purple socks, so dark they almost looked black. Noticing Skip glance at her feet, she looked him in the eye. "If my parents were alive, you wouldn't be wearing shoes in the house either."

Bud sat down on the sofa next to May and spoke in a calm voice. "May, we're sorry for your loss. Truly, we hate that you're going through this, but in order to launch an investigation, we need your cooperation."

"I'm answering your questions, aren't I?"

"Yes." Bud nodded his head.

"But there's more I take it?"

"Yeah," he answered. "We have to follow procedures with this thing before too much time passes. The first twenty-four hours are critical to an investigation, and we need to eliminate you as a suspect."

May frowned.

"It's normal," Skip said. "You're not being singled out, and you're not even a suspect. You're not in trouble, and you're not under arrest."

"But?"

"You can help us by agreeing to a few things," he said. He turned towards one officer who'd remained at attention at the edge of the sitting room. "Can you call out a tech?"

"Yes, sir."

"Have him bring the UV."

The officer nodded and left the room.

May turned towards Skip. "UV?"

"I'm going to ask your permission to run the UV light over your clothes. It's just a procedure."

"Um," she said. "I guess so."

"The tech is also going to swab your hands," he said. "With your consent, of course."

"And that's for—?"

"May," he said. "This is just standard procedure. We have to dot our I's and cross our T's, or the DA will have a fit. You understand?"

She barely nodded.

Bud moved slightly towards the edge of his seat. He turned towards her. "You haven't fired a gun today, have you?"

May's back arched a little. She blew out a lungful of smoke. "Don't be crazy. My parents would never let me touch a gun, much less fire one."

"So, that's a 'no'?" Skip asked.

"Obviously."

"Okay," Bud said. "Then it's no problem. We have your consent?"

"To do what, exactly?" she asked.

"We're going to run a UV light over your clothes and swab your hands. It's very simple and quick. This will go much easier, and we can get out of your hair—"

"I said I'd do it."

"Okay," Skip said.

"Thank you," Bud added.

The tech walked into the room and said, "Detective Malloy?"

"Go ahead," he said. "She's given consent."

The tech politely asked her to stand. He then waved the UV light over her front and back. Next, he opened a small package that contained a wipe. He unfolded the wipe and ran it over both her hands. "Okay, Detectives," he said. "All good here."

May began crying again. "They shot my parents."

"Yes," Skip said. "We're very sorry."

"I've never fired a gun in my life."

"We believe you, May. It's just procedure."

"The light?" she asked.

"It's used to reveal—"

"Blood." May reached for a tissue. "I get it and understand. I hate this. When can I leave?"

Skip looked at his notes. He wanted to understand why the home was invaded. Was it random? Were they targeted? Did the killers expect the family to be home? Was May lucky to be alive, or had the killer or killers known her schedule too?

"Were your parents normally home on a Sunday evening?" Skip asked.

"Yes, that's our usual routine," May answered. "I'm expected to be home for an early Sunday dinner."

"And tonight?"

"I'd passed a test last week. Got a perfect score. It seems pointless now, doesn't it?"

"What's that?" Bud asked.

"School. Grades. Life." May stubbed out her cigarette. "I'd got permission to go see the premier of *The Man, The Woman, and the Gun*. It's a thriller with Jack Mason-Smith."

"So," Skip asked, "normally, you'd have been home?"

"Fifty Sundays a year," she replied. "Or maybe, forty-nine. Yes, I'm normally home. But, as I said, it was the premier of, well, you know—the new Mason-Smith film."

"So, you had permission to be out this evening?" Skip asked.

"Did anyone else know?" Bud threw in.

"Yes, and yes," May answered. "My best friend, Heather. She was at the movies with me."

"Okay, May," Skip said. "I'm going to ask you to sit tight a little longer."

"All right."

"Do you have someplace to go tonight?"

"Yeah, Heather's place. She and her dad will pick me up as soon as I message them that I'm free. My grandmother is getting a flight out of China tonight. She'll be here tomorrow. When can I return?"

"Here?" Bud asked.

"It's my home," she said. "Isn't it?"

Bud nodded.

They went back over the scene for another hour. It served a couple of purposes. The first was to make sure they'd not missed anything the first time around. The second was to observe May and question her one last time before she left the scene.

Out of earshot, Bud asked, "Any feelings?"

"Not the girl," Skip replied.

"I don't think so either. You sure?"

"Nothing is ever certain."

"Until it is."

"Until it is," Skip said. "Let's question her again. A short round—see if she rattles. You remain the bad cop."

"I'm a softie."

"You're a monster." Skip smiled. "Let's go."

May remained on the couch. She lit another cigarette when she saw them approach. "Can I go?"

They told her they had a few more questions and repeated the basic ones. They weren't looking for new answers, only new body language or changes in attitude. After fifteen minutes, Skip said, "Okay, I think we're good. Anything else, Detective Smith?"

"I'm good, Detective Malloy," he answered. Turning to May, he said, "You go ahead and message your friend."

"Could we get that number?" Skip asked. "Just in case, you know, something comes up?"

May held out her cell phone with Heather Campbell's contact on the screen, and Bud took a photo.

Another twenty minutes passed while May waited. She smoked three cigarettes and sent a few text messages. When she stood to leave, she said, "My friend's here. Who will lock up the house? Set the alarm?"

"We're on it," Skip said.

"Okay." She walked to the door and turned the handle.

"Excuse me, May," Bud said.

She turned.

"How was the movie?"

"What mov—oh, yeah, good. Why?"

"Just curious," he answered.

"Have a safe night," Skip said. "We'll likely be in touch tomorrow."

They watched her walk out and shut the door behind her.

The big red door.

The one that was supposed to bring good luck.

"Not a very lucky door," Bud said.

SIX

Echo sat in her BMW and stared at the house.

It was a plain tract home on a street named Elm. A starter house in a bedroom community, not dissimilar to those in rows on both sides of the street. There were hundreds of them in the dozens of blocks surrounding her. Baby Boomer homes, built in the 1950s like so many cookies being stamped in the same shape.

It was a different era. The original residents of the house had lived in a period of unprecedented American prosperity. Eisenhower was President. There was no inflation, and Vietnam was a place few people knew existed. Two-parent households with a working-class dad and a stay-at-home mom dominated. Puppies, white picket fences, and a new Ford or Chevy in the driveway. It was a world Echo couldn't comprehend.

At the time of her birth, her parents lived in a time of massive debt, crippling inflation, and an uncertainty about the future. Buying a home wasn't a given, and most families had two working parents—and that was if they were even intact.

John and Clara Weston had lived in this house. It was their residence when they died.

Echo had asked Lee Callaway for help in her search for clues about her parents. Where they'd lived. Where they'd worked. Anything that could help her uncover a picture of her life as a baby. She wanted to accurately imagine her childhood had they lived.

Callaway called in some favors with his law enforcement buddies and gave what little information he found to Echo. She stared at a photocopy of her parents' driver's licenses. They both looked young—years younger than their ages when they died. It was likely they'd had these for a few years, maybe longer if they'd auto-renewed them. That meant the age of her mother in the photo was close to her current age.

Nothing looks worse than a DMV photo.

Her mom's picture looked like it belonged in a criminal lineup. But, even with the crappy picture, Echo could see herself. It was uncanny. She recalled a dream that she'd had as a teenager. She'd stood in front of a silver-framed mirror, and this exact face had stared back. It made the longing in her heart even stronger.

She wished she could hug her mother. Feel her arms around her. Whisper "I love you" in her ear. *I'd give anything for a moment. Just a moment*, she thought.

There'd been an expectation on her part that once she knew who her parents were, once she'd found out about their past, she'd feel more complete. That there'd be closure. But instead of peace and comfort, she now felt worse. Hollower. Lonelier. Sadder.

Maybe Callaway was right...

The private eye had warned her. He'd said she'd likely regret chasing down the shadows of her past. "Sometimes," he'd said, "it's better to leave the past in the past and focus on the future. You might not like what you dig up, and once uncovered, we can't rebury it."

Echo knew he was probably right, but she couldn't help herself. It was part of the reason she was an amazing investigative reporter. She didn't let the past stay buried, and she didn't ignore where the evidence led, even if the path was dark.

Especially if the path was dark.

Echo thought about her birth parents, Edward and Didi, who were on a scuba diving vacation in Belize. They'd invited her, but her feelings of moodiness and uncertainty about her future caused her to decline. Maybe she should have gone, after all. Instead of sitting alone staring at ghosts, she could be floating above a reef watching beautifully colored fish. Not a care in the world.

But that wasn't her.

Someone had freshly mowed the front lawn of the house. The place looked well cared for—the roof, the siding, the windows were all in excellent shape. An older model Buick sat in the driveway. She wondered if the owner knew her folks. It wasn't uncommon in these old suburban middle-class neighborhoods for residents to live a lifetime without moving.

She decided she'd find out.

But not today.

She wasn't ready to feel any more pain or loss at the moment.

Driving away, she wiped her eyes, turned on the Bose sound system, and cranked up the volume.

SEVEN

Skip thought it was unreasonable to suspect May.

A teenage girl with high academic marks and an upper-class lifestyle was not much of a suspect in any crime.

"What do you think?" he asked his partner.

Bud had gone with one of the patrol officers to run May through the squad car's onboard computer. Officers needed to run license plates and IDs quickly when out on patrol—discovering if a motorist had a criminal record or outstanding warrants could be life-saving knowledge. Bud shook his head. "Don't see her involved," he answered.

"No records?"

"She had a speeding ticket a couple of years back. Going forty in a thirty zone."

"Probably wanted to give her a scare since she was on a provisional license. Nothing else?"

"Nope. No known associates, no other tickets, nothing."

Skip reflected on the options they had to pursue. Both of the Lau's cars were parked in front, visible from the street. Their normal routine would put the family home on a Sunday afternoon—it was looking like the job was targeted. *Somebody knew about the safe,* he thought.

"They must have needed them home," Bud said. "They needed them for the safe is how I figure it."

"Makes sense. So, an insider? Pool guy? Gardener? Maybe they had a home improvement company out to fix something."

They split up the immediate tasks. Bud left with two patrol officers and went to knock on doors. There was a chance a neighbor witnessed something. Skip went to check on the security system and cameras. Maybe they'd get lucky.

An hour and twenty minutes later, they regrouped in the kitchen.

"Any luck walking the 'hood?" Skip asked.

"This hardly qualifies as a 'hood'."

"Any luck walking the upper-class suburban neighborhood?"

"Not much," Bud replied. He frowned and scratched his head. "I don't know if this is a lead or not…"

"What?"

"One neighbor, a couple of doors down, saw a black G-wagon with tinted windows speeding south."

"And they didn't get any plate numbers or a description of the driver. Am I right?"

"Yeah, but that's not the weird thing."

"What's the weird thing?"

"The neighbor's wife came to the door. I didn't know she was even there, but she'd been listening to our conversation. She spoke to her husband in Chinese, and he clammed up."

"You got a name?"

"Nope. His wife told me to get off their property."

"Strange," Skip said. "Something spooked them."

"Officer Bartkowski—he's the tall ugly one by the door—"

"I heard that, Detective," Bartkowski said.

"He said we'd better talk to a Detective Wong with the Asian Task Force," Bud said.

"Why's that?" Skip asked. He walked over and shook hands with Bartkowski. "You think there's a connection?"

"I did some canvassing with *Above The Fold* last month. In Little Shanghai. Black G-wagons with tinted windows, those are the favorite cars of the Chinese mafia."

"Really?" Skip wrote the name down. "That's a Detective Wong, you said?"

"That's it. First name, Steve."

Skip and Bud went over their notes. It was best to double and triple-check anything on a crime scene that could later be important. The security cameras, as expected, had not been recording since the family was home. The alarm system had a panic button, but it had not been activated. Skip called the alarm company, and they verified everything was working properly. No alarms were triggered that Sunday.

Nothing appeared missing besides the contents of the safe. They'd call the insurance adjuster on Monday to get a list of insured items. They'd also re-interview May. She'd be less distraught. It was probable she'd remember more after the initial shock of the day's events wore off. Maybe she'd recall something important.

Skip eventually felt like they had checked out everything they could on the property. He gave Bud a slap on the shoulder. "Okay, let's see if the ME has any helpful preliminary findings."

EIGHT

Sabine Werner, when asked about her height, always said, "I'm a hair over a hundred and fifty-two centimeters." She was a smidgen over five feet tall and had a husky frame she attributed to her German heritage. Sabine was named after her French maternal grandmother, who passed on the genes that gave her a complexion akin to Snow White's.

Her voice was raspy and commanding. She had an IQ of 140.

She'd graduated with a dual major, mathematics and biology, at Amery University. Next, she attended medical school at the University of North Carolina at Chapel Hill. Being an introvert, she quickly realized she would not enjoy practicing medicine on the living—so she applied and was accepted into an anatomic pathology residency in Fairview. She'd never regretted returning to her hometown.

Her ties to the community, coupled with her workaholic personality, naturally led her into the position of the top forensic pathologist, otherwise known as the medical examiner. The position meant she was the Chief Coroner of the City of Fairview.

"So, Doc," Skip said. "You see anything beyond the obvious?"

"Obvious to me or obvious to you?" she answered.

"Obvious to Bud."

"We got ourselves a double murder. Gunshot to the head, both vics."

"Actually, Bud found the entrance wounds first. Looks small caliber. You find an exit wound?"

"Nope. You're probably right—I think a twenty-two. We'll find the slug."

"Dirty business, this thing," Bud said. "The wounds are all antemortem?"

"Look at you with the big words," Sabine answered. "Yeah, appears they were tortured pretty badly. Both were gagged. Probably didn't want the neighbors to hear the screams. At their ages, well, look how small they are—"

"They wouldn't have fought back," Skip said. "That's for sure. Any evidence there were multiple assailants?"

Sabine nodded. "The techs have identified three different shoe print types in the blood evidence on the stairs and in the hallway. Hopefully, you'll get something there, but unless they were idiots, all you'll find are common off-the-shelf marks from brand new shoes."

"Criminals have been known to be dumb," Bud said.

"Could be one set is the daughter's. She came home and found the bodies. Gotta assume she checked to see if they were alive."

"All right, we'll catalog the shoes she owns. Not likely off-the-shelf cheapies."

Sabine pulled off her latex gloves. "It's a tough job, being a rich person."

"Until someone wants your stuff," Bud and Skip said in unison.

"You two practicing for Hollywood?" Sabine picked up a folder and looked over her notes. "I see nothing else notable, guys. Sorry. Y'all noticed the missus wrote something in blood? The tech guys got plenty of photos, but nobody here can read Chinese."

"Yeah, we saw it," Skip said. "We'll find someone."

"Something was bothering me," Bud said. "Did you find their cell phones on their persons?"

"Nope," she replied. She opened another folder labeled "Evidence Log". "Nothing listed in here, either. Strange. Maybe the bad guys didn't think any of this fancy art was worth trying to pawn and decided a couple of high-end phones would make their quota."

"Okay," Skip said. "So, we've got no 9-1-1 calls by the victims, and they didn't activate their alarm's panic button. Maybe the mister was trying to crawl to a phone."

"I think he was dragged up here," Sabine said. "He wouldn't have been able to use a phone, not after what they did to his fingers."

"How soon can we expect some copies of the shoe prints and viable matches?"

The FBI had catalogs available to law enforcement through a national database. There were listings of shoe prints, tire tracks, carpet fibers, and thousands of other items that could end up as evidence.

"I think by early afternoon tomorrow," Sabine said. "I can let the tech team know to make it a priority."

"Please." Skip thought it was their best potential identifier at the moment. Unless the team discovered the intruders had left some of the bloody fingerprints they'd seen.

Bud leafed through his notes. "So, tomorrow, we'll hunt down Detective Wong in the morning?"

"You got it," Skip said. "Nothing like starting the week off with a double-homicide with a potential link to the Chinese mafia."

"It could still be the daughter's involved," Bud said. He didn't sound convinced. "Or random."

"Or the pool cleaners, the gardeners, the window screen company that was out here last month, or the caterers for this luncheon Mrs. Lau held two weeks ago."

"Sounds fun being rich."

Skip had a nagging feeling that he was missing something. "Let's make a call to the insurance guy the priority. Whatever was in that safe might be our biggest clue."

NINE

Echo drove into the expansive parking lot of the Camden Mall. The lot was half empty. She sat for five minutes, clearing her head before she went inside. She needed to think.
The loneliness she was feeling would pass, she knew—but it was also something she would have to allow herself to work through.

She ordered a coffee and sat on the edge of the food court. After booting up her computer, she began editing her latest article for *Above The Fold.* While no longer an employee —she was freelancing—she felt a sense of loyalty to Frank, the owner of the independent paper.

Times were hard for newspapers. Revenues were down, advertisers were reluctant to continue to pay for ad space, and readers were changing their habits.

Despite her status as a freelancing writer, if Frank didn't pick up and pay for an article she wrote, she'd just file it away. She couldn't bring herself to offer her work to a different newspaper. It just didn't feel right. It would seem like a betrayal.

To make ends meet, Echo was relying on her trust fund. Her parents had set up the fund when she was only months old. Her father was a smart investor, and a few of her tech stocks had exploded in the two previous decades. The fund was large.

She could have taken a lump sum payment at twenty-one, but she had refused the money then. Now, the fund was saving her from having to go back to a menial job. She loved being an independent investigative journalist, but she also had fallen in love with working at *Above The Fold*. The option of moving back home had crossed her mind a few times. Her old bedroom hadn't changed.

But, until she got really desperate, she was going to continue working on staying on her own. She loved her parents. They'd given her a good life.

However, it was time to grow up on her own terms.

The article she was editing and putting the finishing touches on was about a rise in the activities of Chinese gangs in the Little Shanghai part of Fairview. It was both interesting and complex.

The idea there was a monolithic Chinese mafia was false. No such hierarchical cartel existed among the Chinese communities. What existed was a plethora of groups ranging from street gangs of teenagers to secret societies of wealthy business owners. There were parent organizations called tongs which operated in the open with legitimate non-profit status. They owned properties in which the gangs under their umbrella could meet and organize.

Like all cartels and syndicates, the Chinese gangs, triads, and criminal groups operated in geographic areas, usually cities or counties. Those areas were strictly controlled. Violence was common when rival gangs tried to operate across each other's boundaries.

Because Fairview was a large enough city to accommodate three territories, there'd been a climb in violence over the last couple of years as competing interests fought for control.

That was the object and focus of Echo's article—actually a series of articles—if Frank approved the work.

She'd discovered that the most powerful tong was the Ching Lóng Benevolent Society. Obstinately, it helped poor immigrants adjust to their new life, worked to influence politics in their district, and gave aid to widows and orphans. Underneath their protective cover of legitimacy, however, two street gangs operated.

The gangs ran various gambling operations and trafficked drugs, mostly opium. There were credible rumors they also controlled prostitution. Law enforcement had made no indictments regarding trafficking in sex workers. Echo believed there was proof out there, but she hadn't uncovered it.

Her first article would concentrate on the known offenses. There were dozens of low-level street gang members in prison for a variety of offenses, ranging from extortion to illegal gambling and pimping.

As always, her journalistic sixth sense was buzzing from all the little connections that she'd uncovered. If she could find concrete evidence, the bigger connections, the tie-in between the apparently legitimate entrepreneurs and the low-level criminal members, she'd have a breakthrough article. She'd see her story at the top of *Above the Fold.*

Getting a story above the fold on the front page of a newspaper was an investigative journalist's goal. A breaking story, especially an exclusive one, with a huge typeface headline and a byline with your name—that's what set the standard in the industry.

If you did it often, you became a star.

Echo re-read the article a final time. She made one slight change and then emailed the piece to Frank. She was confident he'd buy it; it was a good story, timely, and addressed a societal problem that people knew existed.

Newspaper articles like this could force the government to work harder for change. Positive change.

Echo considered her next move.

She'd have to go into Little Shanghai and start asking dangerous questions.

TEN

Skip and Bud walked towards the street. There were two news vans from local stations and a small group of reporters. Murder wasn't a rare occurrence in most cities, but a double homicide in an upscale community would be a leading news item.

"I'll flip you for it," Bud said.

"Sure." Skip didn't want to give an interview or answer questions, but they'd been under pressure to be more accessible to the media.

The Fairview mayor was in the middle of a spending scandal. He'd wasted thousands of taxpayer dollars on questionable expenses. Apparently, he believed the citizens should fork over money for tanning salon visits, gym memberships, and even his haircuts. When he remodeled his office—it had been upgraded only two years before—someone inside the mayor's office leaked information to the press.

The mayor called a meeting. Skip and Bud were instructed, along with the rest of Fairview's detectives and public servants, to be more forthcoming and interesting to the media. The mayor wanted the heat removed from himself, and he was using city employees to help him.

"It's not that I hate the media," Skip said. "I just feel like this isn't my job."

Bud flipped a quarter and said, "Call it."

"Heads."

Skip frowned when Bud revealed the coin had come up tails. "Crap. Well, I guess I lost fair and square."

"You aren't very lucky, are you?" Bud asked.

"Maybe I can find Echo," Skip said. "At least I don't mind so much talking with her."

Bud's head turned left to right. "I don't see her."

Skip scanned the crowd. He saw Conner, the reporter with *Above the Fold*. But no Echo. He frowned, and his shoulders slumped.

Bud patted him on the back and said, "Don't worry, Detective Malloy. I got this one."

"Really?"

"Yup," Bud said. "I'll give a quick statement and then shoot the breeze with Conner over there. He's not such a bad guy, and it'll give you a chance to sneak out of here."

"Thanks, man. I owe you one."

Skip and Bud had a working relationship that was common among partners in dangerous professions. They had each other's backs. They knew they could trust one another, no matter what. But Skip knew their friendship was deeper. Bud used to come over for breakfast every morning. He only stopped when he started getting serious with Janice. Skip's wife, Vivian, a defense attorney, had set up her best friend with Bud. Skip helped. So far, it seemed like a brilliant match.

Skip watched Bud cross under the yellow police tape. He stood facing the news cameras. Two competing field reporters barked questions at him. Skip ignored the interaction. He knew Bud could handle them and wouldn't give away any information that would hinder the investigation. He got into his car and phoned Vivian.

"You're running late," she said.

"A big case. We caught a double murder up here in the hills."

"It's usually quiet up there."

"Yup. There's a little media circus, but Bud's handling it. I'll be home in twenty-five minutes."

"Okay, honey. You hungry?"

"Does the Pope know Latin?"

"I'll heat up a plate," Vivian said. "The twins are watching a movie, so don't rile them up when you walk in. I've had just about enough of them today that I can handle."

"You want me to call the Gypsies?"

"Can you get a good price?"

"I'll use my awesome negotiation skills," Skip said. "Maybe a two-for-one deal. They're both healthy. Maybe the circus will take them."

"I don't think there's much demand for circuses anymore. Too many people have realized that animals deserve better."

"Maybe we can just ship them off to the military."

"They're too young."

"Well, okay. Let's give them another chance."

Skip's mind switched back to business. "Hey, Viv, you know anything about the Chinese mafia?"

"A little," she answered. "First thing, there's not a single controlling organization. I've had to defend a few low-level gang members who the DA wanted to press for information."

"They talk?"

"No way. The Chinese, at least from the stories I've heard, are even more violent and less forgiving than the *mafia* mafia. Nobody talks. I couldn't cut any deals for them."

"Okay. What else?"

"I heard something," she said. Her voice was deadpan, cold.

"And?"

"Let's talk when you get home."

ELEVEN

Echo left Camden Mall and drove randomly.

She felt a connection to the city because her birth parents had lived there. She had lived here, too. There were things she thought were familiar when she saw them. But that was silly. She'd been stripped away from her birth parents when she was only months old. She couldn't possibly remember anything about the city from then.

Besides, the town had transformed.

Camden used to be smaller, a factory town.

Then, around the time her parents were alive, the city fathers gave massive tax breaks and land grants to corporations. Many of them foreign entities. That led to an employment boom and massive immigration.

There were now corporate offices for a variety of online entities: social media companies, virtual reality software, and hardware companies, as well as accounting firms and banks. A few of the old factories, car part manufacturers, and beer brewers, remained.

Camden was a blend of old-school blue-collar industries and innovative tech firms that set up offices to take advantage of cheap land, tax breaks, and a growing workforce of immigrants.

As it got late, Echo realized she ought to head home. Since it was Sunday night, the streets were mostly empty, and most of the businesses besides liquor stores and mini-marts were closed. She drove out of an industrial area into a poor residential neighborhood. She passed run-down apartment buildings, most of which had bars on the windows. Gang-related graffiti covered the walls. Streets and alleys were strewn with garbage.

She drove for another mile, and the atmosphere changed as if she'd passed an invisible barrier.

There were new office buildings and manicured green belts with trimmed trees. After another mile, she came across the new high school that had triggered much controversy due to cost overruns. The football stadium had gone over budget by more than a million dollars. Some felt that it was worth the money. It was for the students, after all, they'd argued. Others complained it glorified sports at the cost of science and the things that most students needed to get into a good university.

Echo was on the fence. Of course, she felt the core subjects should be priorities, but she wasn't against sports. What she decided was that she didn't object to the city building football stadiums, basketball arenas, and baseball diamonds, as long as they gave equal attention to computer centers and science labs.

She drove a couple of miles, and then she decided to swing through Little Shanghai.

She turned left onto Main Street and headed through downtown and thence to Little

Shanghai. The transition was like she'd left America altogether. Business signs were in Chinese. Traffic and bus stop signage were written in both languages. Streets running perpendicular to Main had names like *Bái jiē* and *Dì sān jiē*.

A left turn on *Chéng shù jiē* took her to a city park. It was well-lit, immaculate, and had a life-sized bronze statue at its entrance. A wooden sign declared it Yue Fei Park. The area was graffiti and trash-free. The lawns were lush, the trees neatly trimmed. It reminded Echo of Disneyland.

A group of young Asian men were playing basketball on one of the courts. She stopped and watched.

Echo's sense of time got away from her, and she jumped when a siren sounded for a single whoop. Red and blue flashing lights bounced inside her BMW. A squad car pulled up alongside her. An officer on the passenger side rolled down his window.

"Is something wrong, officer?" she asked.

"No ma'am," he said. "What are you doing in this part of town at this hour?"

"Am I breaking some law I don't know about?"

"No ma'am."

Echo slowly brought out her press credentials.

"Echo Rose. Freelancer for *Above the Fold*, officer," she said. "Care to answer a few questions?"

"No ma'am," he replied. "This isn't the best place for a pretty white girl in a fancy car to be parked at this time of night. You be safe." The cops drove away.

The City of Camden used a simple system for identifying all city-owned vehicles. Echo made a note of the squad car's number.

The basketball players had stopped playing and were staring at her. She felt a chill and pulled away from the curb. A few minutes later, in a maze of small side streets and alleys, she was lost.

She opened a driving app and clicked her apartment address.

A computerized voice announced, "In three hundred feet, turn left." As she made the turn, a figure glided between two parked cars. He blocked her way. She slammed on the brakes. He was wearing a black hoodie, his face in shadow.

He lifted his arm.

Echo flinched, preparing for violence. But it wasn't a gun the man was holding—it was a cell phone.

The flash blinked twice, and the man disappeared into the shadows.

Echo sped away.

TWELVE

Skip sat at the dining room table and drank two glasses of water.

"That must have been some interview," Vivian said.

"Yes. Tiring," he said. "And she was chain-smoking."

"A suspect?"

"Everyone's a suspect."

"Even me?" Vivian smiled and set down a plate of lasagna.

"I suppose you have an alibi for this one."

Skip started eating and didn't say another word until his plate was empty.

They sat in the living room and made small talk about their upcoming move. Their old home was finally going to be demolished. Skip imagined what it would be like to live in a brand-new house. He could barely comprehend the luxuriousness of how that sounded. "So," he said. "Tell me more about the gangs in Little Shanghai."

Vivian frowned. "The public defender's office doesn't deal with very many cases. The gangs seem to be well-funded from higher, but secret, sources."

"You're saying they usually have private attorneys?" Skip asked.

"Yes. There's obviously a network and hierarchy," she answered. "The different organizations have different lawyers. They don't cross the line—whatever it is—between groups. I only heard a bit of gossip because a couple of young thugs were complaining to each other about the tardiness of their attorney."

"They weren't speaking Chinese?"

"You know, I don't think all the teens know Chinese. A lot of them were born here, and they've adopted American culture pretty thoroughly. They listen to rap and play basketball."

"So, you overhead something?"

Vivian explained what she understood from their conversation. She also had asked around the office, mostly out of curiosity. Apparently, the biggest gangs had united under one banner, and they were taking over the territory of the lessor ones. There'd been bloody gunfights, a rise in hospital visits, and a handful of arrests. Only one murder had made it to the books. "So, the consensus at my office is leadership wanted to keep the violence off the radar as much as possible," Vivian concluded.

Skip nodded. He reflected for a minute on how this information might provide a clue in his current case. "You think they made the bodies vanish to keep a lid on the territory grabs?"

"That's exactly it. One of these kids I was eavesdropping on was speaking bitterly about one of his cousins. He said his aunt and uncle were upset because they knew there'd be no funeral."

"Interesting," Skip said. "It gives me an idea about what questions to ask."

THIRTEEN

Echo woke up on Monday morning with a chill. She had a foreboding sense of dread—her investigation into criminal behavior in Little Shanghai had caught someone's attention. She'd even taken a step down the path of discovery regarding her birth parents. Both things carried potential danger. One was physical, and the other, emotional.

She'd gone with modern design when furnishing her apartment. The furniture had clean lines and proportions. Metal, wood, and glass. Recently, she'd added a few houseplants, things that required care. It was a big step, and she wondered if she'd ever be ready for a pet.

Probably not.

But, then again, regardless of the uncertainties of her employment and the sometimes dangerous aspect of her work, she yearned for a piece of normalcy. Normal families had pets. Maybe she could care for a dog or a cat. Perhaps a fish tank, or a snake or a lizard, was more her style—but regardless of the species or breed, having something living in her place besides plants would probably lift her spirits.

Echo didn't want to go into the office. Too many people, too many questions. She wasn't exactly fired from *Above the Fold*, and Frank was good about purchasing a lot of her freelancing efforts, but things had changed. The paper was going through a financial upheaval. Rumors were rampant that it would close. The newspaper business wasn't what it used to be.

A thought crossed her mind. *What if I invest?*

She had her trust fund sitting there, a large portion in tech stocks and a few in blue-chip companies. She knew there were opportunities for it to grow in crypto, options trading, or other risky ventures, but she didn't want to become an active investor.

Those who didn't know exactly what they were doing with their investments were just gambling.

Gambling with her life savings didn't appeal to her in the slightest, but neither did studying companies' P&L statements and industry reports. She had no desire to learn technical analysis. Her love was journalism, specifically crime reporting and breaking stories that affected people's lives.

She decided she'd talk with her parents. Her father was a smart banker and knew his way around the investment world. He'd be able to discuss the pros and cons of her investing in *Above the Fold* and becoming part of the leadership in a paper that would provide her an outlet to work in a field she loved.

Edward and Didi would be home from Belize in less than a week. She messaged her mother: *I hope you're having fun. Take lots of fish pictures. Let's have dinner when you return.* Her mom would be happy to get a message and even happier knowing Echo wanted to have dinner with them. She wrote nothing about wanting investment advice. She'd spring that on her dad after he'd had a cocktail.

They didn't know their daughter had discovered her birth parents. Echo didn't want them to be jealous or slighted or hurt. But sometimes, those things couldn't be avoided when hunting down the past. Her adoptive parents cared for her as if she was born to them naturally. She was certain of that. But nevertheless, for better or worse, she now knew the details of the tragic reason she'd been given up for adoption.

Her investigative tendencies and curiosity wouldn't allow her to let it go. When she pursued a story, she was like a bloodhound chasing down an escaped convict—even when it meant running through a swamp.

The second bedroom in her apartment was set up almost like an office. It had a desk and a comfortable chair. Enough work space for her laptop and a powerful desktop that she used when she had to do untraceable things online.

There was a tall silver floor lamp and a few photos on the walls.

One old photograph in a plain frame held a picture of her birth parents. She also had several pictures of her adoptive parents and herself. Graduation photos and a couple of family vacations. Wonderful memories mixed with some tragic ones.

If her search for the past and her genealogy hurt her parents, she'd be upset—but she couldn't stop. There were things she knew she would never let rest.

Echo opened her desktop's portal into the dark web. She needed some answers, and she knew who to ask.

Anlt984snk: *What's up ER?*

ER43seer: *I'm looking for anything relating to the Ching Lóng Benevolent Society.*

Anlt984snk: *What's that?*

ER43seer: *It's a Chinese organization called a tong. It's a cover for criminals. I think it oversees street gangs in Fairview and Camden. I need to know more.*

FOURTEEN

Skip and Bud reviewed their cork board. Its pictures and clues were hastily thumb-tacked in what appeared to be a logical arrangement.

The murder book sat open between them on a Formica-topped table. They were still early in the investigation, but the first few days were the most critical. Skip flipped through the pages. A murder book was a three-ringed binder. Homicide detectives kept all the written evidence inside it. Pictures, notes, photocopies, observations, and contacts. Anything that might be helpful at some point was included.

Below the office they'd occupied for the investigation of the Lau murders was a basement that contained cold cases. Murder books remained because murder didn't carry any statute of limitations—technically, a case was open indefinitely—but realistically, there was a point when everyone involved, the unknown murderers, the victims, the cops, and all the witnesses, were all dead and gone.

Every city had horrible crimes on the books that would never be prosecuted—at least in human courts.

Skip read through a list of people they needed to interview.

The insurance company representative, each of the various service providers, May Lau, as well as her best friend, Heather Campbell. They'd reach out to Detective Wong in the Asian Task Force.

The Lau's also had a business partner.

"You think the partner should be a priority?" Skip asked. "Seems he's likely to have a motive."

"Agreed," Bud said. "Add pawn shops to the list. I'm curious to know if anyone shows up trying to pawn any Asian art."

"It appeared nothing was missing to me."

"What about the contents of the safe?"

"Doesn't seem big enough for art pieces. Maybe jewelry." Skip flipped through pictures of each room that the tech crew had put into their "in" box early that morning. "I don't see any empty spots. No empty picture hangers."

"We need to talk to May again soon." Bud tapped the photo of the empty safe. "No way she's clueless about what was in there."

"Okay. We talk to May and the insurance guy, get a better idea of what was missing. If it was only cash or documents, then we look at the business partner. If there was jewelry, we canvas pawn shops. Maybe roust some fences."

"We need to request phone and banking records."

"I'll write up a memo for the sergeant."

Their research had revealed the basic history of Lee and Ming Lau. The couple had come to the United States thirty-five years earlier. He'd worked his way through college, and together they'd mastered English and entrepreneurship. They built the American Dream for themselves, eventually owning a small chain of laundromats and dry cleaners.

Once the businesses were prosperous, they'd had a daughter. May was an only child. She had no other family in America. Only her grandmother, who was due to arrive sometime late that night, was a known relative of the Lau's.

Immigrants to America often suffered through many hardships and prejudices. It was better today than it was thirty-five years ago, but that didn't mean it was easy. The Lau's had built a successful life only to see it cut tragically short.

Skip wanted justice for the Lau family. It was the driving force behind why he'd become a cop. Now, as a homicide detective, he felt it was his duty to catch murderers and put them in prison so they couldn't hurt anyone else. He flipped through more pages until he came to the photocopied picture of the bloody symbol.

Bud tapped the picture with his index finger. "That's what you call in the business, a clue."

"A bloody clue," Skip said in a British accent.

"What, you're Sherlock Holmes?"

"Nope. I'm Idris Elba, OBE," he replied.

"Huh?"

"Only the greatest black British actor in history. Don't you watch anything on television?"

"Not enough, apparently."

"About this bloody clue," Skip said. "We need to find someone who can tell us what it means."

"On it." Bud opened his departmental laptop. After entering his passwords, he looked up the email and phone number for Detective Wong in the Fairview Police Department directory. He emailed him an introduction and explained he was working on a double homicide that might have a connection to Chinese gangs. He included an attachment, a jpeg of the bloody Chinese character. Then he called Wong but got voicemail.

He left a message requesting a meeting as soon as reasonably possible. “This is one of those ugly cases that is going to get a lot of media attention,” he concluded. “If you can help narrow the search, it’ll look good for both our departments.”

Skip’s cell phone rang. “Hello, Detective Malloy here,” he said.

Bud listened to Skip’s side of the conversation. It was mostly a lot of yes’s and no’s, and then Skip gave his email address to the caller and asked for the list of insured items they’d been discussing.

“Our first lead,” he said after he ended the call. “The insurer is emailing a list of insured items, but he also expressed some concerns about the Lau’s policies. Put a visit on our to-do list.”

Bud looked hopeful. “And? What else? What was in the safe?”

“The contents of the safe included two-hundred and seven ounces of gold.”

“Holy smokes. A solid lead.”

“Solid gold.”

“Wow,” Bud said. “Any idea of the value?”

“Insured for half a million.”

“That’s some motive.”

“Let’s hit the pawn shops before the perps,” Skip said.

FIFTEEN

E-Z Pawn was Fairview's biggest and most popular pawnshop. It was owned by Teddy Anderson, known around the city as "Big Ted." He'd become a minor celebrity after running late-night television commercials back in the late 80s that featured a Bengal tiger and a Grizzly bear. He'd once appeared on a cable series that featured a couple of treasure hunters who scoured pawn shops across America for undervalued antiques and vintage collectibles. That appearance solidified his celebrity status.

He also had a reputation, perhaps deserved and perhaps not, of being a fence for high-value items.

Big Ted had his finger on the pulse of Fairview's underworld. He knew who moved stolen items, even while he'd insulated himself from ever being prosecuted. There were various signs posted outside the pawnshop. WE BUY GOLD, a bright yellow sign with black lettering, was the one Skip and Bud noticed first.

A slender woman, wearing excessive makeup and gaudy jewelry, sat near the entrance. She controlled the double entry—in order to get inside, a customer would have to walk through exterior glass doors and then wait inside a caged area.

"You look like cops," she said.

"Got it in one," Skip said.

Bud rattled the door. "Buzz us in."

"Need to see your badges, fellas," she said. "Nobody gets in carrying without verifying they're really the police."

Skip and Bud pulled out their IDs and badges at the same time.

"Hold them under the camera, fellas. That's the policy."

Bud groaned, but he followed her instructions. Skip did the same. A minute later, the lock buzzed, and they walked inside. The iron door slammed behind them.

"We had a couple of fake cops about a year ago," the woman explained. "They got out of here with about a hundred and fifty grand worth of merch. Big Ted is more cautious these days." She gave them a fake smile. "How can I help you fellas today?"

"We need to see Teddy," Skip said. "Sooner, the better."

The woman was wearing a wireless headset. She pushed a button on her computer and a moment later explained to Big Ted that a couple of Fairview's finest were asking for him. "He'll be right out, fellas. Can I get you a drink? Coffee? Tea? A sip of bourbon?"

They both shook their heads and walked past the reception desk. Because it was still early on a Monday morning, the place was empty. Big Ted approached them and smiled with a perfect set of teeth. *Probably dentures*, Skip thought. The tall, large man stuck out his hand.

"How can I help you two gentlemen this beautiful morning?" he asked. His warmth seemed genuine, but Skip remained skeptical. "You need to pawn something you may have found during a routine search or something?"

Skip told him they weren't there to sell anything. They'd come to ask if he'd heard anything about a gold heist. Bud added a few details about the crime, and then they waited silently for him to answer.

"It's a bit early for criminals to come in," Ted joked. "The bad guys are still in bed. Seriously, though, no, I haven't had anyone come in asking about selling gold. Nobody has called, either, for that matter, about a large quantity of gold. I'd know about it."

"What if the perps went to another pawn shop?" Bud asked.

"You mentioned it was a significant amount," Ted said. "Care to elaborate?"

Bud looked at Skip, and he nodded his head. "About two-hundred ounces."

"That's a lot of yellow metal. Nobody in town, except me, will have that kind of cash available. If another shop gets approached, I'll hear about it."

"Okay," Skip said. "Keep this under your belt. Call us if you hear anything."

"You got it," he said. "I'm always a friend to law enforcement. I run a clean business."

"If you say so," Bud said. "We'll have to take you at your word."

"I have all my files and city requirements in order, boys. If you'd care to head back to the office—"

Skip held up his hand. "No time." He handed his business card to Ted and turned to leave. "Thank you for your cooperation on this one. It's going to hit the press today and make a lot of people uneasy. A home invasion and a double homicide aren't good for the city."

"Understood," Ted said. He shook his head. "Terrible business. Hey, is there more you can tell me about the gold? Is it bars? Coins?"

"Pandas," Skip replied. "Various denominations."

"Hell." Ted appeared to be pondering something. "Pandas are collectible. They can be worth more than just the weight value of the gold. Also, people track that kind of thing. Few collectors out there with hundreds of ounces sitting around. This doesn't sound like a regular B&E guy or a lone cat burglar. These guys don't commit this kind of violence—it's bad news when they're eventually busted. Most of these rubes can do five years standing on their heads, but the Big L is another story."

The Big L was a life sentence. Skip knew Ted was right. Smart thieves rarely broke into a house when the residents were home. If it was a heist job, they'd usually be smart enough to wear masks and leave the victims alive. Why turn a potential nickel or dime sentence into life?

There had to be more to the case.

Big Ted coughed. "Sounds like a triad hit. I'd ask around Little Shanghai if I was you. But, be careful. This kind of violence comes naturally to these people."

"These people?" Skip asked.

"I was in Vietnam."

“The Lau’s were Chinese. Little Shanghai is Chinese.”

“Same smell to me, fellas.”

“That’s very enlightened of you,” Bud replied with dry sarcasm. He turned to Skip. “Let’s get out of here.”

“You should hit up the Laughing Bandit.” Big Ted spread out his hands. “There’s an idiot with some stones on him. He’s a fan of vicious beatings just because he likes it. A real sociopath.”

SIXTEEN

Echo's dark-web contact was going to need some time to research the tong and any people that were connected to it. Patience was a hard but necessary element in her profession.

Needing to stay busy, she opened her *Above the Fold* email account. She scanned the inbox and ignored things that weren't important at the moment. Pablo had forwarded her a list of assignments she could choose to work on—if she wanted—which she didn't.

With her being let go by the paper, Pablo was the most junior staff member again. He looked like a Latino hipster with a goatee and a single earring. He always wore well-pressed button-down shirts and maintained a neat appearance. His job was to make sure the paper's pages got filled. There were always extra local interest items and minor crime reports that could be written up if needed. Pablo liked Echo and wanted to help her stay busy.

Before she'd begun working on the series about Chinese gangs and organized crime in Little Shanghai, Echo had been filing stories on hit-and-run accidents, DUIs, domestic violence, and other things she'd vowed to not ever work on again.

Not that any of the routine incidents weren't important to the people involved. Not that the issues weren't major problems in America taken as a whole. But Echo wanted to work on the kind of stories that became above-the-fold articles. She wanted to spark change in the world, or at least in her little part of it in Fairview.

Because she had access to her trust fund, she didn't have to work just to pay the bills. She could be selective. Echo replied to Pablo's email and politely declined the potential assignments. Opening her access to the LexisNexis database, she began searching for connections to known companies and names that she'd already uncovered.

Sometimes being a journalist was like working on a *Find the Word* puzzle. Often it was like a *Where's Waldo* picture.

Nevertheless, it was the job. She kept searching and reading. Then she heard a ping.

A new email.

It grabbed her attention.

SEVENTEEN

Skip drove while Bud contacted a parole agent named Tony Gallo.

"Whadda he tell you?" Skip asked, using a heavy accent.

"He said we should stop by his uncle's place for spaghetti. *Capiche?*"

"That's Nick's Diner, right?"

"No, that's the Greek place. Great gyros. Tony's uncle's place is Callo's Ristorante. They have the best pizza in Fairview."

"Okay, but what did he say about the Laughing Bandit?"

"Ricky Ortega. He's in a halfway residence over near Fourth and Spring."

"By the bowling alley?"

"Exactly," Bud said. "It's only fifteen minutes from here. Let's go beat the bushes a little."

Ricky Ortega had served twelve years of a sixteen-year sentence. His last known territory was in the Fairview Hills neighborhoods, one of which was where the Lau's residence was located. He'd been picked out of a lineup partially because he had a distinct laugh, a cross between a hyena and a donkey's bray. After serving a warrant, Fairview's finest had discovered a match to a stolen property inventory. This discovery tied him to a beating of an elderly woman. She'd woken up in the middle of the night and surprised a cat burglar.

Because they didn't have concrete evidence that Ortega was the assailant—only that he possessed her property—the DA worked out a plea deal that was less than satisfactory to all parties.

Sometimes justice means splitting the difference, Skip thought.

Bud used the drive to make calls.

"Allen Security. We're your home defense specialists. How may I help you?" the voice on the other end of the line said.

"I need to talk to someone about the Lau residence," Bud answered. He gave the representative their address and waited. After a moment, a manager came on the line. "This is Detective Ralph Smith. I'm calling to follow up on a request for information." They talked for five minutes, and he ended the call. He looked at his partner. "Nada. They didn't get any calls or alarms."

"Figures," Skip said. "People spend a lot of money on these systems and then don't take full advantage of them."

"Exactly," Bud agreed. He explained to Skip that the home had two stations with panic buttons. All three residents had speed dial codes on their cell phones that operated similarly to a panic button. If punched, an armed response would follow, even if nobody was on the line asking for help. If someone did answer, they'd still send out a team unless a special code word was given.

The Lau's didn't call or hit a panic button.

"You think the intruders knew they had this service? Maybe that's why they grabbed the cell phones?"

"Maybe," Bud said. "It doesn't explain why they didn't dial the panic codes."

"They knew the perps?"

"Maybe. Maybe they just didn't have time."

Skip found a parking spot near the halfway residence. They announced themselves and waited in a plainly decorated living room. It had two dirty couches and several unmatched chairs.

Ricky Ortega walked into the room. He used a cane and crept towards them.

"Arthritis," he said. He sat on a green recliner. It was spotted with stains and had a couple of cigarette burn marks. "People got no respect."

"Respect had you pistol-whipping that old lady?" Skip asked.

"I never hurt nobody," Ortega replied. "I only took from the rich."

"A real modern-day Robin Hood," Bud said. "A hero."

"Hey, looky here." He coughed and spat some phlegm into a handkerchief. "My PO says I have to talk to you, so here I am. But I don't have to be nice, only cooperative. I'm being cooperative, and it's almost time for my favorite show."

"You know anything about a break-in last night?" Skip said. "Up in the hills. A couple of thugs with a violent streak. They left two bodies. And a mess."

"That was never my style, officers," Ortega said. "The incident in question on my record was a mistake. I was an in-and-out kind of guy. I never worked with anyone violent. Violence gets you locked up."

"Okay," Bud said. "Let's say we buy this. What can you tell us about anything you've heard? Must be some gossip in the wind."

"I've been out of the game for over twelve years now. I don't know squat, except I'm gonna miss my show."

It was obvious that Ricky Ortega wasn't involved with the Lau's break-in. He was too arthritic, and besides, the PO had verified that he'd been on the premises the entire day on Sunday. Skip and Bud had hoped he could give them something. Anything.

"Think harder," Skip said.

Ortega closed his eyes and said, "Describe the house and what was taken. How did the deceased get that way?"

Skip went through the basics. He was careful not to give away the few details the office had agreed to keep from the public. Law enforcement needed ways to eliminate crackpots, so they always held back some details on big cases.

After Skip finished, Ortega tapped his cane on his head. "This is reminding me of something. Wait for it—wait for it."

Skip and Bud kept silent.

Finally, Ortega spoke. "Chinese neighborhood and victims. A pile of gold. Massive violence. This is triad stuff. No teenage street gang is pulling this job. It smells to me like something out of the Chinese mafia handbook."

When Skip and Bud drove away, Bud said, "You think there's a Chinese mafia handbook?"

"I don't know," he answered. "But we need to talk to Wong before the end of the day."

EIGHTEEN

Echo opened the email. It was from an editor of a feminist magazine, *Soft Vanda*, that was breaking out in popularity and influence. It was even getting international attention, which Echo thought was cool for a Fairview-based woman's journal that wrote about everything from teen social anxiety to sex trafficking between the third world and the first.

The editor, Courtney Baily, had written to ask Echo if she'd be interested in discussing a position as a staff writer. The focus of the position would be to write about women in third world nations and the challenges and abuses they faced. Everything was open to discussion: the lack of equal rights, equal pay, representation in government, forced child marriages, and how law enforcement often ignored assault, rape, sex trafficking, and the murder of women.

Echo took a deep breath and sighed.

The issues the magazine covered were exactly the type that she knew could have far-reaching influence on people—especially voters who ultimately empowered those who could bring change. She opened the magazine's website and read the "About Us" section, and then browsed through the recent headlines.

A window popped up, asking for her email address. She entered her personal email and went back to reading. A paywall popped up explaining how independent media outlets depended on subscribers for financial support. Feeling both curious and supportive, she signed up for a trial subscription. It was only ninety-nine cents.

She returned to browsing articles and liked what she saw. They were current and hard-hitting. The articles named people and were well-referenced. Echo replied to Courtney Bailey's email and agreed to a meeting.

Before she could get back to her gang research, her email pinged again.

The editor wanted to meet that day if possible. Because everyone was working at home, Bailey suggested that rather than meet at a coffee shop, Echo should come to her home.

Echo agreed.

NINETEEN

Skip and Bud's next stop was Chang's Insurance in Camden. The offices were in the center of Little Shanghai. They drove past the new football stadium, and Skip thought about his son's transition from sports to theater. "It's a shame the school system doesn't support acting and music like they do sports."

"Football and basketball bring more money," Bud said.

"I know, but I wish the voters weren't so biased towards touchdowns and slam dunks."

"Don't let Lucy hear you say that."

Lucy Malloy was an athletic star—her twin brother, Lew Jr., sometimes got teased for being a thespian instead of a power forward. Skip and Bud were strongly supportive of Lew Jr.'s decision, but kids his age could be cruel and judgmental.

"I'm not against the district's financial support of athletes. I just want it to be fair."

"Life's not fair," Bud said. "Hey, turn left. You're gonna miss our turn."

"Sorry, I get confused by the street names."

Bud laughed. "I thought you were the language expert."

"I wish, but I don't think knowing a few Cajun slang words counts. I know how to say 'Kung Pao Chicken', so I'm thinking Chinese instead of Italian for lunch. Besides, I had lasagna last night."

"Fine with me," Bud said. "I love Chinese."

"You love *food*, period."

"Guilty as charged, officer."

The agent who handled all the Lau's insurance policies went by the nickname, Xiao Pang. He was short, chubby, and jovial.

"Please, please, sit, my friends," Pang said. "I'm always a friend to the men—what do you Americans say? 'Men in Blue'?"

"That's one term," Skip answered. "We're detectives, and—"

"Please," Pang interrupted, "let me get you something to drink. Coffee?"

Skip and Bud agreed to coffee but refused the additional offer of doughnuts.

"You really wanted a donut," Skip said. "Didn't you?"

"Yes, honestly," Bud admitted. "But I didn't want to live up to some dumb stereotype."

Pang had left minutes earlier to make photocopies of his files on the Lau's insurance policies. When he returned, he sat first, then handed over a stack of papers. "You sure about the ham and cheese croissant? I'd be happy to have Caihong heat them up."

"No." Skip looked through the papers. "Thank you, but we have a tight schedule today."

Bud said, "You mentioned to my partner on the phone this morning that you had some concerns. Is that right?"

"Yes, yes," Pang answered. "Let me see…" He flipped through some papers while humming to himself. "See here, officers. This life insurance policy. It's a whole life policy and had accumulated fifty-seven thousand, four hundred twenty-two dollars. And, well, nineteen cents." He looked up from the paper. "You see?"

"See what?" Skip asked.

"Last month—I think it was Tuesday the—no Wednesday, let me…"

Bud coughed. "The exact day isn't important right now. What happened?"

"Mr. Lau cashed this policy out. He also canceled the term-life policy he had on himself and his wife. A quarter million-dollar policy that had been in place for years. It was sort of abrupt, and, well—"

"The benefactor?" Skip asked.

"The daughter, of course," Pang answered. "In fact, she was the recipient of the whole life policy. The fifty-seven thousand, four hundred twenty-two dollars, and yes, nine—"

"We get it," Bud said. "So, they made the check out to the daughter?"

"Let me see." He rifled through his notes. "Ah, yes, we had an appointment. It was right around her eighteenth birthday. I tried to convince her it was a smart move to put the money back into a new policy, you know, for herself, and—"

"Why would a healthy eighteen-year-old need life insurance?"

"Well, it's not just life insurance, it's whole life. It's asset and tax protection. Let me explain—"

Skip held up his hand. "Stop right there. We don't have time for a sales pitch. So, the daughter turned down re-investing and took the check?"

"Yes, that's exactly right," Pang answered.

"And you think it's strange?" Bud asked.

"The strange thing was how she was behaving and how weird it feels that her parents died right after canceling their insurance."

"Canceling the policy is hardly a motive," Bud said to Skip. "I mean, if you're gonna whack mom and dad, you do it before they cancel their life insurance, right?"

Skip nodded. "Pang, you said she was acting strange?"

"It's not uncommon for Americanized Chinese teens to act different. I mean, from how our traditions would normally allow for, but this girl…" He flipped through his notes again. "May. May Lau. She was exceptionally curt with her parents and refused to listen to their advice about securely investing the money. She said she was putting the money in her own account, and now that she was eighteen, it wasn't their business anymore."

"And that was unusual?"

"If I'd said something like that to my parents at eighteen, I would never have seen nineteen. It's a different age and a different culture here in the states. But, you know, traditions with people like the Lau's are hard to break. They weren't born here."

"Okay, we understand," Skip said. "Let's move on. Can you tell us anything about what they kept in their safe?"

"I can't be sure what was in or not in the safe, officer," Pang answered.

"Detective," Bud said. "We're detectives."

"Sorry, sorry," Pang said. "I get confused sometimes with titles and translations. Forgive me." He held up a list. "The Lau's had eight pieces of heirloom jewelry insured. Total appraised value, twenty-six thousand, three hundred—"

"Rounded up values are good enough," Bud said.

"Ah, yes, I see. Forgive me, please. It's a habit. I see, okay, so there's a list of paintings and sculptures. Did you see that?"

"Yes," Skip said. "We'll go over that list. And the furniture. But, there's nothing to indicate any art was stolen. What we're most concerned with is the gold."

"Ah, yes," Pang said. He smiled fully and revealed a mouth full of gold crowns. He laughed and pointed to his mouth. "The gold. We can assume it was in the safe—that would be the smart thing, don't you think?"

"Yes," Bud answered. "We'd assume that someone with two-hundred ounces of gold—"

"That was two-hundred and seven ounces, offi—I mean, detective."

"Two-hundred and seven. Fine," Bud said. "I don't think that detail matters at the moment, so let's move on. What can you tell us about this gold?"

"It was gold pandas. Are you familiar with them?"

Skip looked up and said firmly, "Assume we're not."

"Yes, okay. Pandas are minted as legal currency in China, although it's not common to spend them like money. Not so much today. Chinese pay for things with their phones now, mostly. Apps, you know. I'm sure there's an underground market for some things—of course, you're the police—you know how people get things. It's not that different in China."

"So the pandas?" Bud asked.

"Yes, okay. They're stores of value, like collector coins, but of course, they're gold. They track the value of gold in the world market, so even a poorly treated coin is still worth its weight in gold—as they say—even if it's not desirable to a collector."

"You've been very helpful, Mr. Pang," Skip said. He stood and motioned to Bud. "If you have no further questions, partner?"

"No," Bud said. "Unless you know where we can get the best fried rice around here?"

"Yes, yes," Pang said. "Of course. Of course. Here, let me give you gentlemen my card. I handle auto, life, health, home, renters—"

"We're good," Bud said.

"Wait a second." Skip took a card from a dragon-shaped business card holder. "I'm going to be building a new house. I guess I need to think about upgrading my policies."

"Oh, yes, sir," Pang said. "I can guarantee you the best rates. If you combine policies, it's even more economical. May I ask if you're married? Do you have children?"

Bud laughed. "You've opened a can of worms, Skip. And I'm getting hungry."

"Always being led around by your belly."

"Better than other things."

"Mr. Pang, I'll take your card."

They walked out of the office onto a crowded sidewalk. "Where did he say we'd get the best fried rice?" Bud asked. He looked up and down the street. "I forget."

"He didn't say," Skip answered. "He went off on a tangent about insurance."

"Oh, well, um, that is important."

"I know it's important, but it's not a pressing issue. We need to follow up with the Asian Task Force. Maybe there's something there. We need to find out what that symbol means."

"We need to know if the pandas were really in the safe," Bud said. "It makes sense, but until May files a claim—"

"And she said she didn't know what was in the safe."

"Maybe she doesn't even know about the pandas."

"She will soon enough."

"So, next move?"

Skip said, "Let's go back to see Big Ted. We can give him a copy of the list of jewelry. At least there are some unique pieces on the list. If someone walks into E-Z Pawn with a gold panda, we can hardly prove they stole it."

"I'm thinking Walnut Shrimp and—"

"Can't you stay serious for a minute?" Skip asked.

"I'm hungry. It's hard to think on an empty stomach."

"Your stomach hasn't been empty since nineteen-eighty-seven."

After they argued about whether to eat at Chang's or Wang's, Bud won, and they got a table at Wang's Buffet. They ate lunch in silence. Then they drove towards Big Ted's E-Z Pawn. Maybe he'd made some calls.

TWENTY

There was a crowd in the E-Z Pawn.

"I see business is brisk," Bud said.

"Let's see if anyone has asked about Chinese pandas," Skip said, "and get out of here."

"And the jewelry," Bud added.

"Yeah, and of course, the jewelry. I still think Chang's would have been the better choice."

"I like buffets."

"Of course you do, Bud. Of course. And I can see buffets like you, too."

The receptionist buzzed them in without asking for ID. "Hello detectives," she said. "You need Teddy?"

"Yes, ma'am," Bud answered.

Ted was appraising an antique sword. "I'll be right with you," he said to the detectives. "Please, look around and see if anything catches your eye. I give ten percent discounts to law enforcement, firefighters, and vets."

When Ted was free, Skip handed him a folder. "I suspect you've got a photocopier here?"

"Indeed," he replied. "I'll be right back."

"You think he's legit?" Bud asked when he was out of earshot.

"I don't know," Skip answered. "But I feel dirty in here."

When Ted returned, he handed the originals back to Skip. "Okay, detectives, you've given me a list—from an insurance company—but no police report."

"And?" Bud asked.

"And, legally, all I have is a list. Someone comes in here, wants to pawn or sell any of this jewelry, I got no legal cause to call you. I need a police report."

"A technicality," Skip said. "Have you seen any of this stuff today?"

"Nope," Ted said. "Look, I'm a friend of law enforcement. Like I said. Heck, if someone comes in here ten minutes from now looking to sell any of this stuff, I'll call you. Sure. But I have a license to protect. Ethical obligations to the public. If a woman comes in here looking to sell joint property to get away from her abusive husband and I call the cops, I'd open myself up to be sued. Just saying. Get me a police report. Then it's legit, all the way around. Okay?"

"Yeah, sure thing," Bud said. "You know about Chinese pandas? They're like legal coins over there, but people use—"

"I know what a panda is, Detective," he said. "I've got some for sale, in fact."

"Really?" Skip asked.

"Don't get excited, Detective," Ted replied. "They've been in my inventory for months."

"Okay, well, you call us if anything shows up on that list. We'll get you a police report by the end of the day."

"Is that all, detectives?"

Skip nodded. "For now. Earn some goodwill with the department, Ted. Make some calls."

"You know, detective," Ted said. "I like you. I got a tip, but it can't get around that you got it from me. Give me one of your cards. I'm going to write down a name."

Skip handed him a card.

Ted wrote: Gao Fu Shuai Chin.

"I've done business with him," he said. He whispered the next tidbit as if there might be a spy in the pawnshop. "He's a mid-level gangster with ties to leadership in the Chinese syndicate in Little Shanghai. Look, all my dealings with him have been legit, I swear. He brings in things to sell. I give him a good price. Then I mark them up for reselling. It's a win-win business transaction. All on the up-and-up. Totally legit."

"How do you know he's part of a bigger criminal organization?"

"I had to do an appraisal once on site. It was for a pair of foo dog statues that were smuggled out of China. They probably weighed a ton each, so bringing them into the shop was impractical."

"Okay," Skip said. "I'm listening."

"Before we got into the hills, they blindfolded me. Chin said it was for my protection. You don't mess around with these guys, so I went along. The estate where I was taken was at least a couple of acres. Hidden from the street, too. I counted half a dozen armed guards. I'm talking body armor, automatic rifles, the whole nine yards." Ted lowered his voice even more. "There were four G-Wagons. Black, tinted windows, probably the armored package—you know? Bulletproof plating and so forth. Definitely Chinese mafia."

"And what happened?" Bud asked.

"That's confidential, detective. All I can say is that a successful business arrangement was the result. Keep in mind, while those lions—"

"I thought you said dogs?"

"Foo dogs are lions."

"Huh?"

"Foo dogs are just an English term, like a nickname. They're really lions but look a bit like Chows or Shih Tzu's, so that's why—"

"Okay, I get it. Anything else?"

"Well, as I was saying—the statues aren't illegal here or anything. I'm not sure about Chinese laws, but I helped broker a mutually beneficial transaction. I'm giving you Chin because I know he's connected, and someone in that circle would likely know about a couple of hundred ounces of Chinese gold hitting the market."

Skip and Bud thanked Ted for his cooperation and left the pawnshop.

They went back to their war room at the station. They reviewed all the case notes. It was important to have the facts in evidence memorized so they'd know how critical any new clues were to the case. Deciding what things they needed to prioritize was accomplished by talking about each facet of the case. They argued about what items were important. Bud played devil's advocate and forced Skip to use his logical reasoning powers to develop working theories.

The phone extension rang. Bud picked up. It was the Sergeant. He listened, saying nothing except he understood.

"What?" Skip asked.

"Detective Wong is undercover, and we can't talk to him until he's released."

"When will that be?"

"Anywhere from twelve to forty-eight hours," he answered. "Until then, the Sergeant said, we're to stay away from Little Shanghai."

TWENTY-ONE

Echo sat alone. She had a small private table in the back of Callo's Ristorante, an authentic Italian place with a wood-fired pizza oven. She sipped on the house red and nibbled on a breadstick.

Conner messaged her an apology. He'd been working on a big story and had a lead he couldn't ignore. Echo respected that. It was part of being a dedicated investigative journalist. They were both vigilant reporters who hated giving up a good story, even when following it was perilous. It's how they'd met in person—a dangerous story that nearly cost Conner his life. He'd been attacked and left bloodied on the side of the road.

Echo had tracked him down. She'd then broken into his house and stolen his files so that the story wouldn't die. Conner didn't hold any grudges. In fact, he was happy that her determination helped bring an important story to light.

They started getting to know each other while he was still in the hospital recovering from his injuries. There was a time when the doctors weren't sure he'd walk again.

Echo was there during that period, encouraging and supporting him. That time was when their relationship sprouted like a fragile seedling. She was remembering how terrible his injuries were when she heard his voice.

"Sorry I'm late," he said.

Echo jumped, startled out of her thoughts. "Hey!"

"I didn't mean to scare you," he said.

Connor David Lansfield had sparkling green eyes, a square jaw, and stubble on his cheeks. He was as handsome as the first time she'd laid eyes on him.

They ordered dinner and made small talk. After their plates arrived, Conner asked her how she was holding up. He told her he was worried about her efforts to dig into her past. Conner's parents had also died in a car accident—he understood her pain.

"I visited the graves again," Echo said. "It brings me comfort but also makes me feel worse. It's a two-edged sword."

"You sure it's healthy to keep pursuing this investigation? What do you hope to learn?"

"I know it's painful, but I have to know as much as I can. It's like any big story. Once I started down this path…"

"Understood. I feel that way with my current story, the Lau double homicide. I think it's connected to some kind of organized crime, but all I have are feelings and suppositions. No actual facts. Bud gave a statement to the press—but I could tell he's just following departmental orders. His heart wasn't in it."

"That's interesting. You know I'm working on a series about organized crime in Little Shanghai and the possibility of a mafia or syndicate operating there. It's frustrating because nobody, I mean nobody, wants to talk. Not even about non-controversial topics."

"There's a strong code of silence. I'll share any notes I come up with that are separate from the Lau's case. I'm reserving the right to keep that story under my belt—"

"No need to explain," Echo said. "I'm not concerned about any specific crime, per se. I won't step on your toes. Promise."

"I believe you," Conner said. They finished their meals and sat in silence for a few minutes. He smiled at her. "Let's share a dessert?"

Echo nodded. "I enjoy sharing with you."

Thirty minutes later, as they spooned the last of the crème brûlée, Echo said, "My parents will be back soon from Belize. I want to schedule a dinner so they can finally meet you."

"Just let me know," he said. "I'll put it on my calendar."

"You said you talked with Bud," Echo said. "Did you speak with Skip?"

"No, he snuck off like a thief in the night."

"Hmmm." Echo tapped the table. "Knock on wood that they've got something from the Lau case we can both use."

"That would be great. A two-for-one deal."

"I'm going to call and press him for details," Echo said. "If it's purely about the murders, I'll hand it off to you. If it takes me down the path I'm headed with my series, I'll work that alone. Agreed?"

Conner nodded his head.

He scooped up the last raspberry and fed it to Echo.

TWENTY-TWO

Skip walked into a mess.

"Watch your step," Vivian said.

"Dad, it's not fair," Lew Jr. said. "I need to keep all my Legos—"

"Hold your horses!" Skip looked over the disaster. Boxes were piled along the wall. Open boxes sat in the center of the living room. Piles of clothes, toys, and small appliances were arranged on the floor. He hoped Vivian was using a method he could follow in her sorting of his things.

Lucy tugged on his arm. "Dad, I really, really, really need—"

"Stop!" Vivian commanded. "Give your dad a minute to get his bearings."

"But mom, it's not fair," Lew Jr. said. "I'm a part of this family, too."

"Yes, of course, you are, son," Skip said. "But slow your roll, buddy. Let me talk to your mother for a few minutes. I haven't even—"

Lucy interrupted. "I'm not helping anymore. I quit, and I want a new family." She ran to her room.

"If she doesn't have to help," Lew Jr. said, "I'm quitting, too." He sat on the couch between a stack of books and a box of Christmas decorations. He sulked and crossed his arms.

"Go to your room, too," Skip said. "I need to talk to your mom in private."

Lew Jr. stormed off without saying another word.

"Did you hear from the Gypsies?" Vivian asked.

"No."

"They're not very reliable."

"They're Gypsies," Skip said. "What did you expect?"

"I meant the kids."

"Oh." Skip went to the refrigerator and opened a light beer. "They're kids. Their job is to be unreliable."

"I want to trade them in and get helpful, obedient children."

"That get good grades, go to university, get good jobs and support us in our old age?"

"Yeah," Vivian said. "That's the kind of children we should have ordered in the first place. What's wrong with us? And how did we accumulate so much junk?"

"You're the shopper," Skip said. "I don't—"

"You better think carefully about your next words, Detective Malloy."

Vivian used his work title when she was on the edge of getting mad. Skip knew that days off work to sort and pack were difficult on her. He moved two boxes and patted the sofa with his left hand. "Come, take a load off. Let's talk."

Vivian sat next to him.

He took her hand. "I'm proud of you. It takes a lot of patience to pack up years of accumulated junk and not commit child-a-cide."

She wiped her eyes. "I'm not going to cry, but I feel at the end of my rope."

"It's okay to let your guard down," he said. "This isn't going to happen in a day."

Skip and Vivian had signed all the paperwork for the construction loan. His old friend Angela, who worked at the bank, had helped. They'd hired a contractor after weeks of interviews and lots of phone calls to verify references. They'd even driven by a couple of ongoing projects before finally agreeing to hire Conceptual Construction, a local general contractor with nearly thirty years of experience working in the Fairview community.

"We need to rent an apartment soon," Vivian said. "We can't keep kicking that can down the road."

"I know. It's just the prices for rent. They're unbelievable." Skip hated wasting money and renting seemed like burning cash with gasoline. If he had his way, they'd find a campground and pitch a tent while the new house was being built.

"We're not going to live in a tent, Skip," Vivian said as if reading his mind.

"What about a—"

"No RV either," she said. "Be serious, Detective."

"Okay. We'll rent a place this week. Or the week after. I promise. How long did the contractor say this was going to take?"

"He said a year."

"A year!" Skip stood up and put his hands on his hips. "A year? Seriously?"

"That's if we don't make any changes during construction. If we give them any change orders, he said it would take longer, so we have to decide if we're happy with the plans before they begin working."

"I certainly don't want this to take more time. We'll end up going crazy."

"Agreed," she said. "I'm happy with the plans."

"Promise?"

"Promise," she answered. "Now sit down again, and let's talk about renting that apartment."

TWENTY-THREE

Skip attended funerals with a heavy heart.

They came too often in his line of work. It wasn't necessary in every case to attend the services of a victim, but sometimes it was part of the job. Killers often showed up. People offered clues via body language and things they said. New characters sometimes showed up, people under the radar until they came to the church or gravesite and made an impression.

Because there were so many items to follow up on, Skip and Bud decided they'd split up. Bud stayed at the precinct. He'd work the phones, review their notes, and brainstorm new avenues of attack.

That left Skip with funeral duty.

An ancient-looking woman used a cane to approach the annex of the Chinese church. May was with her. Skip thought she looked to be about a hundred and ten years old. Her back caused her to hunch over, and she stopped every few steps to catch her breath. She wore white.

"I'm very sorry for your loss," Skip said.

May nodded. "Thank you. My grandmother doesn't speak English, but I'll pass along your condolences."

Skip gave her an awkward smile. He waited until they passed into the building, and then he took a seat. He sat in the last row so he could see everyone in attendance pass. They dressed mostly in white or brown burlap clothes, although a few of the American guests wore black. He'd worn a black suit as well, rescuing it from a box Vivian had destined for storage.

It was common for red or pink to be worn at a traditional Chinese funeral, but only when the deceased was older than eighty and died naturally. Family and friends would then show their happiness for a long life lived by the loved one who'd passed. Skip reflected on why they were there. It was anything but a joyful event. Losing one parent prematurely was emotionally devastating, and losing both parents in a double homicide was a tragic nightmare. The kind nobody should ever have to experience.

Skip and Bud had discussed earlier in the day whether it was likely that a connection to organized crime existed and, if so, would any of the players be in attendance. They agreed it was possible, but they didn't have any concrete way to establish who was who without being disrespectful. So, they'd assigned an officer with the tech team to set up outside the church and photograph every one.

It was a long shot, but they agreed it was better to cover all their bases.

This case would stay alive in the press, and there'd be political pressure to get results.

After the service, Skip positioned himself outside to watch attendees exit. He knew what he was about to do next could backfire, but his gut told him it was worth the risk. Solving a crime wasn't always pretty.

"Excuse me, May," he said. "Could you ask your grandmother if she can understand this symbol?"

He held up the scribbled Chinese character that Mrs. Lau had written just before she expired. The photocopy was not in color, and he'd purposefully blurred the image so that it no longer resembled blood. It looked a bit like a child's fingerpainting, but it was clearly an Asian character.

"This is vulgar, detective," May said. "We're at my parent's funeral."

The old woman spoke to May.

"What did she say?" Skip asked.

"She said you're a very rude American and that you should leave."

Skip folded the page and put it in his coat pocket. He nodded, apologized again, and excused himself. Scanning the crowd after May escorted her grandmother into a white limo, he spotted a face he recognized: the business partner.

The man approached him.

"Hello," he said. "I'm Fu Jun Li. The Lau's and I were in business together."

"Sorry to meet you under these circumstances," Skip said.

"I've been expecting a call."

"You're on our list of people to speak to. We could set it up if you're free tomorrow?"

"I have a few things I'd like to get off my chest now," he said.

Skip nodded. "Go on."

TWENTY-FOUR

Fu Jun Li was seventy-four and in great shape. He practiced Tai chi each morning, avoided unhealthy foods, and played tennis three days a week. His friends expected him to live to a hundred and twenty, at least.

He'd been born and raised in New York. During his first year at Columbia, in 1967, he'd joined ROTC. He loved the comradery, despite the prejudice of the times. In 1968, the students and faculty protesting Vietnam succeeded in getting the ROTC removed from the campus. Li promptly quit in protest. The end result was a transfer to the private Jesuit university, Fordham. He continued earning top grades, but the military became his passion.

Li graduated with honors. He received his commission into the US Army and worked his way into Ranger school. They sent him to Vietnam.

Asian Americans serving in Vietnam as part of the Ranger's Special Forces were called Team Hawaii. Because they could blend into the environment, the military sent them on long-range reconnaissance missions. They faced discrimination and hatred from both sides—but through all the hardship, Li served with pride and conviction. The Army awarded him the Medal of Honor in 1972.

Li retired in 2001 and settled down in Fairview. After thirty years of service in the United States military, he felt he deserved to retire with some comfort. Using connections and friends to find the best place to park his money, he invested with the Lau's.

Their death was a devastating shock. He carried more than a little fear about the security of his life's savings.

"The Lau's were good people. Devoted to their community, each other, and their daughter," he said. He'd been crying earlier, and he tried to conceal his emotional state from Skip. "I'm sorry."

"It's perfectly understandable, sir," Skip. "I'm sorry for your loss."

"Thank you. I'd been business partners with them…" He stopped to compose himself. "We became good friends. My wife and I played mahjong with them weekly. We celebrated holidays together. I… it's hard to believe they're gone."

"My condolences," Skip said. "Normally, I'd set up an appointment to talk to you, sir—"

"Please, my friends, call me Fox. It goes back to the army."

"Hey, that goes both ways. You can call me Skip."

"Okay, Skip, thank you. I put in a Triple X starting with 'Nam back in the day."

"Thirty years…" Skip put his hand out and said, "Thank you for your service. That couldn't have been easy. Not in the seventies."

"No, sir—I mean, Skip, it was brutal at times. But, you know, I felt it was my duty to my country, and regardless of what people see when they look at my skin, I'm red, white, and blue on the inside."

"Aren't we all?"

"Ain't that the truth," Li said. "I have to join the…" He pointed at the other mourners and looked down. "This is really hard for me, detective. But, I…"

"Go on," Skip said. "This is just between us."

"It's about May. She's been problematic. Troublesome. I don't entirely trust that she's as innocent as she pretends to be."

"Can you be more specific?"

"For starters, like most immigrant parents, especially the Chinese—they put a lot of pressure on her to excel at school. My parents did the same. I credit them with who I am today. But it wasn't easy. Kids today have a different attitude. The internet, sex, alcohol, drugs…"

"You're saying May was into the party scene?"

"She cut school. I know that. They caught her once, smoking weed. Her parents flipped. Her dad called the police department, and a couple of well-meaning officers came out and read her the riot act."

"Did it help?"

"I don't think so. She acted like she'd changed, playing the straight and narrow, putting on a show for her parents. Lee and Ming were good people, Detective. Really good people, but they were strict, and I think a little naïve. They believed in May, and I think she betrayed them."

"You think she had something to do with her parents—"

"Oh, no, no. Not directly, anyway. I mean, I think her behavior was outlandish and irresponsible. She openly defied them. Maybe she did something inadvertently. I don't know, Detective. I just don't know."

"Can you read this?" Skip asked. He unfolded the photocopy of the Chinese symbol and held it up for Li to view. "It's a clue, and I'd appreciate you keeping a lid on this. I mean, if you can tell me what it says."

Li laughed. "I'm one hundred percent born and bred American, Skip. Sure, I play mahjong and tennis and eat dim sum regularly on Sundays. I practice Tai chi, and I'll have to admit all my close friends are Chinese, but I'm American through and through." He pointed at the picture. "I'm saying I'm not multilingual."

"Ah," Skip said. "American schools. I get it. I think I remember about a dozen Spanish words. Ten of them are numbers."

"I took a little French," Li said. "But all I remember is *bonjour* and *oui*."

Skip put the photo back in his pocket. "I'll let you go, but thank you. Here's my card. If you think of anything else, call me."

Li took the card and carefully put it in his coat pocket. He looked up at the sky and shook his head. "What a shame."

"That it is," Skip said.

"I wanted to tell you a couple more things, Detective. One, the boy May dated. Oh, man, did she cause her parents fits. She dated rich white boys. Spoiled ones. Entitled. Her parents forbade her to date—but she defied them. It was impossible for them to stop her at the same time they were demanding she attend lessons and extra classes."

"Like what?"

"They pushed her, I'll admit. Tennis, swimming, music. She had a math tutor and, I believe, a couple of language tutors. Her parents would not accept her growing up without knowing Mandarin."

"She knows Chinese?"

"Well, the basics. It's a hard language to pick up when your first language is English. The sounds are so different."

"And the spoiled rich kids? You got any names?"

"I'll find out, and um—your email was on that card. I'll send you anything else I can think of, Detective. It was nice to meet you."

"Likewise, Fox," he said. Skip thought for a minute and then asked one last question. "Do you know anything about the Chinese Mafia?"

Li frowned. "Not here," he said and walked away.

TWENTY-FIVE

Echo pulled her BMW into the long drive that led up to the Bailey residence.

"Welcome!" Courtney Bailey said. She flashed a friendly smile and motioned for Echo to enter through the tall bronze and beveled glass front door. "Thank you for meeting me on such short notice. There's so much to discuss, but first, please let me give you a little tour."

"Okay, sure," Echo said. It seemed a little unusual for a job interview, but it wasn't as if she had a pressing deadline waiting for her attention. The entry was round like a castle turret and extended well above the second story. A medieval-style chandelier hung on a thick chain from the apex. Echo half expected to see a suit of armor as they walked down the hallway.

"My husband is an art dealer," Courtney said. "We travel to Europe quite often for auctions. Oh, this piece here—" she pointed to a knight on horseback fighting a dragon "—it's a Saint George motif, early…" She scratched her head and looked closer at the piece. "I can't recall now, silly of me. I'll find Kenneth. He knows everything about this era."

"It's okay, really," Echo said. "I do love art, but I'm more interested in talking about the position. Journalism is my love. As you know, I'm sure."

"Yes," she said. "Yes, of course. I've researched you, as I'm sure you've guessed already. I like your style. Follow me, dear. This way." She walked through another door into an enormous kitchen.

A short, portly man with sagging skin and several chins sat in the breakfast nook. He chewed off a piece of what looked like a roast beef sandwich. It was obvious he was much older than Courtney. At least twenty-five years, by Echo's estimation. He wore an ill-fitting toupee and had a mustard stain on his shirt.

"My husband, Kenneth Bailey," Courtney said. "Ken, this is Echo Rose. She's come to interview about a position with *Soft Vanda*."

"Oh, that's nice, dear," he said with his mouth full. He glanced at Echo before leaving the room with his sandwich. "Nice meeting you."

"He's got a lot on his mind," Courtney said. "The art business took a hit recently. But, well, never mind about that. Please, have a seat in the dining room. Can I get you something to drink?"

Echo declined and took a seat. There were eighteen chairs around the biggest table she'd ever seen outside of a banquet hall. On all the dining room walls were paintings that looked like they were from the Middle Ages. King Arthur and the Knights of the Round Table, she assumed. She decided not to ask because she didn't want the discussion to go down a rabbit hole.

"I met Ken at an art show," Courtney said as she sat across from Echo. "In Paris. What a coincidence, don't you think?"

"Coincidence?"

"Yes, can you imagine flying all the way to France and meeting the love of your life at an art show and finding out you're both from Fairview?"

Echo shook her head. "That is pretty crazy."

"I've wanted to start a family for a few years, but, unfortunately…"

Echo waited for her to finish. Courtney was a tall blonde with striking blue eyes, and she couldn't imagine the two as a couple. But love is blind. *Isn't it?* After another moment of awkward silence, Echo said, "Unfortunately what?"

"I'm his third. Wife, I mean. He's got five kids already. It's expensive these days. You wouldn't believe what he spends on those kids." She frowned and shook her head. "Cars, clothes, shoes, trips, private schools, vacations—it never ends."

"I bet," Echo said. "Shall we get down to business?"

"Oh, yes, sorry." Courtney worked to regain her composure. "We've been all over, you know, collecting art, going to auctions." She opened her cell phone and showed Echo pictures while she scrolled. "Paris—well, I told you that, but also all over. Berlin, London. Ummm, we went to Greece once, and to the South of France. Spain, Portugal, and, well, just about all over Europe."

"Okay," Echo said. "That's really nice."

"You know, I've always wanted to go to Tahiti or Fiji. But it's sad, they don't really have a lot of art auctions there. I guess the natives don't collect art. Well, anyway, someday I think we'll make it to New Zealand and Sydney, and, what's the place where they…" She flipped through more pictures. "Ah, Malaysia. That's the place. I think they have a famous museum there."

Echo nodded.

Courtney then looked up from her screen and said, “Echo Rose, I really and truly need your help.”

TWENTY-SIX

Skip returned to the station and found Bud talking to a man who appeared out of place.

He was Asian. Skip thought he looked Chinese, but he wasn't sure. His hair was messy and hung to his shoulders. Tattoos covered both arms. He wore jeans and a concert tee-shirt that listed the cities of the band's last world tour. Skip didn't recognize the group.

Bud turned towards the door. "Hey, Skip, you're back."

"What happened?" Skip asked. "I go to one funeral, and you get a new partner?"

"This is Steve Wong," Bud replied. "He's undercover with the Asian Task Force."

"I figured that."

"You're a brilliant detective."

Detective Steve Wong held out his hand. "Either that, or you just know they don't let delivery guys past the front desk."

Skip shook his hand. "Another comedian."

"So," Steve said, "you just attended your first traditional Chinese funeral?"

"And I hope my last," he said. "No disrespect to the deceased."

"I hate funerals," Steve said. "The worst part of this job."

"How long have you been undercover?" Skip asked.

Bud put up his hand. "Before you two become new best friends, why don't we take a seat. I'll get you up to speed, Skip."

They all sat. Bud took the lead and gave Skip an overview of what they'd discussed before his arrival. Steve had been undercover for nearly eighteen months, working with the Asian Task Force in Fairview, Camden, and the surrounding communities. Little Shanghai was the main area of operations, and Steve knew the place as if he'd grown up there, which was, in fact, the case.

As part of his cover, he'd developed a convincing lie about traveling out of state to attend university. His work was currently indispensable for law enforcement's attempt to crack open the various gangs and criminal organizations.

"Skip," Bud said. "He's interpreted the bloody symbol."

"Really? Great news, what's it say?"

"Daughter."

"No." Skip frowned and thought about the implications of that revelation. He didn't think the daughter could have shot her parents. It was too far-fetched. "We need to confirm and triple check her alibi," he then said. "But I still can't see the daughter pulling the trigger."

"I don't think so, either," Steve said. "Based upon my experience in the community, I'd be shocked to discover she was there, in the house, during the murders. But that doesn't mean she wasn't involved."

"I don't buy it," Bud said. "But stranger things have happened. No stone unturned here, of course, but I'm still convinced there's a connection to the Chinese Mafia."

"There is no mafia," Steve said. "Lots of organized crime, but they run things differently than the Italians."

"Okay, organized crime. Syndicates. Gangs. Tongs. I don't care about the names. They still extort businesses, smuggle drugs, promote gambling, and pimp out women—some who might be victims of sex trafficking from outside the country," Bud said.

"What more can you tell us?" Skip asked Detective Wong. "Did you two discuss the pandas and the heirloom jewelry?"

Detective Wong stood. "I can think better if I'm not sitting," he said. Then he paced for a minute. He explained it was a delicate situation at the moment. The FBI had a joint task force working with the Fairview PD. Tempers flared, and jurisdictional fights were common. "So, bottom-line, Detectives, you're going to want to tread lightly."

"We've got a double-homicide," Skip said. "I'm not neglecting my duties because of the feds or anyone else."

"I feel you," Steve said. "I do. But there's a lot of rank over our heads, if you know what I mean. I'll help steer you however I can, but don't burn me on this. We've got more agents out there. Undercover. People I can't reveal to you."

"The feds, the sheriff, the state police," Bud said. "I swear we spend more time infighting or trying to figure out who's who sometimes than fighting the criminals."

"But," Skip added, "we respect your position, Detective. We don't want to mess up your investigation. We'll keep you in the loop, but we hope you can do the same. A couple of law-abiding, taxpaying citizens were murdered. It's our duty to find those responsible and put them in one of the state's concrete and razor-wired hotels."

"You have my number," Detective Wong said. "I'll see you two around."

When the door closed, and they were alone, Skip looked at Bud and asked for his opinion.

"He seems like he's being straight with us," Bud said. "I've got a file here with names and connections. Some of the hierarchy involved and so forth. It's a start."

"Other than we now know the symbol means 'daughter'," Skip said, "is there anything helpful? The gold? Any connections to the Lau's or their business partner?"

"None," Bud said.

"So, what's next?" Skip asked.

"We need to interview the boyfriend."

TWENTY-SEVEN

Echo looked at Courtney Bailey. *She wants a favor?*

They hadn't started the interview—if that's what it really was about—and the woman was asking her for help. Echo looked her in the eye. "I think I'd like a glass of water," she said, "if you don't mind?"

"No, of course not," Courtney said. "You sure you don't want something stronger? A cocktail? Beer? Wine?"

"No," Echo replied. "No, thank you. Just water."

Courtney returned with two wine glasses, one with ice water and a second with white wine. She raised her glass and said, "To our new venture."

"Well," Echo said, "You haven't even explained what it is you'd like me to do."

"Oh, those salesmen. I blame my husband. Ken always says, 'assume the sale' and you're halfway to closing."

"I don't want to be closed, Courtney. Please explain what it is you'd like me to do."

"There's this terrible website. It's called 'Amanda's Secret', and it's so married people can cheat." She'd lowered her voice as she said the part about married people. Then she glanced around the room as if to check to see if they were still alone.

"Okay," Echo said. "Please. Continue."

Courtney explained how Amanda's Secret worked. It was an app for people in relationships, married or not, to cheat on their partners. It operated like regular dating and hook-up apps, but they specifically designed it for people who wanted privacy and no entanglements.

Since both people involved would have something to lose if their liaisons became public knowledge, the app advertised that it used many steps of security to thwart hacking attempts. The company headquarters were in Camden.

"I know your reputation," Courtney said. "I've heard stories about you, and I need a writer who can really dig deep into this thing and find out—"

"Hold it right there," Echo said. "I think cheating is wrong, but this isn't really my area of passion. I work in criminal investigative journalism. This story sounds like something for the gossip—"

Courtney shook her head with exaggeration. "No, you don't understand."

"Okay, explain."

"There are two things I believe the company is doing that is illegal. The first thing is that they're turning a blind eye to prostitution on the app. The second is less serious, I know, but it's still a multi-million-dollar scam. They use bots."

"Bots?"

"Yeah. Can you believe men pay hundreds of dollars a month to talk to these programs that pose as actual women?"

“And the company is a front for prostitution?” Echo asked.

“The company isn’t providing hookers. That’s not what I meant. By federal law, a company cannot let its platform be used for solicitation. It doesn’t have to be providing prostitutes. It only has to turn a blind eye to pimps and hookers to be violating the law. I believe they know for a fact that prostitution is going on. They just don’t care. Profits over people. That’s what *Soft Vanda* was created for—to shine a light on darkness. We want to help stop the exploitation of women.”

“So, let me get this straight,” Echo said. “You want to hire me to work on this story alone? As a freelancer? Or something else? I was under the impression you were looking to hire a staff writer?”

“Yes, yes, of course,” Courtney said. “The magazine has a need for a woman writer like yourself to step up and seek important stories. The thing is, the budget, the times… We’re underfunded. It’s part of the reason we’re meeting here and not in a fancy downtown office.”

“So, this isn’t a job interview?”

“Think of it as a freelance offer that we hope will lead to a full-time position.”

“All right. I’m not opposed to considering this idea.”

“I figured you might like your independence.”

“True.” Echo thought about the situation. She felt a little blindsided and misled; however, the story sounded intriguing, at least the exploited-sex-worker angle. She wasn’t so concerned about men wasting money chatting with bots they assumed were real people. *Fools rush in*, she thought.

"Penny for your thoughts?" Courtney finished her wine. "You sure you won't join me?"

"I'm sure, thank you. I'm curious about the sex workers involved in this because I really don't want to go down a path that hurts women even more."

Courtney nodded. "I knew you'd feel this way. These aren't free-thinking mature women who are expressing their right to use their bodies as they want. That's a different subject and a fiercely debated one."

"Especially in feminist circles and women's rights groups," Echo said. "So, what are we talking about?"

"Sex trafficking of young women. Some of them are undoubtedly underage. They aren't free to make their own choices. They're from foreign countries, and they get stuck in these illegal schemes and can't get out. That's the story I want you to pursue."

"And you have evidence?" Echo asked.

"Some," Courtney replied. "We've been shorthanded and underfunded, as I mentioned, so I only have circumstantial evidence. If you agree to a freelancing contract and an NDA, I'll get you all I have. The focus at first will be sex trafficking in Little Shanghai. There's a veritable epidemic going on. In fact, I've met—this is off the record—with a cop at the Fairview PD. Detective Steve Wong. He works in Little Shanghai with the anti-gang unit."

Echo felt butterflies when Courtney mentioned Little Shanghai. "Okay, I'm interested," she said. "But before I commit to anything, let me dig a little first."

TWENTY-EIGHT

Bud said, "Let me be the good cop this time."

They were on their way to interview a nineteen-year-old college freshman named Gary Turner. He was the former boyfriend of May Lau. According to their research, he was a business major and an athletic high-achiever from a wealthy Fairview family. He was tall, white, and handsome. They'd also discovered that a math tutor that May had been seeing was going to be on campus as well. Perhaps they could pry a clue out of one of them.

"You're better at being the bad cop than I am," Skip said. "This kid is going to be too smart to think I could be a bad cop."

"You're giving him too much credit," Bud said. "He grew up in an upper-class neighborhood."

"So?"

"So, he's preconditioned to think black men are scary."

"Is that right?"

"It's in the handbook," Bud said.

"What handbook?"

"You're totally changing the subject. Let's just try it my way for once and see."

"You're making me a little angry," Skip said.

"I know I am. It's part of the process."

"What process?"

"Getting you ready to be the bad cop."

"We don't even know this interviewee will be evasive or hostile." Skip put his attention back on driving.

Bud turned on the radio. He found a station playing old country music and whistled along. He turned off the climate control and rolled down his window.

"You're too much," Skip said.

"Just getting you into character."

Skip ignored him the rest of the way to the Amery campus.

When they began the interview with Gary Turner, Bud felt his efforts were wasted. Gary was polite and cooperative. *Maybe we'll get lucky*, he thought. *Maybe it was all a façade.*

They'd been talking informally for twenty minutes when Gary said, "I really do have to get going soon. I have a class and practice after that, but you have my cell number."

Gary had explained that he broke up with May months ago. May's parents were strict. She got good grades. They'd put her in piano and tennis lessons and had expected her to study Chinese and French.

"Do you think they were unhappy she was dating you?" Skip asked.

"Oh, for sure," Gary answered. "There was no question. They didn't want her dating until after she finished high school. And, I hate to say this, but they were prejudiced against me."

"For being white?"

"Yes. Traditional Chinese families expect their children to marry—you know—other Chinese. It's kind of embarrassing to say that."

"Did they treat you badly?" Bud asked. "Like when you were in their home?"

Gary showed a crooked smile. "I was never in their home. Well, at least not when they were there, which was most of the time. Me and May only saw each other away from her parents. They basically forbade her to see me at all, but May was too stubborn to control that much. She had too many lessons and tutors and practices to attend, so there was always a little wiggle room for us to get together."

"Did they ever threaten to call the authorities?" Skip asked. "What I'm saying is: you were an adult, and she was seventeen. They could have used that against you."

"I started kindergarten early, so I wasn't that much older than May. We actually broke up close to my eighteenth birthday. Most of the time we dated was when we were in high school together. We were both minors."

"Did she ever talk about killing her parents?" Skip asked.

Gary looked at him with a startled expression. "Excuse me?"

"Did May ever talk about getting rid of them?"

"No, of course not," he said. "She loved her parents. They were overbearing and controlling, and I broke up with her because I couldn't handle the third person in our relationship."

"Third person?" Skip asked.

"Yeah, what third person?" Bud added. "I don't have anyone else involved, according to my notes."

"Them: Mr. and Mrs. Lau. They were the third person. She essentially brought them along everywhere she went."

"So that resentment didn't lead to anger?" Skip asked. "I'd be real mad if I had to live that way."

"Of course, it did. Her parents started pushing her as a little kid. Chess lessons and spelling bees. They even tried to get her to learn golf, but she couldn't get the coordination down. May had no time for herself—she left the house at seven in the morning most days. She got home, did homework, played the piano, and was lucky to go to bed before midnight."

"Sounds tough," Skip said. "That could drive someone mad. Maybe make them think about ways out. Maybe she said something to you and—"

"No way," Gary said. His face reddened. "She hated them. I'll admit. She hated her parents and wanted to escape. But kill them? No way. May's not capable of inflicting that level of violence. You don't know what you're saying."

They left him standing there cursing under his breath.

"I think you got to him," Bud said. "I knew you could do it."

"Let's go talk to the math tutor."

TWENTY-NINE

Echo, back in her apartment, opened a browser and found the Amanda's Secret website. It directed her to download an app onto her phone. She had several smartphones with non-registered phone numbers, like burners, except she didn't throw them away. They came in handy when she didn't want to use her personal contact information when researching a story.

Amanda's Secret was well designed and easy to use. Echo built a fake account using an alias and twenty-year-old stock pictures of a European model who appeared to be in her early twenties. Using the app was free for women, but it required men to pay a monthly fee. There were also other features, profile boosts, and greater access that cost extra.

Echo set up a second account using a different phone, this one for a man's profile. She also used old pictures of a minor celebrity that were unlikely to be recognized.

The app allowed her to set a maximum distance for matches; she used fifty miles at first. That covered Fairview and the surrounding communities. The women that came up while she used the male profile ranged in age, so she altered the settings. She was interested in those under thirty—based upon her research, she figured it would be unlikely to find older women who were sex trafficking victims.

There was no way to know by a cursory look if a woman's profile was legitimate or not. Any of them could be faked, just as Echo had done herself. They could be bots, or perhaps they were pimps, as Courtney had suggested, who created fake accounts to surreptitiously offer sexual services to men on the site.

The potential for scams and cons to thrive always existed on the web. It would be Echo's job to search for facts on which to build a story.

In order for a connection to happen, both parties had to interact with each other's profiles. Once that happened, they'd each receive notice that a potential affair was in the making. The idea made Echo sick to her stomach, but in order to create realistic messages, she forced herself to imagine what things she'd write if she was actually interested in adultery.

Her story would require her to see the transaction from both perspectives, so she played the deception using both fake profiles. Then she put aside the phones. Her targets would need time to find her profiles and reciprocate.

Next, she opened her laptop and did some digging. The company website was heavily encrypted—she wouldn't be able to hack into it on her own. Amanda's Secret's marketing announced that people trying to cheat could trust the website and app to keep their information totally secure.

They weren't kidding: they'd locked it down like a bank. No security was ever one-hundred-percent fail-safe, although many times successful hacking required an insider. That gave Echo an idea. She went to the company's main web page and found a "Work for Us" link. They were hiring marketing specialists and content writers.

She created a fake CV and applied for the writing job.

Looking at the phone with the female profile, she saw there were already four notifications—the male profile had three. *That was fast.*

Ignoring it for a moment, she opened the secure messaging platform on her computer and typed a message:

ER43seer: *Hey, are you online?*

Anlt984snk: *Of course. Where else would I be?*

Out getting some fresh air?

What's that?

It's this stuff you find outdoors along with trees and clouds.

Overrated.

There's also the Chili-Chili Hotdog Cart.

They do home delivery.

No, really? Since when?

It's a new age, ER, everyone delivers. If house calls return, I'll never have to leave my sanctuary.

How's the diabetes?

I'm fine. Really, thanks for asking. What's up?

I have a job for you.

On top of that Chinese thing?

Yeah. This is different.

Okay. Same rate?

Yup.

You got it. What's the target?

Amanda's Secret.

Hold one sec…

Echo looked at her phones while she waited. Both profiles had each received another message. *I'd never imagined there were so many cheaters,* she thought. *Humanity is doomed.*

Anlt984snk: *I'm back.*

And?

This will take some time. It's heavily encrypted. But you probably knew that.

Yes. I also applied for a job. I'm going to get myself inside the building.

That will work. Keep me updated.

Will do. Take care and avoid carbs.

Echo closed the program and considered her next move. She opened the app connected to the male account and began writing to women.

The only way to set a trap was with good bait.

THIRTY

Skip had made an appointment with a math tutor named David Chang. He was waiting for them at the campus cafeteria.

"Thank you for meeting with us," Skip said. They'd agreed on the walk over that Bud would take back the job of bad cop if needed. Neither of them thought the tutor would be very helpful, but they were already on campus, so it made sense to talk to him.

"That's okay," David said.

He appeared nervous to Skip, but it was common for completely innocent and unknowing witnesses to have anxiety when talking to a couple of homicide detectives. It wasn't every day that a murder affected someone close.

"We're just covering a few bases," Skip said. "May we sit?"

David nodded, sat, and closed his laptop. "I've got an appointment in twenty-seven minutes. Will this take long?"

"No, I don't think so. Can you describe your relationship with May Lau?"

"I've been her tutor for nearly three years. We meet weekly, usually on Thursdays, but sometimes that changes."

"Where do you meet?"

"Here sometimes. Sometimes at the public library. It kind of depends on her other activities, so it changes season to season."

"Do you ever tutor at her residence?" Skip pulled out a notebook and pretended to take notes. It was a ruse simply designed to make sure the interviewee took the questions seriously.

"No, never," David said. "She lived up in the hills, from what I recall. It would have taken me too much time to get there and back. I have other students and classes."

"So, you never met her parents?"

"No."

"Did May talk about them to you at any time?"

"She complained a few times. I mean, normal teenage complaints. We weren't friends, Detective Malloy."

"Okay, fair enough. Did you ever speak to either of them?"

"I got a phone call once. From her father."

"How did that go?"

"He was upset that May's test results and grades weren't perfect. He seemed to think that it was my job to make her good at mathematics, but that's not how it works. Math is a passion for some people—others hate it and only do the minimum amount of work they can to get by."

"So, May was in the second category?"

"I wouldn't say she hated math so much. Instead, I'd say that she didn't have a natural affinity for it. There's only a handful of us, you know, who really love and study math as a passionate subject. It's not like marine biology or astronomy."

"Okay, so her father wanted better results, and you told him it wasn't your job to make her a math expert. How'd he take that?"

"He wasn't happy with me, but I think he got it. I think he realized I could help her pass her classes if she did the work—but I couldn't turn her into a math prodigy."

"Let's return to things May might have said to you or perhaps something you overheard her say, like on the phone," Skip said. "Was there anything that would show tension in her relationship with her parents? Anything to indicate a substance problem or anything she might have been hiding from them?"

"There was tension, for sure. It's common with a lot of my students who have old-school traditional parents. Not just Chinese, but others, too. I tutor a Jewish kid whose parents get upset if he gets a ninety-five on a test. I once had a Korean student, a senior, who showed up with a black eye after a poor test result. My students almost always feel a lot of pressure to get into a top university—it's axiomatic that a parent who hires me has high expectations. I'm not inexpensive."

Bud said, "This isn't leading us anywhere. You ready, Skip?"

"One minute," he said. "What was your childhood like, David? If you don't mind me asking?"

He blushed. "I was a straight-A student and had little life outside academics if that's what you mean."

"Your parents were strict?"

He nodded his head. "They came to America only two years before I was born. It was a hardship. They wanted a better life for me."

"And they pushed you to excel in school?"

"I got an A-minus once, Detective." He looked down, embarrassed to be talking about it.

"Go on," Skip prompted. "What happened?"

"My parents didn't let me listen to music, watch TV, or talk on a phone for months. Not until my next report card came back. My mother lectured me every night at dinner about how important it was to work hard and secure a good future."

"But, David," Bud said, "you never considered hurting them, correct?"

"No, of course not. I'd never. My parents love me and only want the best. I'm headed to an advanced degree, and I'll be in an elite group. I mean, in the entire world, Detective. If math were like football, it'd be like if I was going to get drafted by the Dallas Cowboys or the Los Angeles Rams."

"And what about May?" Bud asked.

"I can't see it, Detective. No way. A Chinese daughter killing her parents? It's just not done. She might have hated them but hurt them? Kill them? Not a chance."

Skip and Bud thanked him and left the campus.

"Well, that was unproductive," Bud said.

"Can't win them all."

"You have any reservations about crossing May off the person of interest list?"

"Yeah, I'm not ready," Skip said. "I'm not saying I think she's a suspect at this point in time. No. But my gut tells me she's not being totally forthright."

"We need her to file a police report about the stolen goods, too," Bud said. "Maybe we should go talk to her?"

"I think that's prudent."

THIRTY-ONE

Echo drove to *Above the Fold*'s offices because Frank Walsh had requested a face-to-face meeting.

She liked Frank and missed the feeling of belonging to a team. The office had changed little. It just had fewer people and less activity. The idea of investing crossed her mind briefly, and she made a mental note to bring it up with her father.

"Hello, Echo," Frank said. "Please, come in."

The owner and managing editor of *Above the Fold* wore a dark gray wool suit. His silk tie was a deep purple. It reminded Echo of royalty and prestige. The office had the lingering odor of an expensive cigar.

"Please, close the door behind you," Frank said. He spoke with authority and confidence. "Have a seat. Can I get you a coffee or anything?"

"No, thank you, Frank," she said. Echo sat across from his expansive metal desk and looked out the windows towards the city center. "I love this view. I miss the office, you know?"

"I understand. I'll miss it, too, if I'm forced to retire early."

"I can't imagine you retired," she said. "What will you do with your time? Fish?"

"Hardly. I hate worms, the sun, and boats. But, you know, you're right. I'd get bored in less than a week. It wouldn't take me long to start scrolling through job postings for anything I could find. Maybe I'll end up in the mailroom at a surviving paper's offices. Wouldn't that be ironic?"

"I'm sure it'll never happen," she said. "How's the investor search?"

"It's slow going. A newspaper isn't exactly a bright and shiny tech stock."

"Yeah. Times have changed, haven't they?" Echo recalled how she'd met Frank—his daughter had been kidnapped many years previously and then disappeared without a trace. It wasn't until Echo had been working on the story of a kidnapping that the truth finally came out. While it didn't heal his pain, of course, she knew that having the closure that came with knowing the truth helped. It was one of the reasons she continued pursuing the story of her own past and her birth parents. Closure. It could really hurt to know the truth, but not knowing was an unacceptable alternative.

"I'm still torn up about you not working here anymore," he said. "I'd like to hand you more leads, in fact—"

"Hold on, Frank," she said. "I'm working on that crime series already. There's a lot there."

"Okay, understood. You know, I appreciate you not selling stories to rival papers."

"Although, I miss being part of a team," she said. "I can't promise you I won't work for anyone else. You do know that, don't you?" She didn't want to tell him about the potential story she had. If she came to terms with Courtney Bailey and signed a contract, she'd be ethically obligated to keep everything she discovered away from *Above the Fold*.

"I understand," Frank said. "Totally and completely. You need to work. Heck, you have to work. It's in your blood. I get that. I respect it, too."

"Thanks, Frank."

"I'm disappointed, of course, but if you've got your hands full—well, that settles it."

"I'm going to hang out and wait for Conner," she said. "You don't mind?"

"Make yourself at home, Echo."

THIRTY-TWO

The older of the two brothers was stocky. He worked out whenever their schedule allowed and had the muscles to prove it. He had a dozen tattoos and was planning to get the next one as soon as they could clean up the loose ends resulting from their latest job.

"When are we going to get out of this crappy motel?" the younger brother asked. He was slender, almost to the point of being too skinny, at least in his brother's eyes. He didn't have any tattoos because he thought getting inked was tacky and low-class. Not that he ever gave that opinion to his older brother.

That would lead to a beating.

Ever since they were kids, the older ruled the younger. It was tradition, in a way. At least that's what their father had told them before he was killed during an armed robbery. They didn't grow up thinking they were involved in a crime family or that anything their uncles did was unusual. It was just the way it was.

They were inseparable. By the time they'd reached adolescence—they were only eighteen months apart—they'd both been arrested multiple times. Because of their ages and the minor level of the crimes they got caught doing, neither had spent much time locked up.

But, even a few nights behind bars makes an impression.

By their late twenties, they'd become ruthless but also very cautious. It'd been five years since the last arrest, a little side job in Houston. That experience drove home a few lessons: trust nobody, plan every step, stick to the plan, and if picked up by the cops, never ever talk.

At some point in high school, one of their uncles had given them the nicknames, Ying and Yang. Ying was athletic and excelled in wrestling and football. Yang was a straight-A student and a nerd. Both were, according to the school psychologist, budding sociopathic criminals.

The elder brother slapped Yang on the back of the head. "We're not leaving this motel until we've figured out if it's safe. I'm not driving around with thirteen pounds of gold."

"I'm bored out of my skull."

"Here, play with my phone," his older brother said, tossing it onto the unmade bed. "Check out this app where you can find a cheating whore."

"That's not my style. I want to settle down with a nice girl."

"You mean like mom?"

"That's not funny."

"You need to grow up. Swipe through those profiles. There are some hot Asian girls in there who are bored with their workaholic executive husbands."

"You know I like Latinas."

"Don't let mom hear you say that."

"Mom's dead."

"She can still hear us."

"Right. And Dad's ghost is here guiding us, too."

"Don't be stupid. Dad's in hell. They don't let anyone out of hell."

"If he's in hell," the younger one said, "I'm going to church more."

"That train has left the station, bro. Look, if you don't want to arrange a hookup, at least do some work."

"That sounds worse."

"We need a new client."

"You make it sound like we're traveling salesmen."

"We kind of are," the elder brother said. "We provide a needed service."

"Let's sell the gold and take some time off."

"I'm working on it. But we still need to think about the future. We can't retire just yet, little bro. We need a bigger nest egg. Find someone."

Yang opened his laptop and went to work.

THIRTY-THREE

Echo sat at her old desk.

Above the Fold's offices didn't feel like home anymore. Not like they used to. What used to be her spot was devoid of personal things. She wondered if it would be fulfilling for her to invest in the paper. It would be risky, but it would bring her back to a place she loved.

Pablo, walking by, stopped and looked at her. "Everything okay?"

"Hi, Pablo. Yeah, I'm just waiting to meet Conner."

"You look sad."

"Just remembering things I missed about this place."

"I have stories—"

"I know," she said. "And I appreciate it. But those aren't my style, plus I'm working on something."

"You got an assignment from a competitor?"

"No, it's not like that," she answered. "I'm working on something for Frank, that Little Shanghai series…"

"That sounds like an *and* at the end of that sentence?" Pablo asked.

"And I have other things going on too. Don't worry, Pablo. I'm still loyal to *Above the Fold*. But I also have to keep busy."

"I understand."

"Thanks for keeping me in mind," Echo said. She smiled at him. "If I need something, I'll let you know."

Conner walked up behind Pablo and said, "You two having a private meeting?"

Pablo laughed. "Yes, but she's all yours now."

When they were alone, Conner said, "I'm not getting any comments from Fairview PD. Any chance you talked to Skip?"

She shook her head. "We haven't talked except for him saying, 'No comments at this time'."

"That's about all I'm getting from anyone," Conner said. "I don't know if they're being extra careful about something or just obstinate."

"Maybe a little of both," Echo said. "In any case, I'll share anything I can. And I have a small favor to ask."

Echo had agreed not to keep him in the dark about what stories she was pursuing after how close she'd come to losing her life in the Hotel Murders.

"Sure," Conner said. "How can I help you?"

"I might take an assignment," she said. "It's with a national magazine. Before I say what it's about, I want to—"

"You know we have a deal."

"Yes, I know. You'd never steal a story. I wouldn't do that to you."

"So, what's the issue?"

"If our stories overlap, what will we do?"

Conner thought silently for a minute. Then he whispered as if they were conspiring in secret, and someone might listen, "You think the Lau murders are connected with your Shanghai crime series?"

Echo gently nodded her head. "There's more."

"Okay," he said. "Let's hear it."

She filled him in on the meeting she'd had with Courtney Bailey. Echo told him everything she knew. She explained her thoughts on where she'd go next with the investigation regarding Amanda's Secret.

"So," he said, "you think there could be a connection between everything…"

"It's possible. I haven't researched the Lau's case, but it certainly isn't a stretch to think that a Chinese organized crime connection exists. What seems likely, and what I am looking at, is a connection between the potential abuse of women connected to Amanda's Secret and the crime centered in Little Shanghai. It seems there's something there."

"Where there's smoke—"

"—there's fire," she finished.

"You said you had a favor."

Echo explained that she'd need a man to show up for any meetings she could set. She was going to chat with women, pretending to be a man, to see if any of them illegally solicited the invented profile. She said, "I've made fake accounts on the app, a male account and a female one. There's no reason to make a date with any of the men. I'd like to interview some women to see if I can get a lead on sex trafficking, pimping, underaged abuses, or anything nefarious or illegal. I'd like you to show up and break the ice. Build some trust and then introduce me."

"You're using my picture!?" Conner looked concerned and a little upset.

"No, just a guy that looks close enough. People cheat on these things all the time. Someone engaged in illegal activity won't care."

"I guess not," he admitted. "Okay, I'll help. In return, all I ask is that if you find a connection to the Lau murders, you leave that part of the story to me and *Above the Fold*."

"Deal," Echo said. She put out her hand, and they shook on it.

THIRTY-FOUR

Skip and Bud drove to the Campbell residence. May Lau had been staying with her best friend, waiting for law enforcement to release her house. The detectives had permission from her parents to conduct an informal interview with Heather, who was still a minor.

Skip parked on the street in front of the house. "We should interview May first," he said. "You should play bad cop a little—to see if she rattles."

"I don't know," Bud said. "Let's ask her some tough questions, but I don't see her involved."

"I agree she wasn't there during the killings. I mean, unless she left the mall, went home to kill her parents, and then changed out of bloody clothes and cleaned herself up before calling nine-one-one."

"That would make Heather an accomplice," Bud added, "or an accessory-after-the-fact."

"I agree. It's not likely."

"So, she's *not* under suspicion of being there during the killings, right?"

Skip shook his head. "No, I'm not ready to say *definitely* not. Most likely, no, but I still have this weird feeling…"

Bud turned to face his partner. "So you think it's in the realm of possibility she was there?"

"Yes. But I'm not saying I think it's likely. Just a possibility."

"That means we need to press Heather for any sign that she's covering for May." Bud opened the door and stepped out of the car. "I'll get tough in my questions if needed. We can also enlist the parents to pressure her if we think she's lying."

"Agreed," Skip said.

He followed Bud up the drive to the suburban home of the Campbells, who welcomed the detectives into the house. Mrs. Campbell invited them to sit at the kitchen table and offered them coffee. Mr. Campbell excused himself.

"No, thank you," Skip said. "Could you ask the girls to join us?"

"Yes," she replied. "They're watching TV in Heather's room. I'll be right back."

Heather and May came down the hall towards the kitchen. May laughed at something Heather said, but seeing the detectives, she turned solemn. They walked into the room without saying another word.

Skip spoke first. "We'd like to talk to you, May. Alone. We won't be long. There are just a few formalities we need to cover."

"It's just for our files," Bud said. "Heather, if you could join your mother and wait just a few minutes, we'd appreciate that." He turned to Mrs. Campbell and said, "Please remind Heather how important it is that she's completely and one-hundred percent truthful with us today. She will not do May any favors if she isn't forthright about everything."

"Yes," Mrs. Campbell said. "We understand completely. Heather is a very honest person." She took Heather's hand and left the detectives with May.

"I thought I answered everything already," May said. She stared at the floor.

"Please," Skip said, "have a seat." He pulled out a chair for her. "You've been very cooperative, thank you. We need to cover some ground. It's standard procedure. We won't be long."

"I don't need…" May looked at Skip and then Bud. "I don't need a lawyer, do I?"

"You have every right to a lawyer, May," Skip said. "But you're not a suspect in this case. You're not under arrest, and you don't have to talk to us."

"You do want to help us catch the people who killed your parents?" Bud asked. He remained calm and spoke in a soft voice that matched Skip's demeanor. "We often find in cases like this that a family member knows something important. They just don't realize it. We want to talk to you about some loose ends. Maybe you'll remember something like an insignificant detail that will help in the investigation."

"You do want that, don't you?" Skip asked.

May nodded her head. "Yes," she said. Her voice broke, and she sobbed for a minute. "I'm sorry."

"It's understandable," Skip said.

"I'm ready."

Skip set a file folder on the table. He opened it and pulled out a form. "This is a theft report addendum that is currently blank," he said. "The safe was opened. It's logical to assume items of value were stolen."

"I told you," May said. She sniffled. "I don't know what was inside. I swear."

Skip pulled another form out of the folder and set it on the table. He slid it towards May. "This is a list of insured items. Do you recognize anything on this list?"

May read in silence, looked up, and asked Skip if it was true that her parents had two hundred and seven ounces of gold.

"It appears that way," he said. "The question is whether the gold was in the safe."

"Of course, it was," May said. "Where else would it be?"

"That would seem logical," Bud said, entering the conversation. He raised his voice a notch. "However, without a police report attesting that the gold was stolen, then technically, it's not. How would anyone know for sure?"

"Where else would it be?" May asked.

Bud nodded to Skip. They had an arrangement in these situations. Skip took the gentler parts of the interview. Bud would hang back and attack if needed. They orchestrated it to keep an interviewee off balance; this way, if a witness or suspect tried to hide something, they'd have a better chance of shaking them up.

"May," Skip said, "it's likely the gold was in the safe. It's logical to think that. But it could be elsewhere. In a safe deposit box. Buried in the backyard. Good police work requires facts, not assumptions. We can't assume thieves stole the gold merely for you to collect the insurance money."

May tapped the table with her left hand. "I'm not…" Her face changed. She was thinking. She looked up and said, "I'm thinking the gold was in the safe."

"Do you know for sure?" Bud asked. "Are you certain? Or are you guessing?"

"I'm sure. My dad told me," she replied. "I just forgot." She lifted the form up to her face. "I know these pieces of jewelry. They're my mom's. She only wore them on special occasions and kept them inside the safe the rest of the time."

Skip sighed. "Okay."

Bud asked, "So you're willing to sign these property-loss forms?"

May looked at them a third time. "Yes," she answered. "All this stuff was in the safe. I'm sure."

Skip handed May a pen and showed her where to sign after listing the stolen items on the report. When she finished, he put the forms back into the file. "That's settled," he said. "The next thing we'd like to ask you about is the money you received from the whole life policy you cashed out."

"That's for school," she blurted. "It's got nothing to do with my parents."

"Okay," Skip said. "We have to ask."

"We'll need to confirm with your bank," Bud said. He spoke matter-of-factly. It was another thing on a list that required completion.

"You can do that?" May asked.

"This is a murder investigation, May," Bud said. "We're trying to get to the truth."

"It's just routine," Skip said. "Don't worry about it, May. I mean, you have nothing to hide, correct?"

"No, of course not," she said. "But I took cash from the bank. So, it's not in my account right now. It's for school. Plus, I want to take a vacation once this nightmare ends."

"So, you withdrew nearly—what was it, Bud?"

"Over fifty-seven thousand dollars," he said.

"You took fifty-seven thousand dollars—"

May interrupted. "I only took out fifty."

"For school?" Skip asked.

Bud gave her a hard stare. "And a vacation?"

May nodded her head and started crying again.

THIRTY-FIVE

Eventually, May's sobbing ended.

"Could you ask Mrs. Campbell to bring Heather here?" Skip asked.

"Okay," May said. "Is this the last time?"

"We can't say for sure, May," he replied, "because it's an ongoing investigation. We'll only need to talk to you if we think you can help us. Isn't that what you want? For us to find the criminals responsible?"

She nodded her head and walked away.

"She doesn't seem very enthused about helping us solve this thing," Bud said after she left. "I don't buy this story about the safe either."

"Something's not right. No doubt about it," Skip said. "But was she lying before, saying she didn't know what was in there? Or is she lying now and committing fraud with her declaration of loss?"

"I guess we'll find out when we figure out who the killers are," Bud said.

Mrs. Campbell entered the room, followed by Heather. Because Heather was a minor, the detectives needed a parent, guardian, or legal representative present to interview her. Neither of them felt there was any evidence of her involvement, but she was the person providing May's alibi for the night of the murders.

"Please, take a seat here," Skip said to Heather. He pulled out the chair that May had just occupied. "Mrs. Campbell, please sit anywhere you're comfortable. We'd only ask that you observe without comment unless we need to ask you a question. Is that okay?"

Heather's mother nodded and took the chair at the end of the table. She was wringing her hands and appeared to be more nervous than her daughter.

"Let me start by saying that Heather isn't in any trouble, Mrs. Campbell. We just need to make sure she's on record about that night." Skip turned to Heather. "We need you to not only be honest, Heather, but we also need you to stick to what you know factually. If you're not sure about something, that's okay—you can tell us if you have an opinion—but don't give us any opinions as if they're facts, okay?"

"Yes, I understand," she said. "I don't know anything about that night except I was with May. We went to see a movie."

Skip led Heather through a series of questions about the night of the murders. He sought to establish a timeline covering the time from when Heather first met with May through the time they parted. He asked questions about the movie, about anything they ate, if they met any other people, or if May ever left her.

"She went to the bathroom a bunch of times," Heather admitted. "May told me she had a stomach thing—like maybe she ate something bad."

"Did you go with her to the restroom, or did she go by herself?"

"I went once because I had to go to the bathroom too. The other times she went by herself. She was feeling sick, and I didn't want to miss the movie. And I think she wanted some privacy."

"Why do you say that?"

"She kept looking at her phone. I thought maybe it was some new guy she was seeing, but when I asked her about it, she deflected."

"Okay, so she's maybe chatting with a new guy. She's not feeling well. Is there anything else unusual you recall about that night?"

"She was more quiet than normal, but it wasn't that strange, I mean since she was sick."

"What things did she talk about regarding her parents? I'm talking about a normal night when she was feeling okay. Would you characterize her demeanor towards her folks as normal? A little bit angry? Maybe hostile?"

"Well, regularly," Heather replied, "I think…" She looked at her mother and then dropped her eyes.

Her mom said, "Be honest, baby. They just need you to tell the truth, nothing else."

"So, normally," she continued, "May would complain non-stop about her parents. They forced her into doing so many things she didn't like. There were music lessons and sports on top of her school work. And languages. And a math tutor. It's kind of normal, I guess. Every kid complains about their parents. But, she was…" Heather appeared confused. "It was more with her. More than typical, I'd say. Sometimes she even seemed hateful."

"So, this night was different?" Skip asked.

"Yes, for sure." Heather nodded her head and spoke with a tad more confidence. "I thought she must be really, really sick. I mean, not to have anything to say about them. It was weird. But, you know, I remember she got a phone call as we were walking to the car after the movie."

"Did you hear any part of that call?" Bud asked. "Did you know who it was from?"

"No," Heather replied. "She walked away from me. After she hung up, she was smiling. I asked her about it, thinking, maybe it was a boy, you know? Like maybe she got a date or something. But she told me it was nothing, and then she changed the subject."

"And you took her straight home after that?" Skip asked.

"Well, yes, I mean, sort of. We drove through the AJ & Son's Burgers for shakes."

"She didn't bring up the phone call again? Or say anything about her parents the rest of the drive?"

"Nope. We went up Fourth Street and drove right to her house."

Skip stayed on the lead. He knew Bud would jump in and interrupt if he noticed any deception. Or if he wanted to shake her memory. "And you dropped her off, right? Our initial report says that you didn't exit your vehicle. You just dropped May off in the driveway. Is that correct?"

"Yes, that's exactly right," she said. "Then I went home. I didn't know anything was wrong until later when May called me. That was when she asked to stay the night."

Bud asked her a series of questions about May's demeanor after she got to the Campbell's that night. He pushed her with rough questions, asking about anything May might have said or done that was suspicious or strange.

Heather insisted May acted shocked and sad. "She went to sleep right away. My mom gave her something."

"Is that right, Mrs. Campbell?" Bud asked.

"Yes, detective. I knew she needed to sleep."

"How did she seem in the morning, Heather?" Skip asked. "Did she make any phone calls? Did she mention this boy she might have talked to the night before? Was there anything unusual about her behavior?"

"She never mentioned any guys. I don't know if she was talking to a boy—she never said. She was on the phone, but mostly with her grandmother. Or maybe one of her aunts in China because her grandmother doesn't speak English and May's Chinese is terrible." Heather laughed. "Her parents insisted that learning to speak Chinese was important, but May hated it. She felt they wanted to dictate every part of her life. I bet if they'd forbid her to learn Chinese, she'd have mastered it."

Bud picked up his notebook and flipped pages.

Skip knew it was a tactic. Bud was thinking of anything else to ask. Skip filled the gap by asking a few unimportant questions. Then he said they could wrap up.

"One more thing," Bud said. "Did May ever mention selling gold?"

Heather said, "Not recently, no."

"But?" Skip asked. "She did before?"

"I went with her once to a pawnshop near downtown. She tried to sell a coin that she said was a birthday gift, but they told her she had to be eighteen."

"Do you remember which place? The name?"

"Not really."

"What about the coin? Do you recall what it looked like?"

"It had a panda on it," she said.

THIRTY-SIX

Skip and Bud drove to the coroner's building, which was only three blocks from the police precinct. In Fairview, the city council and Mayor appointed the Chief Coroner's position. Sabine Werner had held the spot for more than a couple of decades. She was married to her work and liked to help dabble with the forensic and tech evidence when she had the time. Many times, she'd been instrumental in helping homicide clear a case.

"Is this your office or your bedroom?" Bud asked after rapping lightly on Sabine's open door. Because she was a workaholic and singularly focused on her work, Sabine had a sofa, complete with a pillow and blankets, in her private work space. She also had a wardrobe filled with clothes and a pink bathrobe hanging from a hook.

"Both," she answered. "What's the point of lugging files to my apartment when I'm perfectly capable of getting some sleep here?"

"May we come in?" Bud asked. "Or should we chat in the cafeteria?"

"I could use a coffee," she replied. "I'll meet you there in five. Am I correct in assuming you're here about the Lau case?"

"That's it."

Bud and Skip walked down sterile halls and entered the cafeteria.

"I don't know how anyone can eat in this building," Skip said.

"Someone on staff bakes these amazing chocolate and raisin oatmeal cookies," Bud said. "I could eat those anywhere."

"And I see you have," Skip said, "more than once."

"I'm going to ignore that remark and grab a coffee. You want one?"

"Sure, I can do that."

Bud returned, two coffees in hand and a plate of cookies. "Fresh out of the oven. I'm serious, Skip. Eat one of these, and you'll swear that you've died and gone to heaven."

"I don't think you should say 'died and gone to heaven' in the morgue."

"Better than the other place." Bud looked down and stuck half a cookie in his mouth.

Sabine entered the room and dropped a stack of files on the table next to Skip. "Are those warm oatmeal chocolate raisin?" She didn't wait for an answer before taking one. Looking at Skip, she said, "You might want to eat a cookie before you open that."

"I'm gonna pass," Skip said. "You two enjoy." He opened a file and started reading.

Bud took another cookie. "Don't worry, Detective, I'll take care of these for you." He turned to Sabine. "You want to give me the *Reader's Digest* version while Skip plays master detective?"

"Sure," she said. "There were no surprises in either autopsy. In both Mr. and Mrs. Lau, the cause of death was gunshot. The slugs were twenty-two caliber. In Mr. Lau, the bullet ricocheted inside his skull. The trauma to the brain was extensive."

Bud nodded. "Okay, any striation left?"

"That report isn't back yet," she said. "My initial impression is both bullets are too damaged to help. The bullet that killed Mrs. Lau didn't ricochet inside the cranial cavity, instead it hit the top of the spinal column, just about in the middle of the cervical section of the vertebral column. It's pretty much destroyed in terms of getting any patterns off it. Our best bet is the bullet from Mr. Lau, but as I said, it's going to be a long shot."

"Okay," Skip said. He looked up from the files he'd been browsing through. "Looks like the wounds were all inflicted prior to the gunshot, correct?"

"Yes, we didn't note any postmortem cuts or breaks—all consistent with your initial observation. They were tortured and then shot."

Bud asked about the toxicology reports.

"Not back yet," she replied. "I wouldn't hold my breath there's anything there. But we'll see. I can tell you there wasn't anything notable outside the injuries they received, no signs of cancer—no indications of any terminal diseases. For their ages, it seems like they were healthy… You know, until your murderers showed up."

"And we're sure there were two?"

"Let me show you the tech report," she said, picking up a file. She opened the folder and read: "'All evidence supports the conclusion there were two unknown subjects inside the Lau Residence'." She closed the folder.

"The shoe prints in blood?" Bud asked.

"Yes. There were three distinct sets of shoe prints left on the scene. May's shoes left one set. Techs discovered the pair in her walk-in closet. They were entered into evidence. The second and third set left marks in blood, but more importantly, because of the highly polished hardwood floor, we have full prints from both sets of shoes."

"And did they identify the brands or models?"

"Yes," she said. She opened a folder and showed the detectives what the techs had discovered. "You can see here—" she pulled out a photocopy of a shoe print "—this left shoe has a distinct marking." She pointed to a spot on the print.

"Gum?" Skip asked.

"Probably. Could be gum, candy, dirt, or dog poop. The point is that it's distinct. Find a guy wearing this shoe before he cleans it, and you've likely got one of the perps."

"And the other set?"

"Nothing distinct. It appears to be new. There are faint wear marks. It would be hard to testify that any given shoe is an exact match. You know, beyond a reasonable doubt. That said, find a match to this, and it's likely perp number two. Find them together, and it's ninety-nine percent."

"Okay, it's something," Skip said.

Bud held up his hands and wiggled his fingers. "No luck with prints?" he asked.

"Nothing that's popped up in the system. We have his, hers, the daughters, a housekeeper, some that are likely friends. The team will narrow them down. So far, no felons. Bobby, over in forensics, has a flag on the file. He'll call you immediately if anything they lifted starts ringing bells."

"They had to be wearing gloves," Skip said. "That's crime school One-Oh-One."

"But we might get lucky with the shoe prints." Bud smiled and added, "Maybe they're dumber than we're giving them credit for."

"Looking over the tech's reports," Sabine said, "I'd say the only strong identifier we have is the shoe with the crap stuck to it. Assuming the bad guy hasn't ditched the shoes or cleaned them, that's how you put him on the scene. If you find a twenty-two-caliber weapon, probably a ladies' purse gun, we might get a partial match to one of the slugs. But it's a long shot."

"Okay, let's get a copy of the shoe print photo," Skip said. "Once we find a suspect, we can request a warrant to inspect all their shoes."

"You might consider the choice of weapon here," Sabine said.

"Not a nine," Skip said. "I thought about that."

"I see enough gunshot victims come through the coroner's." She shook her head. "It's sad—but I digress. In most gang-related shootings, or say in cases of execution-style killings, the weapons used are typically nines, tens, forties, and forty-fives."

"So you're thinking it… what? It was the homeowner's weapon?" Bud asked.

"Not my call," she answered. "What I'm saying is that if you go to the ER and ask, sure, they'll have examples of twenty-two caliber injuries: hunting accidents, suicides, and some crime, too. But, for most criminals inflicting death, they're using a bigger weapon."

"Bud, make a note to pull the Lau's up on the state's gun registry," Skip said. "Let's see what they owned."

"And we're sure about it being a handgun?" Bud asked.

"Seems a stretch to think they shot downward on the top of the head with a rifle," Skip replied. "Any forensics confirming a pistol?"

"Yes, two things. First, as you've noted, the angle of the shot and the positions of the bodies. Next, muzzle velocity, which affects how the bullet behaves once it leaves the barrel—I'll confirm and get back to you—but experience leads me to say handgun. Finally, it's just logical, and while that's not a forensic call, it's what I'd bet on in this case."

"Okay, that's helpful," Bud said. "We need a guy who has dirty shoes and likes small guns."

"Maybe one was a woman?" Skip asked.

"Doesn't fit the profile, unless it was the kid. But, our techs did a thorough check. She didn't fire a gun that day."

"Back to square one," Bud said.

"Meanwhile, detectives," Sabine said, "I've got to get back at it. I'll see you two around."

"Not if we see you first," they said in harmony.

"You guys twinsies today?" She laughed and left the cafeteria.

"So, partner," Bud said. "What's next on our agenda?"

"We've got this panda that Heather says May sold. Then we have her unbelievable story about why she pulled fifty grand in cash out of the bank."

"We should follow up with Steve, too," Bud added.

"Let's go find a concrete, actionable lead, Detective Smith."

"Right behind you, Detective Malloy," Bud said, "just as soon as I grab another cookie."

THIRTY-SEVEN

Echo pulled into the corporate parking lot and parked her BMW in a visitor's spot.

The building's address was prominently displayed, but there wasn't anything showing it was the main headquarters of Amanda's Secret. Probably, Echo thought, to evade vandals and spurned wives and girlfriends. She knew it wasn't really fair to blame the company, after all; it was the cheater who cheated. But she felt the company was being irresponsible and providing a service that ultimately damaged society.

Her CV was fake, but she'd enlisted Frank, Conner, and a couple of hacker friends to provide her references and to confirm the made-up jobs she'd claimed. The experiences she'd listed were all things she could have done with her writing skills, so she was prepared to take any tests they could throw at her.

After checking in with the receptionist, Echo waited ten minutes before being called to a conference room. A short, round-faced woman in business attire put out her hand. "I'm Teresa West, and I'll be starting off the interviewing process today."

Echo acted as if she was aiming for an Oscar. "I'm Rhonda Flemming," she said, giving her fake name. "I'm thrilled to be here today. It's a pleasure to meet you."

After further pleasantries and small talk, Teresa got down to business and asked a series of questions about “Rhonda’s” past employment history and experience. Echo played along and answered each question based on how she felt would put her in the best position for the job.

“Okay,” Teresa said. “This part of the interview is over. I’m glad to say you’ve passed.”

“That’s great,” Echo said. “What’s next?”

“Follow me,” Teresa replied. “This way.”

They went to a room with cubicles and banks of computers. “Please, have a seat there,” Teresa said, pointing. “I’m going to push this button.” She started a program and handed Echo a set of headphones. “Please, put these on and follow the instructions. I’ll come and get you in about twenty-five minutes.”

The program started with a short video explaining that its purpose was to test the potential employee's writing ability under pressure and with time constraints. The company’s test emulated situations the employee would face working with clients on the app.

Echo began the first phase. It was a simulation of a conversation with an interested man.

Tom: *I like your profile.*

The test required her to type in a response: *I like yours, too.*

She cursed under her breath for giving such a lame answer, then quickly scrolled through the simulated profile of the account named “Tom” and read that he was a lawyer. He’d been married for ten years and was “kind of bored” with his sex life. He wrote he was looking for some spice and a change.

The work disgusted her, but getting the job was crucial to several steps of her investigation. She reminded herself she was pretending and that it was for a good cause.

Echo wrote: *I'm nervous, but I think it's fair that we get to be selfish once in a while. I work hard, and I'm good to my husband and kids. I just need some me-time.*

Tom: *You understand me exactly.*

Echo continued to write things she thought would qualify her for the job. Eventually, the "Tom" account asked if she'd like to set up a meeting. Echo wrote: *Yes! I'm so happy you asked.*

A window in the program flashed. A new message: *This portion of the test is complete. Please move to the next section.*

Echo did so and completed all the steps. Teresa reappeared and said, "Great. That's it for testing. What happens next is that my supervisor will look over your test scores and application. Security will do a pretty thorough background check. You know, we get a few crazies in here. Then, if it's all good to go—and I believe it will be—we'll call you back for a final interview and hopefully a contract."

"That's great," Echo said.

"Questions?"

"No," Echo replied, and she thanked Teresa for the interview.

Back in her car, she let out a giant breath and called Conner.

"I feel so disgusted," she said when he answered.

"I bet," he said. "Did you find anything you can use?"

"Yup," she said. "When the person interviewing me left me, she entered a room with a massive bank of computers—I saw she used a card reader to get inside. I'll need to swipe that and install a gateway device that'll let my guy in. Easy-Peasy."

"You just have to get offered the job."

"Oh, they'll offer me the job. I nailed the interview."

THIRTY-EIGHT

May Lau opened her front door.

The big red door that was supposed to invite health and prosperity to the home mocked her. She shuddered as she stepped inside. The stale smell of disinfectant hit her nose. It reminded her of being in a hospital.

A specialty cleaning company had finished only an hour before she'd arrived. The regular cleaning woman had refused to enter the house until someone else removed all traces of blood and gore. When the Fairview PD tech teams had finally released the house, one of them gave May a couple of referrals to agencies that worked on crime scene cleanup. May hired the first one she called and then fired her family's regular cleaner. "I'm selling the house," she'd told her.

May got a notepad and pencil from a kitchen drawer and made a list.

Call a real estate company. List the house.

Go to that insurance guy's office. Ask about policies.

Research art auctions. Or maybe talk to the guy at the pawnshop?

Sell the piano. Try eBay?

Look at lofts downtown. Rent or buy?

Sell the cars. Trade-in?

She walked downstairs to the basement. She started to add the pool table to her list of things to sell but then changed her mind. In the office, she stared at the safe. "Damn thieves," she muttered to herself. "Damn. Damn. *Damn!*"

Back upstairs, she called her grandmother. Their conversations were strained, but May knew enough Chinese, and her grandmother understood enough English to get by. By the end of the call, she'd explained the situation well enough. The police had released the house and the guest quarters—where her grandmother always stayed when she visited, and it was ready for her.

She then dialed another number.

One she'd memorized two months before.

It would not be a fun conversation.

THIRTY-NINE

Skip looked at Vivian and asked, “You can’t be serious?”

“I’m not staying in that roach-infested apartment downtown, Detective Malloy. We can splurge for this place. It will give me peace of mind with the kids.”

“It’s way out of our budget. We don’t need an apartment with a clubhouse, a gym, a pool, and an underground parking structure. Nobody is going to steal my car if I park on the street.”

The complex they’d just left had the fancy name, *The Stony Brook Luxury Apartments*. Skip had argued before they set foot on the property that it was out of their price range.

Vivian had said, “It can’t hurt to look, can it?”

Skip opened the passenger door for his wife. “Let’s find a compromise,” he said before closing the door. As he walked around to the driver’s side, he realized she’d brought him here on purpose. After looking at a very expensive place, the moderate apartments she really wanted him to agree to rent wouldn’t look so bad.

He sat and started the car. “I know what you’re doing.”

“And what’s that, Detective Malloy? What am I doing?”

Skip put the car into drive and realized he was falling into another trap. “You’re just looking out for the kids. I love you for that.”

"I don't want them in a sketchy environment," she said. "That's all."

"I know, but look at me," he said. "I'm fine, and I grew up in the 'hood."

"You're a unicorn, Skip. You got lucky."

"I'd say I made my own luck."

"Okay, fine. But my point is that a bad neighborhood and the wrong friends can lead impressionable kids down a path we don't want them to go."

"All right. Point taken. But I'm still not renting a luxury apartment."

Vivian smiled and took his hand. "Agreed. Let's find something in the middle."

They'd looked at eight places over the last two weeks, and Skip was losing his patience. "You sure you won't consider—"

"I'm not staying in a KOA campground in a rented RV. I don't care how nice it is."

"Okay," he said. "I surrender. Let's go look at that place on Montgomery Avenue. It's in a good area."

"That's better," she said. "No more excuses. We need to find something soon. The longer we put this off, the longer it's going to take for them to start tearing down the old house."

Skip reflected on that—it was funny how sometimes, to build up something good, you had to destroy something that you'd lived with for years.

FORTY

Echo entered the Amanda's Secret corporate offices dressed in light blue business attire and sensible shoes. She downplayed her makeup and didn't use drastic colors.

They'd scheduled her to interview with Landon Grimes, the head of HR. Teresa had hinted on the phone that if it went well, he'd offer her the position and want her to start right away. They were short-staffed and had projects piling up.

Before she'd left her apartment, she'd called Conner. "I can't believe the world we live in. We have serious businesses, an important source of news like *Above the Fold*, that can barely afford to pay staff writers while a company that provides cheaters a way to cheat can't hire enough people to keep up with the demand."

He'd reminded her she couldn't save the entire world. She could only do her part to fix the things she could. "You're doing important work, Echo," he'd said. "Don't forget that."

An aide took her to an executive suite on the upper floor and directed her to take a seat. It wasn't long before Landon Grimes walked in and introduced himself. He started the interview with softball questions but eventually got around to asking more direct and hard-hitting ones.

"Are you sure you're okay working with a company that facilitates what many call an unethical and immoral transaction?" he asked.

"I'm not the moral police," Echo replied. "What consenting adults do behind closed doors isn't any of my business. I'm a writer—and a good one—I'm just providing a service. It's not a concern of mine."

"Okay, great. And if you're approached by outside media?"

"I'd say 'no comment' and be about my business," she said. "I have no problem ignoring people who are poking around in private affairs."

Landon smiled. They talked for another ten minutes before he said, "I'd like to offer you the position. If you accept, you can start immediately, once the HR department gets all the paperwork done, of course. You'll begin working on building profiles. These are the bots that need to be created in such a way that they appear realistic. It takes a certain skill that I believe you have."

"Thank you," she said. "I enjoy being creative."

"Later, I'm going to see how you work out in the live response department. This gets a bit trickier because you're often chatting live with someone, and you have to keep up the front that you're really Jane, Sally, Linda, or Heather."

"Sounds fun," she said. "Like a game."

"Yes, it's a bit like a video game."

He stood, put out his hand, and said, "Welcome to the team."

FORTY-ONE

Skip looked at their corkboard and said, "There's got to be something we're missing."

"Let's go see Big Ted," Bud suggested. "I do not believe the story that May's selling about the safe and her knowledge about its contents."

"If she's lying about her knowledge, it just means she's signing the police report with the assumption that the gold was there. Which it probably was—which means there's nothing there to pursue. It doesn't imply she committed murder."

"What if she took the gold and hid it," Bud said, "and now she's filing an insurance claim to double-dip?"

"I'd say that's a stretch. Possible? Sure. But even if it's what she did—"

"It doesn't make her a murderer."

"Probably not," Skip admitted.

"So, we scratch her off the persons of interest list?" Bud asked.

"Let's not say that yet. In fact, I'm calling the Sergeant to ask if we can put a surveyance team on her."

"He's going to yell about the cost."

"I know, but I'll only ask for a day shift to follow and observe her. Just to see if she does anything strange or meets with anyone suspicious."

"He might agree."

"And I'm only asking for a week."

"What do you think she's doing with fifty grand in cash?" Bud asked.

"Maybe there's a connection to the Chinese gangs?"

"You think she's being extorted?"

"Perhaps. Maybe her parents were being blackmailed, and they refused to pay?"

"But for what? And if they didn't go to the police right away for extortion or blackmailing, why would they for theft? What would be the point of killing them? The robbers could have tied them up and just taken the gold, and the Lau's could have filed an insurance claim. Nobody's looking at a life sentence for murder."

"What did the State Weapon Registry report say?" Skip asked.

"The Lau's owned one handgun. Registered to Mr. Lau. It's a SIG Sauer Nine—probably the gun in the little safe under the bed. The tech crew dusted, no prints except Mr. Lau's, so it's not even evidence. May didn't know the combination. A dead end."

"Maybe we should follow up with the partner, Mr. Li," Skip said. "When I asked him at the funeral about any potential gang connection, he acted uncomfortably and didn't want to discuss it."

"Maybe just a bad day," Bud said.

"Agreed, but maybe he knows something. Let's go see Ted, then Li, and then we'll circle back and talk to May again. Maybe we can rattle her."

"You'll be the bad cop?"

"No, stick with what she knows."

"You think she thinks I'm the bad cop?"

"I can tell by the way she was looking at you the last time we talked."

"Okay, partner," Bud said, "let's roll out of here."

FORTY-TWO

HR assigned Echo to a computer station, a cubicle near a window.

The window overlooked a parking lot and not much else. It didn't matter. She wouldn't be there long. She went to work creating profiles: bots luring men into spending more time and money on the Amanda's Secret app.

I'm a dog lover, and I like Italian food.

My home life is difficult, but I can't leave him. We have two children.

He works nights and weekends, so I can get away between 5 pm and 11 pm.

I enjoy movies, wine, chocolate, and hehe...

After a few hours, just before lunch, Echo thought she might go to the roof of the building and jump. Instead, she waited until her lunch hour and snooped. It wasn't risky for her to walk around the building looking lost; it was her first day. Getting lost wouldn't be unexpected. Nobody would become suspicious if they found her in the wrong hallway. Of course, the strategy wouldn't work in a few days—so she took advantage of her newness.

"You lost?" someone she hadn't met asked.

"Oh, yeah, sorry, first day," she answered. "I was looking for the break room where I was hoping I could heat up my..." She held up a paper bag.

"Follow me," the stranger said. "My name is Stanley, but the guys call me Mouse. I'm in IT. You don't have clearance to continue down this hallway. The backup systems are down there. You need a passkey." He held up his ID card. It hung on a lanyard around his neck.

Echo smiled.

"There are two break rooms. Most of the creatives and sales guys stay on the first floor, but there's no reason you can't eat up here with us geeks," he said. "You like computers?"

"Well, of course," she said. "I write for a living, don't I?"

Mouse smiled. It was one of those awkward smiles that Echo recognized from her friendships with introverted computer experts. Guys who didn't get out much into the real world. He laughed and said, "You know Pony and Python are animals, I'm sure, but around here, they're languages. For computers. It's complicated."

"I wouldn't know about it," Echo lied. "I use word processors and email."

"And I bet you're an expert on social media."

"For sure!" She pretended to laugh and hoped he didn't catch on that she was faking. "Well, I'd better find that microwave."

"Let me show you," he said. "This way."

Echo needed a friend in the IT department, so she played along. She felt a little bad about plotting to steal his pass card, but then again, he chose to waste his programming talents at a company that ruined marriages, destroyed lives, and could be helping sex traffickers. She needed a plan to get into the server rooms.

“I’m right behind you,” she said. “Lead the way.”

FORTY-THREE

Bud closed the folder he'd been looking through. "You think there's a connection between this Ching Lóng Benevolent Society, the Golden Dragon's, Gao Fu Shauai Chin, and the Lau's?"

"I want to ask Li about it," Skip said. "And May."

"We'll have to be careful not to interfere with the task force's investigation."

"I know. This might get tricky."

"Let's go see the Sergeant and request the surveillance on May. We can explain to him our concern about tipping off gangsters while needing to know if there's a connection. Perhaps May is just the victim here, and she's scared."

"She didn't seem scared to me," Skip said.

"You're right. She didn't seem scared at all. More like confident and arrogant."

The detectives filled out the required forms and gave them to the Sergeant. They gave him an overview of the case. He said, "Go see Big Teddy and don't hesitate to inform Licensing and Enforcement if you see anything sketchy."

After they parked under the, WE BUY GOLD sign, Skip said, "I'm getting tired of coming here."

"Let's get it over with," Bud said. "I bet there's no paperwork on May. We'll be out of here in ten minutes."

"I think there is," Skip said. "I just have a feeling."

They walked into the EZ-Pawn, and the receptionist buzzed them in. "Hello detectives," she said. "He's in the back. I'll let him know you're here."

"Tell him we're headed back there," Skip said.

They met Ted at the rear of the retail space near the office door. There was an "Employee's Only" sign hanging just under an antique brass plate that read "Office."

"Back so soon, detectives?" he said. "Did you see something you liked last time? I'll even go up to fifteen percent off today only."

"We're not here to shop, Ted." Skip pointed to the office door. "We'd like to see the slips on the pandas you sold."

"Right this way, gentlemen," he said, opening the door. "I run a clean and legal business here, as you well know, and, here, please grab a couple of chairs if you'd like."

"We'll stand," Bud said. "Just pull the slips for those pandas real quick. We've got other places to be."

Ted pulled a ring of keys out of his jean's pocket and opened a filing cabinet. "I think it was a couple of months back. Let me see. One second." He rifled through several sets of folders and then pulled out a single sheet. "This is it. I remember now. Young Chinese girl sold me two coins. The previous purchase was last quarter, different cabinet. Would you like that one as well?"

"No," Skip said. "Let me see this one first."

The paperwork was for a direct purchase, not a transaction involving a loan. A pawnshop could legally take an item of value and hold it for security for a loan. The interest rate and fees were high, and it was often the desperate who used the service. A straight sale, however, was different. A person might sell gold, silver, jewelry, or even a television to a pawnshop just to get quick cash. You'd get more money, usually selling to another party online. However, if you were in a hurry, a pawnshop could offer you cash on the spot.

"It says here, Gary Turner," Skip said, looking at the paper.

"I remember now," Ted explained. "This girl comes in and wants to sell some gold, but she's not eighteen. She complained and made a big fuss when I told her I couldn't buy from a minor. She came back with this guy in tow, and that's who you see on the paperwork."

"So, you still bought gold from a minor," Bud said.

"Nope. You can see right there. I followed the law to the letter. Nothing about an underaged girl on that sheet. I'm cooperating, detectives, by telling you what I recall. Don't forget that. I could have kept my mouth shut."

"Run me a copy of this," Skip said. He handed the paper to Ted.

"Whatcha thinking, partner?" Bud asked.

"So, May, she comes in here to sell a couple of coins. So, she knows about the gold, at least some of it. She lies at first that she doesn't know what's in the safe—"

"Or she lied afterward because she wants the insurance money."

"Right. Bottom line, she lied."

"So, we go see her next?"

"No, let's go talk to Mr. Li and gather more intel first."

When Ted returned, Bud took the copy from his hand and said, "Thank you, Ted. Don't forget. We're your first call if anyone shows up looking to sell any pandas."

"You got my police report?" he asked.

"It's right here," Skip replied. He handed Ted a copy of a police report listing stolen goods. The names and addresses of victims were redacted.

"The girl?" he asked.

"Can't say more, Ted," Bud answered. "Keep a lid on this and call us."

"I'm always a friend to law enforcement, detectives. If something comes up, you'll be my first call."

FORTY-FOUR

Skip and Bud took the most direct route to the hills. Fu Jun Li, nicknamed "Fox," lived only a mile and a half from the Lau residence. He was outside in the front yard when they arrived.

"Detective Skip," he said.

"Mr. Li—"

"Please, call me Fox, or Fu Jun," he said.

"Okay, this is my partner, Detective Smith," Skip said.

"Call me Bud, please. It's a pleasure to meet you," Bud said. "I wish it wasn't under such terrible circumstances."

"Me as well," he said. "How can I help you guys? Would you like to come inside?"

"No, thank you," Skip said. "That won't be necessary. We'll make this quick."

"Were you aware of any guns at the Lau residence?" Bud asked.

"Lee Sum kept a SIG under his bed," Fu Jun said. "I doubt he ever brought it out. It's probably been fired only a few times at the range. He took a gun course."

"That's a nine, correct?" Skip asked.

"Best to my best recollection, yes."

"And as far as you know, there were no other guns?"

"As far as I know."

"Okay, thank you," Skip said. "The other topic is something I touched on at the funeral."

"The organized crime connection," Fu Jun said. "That's a dangerous topic. Can we go inside?"

Skip looked at Bud, and his partner nodded. "Okay, lead the way," he said.

After they entered the house, Fu Jun pointed towards a living room. "Please, have a seat," he said. "Can I offer you anything to drink?"

The detectives declined and sat on opposite sides of a long black sofa. The room was decorated minimally, with only three other pieces of furniture. Fu Jun sat on one of a set of red chairs across from a coffee table. On the table sat several enormous books about military campaigns.

"I can't get away from it," he said, pointing at the books. "My wife complains that I still watch military documentaries and war movies after giving most of my life to the service of the country. 'You were there,' she says to me. 'Why do you need to watch more?' I have no real answer. It's an addiction, I suppose."

"Thank you for your service," Bud said. "Detective Malloy mentioned your career and medals."

"It was a job," he said. "I did my duty. Now, what exactly do you want to know about the Ching Lóng Benevolent Society?"

"What can you tell us?" Bud asked.

"What my partner means," Skip added, "is that we know little about how organized crime works in Little Shanghai. We've been told that this thing called a tong is a cover for various street gangs and others who do the dirty work."

"That's basically it," Fu Jun said. "The tong has a community center. They're a legitimate charity, at least on paper. They help immigrants and widows, but they also provide cover for street gangs. That's where it gets dangerous looking into this stuff. Everyone knows they can't talk to the police without consequences."

"Does the name Gao Fu Shauai Chin mean anything to you?" Skip asked.

Fu Jun frowned. He closed his eyes and appeared to be meditating. When he opened his eyes again, he said, "You know, I'm not afraid. It's not me I'm worried about. I have a wife. I don't want any of this to touch her."

"We understand," Skip said.

"I don't think you do. It's unlikely they don't know you're talking to me—you were seen at the funeral. If they don't know you're here at the moment, they'll likely find out."

"You think—"

"No, Detective," he said. "I know. That you're here asking questions isn't a problem for me. They know you guys have a job to do, and they respect that. Everyone's got to eat. But they expect me to say nothing. If you drive out of here and go hassle Gao Fu Shauai or his crew, they're going to connect that to your visit here."

Skip nodded his head. "I can see your concern. It's not our intention to bring you grief. One thing I can say about all of this is that we've been directed not to dig around in Little Shanghai. That's out of our hands. We're not in an anti-gang unit or with financial crimes. We're homicide cops."

"What our agenda is right now is trying to discover what the connection is to the Lau's—or if there even is a connection at all," Bud said.

"Nothing about this crime seems like the Golden Dragons to me," Li said. "They're criminals, not above murder, but they're not messy. They don't leave loose ends either."

"The daughter?" Bud asked.

"Exactly," Fu Jun replied. "This looks like a crime of opportunity—"

"You're saying you think May's involved?"

"No, Detective. Not at all. She was disrespectful and a bit out-of-control—but murdering her parents? No, I don't think that at all. What I'm saying is that maybe she told the wrong people about her parent's wealth. Maybe she posted pictures online of her home, and some thugs took advantage. That's all. This crime doesn't leave me with the impression that the Chinese orchestrated it. It's too undisciplined. It's the kind of crime that draws a lot of attention."

"The opposite of what a criminal organization trying to avoid attention from the feds would do," Skip said.

"Exactly."

Bud stood. "So, we're back to square one." He looked at Skip and said, "I guess we should thank Fu Jun and get back on the road."

Back in the car, Bud asked, "May first? Or do we want to track down Gary Turner and ask him about the coins he sold?"

"Gary first," Skip said. "See if you can locate him."

"You got it."

FORTY-FIVE

As the end of Echo's work day approached, Mouse came to her desk.

"How was the first day?" he asked. He had that awkward smile and uncomfortable posture that Echo recognized. He was flirting—in any second, he'd probably ask her out for a coffee or lunch. If he was one of those guys who watched "Pickup Artist" technique videos online, he'd try to manipulate her into leaving the office with him at that moment.

She had a dilemma but decided she'd play along. The security card he wore was her key into the server rooms. "I had a great day," she said. Echo smiled and batted her eyelashes. Playing games worked both ways. "It's going to take a while to get into a rhythm, but I like it. It's like being a romance novel writer." She giggled like she imagined a silly school girl would.

"So," he said awkwardly, "you from around here?"

Echo answered and engaged him in small talk. She put her flirtation skills into overdrive. At one point, she thought maybe she was overdoing it. Going too far. But no, Mouse didn't show any sign of suspicion. Eventually, he took the bait.

"I was—um—thinking, you know," he said, stumbling on his words, "that maybe, you know if you were hungry? The little café down the block, you know, the place with, it's got… well, could you consider going to get some food?"

"A girl's gotta eat," she replied. She blushed and giggled again, while inside, she forced herself not to laugh. "Let me just log off, and I'll be ready."

A few minutes later, they were in the parking lot. Mouse said, "Um, do you want—"

"I'll drive," she said. "I've got a fancy BMW, and I hardly ever get to show it off."

Echo directed him to her car. "That's her." She opened the passenger door and nodded her head. "Get in," she said. "The passenger seat belt is sticky. Let me show you."

Mouse sat, and Echo fiddled with the seat adjustments and the safety belt. While doing this, she swiped his pass card. He didn't notice, perhaps because she'd placed her chest uncomfortably close to his face. "There," she said, "all set." She walked to the driver's side around the back. The moment she was behind the car, she sent a fast message to Conner. "Call me ASAP!"

"I like your car," he said. "Thanks for driving."

"What kind of music do you like?" Echo asked. She started the car but didn't put it into gear. Instead, stalling for time, she fiddled with the BlueTooth.

"Oh, I'm a fan of all kinds of music," he replied. "What do you like?"

"How about—" Echo's phone rang, cutting her off. The ringing was coming through the car's sound system, so she disconnected before answering. It was Conner. "Hello," she said into the phone. To Mouse, she said, "One second, I have to take this. Excuse me."

She got out of the car and told Conner she was using him for an excuse. He asked if she was safe. She said, "I'm fine." They'd worked out a code for times like this. If Echo said that everything was "peachy", he'd know she was in trouble and couldn't speak openly. If she said anything else, he knew she was fine—but using the call as cover.

"I'll talk to you soon," he said.

"Bye." She hung up and put on a sad face. She walked around the car and rubbed her eyes.

"Is everything all right?" Mouse asked when she opened his door.

"It's my… my grandmother," Echo said while acting as if she was forcing herself not to cry. "She's in the hospital. I have to go. I'm so sorry."

"I understand," he said. "Is there anything I can do?"

"No, it's okay. Raincheck, okay?"

"Um, sure, yeah. Maybe we can go to lunch tomorrow?"

"That would be real nice," Echo said. "How about you give me your number?"

"Sure."

Echo saved his number.

He didn't realize, of course, the true reason she needed it.

FORTY-SIX

Skip and Bud pulled up to a shabby student housing apartment.

Gary Turner was home studying. He opened the door and pulled out earbuds. “Come in, I guess,” he said. “My roommates aren’t home. Sorry about the mess.”

The living room had a brown sofa that was torn and stained. A pile of pizza boxes sat on the floor, along with a dozen empty beer cans. “College kids,” Bud said.

“Sorry,” Gary said. “If we go to the kitchen, there’s a table. It’s sort of clean.”

The detectives followed him.

“How can I help?” he asked.

“Your parents,” Skip said, “they…” He motioned at their surroundings.

“Yeah. I get it. It’s tough love, Detective. My parents want me to struggle.”

“Why don’t you take a seat?” Bud said. It wasn’t really a question, and Gary took the hint.

“Tell us about the gold panda, Gary,” Skip said. “We’re curious why you left that out during our last visit. You know, when we asked you about whether you knew anything that could be helpful.”

“I don’t understand, Detective,” he said. “I helped her, I think months ago, to sell a birthday gift from an uncle. She wasn’t old enough yet to sign the paperwork.”

“You didn’t think it was something her parents should have been part of?”

"She was nearly eighteen at that point," he said. "Practically an adult."

"But not," Bud said.

"Did I do something wrong?" Gary's posture fell. "I don't see the problem."

"Let's move on," Skip said. "It doesn't appear you broke any laws, assuming the gold was May's to sell. Where exactly did she say she got the gold?"

"We know she has no uncles around here," Bud added.

"She always called close family friends her aunts and uncles. She didn't say a name. It was only a couple of small coins. I think she got about six hundred dollars or something. It wasn't some grand heist. Does this have something to do with what happened?"

"That's what we're trying to find out here, Gary," Bud said. "You need to be more cooperative if you don't want us to think you're hiding something."

Skip said in his good cop voice, "What my partner is trying to say, Gary, is that we need your full cooperation. We don't think you've done anything wrong, but if you're not telling us everything you know, it could lead to something else bad happening. Do you understand?"

Gary nodded his head slowly. "Her parents thought she'd been accepted into Amery."

"And?"

"And it was a lie. She didn't even apply to college. Not a single one."

"What did she tell her parents?"

"She took my acceptance letter and made a fake copy. It was easy to fool them. She used some of that correction fluid and removed my information. Then she added her name and made a copy."

"So, her parents thought she was going to be attending Amery next fall, but in reality, she was going to do what?" Skip asked.

"I'm not sure," Gary replied. "We broke up, and she wouldn't talk to me about anything else. When she was talking about her plans before, she was all over the place. One day, she was going to move to Paris or London. The next week, she'd be talking about getting a loft in the new downtown complex. You know the one? By the river?"

"I know those," Skip said. "I've been apartment hunting recently. That place is all high-priced, luxury units, water views, club houses. How did May say she was going to pay for these dreams? Paris ain't cheap."

"She never said. I dismissed it all as a teenage girl fantasy. I thought she'd change her mind eventually. It was just a phase, I thought. Her parents were so controlling, so she was just trying to gain control of her life, I think."

"Did she ever say anything about having more gold?"

"No. Like I said, I thought she was just dreaming about things. I was sure she'd make up with her parents and go to college like everyone else we know. May used to spend some time at my house when she was evading her parents. They thought she was at lessons most of the time. But she wasn't. She was with me."

"And she never mentioned gold or insurance or any plans she had to get money to pay for these things she was talking about?"

Gary's face changed. Embarrassed. He looked down. "I just thought she was angry when she said it."

"What?" Bud prompted.

"We were talking about a friend's mom who died of cancer. She said all her problems would be over if only her parents were the ones in the hospital. I know she didn't mean it."

"Mean what?"

"That she wanted her parents dead."

FORTY-SEVEN

Skip knocked on the giant red door.

"There's an intercom button right here," Bud said. He pushed the call button.

"I heard it was good luck to knock on a red door," Skip said as he knocked again. Cops often knocked on doors aggressively to throw a suspect off balance or to surprise them. Skip wasn't ready to call May a suspect, but in his mind, there were doubts floating around.

A sleepy voice came out of the intercom's speaker. "Um, hello?"

"May, it's Detective Smith and Malloy. Can you please come to the door?"

"I'm not dressed."

"We'll wait."

When the intercom disconnected, Bud shook his head and said, "I think I'm going to have to be mean this time."

"Don't push too hard unless she's obviously evading questions." Skip knew time was passing too quickly, and in a murder investigation like this, each that passed without a solid lead or suspect meant the chance of resolution steeply dropped. Closure rates in old cases were low. He thought about what it would take to make a child wish their parents were dead. It was normal for teens to fight and argue with and sometimes even hate their mothers or fathers. Or both, in the worst cases. But to want them dead and gone forever—not as a passing angry thought—but really dead, that would be rare.

To murder them in cold blood was extremely rare.

When a child was found guilty of murdering a parent, it was usually patricide committed by a male child. Usually the eldest child. It was common for district attorneys and defense lawyers to be forced to figure out a fair solution in plea bargaining because the cases were usually not cut and dry. They were always tragic stories of abuses. Alcohol and drugs featured prominently in those dramas.

But May Lau wasn't a victim of drug-fueled abuse.

She wasn't raised in the inner city or even in a poor, middle-class neighborhood. She was raised by wealthy parents who provided her with everything needed to succeed in life.

The door opened. May was in baggy gym clothes. She wasn't wearing makeup. "I'm going to make a coffee," she said. "You can sit in there—" she pointed to the living room where they'd first interviewed her "—or follow me to the kitchen."

Skip looked at Bud and nodded towards the kitchen. They followed May and sat at the breakfast nook table. A pile of newspapers sat unopened.

"Another thing on my list," May said. She pointed to the papers. "Cancel newspaper subscriptions."

"It must be a hard adjustment," Skip said.

May sat while the coffee brewed. "My parents were super organized. Their lives followed a pattern. I just have to look at my mom's calendar, and I can see each day something to cancel, change, or deal with in some fashion. The gardeners, the pool people, the guy who came out to wash the cars. Then there's the friends—well, they all know they're dead, so I don't have to tell them my parents aren't hosting mahjong on Thursdays. Mom won't be hosting the Orchid Club's meeting next month."

"You seem very organized yourself." Skip smiled.

"They taught me well."

"May, I have to be honest with you," Skip said in a serious tone, "we're having a problem with that fifty-thousand in cash. It doesn't line up with being conservative, careful, and structured."

"Well, I told you," she said, "I was thinking of doing some traveling."

"And school," Bud added.

"Yeah, and school."

"Tell us about these plans for school," Skip said.

"I was thinking of going to school in Europe. It's not expensive, but I'd need an apartment and supplies. A new computer, a laptop. Traveling things. I don't know why this is a problem."

"We're just trying to understand, May."

Bud coughed and then said, "You know, if my house was just robbed, I'd be worried about keeping fifty thousand dollars lying around. Wouldn't you, Detective Malloy?"

"Certainly," he replied. "It's not safe to keep so much cash around. Besides thieves, there are fires, flooding, natural disasters… That's why people use banks. Wouldn't you agree, May?"

"I guess." She poured herself a piping hot cup and sat back down. "You're right. I'll put the money into the bank or maybe buy traveler's checks or something."

"Or something?" Bud asked.

"You know, May," Skip said, "I've never seen fifty thousand in cash all in one place. Like it must be impressive, to look at, I mean. You think we could see it?"

"I don't understand," she said. "It's my money."

"Yes, of course. I'm just asking if I could look at it."

May stared. After taking a sip, she said, "I don't have time to get it, Detective. I need to make my grandmother breakfast."

"That's right, your grandmother is staying with you," Skip said. "Do you get along with her?"

"It must be tough not speaking the same language," Bud said. "How do you manage?"

"We understand enough. I know a little Mandarin. She gets enough English to get by. It's not that hard. She's leaving for China in a few days, anyway."

"So, no, you won't show us the money, May?" Bud asked. "I mean, it'll only take a second."

"It is here, right?" Skip looked around the kitchen. "Don't tell me you put it in the freezer."

"That's the first place burglars will look," Bud said. "First the freezer and then the top shelf of your closet. Next, they—well, never mind. You *do* have a safe."

"Not that it was very helpful the last time," Skip said.

May glanced at the freezer. "It's not in the freezer."

"May, do you think your parents were being extorted by anyone?" Bud asked.

She stood and walked to the sink. She set the cup on the counter and looked up. "I don't want to talk about Gao Fu Shauai."

"But you do know the name?" Skip asked.

"Of course. Everyone in Little Shanghai knows him and the Golden Dragons."

"And?" Bud prompted. "Tell us more."

"They're minor criminals."

"Minor?"

"Okay, I didn't mean it wasn't serious. They deal in drugs and women. I heard they have underground casinos, but I don't know anything about that kind of thing. I just heard stories, like everyone else."

"Did you hear anything about extortion?"

"Sure. Those street gangs are always asking for money for protection."

"And your parents paid?"

May was quiet for a moment. She was thinking—but Skip couldn't decide if he felt she was thinking up a lie or thinking about how much truth to tell. *Dealing with violent gangs is a tricky business*, Skip thought. *Even Fu Jun Li wasn't comfortable talking about it. And he's a war veteran, not a teenage girl who lost her parents in a vicious double murder.*

Finally, she spoke. "I'm pretty sure they paid."

"But you're not certain?"

"My parents never told me," she said, "if that's what you're asking. I never saw money change hands or anything like that."

"But your parents knew Gao Fu Shauai Chin, correct?"

"Yes, of course. Anyone who does business in Little Shanghai knows Gao and the Golden Dragons. I said that. It's not a state secret, believe me. Everyone knows. Nobody talks. That's how it works."

"May," Skip said, "if you were being extorted or threatened, you could tell us."

"We'd help you," Bud added.

"You're out of your league," she said. "I'm going to prepare my grandmother's breakfast, and I'd like you to leave."

"May, if you've been threatened—"

"Detective Malloy, if you were part of the Chinese community here, you wouldn't even be talking about this subject. Now, this is my house, and I'm asking you to leave. Please."

Skip stood. "Okay, May. We'll let ourselves out. Please, if you change your mind about—"

"I'm going to be fine, Detective."

The detective duo walked slowly down the polished hardwood floor. Skip looked back and noticed faint marks from their shoes. He looked into the living room as they passed. He recalled part of their first interview with May on the night of the murders. *"If my parents were alive, you wouldn't be wearing shoes in the house either."*

FORTY-EIGHT

Echo didn't waste any time.

She raced downtown and pulled to a stop in front of Dan's Computer Repair & Parts. A neon sign with the words "Sorry, We're Closed" glowed in red. As she pounded on the door, she called Dan.

"Is that you banging upstairs?" he asked in place of greeting when he answered the call.

"Yes, open up," Echo said. "I've got a rush job."

A moment later, the locks turned, and she pushed open the door. She stepped inside. The door closed, and she could hear tiny motors whine as the locks re-engaged. Echo walked to the back and down old creaky stairs. When she reached the basement, she heard loud voices arguing about demons and treasure.

"Hold a sec," Dan said, barely looking up. "I'm about to—wait, wait, hey, Echo, come and blow good luck on these dice."

A fat guy holding a paper plate covered in pizza spoke with his mouth full. "That's cheating."

"It is not," another guy said. "House rules."

Dan held his cupped hands under Echo's face, and she blew on the dice. "Good luck," she said. "Now hurry up and win. I've got a little job for you."

Dan rolled, and the fat guy, looking at the result, said, "I told you it was cheating."

"What happened?" Echo asked.

"I just rolled triple sevens." Dan raised a fist and shouted. "That's three in a row, suckers. Losers clean up. I'm going to help Echo do something that's probably highly dangerous, illegal, and might cause the government to raid my shop."

"Not asking that much," she said. "It's just a pass card. I need it copied real quick."

"Hand it over."

While Dan worked, Echo called Mouse.

"Hey, Rhonda," he said. "You miss me already?"

"Oh, yeah, well, sure, but that's not why I'm calling," she said, adding a sadness to her voice. "I'm at the hospital, and when I parked, I noticed your pass card and lanyard. On the floor. Under the seat. It must have fallen."

"Oh, crap," he said. "I've got to call security—"

"No, wait," she said. She forced herself to think sad thoughts and cry. It wasn't her best performance, but over the phone, she knew it would sound authentic enough. "I don't want you to get in trouble. And I really need a hug. Can you come over to the hospital?"

"I suppose," he said. He hesitated as if trying to decide what to do.

"You there?" she asked.

"I really should call security," he said.

"Mouse, I know. But it's only been minutes. Nobody was in my car. There's no risk, I mean if you come here right now. Have you eaten yet?"

Thirty minutes later, Echo, pretending to be Rhonda Flemming, and Mouse ate cheeseburgers and fries in the hospital's public cafeteria. "I'm sorry about this," she said. "It's not very romantic."

"It's a great story," Mouse said. "Our first date, in a hospital cafeteria, but…"

"Oh, it's okay," Echo said, sensing his apprehension. "My grandmother's going to be okay. False alarm, not a heart attack—my mom's up there, and we can't have too many people in the room, anyway. So, I'm glad you came."

Mouse held up the card that was now secure around his neck. "I'm happy too. If I had to report this, it's a write-up. Didn't need that on my record. Thank you."

"No problem," she said. She smiled wickedly.

FORTY-NINE

Echo made it back to her apartment without, she believed, leaving Mouse with any suspicions.

Conner met her, and they sat together.

"What a close call," she said.

"You want to talk about it?" he asked.

She needed to unwind and relax, but she also wanted to keep Conner up-to-date with the progress on her stories and with her life. Echo told him everything, right up to the awkward moment when she told Mouse she had to leave.

"He's going to expect you to go on another date."

"I know. I'll blow him off for a few days. Hopefully, it won't take long to find what I need for my story. Once I have what I need, I'll quit that terrible job."

"Do you think you'll take a staff writing position at *Soft Vanda*?"

"I'm excited about the prospect of that, yes. It's a job working on stories that can make progressive changes in society. Not just our society, but the world."

Conner took her hand. "This is one of the things I like best about you. You actually care about the people and subjects you write about."

"And you forgive me for, you know—bending the rules a little?"

"You only do it for a good cause."

"Sure. But sometimes these things aren't exactly legal."

"Don't get caught," he said.

Echo changed the subject by asking about his progress on the organized crime connection to the Lau murders.

"If there even is a connection," he said. "I'm not sure at this point."

"Why's that?"

Conner explained it wasn't common for the Chinese street gangs or mid-level crime organizations to act in such a visible fashion. They were violent, nobody disputed that, but they kept the kind of newsworthy violence displayed in the Lau case off the radar of the police. People disappeared. Sometimes, a building fire would break out in a shop or restaurant, but those were usually warnings and done without inflicting injury. Fear of what might happen was usually enough to force compliance.

"Nobody I've talked to thinks a street gang did the Lau murders," he said. "There is little doubt, though, that if they were being extorted and they refused to pay, that violence would result. Normally, I'm told, someone would get hurt bad, not murdered."

"What if something like that did happen first and the Lau's didn't report it?"

"My sources tell me that the Lau's made no hospital visits of late, and there were no fires at any of their business locations. They have a few laundry and dry-cleaning centers —I checked, nothing sent up a red flag. I'm not even sure they were being extorted or threatened at all. Apparently, there're some families with connections that are just simply off-limits."

"You think they were one of those?"

"No way to know without an insider talking."

"And they don't talk, do they?"

"Nope," Conner said. "It's one stone wall after another."

"The police?"

"They got nothing. Or, at least, they're not talking either. So, what about you? Do you have any leads or insider info?"

"Not really. I've come up with some names. Gao Fu Shauai Chin. He's high on the food chain, not a street thug. He's also not the top dog, either. The Golden Dragons are a street-level criminal organization. According to my sources, they take orders from this Gao character, but that's only an unconfirmed rumor. Getting two solid sources is like hunting for diamonds at the baseball stadium."

"Have you heard of a group called Fist, or the Black Dogs?"

Echo nodded her head but said nothing.

Conner said, "They're low-level street gangs. Teenagers. They use underage kids as runners and for handling drugs, money, and weapons. If one of them gets popped, they're back on the street in no time."

"That's all I've heard," she said. "And, of course, they don't talk."

"Have you heard the name 'General Zhang'?"

"In passing," she said. "Supposedly, he's the apex predator in Little Shanghai. On the surface, he's a legitimate businessman with interests in dozens of restaurants, bars, and clubs. A source told me he's actually the Godfather of Chinese organized crime in the entire state. Of course, getting legitimate sources to confirm this is looking impossible."

"It's not likely he knows anything about the Lau murders, so it's not something I'll be pursuing," Conner said. "But if I uncover anything, I'll pass it to you."

"I'm going to see if I can find a link between Zhang and Gao or anything shady."

"Be careful."

Echo winked. "Aren't I always?"

FIFTY

Echo walked into the Amanda's Secret building like she'd been working there for ten years.

She said, "Good morning," to the receptionist and then heard someone shout, "Rhonda!" Echo ignored the shout at first but then remembered "Rhonda" was her alias. She looked towards the voice.

Mouse was standing in the reception area, near the elevators, with two security officers. "Good morning," he said. He smiled mischievously.

"Good morning, Stanley."

"Look, she's calling him Stanley already," one of the security guys said to the other.

The other guard chimed in with a laugh. He hit Mouse on the shoulder. "Must be true love."

"These are my friends," Mouse said to Echo, ignoring the taunts. "Freddy and Joey. I wanted to introduce you and…"

Echo didn't hear the rest of what he said. Her heart was beating too fast, and she thought for sure they'd caught on to her. But, as it turned out, the security guys were just there to meet her.

"As I was saying," the first guard said, "it's every Thursday night. At my house."

"Excuse me?" Echo asked.

"Poker," he replied. "We're talking about our poker game."

"Texas Hold-em," the second guard added. "We were asking you if you played."

"Oh, sorry," Echo said. "I have a lot on my mind, plus my grandmother, and it's just overwhelming. Sure, I play poker. But I'm not very good."

"That's perfect," the first guard said. He had a name tag that read "Frederick Brown." "Well, we have to make our rounds. We'll see you Thursday night. BYOB." He slapped the other guard on the back. "That's more dead money, Joey. What did I tell you?"

"Sorry about my friends," Mouse said. "They're just excited for fresh blood."

"What's 'dead money' mean?"

"It's when a player is new or bad, and they have no chance to win. The other players know they'll win whatever the sucker is willing to lose. *Dead money*."

"So I'm the sucker?" she asked.

"No, they're just goofing around," he said. "Heck, I can teach you to play in a couple of hours, and you'll be better than those two clowns."

"Okay," she said. Inwardly, she hoped she could get the gateway device installed in the server room that day. Then she'd be free to quit. She'd decided that she'd make up another lie to Mouse when she left. Maybe she could spare his feelings and keep his security breach from becoming known. Echo figured she'd tell him that her ex-boyfriend wanted her back. She'd elaborate that they'd decided to get married and move to Miami. Or maybe Tampa. No, *New Jersey*, she thought.

"I'd better get to work," Mouse said. "Meet you for lunch?"

"Let me see how the day goes, okay?"

"Yeah, sure," he said. "I'll message you."

Echo went to her station, logged in, and began writing things that made her feel nauseous and a bit depressed. The day passed quickly—she agreed to meet Mouse for lunch. She used the time to ask a few questions about the servers and security. Having met Freddy and Joey helped, as she could feign interest. It was always easy for her to play the role of a naïve girl asking about complex computer issues. So, by the end of their lunch, she'd determined the best place to locate the device that would allow her hacker friend access to the company's servers.

When the day ended, she raced to the woman's restroom and turned off her phone. She wanted Mouse to think she had left the building and that maybe her battery was dead. As long as he didn't stay around, she felt confident that she could talk her way out of getting caught being in the wrong room.

She waited twenty minutes and then went back to her desk. If Mouse was still around waiting, she'd complain that something had given her an upset stomach. Ten minutes passed, and not a soul passed through the room. Everyone had gone home except the night tech crew and security.

She passed the elevator and took the stairs up one level. When she entered the hallway on the second floor, she pretended to be lost. But nobody was around. The server room she needed was three doors down to her right, but she turned left instead and entered the woman's restroom.

With her heart beating out of her chest, she waited. Three minutes passed. Four. Then she heard voices and someone began opening the door. Echo dashed into the first stall and locked the door.

"I'll be right out," a woman's voice called. "Don't leave me. It's creepy on this level when everyone leaves."

A man's voice shouted from the hallway, but Echo couldn't make out what he'd said. She froze. The woman tried the door.

"Um, occupied," she said.

"Lisa, is that you?" the woman asked. "I thought you went home fifteen minutes ago."

"No, it's um, yeah, I'm new here," Echo said. "Rhonda, from downstairs."

"Whatcha doing up here?" the woman asked. She moved into the next stall and shut the door. "We don't get the creatives up here."

"Oh, yeah, well, the toilets down on the first level. They're backed up."

"Maintenance is lousy here," she said. "That happens a lot when it rains. How long?"

"Excuse me?"

"How long have you worked here?"

"It's only my second day," Echo said.

"Well, word to the wise," the woman said, "whatever you do, don't get suckered into Thursday night poker. Trust me on this." The woman laughed, flushed the toilet, and walked to the sinks. Her heels clicking was the only sound as she left the restroom.

Echo breathed to calm herself. She waited another ten minutes. When she opened the restroom door, the hallway was barely lit. The energy-saving sensors had turned off the lights. *It is spooky*, she thought. She stepped into the hall, and the lights above her flashed on. She paused. If someone was watching, they'd know an unauthorized person was on the floor.

After another minute, nobody had arrived. She moved with purpose to the server room door and held up the card reader. The light moved from red to green. She heard a click.

Success.

Stepping into the room, she saw rows and rows of computers. The room was chilly and dim. Knowing she'd passed the point of no return, she acted quickly. The gateway looked like a thumb drive. It plugged into a USB port the same way a thumb drive would on cursory inspection, and it would appear to be nothing more than an innocuous storage device. Of course, it wasn't.

The device would allow her hacker friend to get inside the servers that ran Amanda's Secret—all she had to do was exit the room without getting caught. If she could do that and get off the second floor without arousing any suspicion, she'd be able to quit pretending to want to work there.

She'd be able to write her story.

Leaving the room, she discovered the door was locked. She shook the handle. Nothing.

Don't panic.

She took a deep breath. *The card.*

The room's security required that she swipe the pass card on the way out as well. She pulled the card from her purse and swiped. The little red light blinked off, and the green LED flashed.

She closed the door behind her, took a few steps towards the stairs, and then the elevator opened. A rough voice echoed, "Hey, you!"

She turned.

"What are you doing up here?" a guard demanded.

"The toilet downstairs," she said. She looked him in the eye and prepared herself to lie with conviction. "The toilets in the woman's restroom downstairs are backed up. You know, the maintenance here is shabby. I needed to, you know, use the ladies' room. Too much coffee."

"I've got to report this," he said.

He lifted a walkie-talkie to his mouth. "Hey, Freddy, you copying me?"

"Go ahead, Jake," a voice said over the two-way. "You scared up there? Ghosts? Demons? Witches? It's not even that dark outside yet. Seriously."

"No, Freddy," the guard said. "I've got some newbie wandering around up here."

"What?"

"I said, there's some new employee—what's your name, honey?"

"Rhonda," Echo said. She added, "And don't call me honey," but the guard wasn't listening to her.

He looked at her and said, "Wait here."

A minute later, the elevator opened. "What the hell, Jake? It's just Rhonda. She's Mouse's new friend."

"Well, I don't know her."

"Hi Freddy," Echo said. "I was just about to ask this guy if he was any good at poker or just some dead fish."

"You mean dead money?" Freddy asked. He didn't wait for an answer. "Yeah, he's dead money, all right. Jake still doesn't remember if a full-house beats a flush."

"You lost, Rhonda?"

Echo explained for the third time about the backed-up toilets. Apparently, the building maintenance was shoddy because not one time did anyone question her story.

"Yeah, okay," Freddy said. "I'll walk you down. Jake, get back to your rounds and watch out for goblins."

Jake said, "Haha." He turned and walked away. "A bunch of jokers at this place. It's a wonder nobody has broken into one of the server rooms and installed malicious hardware."

"Not on my watch," Freddy said.

FIFTY-ONE

Echo's alarm went off early.

She'd ignored four phone calls from Mouse. The last had been at ten minutes past midnight. He'd also sent seventeen messages. The last of those came just before one a.m.

Men.

She emailed Teresa in Human Resources at Amanda's Secret.

Hello Teresa,

I'm very sick, sorry. I can't come in today. I've got a hundred and two fever and laryngitis. I'll probably be out a few days. I'll know more after I see my doctor.

Sorry, Rhonda.

Echo made herself a cup of coffee and then emailed Courtney Bailey.

Hello Courtney,

I'm interested in discussing more.

Can we meet today? Perhaps in the afternoon, I'm free after 1 p.m.

Thank you. Echo Rose.

Those two things settled. She made herself breakfast before sitting down in front of her desktop computer to begin communication with her hacker contact. Assuming nothing went wrong during the middle of the night, it was likely he'd pulled all the files she'd need for her investigation.

If that was the case, she'd email her resignation and tell Mouse the story about the ex-boyfriend. If there'd been a problem, she might have to risk going back to Amanda's Secret. That, however, would be a risk. If they'd found the device, using a simple process of elimination, she'd be the prime suspect. The police or FBI could already be there waiting for her.

Corporate espionage was a serious crime.

Echo broke two eggs into a bowl. *They shouldn't be ruining marriages, and if I find any indication of underage girls or sex-trafficked women, then it's not me the FBI will be showing up to arrest.* She beat the eggs into a frothy foam and dumped them into melted butter.

By the time she had washed her breakfast dishes, she was so eager to hear if the hack was successful that she didn't bother to change out of her bathrobe. She sat, logged in, and messaged him.

ER43seer: *Well? Good news?*

Anlt984snk: *Of course. You've hired the best.*

And?

I'll send over your packet the second the invoice is covered.

Echo opened a new tab, found the invoice—which was sent through an encrypted email program—and paid it. No names. Payment in cryptocurrency. Easy. Secure. Untraceable.

There.

Got it. Your info is on the way.

Echo opened another window, and a moment later, a file arrived. She opened it and read through the directory.

That's a lot of data.

A few years, actually. You're going to be busy.

How much of a footprint did you leave?

Not much, but that was what you'd call an epic data breach. They might discover it in an hour. Or next week. Either way, I wouldn't expect more than a couple of days. The media will find out sooner than later, ER. Be ready. This is FBI territory.

Okay. I'll start reviewing and let you know if I need anything else.

And I'll ping you if they discover the gateway.

Thanks. I appreciate your help. How's the Chinese thing going?

That's another story. For one, the tong is clean. Not a single bread crumb out there leading to anything criminal. Assuming your instincts are correct and they're actually dirty, these guys are cautious.

They're dirty.

Okay, well, I can't recommend anything so risky as what you did with the cheater's helper people. Corporations sue or try to get you arrested. These mafia guys make you dead.

Understood. I'm using low-level intrusion only on this one right now. If you find anything, ping me, and I'll get to work.

You got it, ER. Be safe out there!

I will.

She closed down the chat and clicked over to the file. It included a massive amount of data: client's personal information, employees, bots, company emails, and records of all peer-to-peer chats, messages, and uploaded pictures. It was going to be a long day.

FIFTY-TWO

Echo didn't hear from Courtney until after two in the afternoon.

She'd been swamped working through the files, so she was happy to put off the meeting until that evening at six. The sheer amount of information she'd have to sort was daunting. She broke down the task by assigning data to different folders. One she named P.M., which stood for "Probably Meaningless."

Then she separated things like client info, names, numbers, billing addresses, and credit card numbers into another folder. She'd cross-reference that folder if someone came under suspicion.

She made another folder for company emails that referenced things that were likely illegal and another for things that were shady but probably not against the law.

There was a story in the data, that was for sure.

When she arrived a little after six at the Bailey residence, Courtney met her at the door. She'd been crying—it was obvious—but she'd tried to hide it. Echo said nothing to show she noticed.

"Ken's off to Europe," she said. "An important art auction."

"Are you all right?" Echo said.

Courtney nodded and walked into the formal living room. "I'm drinking white."

"No, thank you. I've got a ton of things waiting for me. Nothing but coffee for a few days. Maybe a week."

"That big, huh?" Courtney set down her glass. "Publishing has become a new beast. It's not anything like it was when I graduated from the university. I'm going to guess you're here to negotiate?"

"Well, like I said," Echo said, "I needed to do some digging before I commit to anything. I'm definitely interested in the staff writing position. If it's still a possibility?"

Courtney frowned. "Yes. It's still possible. But. Not…"

"Yes?" Echo asked. "Go on."

"We need more time. We're trying to raise money. This story you're investigating could help get us some national attention. Maybe bring in some investors. Can we discuss a freelancing contract for this story alone? You'll promise it exclusively to us, no shopping it around. We'll guarantee a fair price per word and a generous kill fee if it doesn't work out."

"And you'll be working as the editor?"

"Yes. That's another exclusivity. Nobody else, not even any of my other writers, should hear a peep about this story. You only show me. You only talk to me."

"I can do that," Echo said. "As long as the price is fair."

"I'll write up a contract and email it to you in the morning. Fair enough?"

"That will work," Echo replied. "I'm going to do more digging tonight."

"What have you got so far? I mean, in loose terms?"

"I can see they're doing some illegal things—that's nearly certain—but getting solid proof and finding out if there's anything with solicitation or underage girls, that's going to take me more time."

"Rome wasn't built in a day," Courtney said before shaking her head. "Listen to me, spouting clichés like a freshman English major. No wonder I'm the editor. You sure you won't take a glass of wine?"

"I've got to stay alert and focused, Courtney. I'm gonna go," she said. "I'll look for your email in the morning and run it by my lawyer. She'll have it back to me in a day or two. If everything is good, I'll sign, and then we can discuss the story in greater detail."

"I'm looking forward to that, dear. Have a good night."

Courtney Bailey walked Echo to the door. She stumbled and kicked off her shoes. "Wine and high heels do not, I repeat, do not go together. Remember that when you get to be my age, Echo. That and life isn't fair. Men cheat. And the IRS is unforgiving."

"I'll remember, Courtney," she said. "Good night."

Echo drove away thinking that something about this assignment was off by a notch, and she decided on a plan of attack to see if she could figure out what it was.

FIFTY-THREE

Skip applauded as the curtain closed.

Lew Jr. had a supporting role in his first public performance. The school play was performed in the community center near the Walton's residence. Everyone in the extended family had attended—even Bud and Janice Stuckley.

Stacey Nelson-Walton, Skip's ex-wife, and her husband, Robert Walton, were also there. Robert treated Layla, his step-daughter, as if she was his own. Skip, at times, felt pangs of jealousy, but mostly, he was happy that Layla had so much support. The program for the night's performance listed the Walton Family as a contributor and supporter of the arts.

Robert's generosity even extended to Lew Jr.

Skip couldn't complain about that.

"Dad, stand up," Lucy Malloy said. She grabbed his arm. "It's not polite to sit during a standing ovation."

"Of course," he said. He stood and continued clapping. The curtain opened, and he scanned the cast and crew. Lew Jr. was just to the left of center. He was beaming.

"Isn't he handsome?" Vivian asked.

"Just like his dad," Skip replied.

Robert and Stacey were sitting two rows in front of the Malloy's. Robert turned around and said, "You should be proud. They really put in a lot of work."

"Hey, Skip!" Bud shouted. He was sitting with his girlfriend, Janice, who was Vivian's best friend. "Are we taking them out for ice cream?"

"Do you ever think of anything besides food?"

Bud turned to Janice, and she blushed and looked away.

"Behave yourself, Detective Smith," Vivian said. "And, of course, we're going for ice cream. It's a tradition."

Forty minutes later, the entire group sat together after spending ten minutes debating what flavors they should order.

"I've never heard this gang be so quiet," Janice said.

"Shhhh," Bud whispered. "There's a sanctity to eating cinnamon raisin caramel nugget crunch. It's a Sacrament."

"Can I get another one, dad?" Lew Jr. asked.

"Of course not," his mother answered. "Don't even think about it."

"Ah, but mom," he whined, "I didn't get enough dinner."

"It's not my fault you refused to come down until five minutes before we had to leave."

"But I was practicing my lines," he said. "It's not fair."

"Life's not fair, little buddy," Robert said. "But if it's okay with your mom, you can finish the rest of my waffle cone. I need to talk privately with your dad."

Lew Jr. waited for his mom's reply.

"Sure," Vivian said. "You can have the cone."

Robert led Skip outside and said, "I've got an idea."

"What's that?" Skip asked.

"Well, there's a property my bank owns now. As you probably know, the market's a bit depressed. Anyway, we don't want to take it off the books at a loss. The owners walked away. All the paperwork is complete on that. So, I was thinking, since it's a hundred percent on our books for the foreseeable future, how about you guys consider renting it?"

"That's an interesting idea, Robert," he said. "I'll have to think about it, of course."

"Look, Skip," Robert said. "I know you probably feel a little weird, but really, it's a favor to me as well because I'd know a good family was living there. In a year or so, when your new place is done, then we can list it for sale. Hopefully, the market will have rebounded."

"What neighborhood?"

"Over by Maple and Elm, still in the twin's school district. In fact, it's walking distance now with the new bridge the city built last summer. It's a good neighborhood, Skip, and the house is practically move-in ready. We'd only need a week for minor maintenance. I can have the paperwork ready in a few days. What do you think?"

"I think I'd better run it by the boss," he said, tilting his head towards Vivian.

"Understood," Robert said, nodding. "Why don't you call me tomorrow, okay?"

"Sure thing."

On their drive home, Vivian said, "Well?"

"Well, what?"

"What did Robert have to say?"

"He's got a house," Skip said. He told her all the details.

"That sounds good to me, Skip," she said. "We have to decide soon, or the construction is going to start off delayed."

"I know," he said, tapping his fingers on the steering wheel. "I know."

FIFTY-FOUR

"Make yourself comfortable," Echo said.

Conner, sitting in Echo's apartment, put his feet up and sipped on a glass of red. "How did your talk go with the editor from *Soft Vanda*? You think you'll take the job?"

"Courtney Bailey has some hidden demons—but I'm intrigued by the potential."

"Concerns?

Echo nodded. She sat next to Conner and asked if he thought she needed more art or more house plants.

He pointed to an empty corner. "That spot could use a tall potted plant. But you're avoiding the question."

"I'm feeling better. The layoffs at *Above the Fold* had me down. I thought I'd found a home. But things are moving along too fast now. This potential job with *Soft Vanda,* and there are other things."

"Like what? Are you thinking about reviving *Merchant of Truth*?"

"I've considered it. But, no, the potential to write hard-hitting, impactful stories with *Soft Vanda* has my attention at the moment. It might work. Also, I could stay busy freelancing. The gang's things… and…"

Conner nudged her with his foot. "Go on."

She shook her head and then snuggled up against him. "This feels nice."

"It does."

Conner's cell phone buzzed. Looking at the screen, he said, "I have to take this." He got up and walked towards the kitchen. "It's Gao? You sure?" Silence for a moment and then, "That's good, but I need you to be careful."

Echo knew not to eavesdrop on a friend. She cranked up the stereo and cleared her mind of conflicting thoughts about her options. When her parents returned, she'd talk to her father about investing in the paper. It would be too risky for his tastes—but he'd be objective about helping her think it through.

Maybe I need a pet?

The apartment needed more life. That was a given. Maybe more plants would be enough. In the meantime, she decided, she'd stop by the pet store and get a fish. Or a hamster. Conner's voice rose above the music, but she couldn't make out the exact words. She knew it was about Little Shanghai. That gave her a thought, and she messaged Detective Malloy.

Hi Skip. Can you meet for lunch tomorrow?

She set her phone down on the coffee table. Skip might return her message in five minutes or five hours. Sometimes it was days. But she was confident he'd meet. She'd grill him about his organized crime knowledge. Maybe she'd catch a break.

"Sorry about that," Conner said when he returned to the living room.

"No problem," she said. "Big break?"

"A CI in Little Shanghai. You know I can't say more."

"I understand. Nothing about our deal has changed. You got the Lau case and anything connected directly to the murders. I got the overall crime story. Speaking of which, I just messaged Skip about meeting for lunch. I'll press him a bit for your story. Maybe they've had a break with the Lau case."

"That would be great. I've hit a brick wall."

Her phone buzzed with a message from Skip:

AJ & Sons' Burgers. Noon. I'll be there.

FIFTY-FIVE

AJ & Sons' Burgers was crowded at eleven-forty-five.

Echo arrived early to give herself time to think. She was deep into her research on Amanda's Secret but didn't want to neglect the organized crime story. If she could help Conner with any information on the Lau murders, that would be a big bonus.

Not long ago, Echo's investigation into missing college girls led her to become instrumental in saving the life of Layla, Skip's oldest child from his previous marriage. He'd been grateful, of course, and Echo knew she could count on his help. Not that she constantly held her good deed over Skip's head, expecting him to feel obligated to always help her, though. That was not her style.

"Earth to Echo," Skip said. "Come in, Echo."

"Oh, hey," she said. "I was just—"

"I could see. Meditation is good." He sat down with a full tray. "I ordered for you."

"You didn't have to—"

"Don't even mention it," he said. "Dig in."

Echo grabbed the chili-cheese burger with mustard he set in front of her. "My favorite?"

"I'm a brilliant detective."

She stirred her milk shake. "Half chocolate and strawberry?"

"I take good notes."

They ate for some time without talking. Echo wondered if he had anything new, and her curiosity got the best of her. "So, the Lau case?"

"You wouldn't believe it," he said. "I didn't pick this place randomly—May Lau and her best friend drove through here on the way home that night. They ordered shakes, and a few minutes later, she found out she was an orphan. Well, that's the working theory, anyway."

"She might have known sooner?"

Skip stuffed fries into his mouth. "I've said too much."

"She's a suspect?"

"No."

"A person of interest?"

"Not so much," he said. "It's more like she's giving us some funky answers."

"It's rare an educated teenage girl from an upper-class family commits murder. Especially both parents. It's practically unheard of, as far as I know."

"That's what people keep telling me. Especially when she's from a traditional Chinese home."

"So?"

"Well…" He took a giant bite of his burger.

Echo decided not to press at the moment, so she changed the subject. "I've learned where my birth parents were living when I was born. And where they were living when they died. I have a couple of leads to follow."

"Lee Callaway helped you with that?" Skip asked.

"Yeah," she replied. "He helped a lot. He told me I might not want the answers."

"He's right."

"I know. But it's my birth parents."

"Assuming, as we do now, that May isn't responsible, she's in the same rare club as you."

"What club is that?"

"Losing both parents on the same day."

"At least she knew them. Not to detract from her loss."

"I know what you mean. This not knowing everything is killing you, isn't it?"

Echo nodded. "You are a good detective."

"If I can help," he said.

"Right now, what I could use is something to take to Conner. He's working the Lau case for *Above The Fold*. Even if it's off-the-record."

"I'm not sure what I can say right now," Skip said. "It's an open investigation, and we're up against the clock with a vicious double murder."

"Is there a connection to the Ching Lóng Benevolent Society?"

"I can't comment."

"What about Gao Fu Shauai Chin?"

Skip stared. He looked away. "How do you know that name?"

"I have sources, too," she said. "So that's a 'yes'?"

"Still no comment," he replied. "But be extra careful throwing that name around."

"Noted." She stirred her shake and took a long drink. "How about the Golden Dragons?"

He put more fries into his mouth and shook his head. "Harrumph."

"What?"

Skip swallowed. "Still no comment."

"You're not being very helpful."

"You know, Echo," he said. "That May is an interesting character."

"And?"

"And you're a journalist. You've lost both parents in a tragic event. You're empathetic, and you also ask good questions."

"Are you suggesting I try to interview her?"

"We have a free press in this country," he said. "I'm not, in my official capacity, asking you to interview May Lau. In fact, as an active detective on the case, I'm asking you specifically not to contact her."

"Officially."

"Yeah. Officially." He smiled. "I'm not suggesting anything."

"But we have a free press."

"We do."

FIFTY-SIX

After lunch with Echo, Skip went to meet Vivian at home.

"You good taking a break, Detective Malloy?" Vivian asked. "I won't want you to hurt your back lifting any of these heavy boxes."

"I wouldn't like that either," he replied. "How's it going?"

"Angela came by earlier. I had to sign a couple of things, no biggie. Everything is done. It's smooth sailing now."

"The permits?" Skip asked.

"Conceptual Construction sent someone over with the permits an hour ago."

"What'd they say?"

"They said the demo crew will be here tomorrow at seven in the morning."

"Tomorrow… *tomorrow*?"

"Yes, Skip. That tomorrow."

"We're not ready."

"We'd better get moving, Detective. Unless you want your old record collection to end up in the landfill."

Skip frowned. "When did this show up?" He pointed to a rented garbage bin that sat next to the curb in front of the house. "Do we really have that much junk?"

"Yup."

"Okay, Viv, I have to call Bud. We have a difficult case."

"Janice will be over to help."

"Don't throw away my records."

"Give me a kiss, and I'll think about it," she said.

"I guess we'd better take Robert up on his offer."

"I already called him," she said. "Okay?"

"Yeah. I guess it's best," Skip said. "You're not serious about tomorrow?"

"No, of course not. We're not ready. But we have a week, or the schedule is going to be off to a bad start."

"We can do that?" he asked.

"I think so. We'll try our best."

"I'd better go."

"Go catch some bad guys, Detective."

FIFTY-SEVEN

Echo pulled out of the burger place onto East Rosemead Avenue.

At Birch Street, she stopped at a red light. In her rearview mirror, a black SUV filled the view. The driver tailgated her after the signal changed. She sped up to sixty, but the driver remained steady on her tail. Then, passing them both, a second SUV pulled back to the right and slowed in front of her.

They were both Mercedes G-Wagons. Shiny black with tinted windows. A flash of fear passed over her, but remembering their location imparted a comfortable assurance. It was early afternoon on a busy street in Fairview—hardly the place to commit a grave felony.

The SUV's drivers turned on their right-hand turn signals. A stretched Escalade, also black with tinted windows, pulled up alongside her. They'd boxed her in and were forcing her to the shoulder of the highway.

Options crossed her mind in a moment of decision-making.

She decided not to resist—but she texted Conner.

I'm going to call you. Answer, but don't talk. Record mode.

Okay.

I'm just east of the AJ & Son's.

You safe?

I think so.

Echo pulled to the curb and stopped. She speed-dialed Conner and put her phone into her purse. Jumping out of her car, she scowled when the door to the Escalade opened from the inside.

"Get in, Miss Rose," a man said. He wore a dark suit over body armor. Muscles bulged, and he returned her scowl with one of his own. He was scarier.

"Please, Miss Rose," an older man said from inside the SUV. "You'll not be harmed. I apologize for this great inconvenience. I understand you're investigating the Lau murders. Please, if you'd like to talk about it, you have ten seconds before I drive away."

Echo clutched her purse after locking her BMW. She climbed into the SUV. The door was closed behind her by the bodyguard, who remained outside. "You are?"

"I'm General Zhang," he replied. "I understand you're investigating me."

The Escalade sped off, sandwiched between the two G-Wagons. Echo looked out the window and turned to the General. "I'm not sure—"

"Don't worry, Miss Rose. My man will stay with your car until you return."

"Um. Okay. I don't normally do interviews like this," she said.

"I'm not comfortable announcing my arrival nor sitting like a proverbial duck. Let's get down to business, Miss Rose."

"And that would be?"

"I'd like to convince you that the terrible murders of the Lau's weren't connected to me. Nor my associates. We don't operate that way."

"And I should just take your word for this?"

"I'm a man of my word," he said. "Miss Fang, please tell Miss Rose my position on trust."

Echo realized they weren't alone. A Chinese woman sat cross-legged near the front. She wore a suit that was feminine and executive at the same time. Next to her on the seat was a black leather attaché with gold trim. Echo wondered if she was a model or a lawyer. *Perhaps both.*

Fang gave Echo a cold smile. "A man who cannot be trusted is worthless."

Echo held her gaze a moment longer than was comfortable, then turned to the General. "But I don't know you."

"You know about me. You were asking Detective Malloy about us and our potential connection to the murders. There is none."

"Okay," she said. "I'd like to take you at your word, General. Really, it would be a different world if people always told the truth."

"Agreed. You want evidence."

"That would be nice."

"I have men looking into this situation. When they uncover who was responsible, I'd like your assurance that you'll stop your investigation into my business when I deliver the evidence to you."

"A trade?"

"As you say."

"Neither I nor my paper pays for stories."

"I'm not offering you money, Miss Rose," he said.

Echo took a moment to think. She glanced at the interior and the custom work that surrounded them. They were blocked from the driver by the dark glass, and there were no visible ways to open any of the doors or windows.

"One-way mirror to the driver," Zhang said. "Windows bullet-proof. That's on top of the armored panels. We're as secure as a president or senator, Miss Rose. I don't take many chances in this life. You only get one."

"What do you really want?"

"Let me tell you a story," he said. "There was a time when the county had a much higher murder rate. More violence on the streets. There were fights over territory. Gangs killed each other's minor members without a second thought. These were dumb conflicts."

"And you think you were part of the change?"

"Ah," he said. "I don't think, Miss Rose. I know for a fact. We're not that different. You investigate, hire confidential informants, and make deductions based upon circumstantial evidence. You search. I search too, Miss Rose. I investigate and use CIs for information on my enemies."

"But I'm not a criminal," she spat. "I don't do—"

"Lies aren't attractive on you, Echo. Tell me, would Amanda's Secret agree with your assessment of yourself?"

Echo bit her lip.

"Yes," Zhang said. "I know about your snooping, Echo Rose. Please, let me properly introduce you to Miss Roulan Fang." He pointed at the woman sitting with them. "She isn't just a pretty face. She's my attorney. Should we come to an agreement today, she's ready to witness our signatures."

"So, what do you want?" Echo asked.

"Your little incursion into Amanda's Secret is likely to cost me some money. But I'm not here about that. I'm going to put that little felony in my back pocket for now. Our little secret. However, rest assured that Miss Fang has a memo, with the necessary documentation, to file a complaint with the District Attorney's office."

Echo gulped. She knew that regardless of her intentions, a crime was a crime.

The General continued, his voice calm and his eyes cold. "After certain powers were merged in the county, areas like Camden and Fairview saw a steep drop in crime. Let's acknowledge that a unifying power center means less violence."

"Okay," she said. "I won't argue with statistics. But I do not agree with your overall business model. You're responsible—if my sources are correct—for many serious crimes. I can't be part of helping you."

"You aren't being asked to directly help me or any of my business interests. What I'm asking for is a deal. I give you the people responsible for the Lau's deaths, and you stop your series about crime in Little Shanghai."

"I don't make deals."

"You don't care about the truth."

"I'm not convinced you have the truth."

"Perhaps not today, Miss Rose. But, eventually, I can find out what I need to. If it involves my interests, I have ways to uncover the truth."

"Take me to my car, please," she said.

General Zhang set his hand on a control console. He pushed a button. "Return Miss Rose to her car." He didn't speak again.

When Echo was safely back in her car, she pulled out her phone. “Conner, you there?”

The call had disconnected. She called him back.

“Echo!”

“I’m here.”

“What happened?”

“Didn’t you hear?”

“No. As soon as you got inside, the call turned to static and then disconnected.”

“He said it was heavily armored. I guess he didn’t just mean for bullets.”

“Tell me what happened,” Conner said.

She told him everything about her ride with General Zhang.

“What’s next?” he asked.

“Nothing’s changed, Conner,” she answered. “I’m going to reach out to May Lau.”

“Our agreement?”

“Hasn’t changed.”

“Be careful.”

“Of course.”

FIFTY-EIGHT

Echo looked out the window of her apartment.

She had goosebumps like she was being watched. It was probably just nerves, she thought, after her encounter with General Zhang. He'd known about her incursion into the hidden parts of Amanda's Secret. *How?*

There must be a leak in her system. Maybe the spies had spies? It didn't matter. If someone had tipped off the feds, men in FBI windbreakers would have greeted her at the door. She powered up her desktop PC and opened her deep-web chat with the hacker she affectionately referred to as Anthony. *Anlt984snk.*

It wasn't his real name, of course. She had no idea about that. But it gave her a way to think about him. Or her, she realized once a long time ago, although he seemed fine with the male pronouns she used.

ER43seer: *You there?*

Anlt984snk: *You're okay?*

You knew something was wrong?

I told you those mafia guys were dangerous.

What happened?

I can't tell you, ER. Sorry. They backtracked me. Don't know how, but it means someone with a lot of money and a lot of pull.

What should I do?

I can't tell you what to do, but don't ask me to do anything that involves them.

Okay. What about Amanda's Secret? They knew about that.

They know you got what you got. The gateway is burned. Use what you have, but don't expect more. If I were you, I'd get what I needed off those files and then scrub. You don't want any trace if the FBI come knocking. Or anyone from Little Shanghai, if you understand my drift.

Okay. Anything in Big Media about the breach?

Nope. Contained for now. I suspect they'll try to keep it that way.

So maybe I'm in the clear?

Maybe you're in the clear. But don't hold on to any of that stuff. Trust me on this.

All right. I'll work fast.

ER.

Yeah?

Those guys are scary. Don't push your luck.

You got it. I'm sorry I got you into this.

I do what I want. I'm a grownup.

Take care, A.

Watch your back, ER.

The window closed. Echo pinched the bridge of her nose, closed her eyes, and considered her next step. She needed days, maybe a week, to go through all of the Amanda's Secret files. It could lead her back to General Zhang and solicitation. Maybe sex trafficking. There were lessor stories about bots, but she didn't care about those as much.

Then there was May Lau. Perhaps she'd provide some light on the connection her parent's murders had to organized crime in Little Shanghai. Unless the General was being forthright.

Maybe, despite his criminality, he was telling the truth about the Lau's. Echo recalled the charismatic way that his gorgeous lawyer had answered him. *A man who cannot be trusted is worthless.*

It made sense.

Everyone seemed to agree the violent and bloody nature of the attack was sound evidence that it wasn't committed by an organization with "low-profile" as one of its core mission statements.

Echo's phone pinged. Detective Malloy. He sent her a phone number and then a message.

Please delete.

She wrote it down on a pad and deleted the message from her phone. Then she called it. After four rings, it was answered by a young woman who sounded shy and a bit uncertain.

"Hello?"

Echo took a breath and then slowly said, "Hello, my name is Echo Rose. I got your number from a friend. I thought maybe we could talk."

"Why?"

"I'm a reporter. I think that—"

"I don't want to talk. Please don't call again."

"Hold on one second. Let me explain why you might change your mind."

"I'm listening."

"I met someone today. Someone powerful who doesn't want to have anything to do with the cops. Think Little Shanghai. He told me he was looking into the deaths. I'm sorry for your loss. My condolences. This man, he was sure he knew something or could find out."

"What's that mean?"

"The organization doesn't want to be investigated. They seem to think they can find out who did this terrible thing. And, frankly, I believe them after some things I witnessed today."

"Why don't they go to the police?"

"You realize who you're talking about here? Right? These guys don't work with cops."

"What do you think I can tell you? I've been interviewed about a hundred times already."

Echo laughed inside, recalling how teenagers exaggerated. It was doubtful they had interviewed her five times, but maybe it felt like a hundred to her, which said something. She considered her next answer before speaking. It would be crucial to give May a reason.

"I think you might give me a clue—something the police missed. Then, I'll be able to work with people outside of law enforcement. Maybe we'll discover something that will break the case."

"Crap."

"What?"

"I guess."

"You guess what?"

"I'll meet with you."

FIFTY-NINE

Echo met May in the late morning after spending the entire night reviewing the files stolen from Amanda's Secret.

She sorted through endless emails, profiles, pictures, and messages. Her most surprising find was a profile using the name "Sally Lin." The picture being used was Roulan Fang, General Zhang's attorney. Echo wasn't sure what it meant, but she doubted the attorney was there looking for a cheating husband. She'd used her fake male profile to "like" Fang's account. Something was fishy about the whole thing.

Maybe Roulan would message back…

"You look tired," May said. They'd been chatting superficially for half an hour, and Echo thought May was warming up to talking openly.

"I was up all night," Echo said. "I have a couple of big stories working right now."

"Is it fun being a reporter?" May asked.

"I love researching and investigating topics that are important to society. Writing in a way that puts the information into words that people will read."

"I'm not sure what I'm going to do." May didn't speak, as if she wanted Echo's advice. She looked confused. She'd tragically lost both parents only days ago, so it was understandable to Echo that May felt doubt and anxiety.

"Tell me more about your routine," Echo said. "Before this terrible thing happened, what was a normal day like for you?"

"I'd get up and be out of the house by seven in the morning on most days. I had school, of course, but also lessons. Tennis, piano, language, and sometimes new thing my parents would come up with. Golf, which I failed at. Martial arts. I hated those. It's so much a stereotype."

"Did you talk to them about your feelings?"

May laughed. "Feelings? What are feelings?"

"That bad?"

"You can't imagine. I had no life of my own."

"Never?"

May shook her head. Then, a thought must have reminded her of something. She said, "I guess there was one thing. I had a boyfriend. We broke up. When we were dating, I had my own life whenever I was with him."

"Were your parents supportive?"

"No," she replied. "Absolutely not. I had to lie to them. We only saw each other when I was supposed to be in a lesson or being tutored. I'd make up these fake study sessions. A few of my girls would send me fake messages so I could show my mom."

"I see. That must have been hard," Echo said. "I used to have a lot of resentment towards my parents. I didn't understand why they had to be so… I guess, controlling of me. Probably all moms do this. But, anyway, I found out they adopted me."

"Really?"

"Yeah. It was a shock. It changed my feelings because I realized these people took me and loved me. They gave me a comfortable life. It wasn't like they had to do it—like they'd had a child and were just being parents. They chose me."

"That's cool."

"It is. I had a better relationship with them after I found out. It's weird."

"I wish parents had adopted me."

"My natural parents died." Echo put her head down. Whenever she told her story in an intimate conversation, she had to keep her emotions in check. She didn't want the tears to start. "I was a baby, so it's not the same as what you're going through. I never really knew them because I was too young to know much."

"I'm sorry," May said. "That's so sad."

The topic changed, and they talked more about boys and school. Echo asked May about her plans for university. She dodged the question. As their time together was ending, Echo decided she needed to pry a little deeper into the events surrounding the murders. It was an uncomfortable topic, but it was also Echo's job to seek the truth.

Even when it was ugly.

"May, before I go, I was curious if you remember anything that would show a connection between your parents and organized crime in Little Shanghai. I'm working on a story about the gangs and—"

"The Golden Dragons?"

"You know about them?"

"Sure, all the Chinese families know about them. It's not like I've actually sat down with Gao Fu Shauai Chin and had lunch." She laughed. "I've seen the General at funerals, but he'd never talk to someone young like me. But, sure, I know about the Dragons—everyone does in Little Shanghai."

"Do you know any of them personally?"

May blushed. "I probably shouldn't say."

"I can listen off the record, May. You have my word that anything you say in confidence will remain that way."

"I dated a couple of the guys. Nothing serious."

"Can you give me any of their names?"

May shook her head. "It's too dangerous."

"Off the record?"

She nodded. "Okay." May glanced right and left. She opened her phone and showed Echo one of her contacts. "You didn't get this from me. He's like a lieutenant in the Dragons. Just below Gao Fu Shauai Chin."

Echo copied the name and number.

SIXTY

After her chat with May, Echo felt an overpowering sense of nostalgia.

Exhausted as she was, Echo knew sleep would be impossible. Or anymore work.

The itch in her mind needed to be scratched. She called the retired police officer, Samuel Figus. He'd been the patrol cop who'd pulled her out of the car wreck that had killed her parents. Echo had stayed in contact with him after PI Lee Callaway had helped her discover more about her past. Hearing his voice gave her a sense of comfort. He was a link to answers.

"Why don't you stop by? Have tea with me and my wife."

"Now?" she asked.

"Sure. We don't get a lot of visitors. Jody will be thrilled."

"Okay." Echo entered his address into her phone's driving app. "I'll be there in sixteen minutes."

"Gotta love modern technology. Okay, I'll get a kettle going."

Jody, Samuel's wife, greeted Echo at the door. "Come in, honey," she said warmly. Jody wore a chef's apron, and there was flour on her left cheek. She closed the door behind Echo and said, "You look like you need a hug."

"You're perceptive," Echo admitted. "There're these stories I'm working on and this connection to my past. It's a lot to process."

"A little tea and some fresh-baked cookies will do wonders."

"It smells wonderful."

Echo followed her into the kitchen. Officer Figus—Samuel—was already sitting at the table. He stood and gave Echo a hug. "Have a seat, Echo," he said. "You have the world on your shoulders, don't you?"

"Yeah," she said. It took a deep breath and a moment of concentration to stop herself from bursting into tears. "I hope I'm not intruding."

"Of course not," Jody said. "Tell her, dear. She's welcome anytime."

Figus nodded and smiled. "If you eat one of these cookies, you won't want to leave."

Echo smiled. They chatted for a while about Fairview and Camden and the weather. Light topics and simple conversation. But, while sipping tea, Echo decided she wanted to dive a little deeper into the past. She couldn't help herself.

"There must be something I can follow up on," she said. "I mean, like, what were my parents wearing? Where did you think we were going? Was it really just an average accident, or could there have been anything unusual going on?"

Figus looked into her eyes. "You sure you want to open doors that might have skeletons behind them?"

"Yes," Echo said without hesitation. "I want the truth, whatever it is. Doesn't matter if it's ugly. I need to know."

"Okay," he said. "I understand." He closed his eyes and thought for a moment. Then he continued. "They'd filled the station wagon with stuff. Like moving boxes and things. It wasn't suitcases, or backpacks, or camping gear, like a family going on a trip. It was more like a move."

"Did anyone investigate?" Echo asked.

"Well, remember," Figus replied. "I was a patrol cop, not a detective. Being first on the scene, I made the appropriate calls. Then I wrote up an incident report, of course. But it wasn't in my sphere of responsibility to investigate. In fact, it would have raised eyebrows if I'd tried. The thing is, I was more concerned about making sure you were safe and that the EMTs checked you out completely. There was nothing to be done at the moment about your folks. I'm sorry."

"Okay. I really do get it. So, you think they were running away?"

"There's no way I can speculate on what they were doing or where they were going. I can't even be positive that they were actually going somewhere. It's possible they were just selling some junk. Maybe that stuff was part of a business. They might have been moving things for a friend. You know how it is, Echo. You're a journalist. It's not good to make too many assumptions without facts."

She knew he was right.

But it was another potential clue, and she was glad she'd come over for tea. They chatted a bit more about the weather and Jody's garden. When she left, Echo said, "I'm going to follow up on this, Samuel. Thanks for being open with me."

"Be careful chasing unicorns, Echo."

She nodded and left with a mixture of hope and dread.

SIXTY-ONE

Skip and Bud sat opposite each other in their war room.

The corkboard had pictures, newspaper articles, and white index cards with important facts. They used blue index cards for writing conjectures and theories. This allowed them to keep the objective facts and their subjective opinions separate.

The toxicology report had come back from the lab. There were no traces of illicit drugs, alcohol, or anything that would require further investigation. Sabine confirmed her initial observation, concluding that it was a handgun that fired the fatal shots. Muzzle velocity comparison charts put the probability at ninety-five percent. Of course, if they didn't recover a probable murder weapon, it wouldn't matter.

The slugs were so damaged that even if they recovered the handgun used and fired it to get slugs for comparison, the results would be indeterminate. It could help them narrow down a suspect, but it wouldn't do for court.

They'd called or visited all businesses that bought gold. Several dealers told them that they'd already talked to Big Ted. He'd been good to his word. One of the gold buyers confirmed it was unlikely any gold transaction that large would happen without Ted being involved. It wasn't common for gold and coin dealers or pawn shops to hold on to several hundred thousand in cash.

Their money needed to be working.

Skip looked up and said, “I wonder if there’s something right under our noses that we’re missing?”

Bud nodded as if he agreed, but he said nothing.

Skip walked to the board. “I don’t want to let this one get away.”

“You know it’s a coin toss, partner,” Bud said. Statistically, about half of all homicides in America went uncleared. Of those cleared, the victims knew their killers about eighty percent of the time. “What’s different about this case?”

Skip scratched his head. “I’m not sure,” he admitted. “And I think it’s worse than a coin toss this time. I don’t think the Lau’s knew their assailants. Obviously, they didn’t kill each other. If we rule out May or any of their friends, what are we left with?”

“The twenty percent.”

“Yeah, I can do the math. If someone murdered them to get into the safe, either somebody knew about the gold, or they took a chance that a wealthy couple would store valuables. Either way, we’re looking at too much randomness.”

Bud continued, adding to Skip’s reasoning. “So, we have three likely possibilities this can fall into. One, random thieves. If that’s the case, they’re likely in the wind. Unless someone shows up at Big Teddy’s with two hundred ounces of gold pandas to sell, we’re going to be left with squat.”

“Not much chance of that,” Skip said. “Unless we’re dealing with fools. If this is our scenario and they’re not idiots, the gold won’t show up at Big Ted’s place. If they're smart, they’ll unload it in New York or Los Angeles in a year.”

"And they'll do it little by little," Bud agreed. "Okay, let's put totally random off the table. Why bother thinking about something we can't do anything about right now? That would leave either May or a known entity, like the business partner or the mafia guys."

"I can't see Fu Jun involved," Skip said. "Can you?"

"He's less likely than the daughter, in my opinion. You've reviewed the last will and testament and the family trust. He's got no motive. In fact, with an eighteen-year-old inheriting the controlling interest in the laundry businesses, he's got a powerful motivation to want the exact opposite of what happened."

"I concur. So what are you saying? That we put May at the top of the list because assuming a random robbery gone bad is going to be nearly impossible to investigate without a miracle?"

"No," Bud said. "That doesn't work. What's the statistics say about parricide? Less than two percent? And for a female to pull the trigger?"

"Yeah, the stats say she's not our perp. The evidence says she didn't fire a gun, so unless she arranged this…"

"I don't buy it," Bud said firmly. "We're going to have to work harder."

"So you want to go get a double bacon cheeseburger?"

"Hilarious, Detective Malloy. You shouldn't be in the police. You should have your own cable show."

"Hello detectives!"

Skip and Bud turned toward the door. Detective Hoffman, retired, stood there with a big grin. He stepped into the war room and said, "Did someone say double bacon cheeseburger?"

"I see you've gained weight," Skip said.

Hoffman patted his belly. "Retirement suits me."

"See, Bud," Skip said, "you have something to work towards before you turn in your weapon and badge."

"What's up, Hoffman?" Bud asked. "You not get your pension check this month?"

"I was just bored. Buffets and cable news are all right, but once in a while, I miss the job."

"You missed sitting at your desk making excuses and eating doughnuts," Skip said.

"Hey, that's not fair," Hoffman said. "My clearance rate wasn't so bad."

"Statistics lie." Bud walked through the door past Hoffman. "I'm going for coffee. Hoffman, maybe you can clear this one before I get back." He pointed to the corkboard.

"You guys got that double murder in the hills?" Hoffman asked.

"Yup," Skip replied. "Ugly and brutal."

"No chance it was a murder-suicide?"

"Not unless the weapon disappeared after a dead guy dragged himself up some stairs."

"Family member?"

"We're considering it, of course. But there's no evidence pushing us in that direction."

"I had a case like this once. Long time ago. Other than the luxury car and the fancy neighborhood, the perps picked the victims randomly. These two sociopaths, childhood friends from down in Texas, killed a clerk at one of those twenty-four-seven mini-marts. They realized they'd probably get caught, so they went on a road trip across seven states. Eventually, they ended up here. Low on money and desperate, they followed a Caddie to the residence of mister and missus Wilson."

"You caught the case and saved the day?"

"I caught the case. Like yours here, it seemed unsolvable. No direct evidence. Both victims were shot at close range. The house was ransacked. We'd later discover the pair got fifty-seven dollars in cash and some jewelry. Maybe five hundred bucks worth."

"What happened?"

"Luck," he replied. "A patrol cop pulls them over for making one of them rolling stops at a four-way. No other traffic around, but you know, this patrolman has one of them feelings."

"Probable cause at the stop?"

"Patrolman asks for the guy's license and registration. The driver panics. He pushes the car door into the officer and takes off, speeding like a bat out of hell. The whole thing ended up being like a scene out of a movie. High-speed chase. Lots of property damage. By the time I arrived at the scene, there were a dozen police, a couple of K-9 dogs, two engines from Fire House Nineteen, and probably a dozen more people on top of the cops. Firefighters and EMTs. Whole day probably cost the county half a million in damages and lawsuits. On top of that, the media arrived in force and started second-guessing everything."

"Sounds like a circus."

"Yeah, biggest one of my career. Turns out this pair had murdered five other people across three other states. The FBI ended up getting involved. There were stolen items from at least ten robberies. Those boys… Man, they knew their days were numbered. They just didn't care."

"I don't think we have a similar situation here."

"No. Probably not. I think you've got them Chinese fellas. The mafia. You know what I mean. You'll never solve this thing if those guys are involved."

"Thanks for the encouragement."

"Just telling it like it is, Skip. Straight honesty is how I like to play."

"Well, I've got a few more cards to play, Hoffman. I'll see you around."

"Not if I see you first, Detective Malloy. Not if I see you first."

SIXTY-TWO

Echo knew she needed sleep.

Instead of going home and putting her head on her favorite pillow, she drove to Elm Street. The Buick was sitting in the driveway. Just like last time. Curiosity was driving her into the unknown. She exited her car and walked past a mailbox with green lettering stenciled across the side: *The Kuipers*.

She approached the front door and let out a breath. *It's now or never*, she thought. She knocked.

An elderly man opened the door. His hands were withered, and his skin covered in liver spots. "Yes, young lady," he said. "Can I help you?"

Echo stood silently. Her throat was dry, and it felt like it was in the grasp of a phantom.

"Young lady?"

"I'm sorry," she finally said. "I didn't mean to disturb you."

"Well, dear, you're here now. What you selling?"

Echo sighed. "This isn't coming out right. I'm not selling anything."

"Okay, then. Is there something you want?"

"I'm doing some research," she said. She fumbled with her purse and pulled out two photocopies, and unfolded them. "Is there any chance you recognize these people?"

He put on a pair of glasses that had been hanging from his neck on a silver chain. "My mind still works, but not so much my eyes." He took the photocopies from Echo's hand. "Hmm," he said as he looked them both over.

"Do they seem familiar?" she asked.

"It's the Weston's. John, I believe, and his lovely wife, Clara."

"You sure?"

"Yes. They rented my basement. It was a long time ago."

"You remember them?"

"*Zeker man,*" he said. "That's a bit of Dutch, meaning I'm certain. Besides, just because I'm old doesn't mean I'm senile. They're the only tenants I've had who died in a car accident. It's not something I'm likely to forget."

"I believe you." Echo shed a tear while standing in shock.

"You okay?" he asked.

"Sorry," she said, wiping her face. "It's just that..."

He stared.

"Those were my parents," she finally said.

"Oh gosh, I'm very sorry. I remember you—just a tiny little thing when tragedy struck. I guess you got taken by the state. Forgive me, but I can't recall your name."

"Echo," she said. "It's the name I use today. When I was a baby, it was Grace."

"I remember. Yes. Well, nice to meet you. I'm Willem Kuipers, but please, call me Will. You were the cutest little thing. I can't remember where your parents were running off to when they left. Sad. I won't dwell on the past, but they owed me a couple of months' rent when they swished out of here like wolves were chasing them. No goodbye or nothing." He took off his glasses. "I'm sorry, dear. I shouldn't speak ill of them. Not after what happened."

"It's okay. It was a long time ago."

"My manners," he said, looking at Echo with a crooked smile. "Please, can I invite you in? Would you like some tea? I live alone these days. No boarders. Only me, now. Me and Daffodil. She's my tabby. Here kitty-kitty! Come, say hello to our guest."

Echo stood at the door for a moment, transfixed, contemplating what this next step could mean. She heard a little bell—and it broke her spell. Daffodil, the tabby cat, wore a pink collar. On the collar hung a silver bell. The cat rubbed against Echo's shin as if to say hello and welcome.

Echo stepped into the house. She closed the door and felt her past envelop her senses as if ghosts had delivered it. She kneeled and stroked the tabby's fur.

SIXTY-THREE

Skip drove to the Lau residence in a state of shock.

Bud sat silently in the passenger seat, gazing out the window. There were no jokes or witty comments between them. May Lau's grandmother had discovered May's body, murdered by gunshot. Because of the open investigation involving her parents, Skip and Bud got the call instead of the team that was up next on the precinct's homicide board.

The moment Skip was notified, he'd asked about the surveillance team. Departmental budget restraints had prohibited putting a twenty-four-hour observation group on May. It'd been a long shot following May, and ironically when it was most needed, they'd been off the job. The team had left the Lau residence at eleven p.m. with a log entry that stated: "No activity to report."

"Now we have three open-unsolved that are tied together," Bud said. "Not what I expected."

"I'm there with you, partner," Skip agreed. "I never would have guessed this scenario."

"This takes May off the board—and I guess it puts the business partner back into the mix. Motive being there now unless May had a will in place that's disadvantageous to Mr. Li."

"There's the grandmother."

Skip looked at Bud and crunched his face. "Are you serious?"

"It's extremely unlikely," Bud replied. "Just throwing out all the possibilities. You know, brain-storming."

"Fair enough." Skip pulled up to an intersection and stopped because the light was red. "The grandmother wasn't in the states at the time of the first murders, so unless we're speculating that she discovered May was responsible and killed her in revenge, or perhaps she did it for the money—"

"Neither sounds likely. We don't even know if May had a will in place, although, let's suppose she didn't—wouldn't that make the nearest relative the grandmother?

"Sure," Skip answered. "Nevertheless, what ninety-plus-year-old lady whacks her granddaughter for money?"

"Not many," Bud admitted. "There's still revenge."

"Okay, but do we really think May was responsible?"

"No." Bud thought for a moment and then said, "There's got to be an organized crime connection. For a B and E crew to come back, I don't buy it. Too risky. They already got away with the gold. Why return?"

"And why kill the kid? Unless, maybe, she's a witness?"

"If she's a witness, why didn't she say anything before?"

"That would fit with the mafia angle. Maybe she's been quiet, but all-of-a-sudden she threatens to talk to someone, or worse, she does talk to someone."

"You asked Echo," Bud said.

Skip frowned. "Crap. Is it possible?"

"Anything's possible, partner. But, let's not over speculate here. We'll talk to Echo. For now, let's get to the scene and see what's what."

"Okay."

"Um, Skip?"

"Yeah?"

"The light's been green for about a minute. Plus, we're the police. I'm not sure why you even stopped. The street's empty."

"Just thinking too much, I guess," he said. Skip drove the rest of the way into the hills in silence. He felt a chill thinking about the possibility that his suggestion to Echo to reach out and talk to May led to her murder. When they arrived, he walked to the red door without waiting for Bud.

"Hey Skip," Officer Wainwright said. "This one shocked me."

"Me too."

"The tech crew are on the way. I think they're calling Sabine out since this is going to attract the media like flies to—"

"Yeah, I get it," Skip said. "The grandmother?"

"She's inside with a couple of EMTs. They're watching her heart rate and stuff—they were actually first on the scene because the grandmother called nine-one-one and said something in broken English about needing a doctor."

"May was still alive?"

"No, I don't think so," Chuck replied. "She was gone for sure before the ambulance arrived. They called dispatch right away."

"What about a translator?"

"That's in the works," he said. "Someone's getting pulled out of bed right now, I'd imagine. And, hey, there's Sabine talking with Bud."

Skip looked back towards the street. Bud and Sabine were making their way toward the house. Before they got to the front door, another squad car pulled up, then a media van. Skip slapped Chuck on the shoulder. "You're in charge out here," he said. "Keep those reporters off the lawn and get that officer up-to-speed on the situation. I want him knocking on doors. Cover this entire street. Anything anyone heard or saw, I want to hear about it."

"You got it, Detective."

Skip put blue booties over his shoes and entered the house. It was apparent right away that the EMT crew rushed in. There were footprints everywhere. That couldn't be helped. He knew they were just doing their jobs. They didn't know it was a murder scene. They'd been called out because a frightened grandmother said she needed a doctor.

May's grandmother was receiving medical care in the living room. Skip didn't stop. They'd wait until the interpreter arrived, and she'd calmed down before talking to her. He entered the kitchen and observed the body.

She was on her back near the door. Shot in the middle of the forehead. There were no signs of a forced entry. Nothing was disturbed. Apparently, May had opened the door, and the killer shot immediately. It's likely the killer didn't set foot in the house. Skip snapped latex gloves onto both hands and felt May's pockets. *Nothing.* Her hands were empty as well.

He didn't need to turn around to sense Bud's presence. "I'm going to check her room, partner. You want to go check the safe?"

"On it," Bud said.

"Let me know when you're ready, Skip," Sabine said. "The tech crew is about five minutes out. I can start on the body as soon as you're done."

"I'm done," Skip said. "There's nothing on the body. It looks like she answered the door and whoever was there fired one shot."

Sabine set down her toolbox and put on gloves. "I'll update you as I can, Skip."

He nodded and left the kitchen. In May's bedroom, nothing appeared disturbed. He searched for her cell phone but couldn't find it. Her computer was off. He felt it was a good bet the killer hadn't come into the house. Unless Bud found any signs downstairs or the tech crew uncovered trace evidence, he was confident that the killer's motive was simply to kill May.

Which meant she was a witness to something or knew something that she hadn't shared with them. A cloud of doubt and fear hung over him as he realized his next step was a call to Echo.

If her meeting with May had led to May's murder, he'd need some time to process the guilt. He pulled out his phone and wrote a quick text message:

I know it's late, but we need to talk. ASAP.

SIXTY-FOUR

The elder of the brothers drove cautiously, staying under the speed limit all the way to their motel.

"That was easy," he said when he parked the van.

"She didn't see it coming."

"No," he agreed. "Let's hope she didn't run her stupid mouth too much."

"Think she's mentioned us to anyone?"

"That would have been really, *really* stupid. No, I think we're good. Keep going through her messages before the phone dies."

Sitting in the passenger's seat, he scrolled through the messages one by one. Unlocking the screen with her dead face was a stroke of genius, he thought. But he didn't mention that to his brother because any type of bragging, real or perceived, was met with scorn. "There's nothing in here," he stated with certainty.

"Go through her calls, incoming and outgoing," his brother commanded. "She who she talked with recently."

Obedient to a fault, the younger brother switched from messages to the call log. "Should I write these—"

"I don't care if you write them down. Figure out who she was talking with. Use the burner in the glove box if you want to take a pic of the screen."

"Good idea," he said, reaching for the throwaway. "There's one in here that might be a problem." He took a picture of the contact using the burner's cheap camera. Then May Lau's phone died. "It's dead. Should I toss it?"

"Wait until we pass the next intersection. There's a section along the highway that's overgrown. In the meantime, wipe it down."

"I know. I'm not stupid."

"Noted," he said, slowing down for a red light. "But sometimes you forget the little details."

"I do not," he said emphatically. "That's a lie."

"Okay, don't get your panties in a bunch."

"Just pay attention. The light's green."

SIXTY-FIVE

Skip left to let the ME and crime scene techs do their jobs.

He held little hope that they'd find any additional evidence.

The translator arrived. Skip told her to let May's grandmother know there were two detectives who needed to speak with her. Bud returned from the basement office and game room with nothing to report. All evidence on the scene showed the killer didn't step inside the house.

"Detectives," the translator called. "She's ready to speak with you."

"Okay," Skip said. "I'm Detective Malloy, and this is my partner, Detective Smith. Please express our condolences and let her know this won't take long."

"I understand," the interpreter said. Then she spoke to Mrs. Lau in Chinese. After a moment, the old woman stopped and stared at the detectives.

"Mrs. Lau wants to know what you're going to do," the translator said. "She says she's disappointed in America. She'd hoped it was a better place. She wishes to return home as soon as possible."

"We understand, and we're sorry," Skip said. "Could you explain to her that in order to do our jobs, we need to gather as much information as possible. Anything she can tell us about what happened tonight will help us. No detail is unimportant."

After a brief exchange, the translator explained what the grandmother had said to her. "She came from the guest quarters above the garage to make tea. She was having trouble sleeping. There was nothing that concerned her until she saw the door open. That was right before she realized they shot May. Her first hope was that she needed help. She called the emergency dispatcher. There was some confusion at first, but she could use enough English to express herself. She needed an ambulance for her granddaughter."

"Ask her if she heard anything," Skip said.

They continued the interview, going back and forth between Chinese and English. Mrs. Lau did not hear or see anything until she found May. Nothing.

"What about the organized crime connection?" Bud asked.

"Excuse me, Detective," the translator said. "Are you asking me to translate that, or are you asking your partner about it?"

"Go ahead," Skip said. "Ask her if she's aware of any connection with organized crime between May or May's parents. Explain to her we've heard something about people that might have been involved in extortion. Little Shanghai has a crime syndicate, that is—"

"Yes, Detective," she said. "I'm aware of the situation. Let me ask her."

They talked for several minutes.

"Mrs. Lau knows nothing of value, detectives," the translator said. "She's aware of the Ching Lóng Benevolent Society. In fact, she says they'll be helping her with her affairs in America before she returns to China. She was quite adamant that neither General Zhang nor any of his associates perpetrated this crime."

Skip looked at Bud and shook his head. "Well, either that's true, and we're back to random thieves, or there's something going on here that nobody is going to talk about. Either way, I think we're running into another brick wall."

"Nobody said the job was easy," Bud said. "Should we ask her anything else?"

Skip turned to the translator. "Be sure to get her contact information and give yours to her. I'd like you to be able to reach out to her. Please ask her to call you if she thinks of anything at all, no matter how small, that might help us."

"Yes, Detective," she said.

"And ask her when she's planning on leaving."

The two women spoke in Chinese. Skip watched as they exchanged contact information. He had little hope it would bear fruit. "She says that she wants to return as soon as possible," the translator said. "However, she thinks with the funeral arrangements and all the financial and business things she must attend to with the passing of her granddaughter, that she could be here for two weeks. She asks if she's free to use the house or if she must leave."

“Tell her the woman in the kitchen and the tech crew must finish their jobs. We cannot say at this exact moment about the release of the main house. However, she’s free to use the guest quarters as she wishes.”

Skip and Bud left the women and walked outside. A light, misty rain had forced the media into rain gear. Officer Wainwright said, “No luck with any of the neighbors.”

“That was to be expected,” Bud said. “Well, I guess I’ll take the media this time, Skip.”

“I think it’s my turn.”

“Yes, it is. But I know how much you hate it, and your phone is buzzing.”

Skip forgot he’d set the phone to silent during the interview. He looked at the screen. Echo was returning his call. “I’ve got to take this,” he said.

Walking away, he answered the call.

“This is Detective Malloy.”

SIXTY-SIX

Echo parked on Elm Street.

The sadness she felt over the news about May Lau gripped her. Skip's text message had surprised her. She'd talked to Connor about it and cried again. Emotions brought about by the news of the latest murder mixed with her feelings about what she might discover at Willem Kuiper's house. Willem had invited her to return in the morning because he thought there might be an old box stored away. "I'll probably need a couple of hours to uncover it," he'd said at the end of their previous visit.

She walked to the door and knocked.

Willem opened the door. "Good morning."

Daffodil rushed to greet her.

"Look who has a new friend," Willem said. "Please, Echo, come in."

Echo scratched Daffodil's head, and the cat purred.

"She likes you."

"She's beautiful," Echo said. "I've been thinking about pets recently. But, I'm not sure about that much responsibility. I think I might just get an aquarium and a few house plants."

"Those are good things. But a cat? You can't beat a cat for a friend, especially when you're feeling a little blue."

Echo nodded. "I guess you can't hold a fish or stroke a house plant and expect it to purr."

Willem laughed. He had a deep and hearty laugh that made Echo smile. "You know, I wanted to tell you this yesterday, but I thought it might be better to let you take things slower."

"What's that?"

"The silver bell on Daffodil's collar. It was a gift from your mother."

As if on command, Daffodil ran off to the kitchen. The bell rang softly.

Echo shed a tear. "She's worn that all this time?"

"Well, no, not exactly," Willem replied. "Daffodil is only a few years old. The bell's a hand-me-down. Two cats ago, actually."

"Really?"

"Yes. When your parents lived here, that was when I had Simba. He was adopted. They named him Simba before I rescued him, and he was a hunter, like a real lion. He had a bad habit of killing birds, so I stopped putting out bird seeds and put plants into the birdbath instead of water. Your mother gave me that bell because she wanted me to feed the birds again."

"So it worked?"

"Sure did. Simba couldn't sneak up on anything after that. And I liked it. The sound, I mean. So after Simba passed, I saved it. Not long after, I realized I was lonely for another cat. I adopted a kitten this time, still a rescue, but not an old cat like Simba was. I named her Luna. After she outgrew the kitten stage, I put the bell on her."

"And now it's on Daffodil," Echo said.

"Yup. Luna lived about fifteen or sixteen years. I saved the bell again. A little oil and polish, and it was as good as new."

"That's a delightful story."

"Let me get you some tea, and I'll tell you what I've found."

They went to the kitchen, and Willem poured Echo a cup of tea. "That's all there is in that box," he said. "Go ahead. It's yours now. I hope it helps you."

Echo sat. She sipped her tea and felt her heartbeat increase. "I'm a little nervous," she admitted. "Have you gone through this stuff?"

"Not really," Willem said. "I was curious why they left anything here at all. That stuff was hidden in a utility cabinet. I'm not even positive they left it on purpose. Anyway, I didn't find it until nearly a decade later. I needed a new water heater and a few other repairs—now that I'm recalling it—it was the contractor who found the box."

Echo removed the lid. Peering inside, she could see there were a few folders. Paperwork.

"When I opened it, I didn't know it belonged to your folks. I thought maybe it was forgotten by the original owners of the house. It confused me at first because the names made little sense, but there's a picture of them in there. A wedding picture and a few snapshots that might be old family photos. There's a newborn baby picture, too."

"What do you mean by the names?"

"You'll see, Echo. This might bring up a bigger mystery. The names you know for your parents aren't the ones on the birth certificate."

"There's a birth certificate in there?"

"Yeah," he said. "I'm sorry. If the certificate had said Echo Rose, I would have found you on the internet. But that's not the name on the certificate. Remember, when your parents had you, the web was still new. When they were born, it didn't exist, so searching for the names I found on the papers in there didn't lead me anywhere."

"So Clara and John aren't my parents' real names?" Echo asked.

"Apparently not," he answered. "I always thought that someday you might show up. I didn't want to throw away someone's original birth certificate. Plus, the photos…"

"Thank you," she said. "I'm going to take this home. I need to be alone when I look inside." Echo put the lid back on the box. She sipped her tea.

"I understand completely," Willem said. "I hope you find some answers."

SIXTY-SEVEN

Hank and Kurt Nelson were of Irish ancestry.

Their family had left Boston a generation ago. It had been their great-great-grandparents who'd left Ireland and come through Ellis Island. Neither of the brothers cared much for their family history, but they kept in contact with a few of their uncles. The criminal ones.

A couple of aunts and their husbands, along with a handful of cousins, were still good churchgoing citizens. Hank and Kurt cut them out of their lives over a decade before.

Hank, the older of the brothers, and one who'd been referred to as Ying by their uncle, had tattoos, some inked while running with gangs during his youth. He'd left that life behind, but not because he found crime distasteful. He didn't enjoy taking orders or following anyone else's agenda.

Kurt, also known as Yang, disdained tattoos. He felt they were too much of a help to law enforcement.

"They have DNA testing and fingerprints," Hank had said many times. "So what if they can identify you with a tattoo?"

"I just don't want the risk," Kurt argued. "What if someone is robbed and says, 'the guy had a Celtic Cross tattoo,' and then the cops pick you up? That can't happen to me."

"Okay, little brother," he'd said. "I won't force the issue."

The morning after they'd taken care of their little problem with May Lau, they sat and argued about what was next. Kurt wanted to pack up and leave immediately. Hank wanted to keep a low profile and not travel until more time had passed.

"I think we're stupid if we stay in Fairview for even one more day," Kurt said.

"You're just bored."

"Well, yeah. Look at this dump."

The motel was certainly a dump. It had curtains from the nineteen-eighties. The television wasn't even a flat-screen. In the bathroom, there were mold stains around the shower and peeling paint on the walls. Golden yellow carpeting covered all the floor except the bathroom and a small portion near the door. It was uncleanable at this stage. Hank wondered if they even bothered to vacuum. He was half convinced to give in to his brother's demand and pack up, but he also felt caution dictated that they learn more before getting on the road.

They might also need, he thought, to change their van for something less noticeable.

"Let's give it a day or two," Hank said. "Meanwhile, maybe we can sell off some gold."

"I know we need the cash," Kurt said. "But won't that involve too much risk?"

"I'm counting on that, actually," he said. "Look, here's my plan. We put on those stupid hats and wear some hick country shirts and jeans. With those wigs and fake glasses, nobody will identify us from security video footage. We go down there to Big Teddy's EZ-Pawn and sell enough gold to get us by for a month. Doesn't have to be much."

"Won't that give the cops a head's up?"

"Well, yeah! I'm counting on that," he said. "See, I've been studying on the internet. There's a way to make a fake thumbprint. I've already ordered the supplies online. They'll be here today."

"Why didn't you tell me about this before?"

"Wasn't sure about it."

Hank didn't like to burden his brother with unnecessary things to think about. Kurt complained when this happened, but not too forcefully. Hank figured Kurt really didn't want to know about things that were only in the *maybe* stage. He just liked reasons to complain. "Let's see that contact. It might be time to make a call."

"Yeah, sure," Kurt said. He handed the burner to his brother.

Hank thought about it for a moment and then dialed the number.

A female answered. "Hello, this is Echo."

"You're the reporter?" he asked.

"I'm a reporter. I don't know if I'm *the* reporter. Who's this, and how can I help you?"

"Never mind who I am. Consider me a confidential informant."

"Okay. What's this call regarding?"

"You had a call with a Chinese girl. May Lau."

"I did. Can you tell me where you got my number?"

Hank continued without answering her question. "May Lau is dead. I have information about it."

"I'm listening."

"The Chinese mafia killed her. I can't say more. They're dangerous. Goodbye." Hank ended the call, removed the battery, and snapped the phone in half. He turned to Kurt and said, "Wipe this down and take it to the dumpster behind the building."

"Sure," he said. "Then can we get some breakfast? I'm starving."

"As long as we go someplace different today."

"Annie's has great pancakes."

"I'm tired of pancakes. Besides, I don't want anyone to remember our faces. Better to move around."

A shrill ring sounded. Kurt jumped. "What the—"

"It's just the land line," Hank said, laughing. "You're on edge. Calm down."

He picked up the phone and grunted out a yes, and listened for ten seconds before setting down the receiver without saying thank-you or goodbye.

"That was the front desk with our supplies. Grab them on the way back from the dumpster. And see if they have a newspaper."

Kurt left without another word, and Hank turned on the television.

The local news station was showing footage from the night before. In front of the Lau's residence, Hank watched a tall black detective walk away from the group of reporters. A chubby, round-faced detective gave a succinct statement that revealed no facts other than affirming there'd been a third murder.

"And that, sadly, is why you've got to kill the talkers," he said to himself as he turned off the TV.

SIXTY-EIGHT

Echo looked at the box.

She'd been cataloging its contents when she'd received a strange call. As much as she was dying to discover everything she could about her past, she knew that professional responsibility needed to be prioritized over her curiosity. The past could wait a little longer.

Skip answered on the second ring. "This is Detective Malloy."

"Skip, it's Echo."

"Good morning."

"It's not that good."

"Point taken. What's up?"

"I just got a strange call." Echo described the brief interaction she'd had with the mysterious caller who claimed knowledge about the Lau murders. She'd called the number after the man had hung up without giving his name or any sign of who he was or what he actually knew. He had turned the phone off.

"It's a burner phone, I'm sure," Skip said. "But I'll run a check, just in case. How easy is it to get your number?"

Echo thought for a few seconds before answering. “Difficult. It’s not public. I don’t have this number listed on *Above the Fold*’s website or anywhere else online. It’s for my personal and private life, except for a few people like you, Connor, and Frank. Normally, for a story, I give out a different contact number. So, I’m not sure how the guy got it. I don’t even know if he sounded credible, to be honest. But I felt I’d better let you know.”

Thank you. I appreciate the tip, and I’ll follow up on the number, although I’m certain it’s a dead-end.

“Anything you can tell me?” she asked.

“Not really.”

“I’d like to give Conner something. He’s still working on the story, and now it’s gotten bigger and more mysterious. It’s not likely a break-in guy or cat burglar is going back to murder the daughter just for something to do. There’s got to be a connection.”

“Of course, you’re right, Echo. But we’ve got nothing I can tell you. It’s an open investigation.”

“I understand,” she said. “I have something else. It’s from a confidential source. I’m not sure of its veracity.”

“Anything could help. Let’s hear it.”

Echo told Skip about her encounter with General Zhang. When she was done, she said, “I wasn’t sure I was going to reveal this to anyone. But I wouldn’t exactly call him a source. He didn’t tell me anything except that he claimed neither he nor any of the people he’s associated with were responsible.”

“It’s a bit self-serving.”

“Sure,” she agreed. “But he had to know that before he picked me up. I don’t see the play for him if he’s lying. Why say anything?”

"Interesting…"

"Still not sure what I'm going to do about it. I'll pass along to Conner what I can. He's investigating only the Lau connection. I'm still working at the organized crime angle. But, of course, they're not the kind of people who like to see articles about themselves in the paper."

"Be careful, Echo."

"You got it," she said. She ended the call and wondered whether she should have mentioned Roulan Fang, the lawyer. *No*, she thought. *I'll keep that one close to the vest for now*.

She opened a file and went back to her investigation of the box's contents. There were insurance papers, medical records, and some bills she couldn't imagine why her parents had bothered saving. Her birth certificate showed her name as Grace Sophia Lasko. It listed the place of birth as Reno, Nevada.

Her parents were Perry and Gail Lasko.

She found a high school and college records. There was a wedding invitation and a certificate of marriage. There were hand-written pages, hastily torn from what appeared to be a diary. The script was flowery, and doodles filled the edges. A cursory look revealed the pages were her mother's thoughts and details about her days. Echo put them aside. She'd need time to read about what might be her mother's secrets.

Gail Lasko's maiden name was Voss. She'd graduated high school in Nevada but attended university in Ohio. That's where she'd met Perry.

Perry had been a business major. He'd graduated high school a year before Gail and stayed in his home state for college. They'd married in his hometown, honeymooned in Orlando, and had gone to Reno at some point near the end of Gail's pregnancy.

"Why did you guys run?" Echo asked.

The papers didn't answer, but she knew they might give up their secrets with a proper investigation. She stepped back and gathered her thoughts. If she attacked this project like it was a story—as if she was an impartial investigative journalist—it would be easier to solve whatever mysteries were buried.

Were they grifters? Scammers? Had they stolen money from the mob?

Was the government hunting them?

Terrorists?

Don't let your imagination run away, she thought. *There's going to be a logical explanation. There nearly always is. I just need time.*

Echo put the lid back on the box. The past had stayed hidden for over two decades, so it could wait a few more days. She still needed to review the Amanda's Secret files so that she could destroy any evidence she'd been the person responsible for the hack. She'd been ignoring the calls, text messages, and emails from Mouse and Amanda's Secret's HR department. The burner cell—the one used by her alias, Rhonda Flemming—needed to be destroyed and discarded.

It wouldn't be long before they discovered she wasn't coming back to work. And then it wouldn't take a rocket scientist to figure out Rhonda Flemming didn't exist. From there, it would be logical to assume that she had placed the gateway device allowing the data breach.

The felonious data breach.

Echo knew she had to be careful. The only thing worse than having the FBI after her would be if the Chinese gangs decided she was a genuine threat. Their solution—it appeared they'd used it with May Lau—was harsh and permanent. It was time to do some serious digging into what really happened to May and if there was a connection to her investigation into the Ching Lóng Benevolent Society, General Zhang, the Golden Dragons, or Gao Fu Shauai Chin.

Maybe she could help herself, Conner, and the police all at once.

SIXTY-NINE

Two days after the murder of May Lau, Skip and Bud got a phone call from Big Ted.

Skip parked under a sign that read, "Gold Bought & Sold! Best Prices in Fairview!"

The receptionist buzzed them through the double entry. Ted met them right away. "A white van, detectives," he said. "I'm sorry, I should have called faster, but we've been so busy I'd completely forgotten about the pandas until they walked out."

"Slow down," Bud said. "From the top, what happened?"

"Two guys came in looking to sell pandas. I bought one. As they were walking out the front, I realized you'd want a heads up."

"This is crappy, Ted," Skip said. "You were supposed to call us while they were still inside."

"Did you get a license plate number?" Bud asked.

"Sorry, Detective Smith," Ted replied with his head held down like a scolded teenager. "I didn't. It all happened so fast."

"I'll go radio this in and see if any patrol cops are around. Maybe we'll get lucky and get a plate," Bud said. He waved at the reception desk. "Hey, buzz me out!"

Skip frowned at Ted. "This doesn't make you look good."

"I didn't have to call at all, you know."

"I know, but—never mind. Show me the paperwork."

In Ted's office, he handed Skip a file folder. Inside was a standardized form that listed the particular details of the transaction. The name on the form was Robert Smith. Written in messy blue ink were an address, a phone number, and a state driver's license number. There was only one item purchased: a Chinese gold panda coin. The denomination, mint date, and grade of the coin had been recorded, along with the agreed-upon price. *One Thousand Seven Hundred Dollars and Zero Cents*. Next to an entry of $1,700.00 was PAID IN CASH, stamped in red ink.

"Probably all fake," Skip said. He closed the folder, having avoided touching the form. Maybe there were other prints. Sometimes cases received a little luck like that.

"Looked legit, Detective." Ted pointed to the file. "There's a right thumb print in there. Required by law. I watched him put it there myself. Even if the name's a fake, you've got your man there. Plus, it's a misdemeanor to give false information on one of these. So now you've got probable cause, Detective. See there, I did you a solid."

"Don't get so excited. We have to find the right guys for probable cause to mean anything. Let me see the video footage." While Ted went to his computer to pull up the feed, Skip took a picture of the thumb print with his phone. He uploaded the file to his email and sent it to the tech department marked "urgent." Then he sent a text message to Sabine and asked her if she could use her influence to get someone on the print immediately.

Ted rolled back the timestamp on the recording. While he worked, Skip asked if the seller mentioned any other gold for sale. "Yeah, he did," Ted answered. "He asked me how much I'd buy in one transaction and still pay in cash."

"What did you tell him?" Skip asked while he watched the recording. It showed two men as they walked into the pawnshop. He knew from experience they were likely professional thieves. They both wore baseball caps, dark-framed glasses, and long sleeves. They kept their bearded faces down—and there wouldn't be any way to tell if the facial hair was real.

"I told them I could potentially, maybe, go as high as a hundred grand," Ted replied as if he wasn't sure of the right amount. "The thing is, I don't keep that kind of cash here. I don't want to be a target for thieves and kidnappers, obviously, so I told the guys my policy. Any high amount like that needs at least twenty-four hours of advance planning, and I bring in security. I told them a check was a different story."

"What did they say to that?"

"He laughed. Guys like that don't take checks."

Skip instructed Ted to copy the footage from a minute before to a minute after and then email it to him. He handed him a business card. "Use that email. Write EZ-Pawn footage in the header." Then Skip had a thought. "Ted, I need you to instruct your receptionist to keep the door locked. Give me an hour, okay?"

"What's up, Detective?"

"I also need you to sit. Tell her to stay behind the desk. Nobody walks on the floor." Skip called the precinct and requested a tech crew. Then he called Bud and told him to stay outside.

"You got it," Bud said. "What's up?"

"The shoe print."

"You've got a print?"

"It's a hunch. Any luck on the patrols?"

"Not yet," Bud said. "There's someone close. He's going to cruise for a bit."

"They're probably long gone," Skip said. "But I've got a thumbprint."

"Let's hope it hits."

"Fingers crossed. However, we need the shoe print to tie him to the crime scene. I'm not here to run down misdemeanors."

"How about the form? You think our guys handled it?" Bud asked. He knew Skip would have avoided touching the paperwork and that sometimes the tech guys could pull prints from paper. Sometimes.

"We're in the same boat there—but we'll have the guys check it out. Hold on a sec. I'm getting another call." Skip switched over and then back again. "They'll be here in twenty."

"I'll be out here to greet them."

Skip ended the call and tapped the desk with his fist. "Knock on wood," he said.

"That's a metal desk, Detective."

"Don't get smart on me, Ted. And take a seat. We're going to be here awhile."

"I hope it's not long, Detective Malloy. I have a business to run."

"And I have murderers to catch."

SEVENTY

Echo sat in her office and thought about how she should prioritize.

Emotions were driving her towards working on discovering more about her birth parents. Her long-term plans required that she used diligence to work on the story for *Soft Vanda*. And then there was the organized crime story and the possible connection it had to the Lau murders.

She checked her fake accounts on Amanda's Secret. The "SallyLin" account had written a brief reply. While the account was using a picture of Roulan Fang, it obviously didn't mean the attorney was actually the one responding. However, there could be a connection.

Echo replied. She needed to be subtle—to avoid arousing suspicion—but also direct enough to discover if the Sally Lin account was being used as a cover for prostitution. If it really was just a lonely wife looking for adultery, Echo didn't want to waste her time.

With her go-to hacker off the job regarding the Chinese crime story, she was at a cross-road. If she hired someone else, they'd likely face similar risks. However, many of her contacts were in the Eastern Block—countries like Estonia, Moldavia, and Ukraine—those hackers were arrogant and wouldn't fear repercussions from over five thousand miles away.

She opened her dark web browser and made some initial inquiries. Her moniker was known, but good hackers were cautious. They'd check out her credentials and the brief description of the job she needed done before responding.

Next, Echo put on a pair of gloves. She took a new thumb drive out of its packaging and inserted it into her computer. All the Amanda's Secret files went onto the drive. She erased all traces from her computer, but not before placing coded versions of documents she still wanted to access into anonymous online storage. Still wearing gloves, she retrieved an untouched express mailing package. Using a disposable pen, she addressed it to a blind drop mailbox and placed the thumb drive inside.

The mailing center was across the city. They'd accepted a fake ID when she opened it, and she'd paid for several years in advance using cash. At some point, the story would break—she'd move on and could safely destroy the last remaining evidence.

Hackers would sometimes release all the information from a data breach, but Echo was looking to build a story about corporate corruption, not one about people having affairs. She had no problems exposing criminals, but she was hesitant to get involved in a story that was lurid and gossipy.

After double-checking her security measures, she changed course and confirmed she had cleaned everything from her computer's hard drive. The mailer went into a new shopping bag. She'd mail it later in the day.

Echo logged into her *Above The Fold* accounts to access information from the web. AP archives, LexisNexis, and libraries. She needed to do some digging.

There were several stories and mentions of the accident that resulted in her parents' deaths. The station wagon crash in Camden was a little more newsworthy than an average traffic fatality because two occupants had been declared deceased at the scene. However, none of the articles mentioned an orphaned baby.

"No wonder," Echo said to herself. That was the reason she'd never realized this story was about her parents. Before she had their names, it was just another sad news item she'd glossed over in her searches. Why the reporters missed this interesting and tragic portion of the story, she couldn't guess. Perhaps there were bigger stories being chased down in Camden. Or maybe the reporter was just being lazy.

There was no recourse now. Over twenty years had passed.

Echo continued searching but switched to her parents' real names.

"Oh my god!" she screamed and nearly fell out of her chair.

SEVENTY-ONE

Bud waited outside EZ-Pawn.

When the tech team arrived, he led them to the entrance. "Skip's in the back office with the owner," he said. "We've asked him and the receptionist to hold tight while you guys work. What can we do to help?"

The lead tech explained that exposure to the UV lights they needed to use were harmful. "I'll need you guys to stay clear," he said. "Unless you want to suit up."

Bud called Skip, even though he was only on the other side of the pawnshop. There was no sense in shouting, and they couldn't walk to each other without risking the destruction of evidence. "They're getting started out here," he said. "Unless you want a UV burn, maybe you should close the door. I can observe the collection out here from a distance."

Skip acknowledged the plan and shut the door.

Bud waited. They had given the team copies of the two shoe prints taken from the Lau Residence. However, knowing what to look for and finding it were two different things. Because the larger shoe print was from a common shoe and had no distinct markings, they concentrated on looking for the smaller shoe first.

Finding them both would be evidence, but not proof, of a connection. Finding the smaller shoe print, however, would be powerful evidence. The gum, dirt, candy, or dog poop on the shoe had made a distinct pattern.

Bud watched with anticipation.

Meanwhile, Skip sat with Ted in the office. "Can you identify, if needed, the exact coin you bought?"

"You mean did I mix it with others?" he asked.

"Yes."

"No, it's clearly identified and labeled. It's linked to that exact receipt."

"Once we get cleared to walk on the floor," Skip said, "I need you to identify that coin for the techs."

"There won't be any fingerprints on it," he said. "It's in a plastic sleeve."

"Perhaps the sleeve will have prints."

"Ah, I didn't think of that." Ted paced the room like a zoo animal. "I probably wiped it down, actually. It's a habit of mine, you know, to clean everything."

"All we can do is check."

Ted went back to pacing.

Skip called Sabine. "You got anything on that print?"

"Hey Skip, I was just about to call. You won't believe this…"

SEVENTY-TWO

Echo opened the door to her apartment.

"I need a hug," she said to Conner.

He followed her to the computer station in the office. "So, what's the big news?"

"It's about my birth parents."

"Lee Callaway warned you about this," he said. "Good news or bad news?"

"They weren't just ordinary people who died in a car accident. Their real names weren't John and Clara Weston. I feel a bit overwhelmed right now."

"Start at the beginning," Conner suggested. "Tell me everything."

Echo told him about her visit to the house on Elm Street. The box that had been in long-term storage and her discovery of her birth certificate. "My parents' real names were Perry and Gail Lasko."

"And you?"

"Grace Sophia Lasko."

"What happened?" Conner asked. He was on the edge of his seat.

"My birth father was an attorney. He specialized in financial laws and worked closely with accountants. During my mother's pregnancy, he was a key witness against an American conglomerate. It was in the banking, manufacturing, and trucking industries."

"Go on," Conner said. "This sounds more and more like a soap opera."

"It was an American company, but it was partially owned, through a bunch of off-shore shell companies, by a Mexican cartel. They used trucks and warehouses to move and hide drugs, weapons, and cash. The really crazy thing was that there were banks and investors involved who didn't realize everything that was going on. And, of course, some that did."

"Wow. So what happened?"

"After the trial started, my parents disappeared at some point. I'm still searching for clues in old stories. I was born in Reno, Nevada. Obviously, they didn't stay there."

"And the trial? Where was that?"

"Southern District of Texas, Houston."

"A federal prosecution, then?"

"Yes. It was a RICO case all the way," Echo said. "Here, let me show you the biggest story I could find. It was in the *Houston Chronicle*. One second, I'll pull it up." She opened a tab on her computer and pointed. "Here, see his name right there?"

"And your mom?"

"Not in the stories. I'm assuming, but I don't know, that she was hiding out. I mean, it's not safe to testify against a cartel."

"Well, anything about witness protection in there?"

"I found nothing," she replied. "But at some point, Perry falls off the face of the earth. He's gone. The trial wasn't over yet. No trace of him anywhere."

"So, since we know he died in that car crash—not as Perry Lasko, but as John Weston—then we can either assume he'd gone into witness protection and the accident was just that, a tragic accident. Or—"

"The cartel killed him."

"Or they murdered him, yes," Conner agreed. "That would be the other possibility. He and Gail tried to hide. The cartel found them. End of their story and the start of yours as a new orphan. In either case, I'm sorry for your loss. I know this is tough."

"I asked for it," Echo said. "And I'm not done. I want to know. Did the government hide them and fail? Or did they run on their own and fail? Or, in either of those cases, was it just a weird coincidence that they died?"

"I don't really like coincidences like that."

"Me neither," Echo said. "And there's one more really strange thing I can't explain."

"What's that?"

"This notebook," she answered. "Here, let me show you." The notebook was hardbound and the size of a children's picture book. There was nothing identifying who wrote the entries that filled nearly all the pages. "It appears to be in some kind of code."

SEVENTY-THREE

Skip had hoped Sabine would have some good news, but what she shared was another dead-end.

"It's a fake.

"You're kidding me?"

"Nope. The thumbprint on that form belongs to Molly Hill.

"The actress?"

"One and the same."

"How did they pull that off?"

"I'll text you over an article on how it was probably done."

Skip pulled up the website. It explained how, using easily obtained ingredients, a person could make a fingerprint using a photograph. He said, "I can't believe this," mostly to himself.

"You can't believe what?" Ted asked.

"That thumb print you took from the buyer wasn't his. It was a fake."

"Molly Hill?"

"How'd you know that?"

"There was a big social media story about it a few months ago. She sold a bunch of super high-def NFTs, and from those photographs, it was possible to capture her fingerprints. Among other things…"

Skip shook his head. "What's the world coming to?"

"Maybe you'll get lucky and find something on the plastic sleeve."

Ted didn't sound convincing to Skip, and he was feeling like the day was going to be a bust when he heard someone yelling to Bud. He looked out the office door into the pawnshop and saw a commotion around a spot on the floor. The techs had a rig set up with lights and a camera. "What's up?" he asked.

"We got something here, Detective," a tech said. "Looks like your guy."

"Excellent," Skip said. "Finally, some good news."

The tech crew eventually confirmed the shoe print was a match to the one taken from the Lau residence on the night of the murders. After more searching, they discovered and photographed six more prints that matched. They also found four quality prints of a shoe that matched the larger print from the Lau crime scene. While not unique, it was good circumstantial evidence the pair were working together.

The tech team mapped out the entire floor of the pawnshop. They wanted to compare the movement on the video footage of the suspects with the locations of the prints on the floor. With those comparisons, combined with the sale of the gold panda, they could establish that the two men were the probable killers.

Unfortunately, the plastic sleeve and the gold panda didn't have any prints. Ted had been right. He'd cleaned the plastic before placing an inventory sticker on it and placing it in the display.

After the techs released the floor, they gave Ted permission to open for business.

"What next?" Bud asked Skip.

"Let's assume we're the bad guys," he replied. "Why do we come in here and only sell one coin?"

"Lunch money?"

"Only you'd think of selling precious metal to buy cheeseburgers."

"I mean, they need money, right?" Bud asked. "They need some cash, so they come in here and sell gold. That doesn't seem like a mystery."

"But why only one coin?" Skip wondered if they were shopping around for the best price. Even criminals could be thrifty sellers. "You think they're so greedy they'd bother shopping for the best offer?"

Bud pointed outside. "There's a big sign that says Big Ted has the best prices."

"But that doesn't mean it's true. Advertising isn't always honest."

"So, what are you thinking? That they came in here to see what they could get for the coin, and now they're going to—"

"Exactly!" Skip slapped Bud on the shoulder. "We need to get on the ball here and talk to the Sergeant about getting the likely gold buying places under surveillance right away."

"I have a list, Detective." Ted opened a drawer and pulled out a sheet. "All my competitors, that matter. If someone is selling gold somewhere besides Big Teddy's—and why they would do that, I can't say—then it's one of these guys."

Skip took the list. "Can I keep this?"

"Always want to help law enforcement, Detective," he answered. "It's all yours."

"Let's get out of here," Skip said to Bud. "We've got to move on this before these guys vanish into the wind."

SEVENTY-FOUR

Hank's childhood was less than ideal.

He watched helplessly as his mother died of cancer. He was seventeen. It wasn't a month later that his father died in an armed robbery. Hank always believed his father was recklessly careless in that heist because of his broken heart.

As he turned from teenager to adult, he blamed his mother's death on the insurance company and the doctors. After a time, he blamed his father, too. It wasn't until he'd reached his mid-twenties that he acknowledged that his mother's chain-smoking was the reason she died young. It took him years to forgive her for slowly killing herself and leaving him and Kurt without parents.

It was a Sunday afternoon, years previously when Hank first got the idea. He was sitting in a popular café that catered to wealthy, upscale university kids. There was a group complaining about parents. Most were mad at their fathers, but some thought both of their parents deserved to be dead. One spoiled blonde girl said, "I could never pull the trigger myself. But if there was a service…"

"What? A parricide service?" another joked.

"What's that?" she'd asked.

"You're so dumb—it's like Oedipus, you know?"

Inspiration struck Hank that day. He followed the blonde and got her name. Over the next several weeks, he and Kurt followed her on social media and eventually sent her a message from an anonymous account. They offered to take care of the girl's problem for a fee.

She panicked and blocked them.

But the idea had merit, Hank thought, so he instructed Kurt to scour social media for wealthy children who were actively expressing hatred and scorn for either or both of their parents.

Fathers with mistresses who were spending all their money.

Control freaks.

Parents threatening to cut children out of their wills.

Eventually, they found a client. Mark Treadhill was his name. His mother had just been committed to an outpatient center for substance abuse. His father was about to remarry, and he'd flat out told his son that he'd get nothing in the new will. "You'll thank me someday, son," the father had said. Mark posted that quote on his social media and wrote in the comments that he wished the old man would get hit by a bus before he had time to cut him out of his will.

Hank and Kurt made a deal with Mark. They'd make sure Mark got his inheritance by staging an accident before the will could be changed. The price was ten thousand dollars.

Later, they'd realized they'd asked for too little.

"What you thinking about, little brother?" Hank asked. They'd returned to the motel from Big Teddy's, and Hank was noticing Kurt's nervousness. "You're pacing like a racehorse at the gate."

"I want to get out of Fairview," he said. "Today. Now. I don't like waiting."

"I hear you, bro," Hank said. "I just want to be sure we're getting a fair price for the gold we need to sell. We can't leave here without some cash. It's too risky. We need to ditch this van and get something different—like a station wagon or a sports car—and then we can leave. New wheels and maybe some new clothes. I think we should probably get our hair colored. Just to be safe."

"I'm not getting my hair dyed. Last time it itched like crazy. I'll get it cut short, or I'll wear a wig. But no dye. That's final."

"All right," Hank said. "Don't get worked up. It's just a suggestion."

"I was thinking," Kurt said.

"Yeah? Is that why I see smoke coming out of your ears?"

"Remember that old guy with the fancy suit?"

"The one the papers said drowned with a forty-thousand-dollar suit on?"

"Yeah, and super pricey Italian leather shoes."

"I remember."

"We should have taken the suit."

"Too risky. We made it look like he fell into the pool after hitting his head. It would have been weird if we took his clothes."

"No," Kurt said. "I don't agree. Rich people go skinny dipping all the time."

"By themselves? In the middle of the day?"

"They're rich, dude. They do whatever they want."

"Too much trouble selling a secondhand suit. Even a fancy one."

"We also left the dogs. Those were high-dollar dogs."

"Taking dogs is dumb. There are tracking devices in rich people's dogs."

"Oh, yeah. I forgot about that."

"And that's why I'm the brains behind this organization," Hank said. "I'll do the thinking, thank you very much."

"How's the searching going?"

"I've got a few potentials."

"Find another like May. With two hundred ounces of gold, it hardly even matters if they pay us."

"You mean, don't ask for fifty grand?"

"No, stupid. We still want fifty grand in cash, but if there's gold or diamonds to take, it's a bonus."

"May wasn't too happy that we took her gold," Kurt said. "And don't call me stupid. I do a lot of research that you're too impatient to do."

Hank knew his brother was right. He could never sit in front of a computer for twelve hours straight, combing through social media posts, looking for potential clients. He was a man of action. It was his job to buy materials, things like non-traceable handguns and fingerprint-making supplies. Getting his hands on burner cell phones and wigs was his specialty. "Too bad for May. She shouldn't have paid hired killers to whack mom and dad if she didn't want criminals showing up."

"I kind of feel bad for her. First, we take her gold, and then we just killed her."

"Yeah, so what?"

Kurt shut his laptop. "I'm done for today. Look, I know May was threatening to talk to people, but I don't think she really would have. I mean, she was guilty too."

"What you don't realize, little bro, is that I wasn't afraid of May going to the police. Or the media. I was concerned she'd go to the Chinese mafia and tell them we had two hundred ounces of gold."

"I didn't think of that."

"And this is why we leave the thinking to me," Hank said. He knew if May explained what happened to the wrong group of people, those who didn't talk to police and wouldn't mind getting their hands dirty, they could be at risk. "This is another reason we need to ditch the van. May saw it when she paid us. If she went to anyone and talked about the gold, they're gonna be looking for it, just like the police."

"So let's get out of Fairview," Kurt said. "Right now."

"We can't get a car without cash."

"So let's sell some gold and get on the road."

"We finally agree on something," Hank said. "Let's pack up."

SEVENTY-FIVE

Echo was driving to *Above the Fold* when a call from an unknown number rang through her car's blue tooth system.

"Hello?" she answered. "Who's calling, please?" She half expected to hear a telemarketer tell her that her BMW's warranty was about to expire. "Hello?"

A female's voice, calm and professional, came through the car's system. "Echo Rose?"

"That's me. How can I help you?"

The caller continued. "We met briefly the other day, Echo. In the General's limousine."

"Roulan Fang?"

"I'd rather not say my name. I have information for you."

"Okay, go ahead." Echo recognized her voice, but only barely. She thought she could be mistaken, but it sounded like General Zhang's attorney. "I'm listening."

"Before May Lau's death, she'd tried contacting our mutual friend. Apparently, she wanted to hire someone to retrieve stolen gold. He refused her call. Our association doesn't operate like that. It's in our mutual interest the police understand the Chinese had nothing to do with the death of May Lau."

"Did he say who was responsible?" Echo asked. But there was no answer. The caller was gone. She thought about the implications and called Skip.

Skip answered on the sixth ring just before Echo was about to end the call. "Hello, Echo. I can't talk long. What's up?"

"I just got another call," Echo said. "I'm near to the precinct. Can I talk to you?"

"Sure, if it's quick. We've got our hands full with the Lau cases."

"It's about that," Echo said.

"I'll let the front know to pass you through."

Echo got lucky and found a parking spot near the front entrance to the police center. There was always traffic in the parking lot because the county court building was across the street, and they shared the lot. She made her way into the building and waited a short time in line to speak to the Desk Sergeant.

He passed her through after viewing her I.D. "Detective Malloy is expecting you. He's on—"

"I know it," she said. "Thank you."

Echo found Skip and Bud arguing about a stakeout. They stopped talking the moment they saw her. "You're staking out gold buyers?"

"We can't really say," Skip said. "It's an—"

"Open investigation, I know," Echo said. "However, the call I just got mentioned gold, so perhaps we should talk." Her intentions were always to put public welfare first, but that didn't mean that she'd forego some leverage when she could gain information for a story.

"What call?"

"What stakeout?"

"This is the kind of thing that gives you guys a bad name," Bud said.

"I have a job and an obligation to the public," Echo said. "I have professional integrity."

"I know you do," Skip said, jumping in to stop an argument. "Bud, I trust her. We can give her the basics because they aren't a secret. Not with Big Ted involved."

"Fair point," Bud conceded.

"What do you have, Echo?" Skip asked.

She relayed all the information from the call. It wasn't much, but it brought an additional detail into the case. May had tried to get someone in organized crime to retrieve the gold.

"Did the caller say when this call happened?" Bud asked.

"No."

"That would make a big difference," Skip said. "If May called before we showed her the insurance documents, it would prove she was lying."

"I think she was lying all along," Bud said. "I don't think we should go much deeper with a reporter in the room. No offense, Echo."

"None taken," she said. She considered the fact that the number was still saved on her phone when Skip asked her about it. "I'm considering this a confidential source, Detective. If I give you the number, they'll just burn it."

"She's right, Skip," Bud said. "Maybe Echo can try to pry a little more information. The date of May's request, for example."

Echo thought of all the possibilities. The caller was likely Roulan Fang, and it made little sense for the General to communicate with her if he was responsible for the killings. Why put himself on anyone's radar more than he already was? Why bring the press into the story? "I think, guys, that the most logical thing here is that General Zhang didn't order the killings of the Lau's. He has nothing to gain by getting me more involved in the story. Surely my reputation proceeds me. He must know that getting me involved means a deeper look into the story."

"You need to be careful here, Echo," Skip said. "These guys don't mess around."

"I know," she said. "But they also don't normally kill cops, judges, and reporters. It's not good for business."

"True," Bud said. "But they don't normally call reporters either."

"Which is why I think that he's telling the truth."

Bud turned to Skip. "So, what? These two guys kill the Lau's for gold and then go back to kill May because they've heard she's called the Chinese to come after them? That's a lot of conjecture."

"What two guys?" Echo asked.

"Really, Bud," Skip said, "stop talking about the case in front of Echo. You're going to get us both in trouble with the higher-ups." He pointed toward the ceiling. "Echo, we've got to go."

"On your stakeouts?" she asked.

"You didn't hear that from us," Bud said.

"Let us know if you hear anything else from the Chinese mafia," Skip said.

"Did someone say Chinese mafia?" Detective Steve Wong said as he entered the room.

"Detective Wong, this is Echo Rose, investigative journalist," Skip said. "She's a friend. But she's also leaving. Bye, Echo."

"Wait a minute. You're in the Asian Task Force, aren't you?"

"I am," he said. "Did Skip just say you're speaking to Chinese criminal organizations?"

"Maybe," she admitted. "I have something to ask you about the task force," Echo said. "Maybe we can trade some info?" She looked at Skip and Bud. "Guys, I'll be seeing you around."

She took Detective Steve Wong by the arm and led him into the hallway. "Can we speak off the record?"

SEVENTY-SIX

Echo waited until Steve had followed her out of Skip and Bud's earshot.

"So, I heard you'd spoken with an associate of mine, Courtney Bailey," she said. "Regarding sex trafficking in Little Shanghai. Can you comment on that?"

"I've never heard of Courtney Bailey," he said. "And while there might be sex trafficking, my focus is on breaking the overall structure of organized crime. Bringing about RICO charges, that's racketeering—"

"Racketeer Influenced and Corrupt Organization Act crimes," Echo said. "I know what it means, Detective. But, hold on, are you sure you never met with or spoke to Courtney Bailey? Editor of *Soft Vanda* magazine?"

Steve nodded his head. "I'm pretty good with names."

"What about *Soft Vanda*? Nothing? No other reporters?"

"Nope."

Echo was confused for a moment. *Why did Courtney lie to me?*

"Care to share with me who you've spoken with?" Steve asked.

"General Zhang and his attorney."

Hearing the name shocked the detective. He regained his composure and said, "You met with them?"

"It wasn't exactly a meeting." Echo explained the strange experience she'd had inside Zhang's limo and how her phone had ceased to work.

"Okay, let me get this straight," he said. "You were asked to drop your investigation into criminality in Little Shanghai in exchange for information about who killed the Lau's?"

"Yes," she said. "Of course, it's not ethical for me to pay for information. It creates biases and goes against journalistic principles. I explained this to him."

"They don't care about rules."

"I know." Echo explained that she wasn't planning to stop her story about the criminal gangs but that she had a priority. Sex trafficking and the possible connection to Amanda's Secret.

"Amanda's Secret?" Steve asked. "Isn't that the cheater's app?"

"Exactly." Echo told him how she'd received information from a confidential source that Amanda's Secret might be covering up the use of the app by prostitution rings and that there might be a connection to sex trafficking. She explained how the company used bots to create the illusion of more women than actually existed—and how that created a higher demand for genuine women. That demand created an opportunity for criminals to exploit.

"And you think there's a connection to Little Shanghai and the General?"

"I believe there might be," she said.

"But you haven't found any evidence yet, have you?"

Echo shook her head. That was the problem of trying to get inside criminal organizations run by rich and powerful men. Because they were so dangerous, people didn't talk. Without hard evidence, there was only conjecture and supposition. Those couldn't be used in a court of law, and they also couldn't be used to write a journalistically responsible article.

"Look," he said. "These guys are super dangerous. I have to caution you, it could be dangerous for your health to pursue this thing."

"I know the risks."

"I'm sure you do. If you get me any evidence on trafficking regarding organized crime in Little Shanghai, I'll follow up on it personally. You have my word on that. Prostitution, without the trafficking, I can't do anything there directly—that's vice. I'd pass that along if needed. As to the bots, that's probably a civil matter. Nothing I can say about that."

"I'm not interested in the bots either," Echo said. "And I don't want to open the can of worms that comes with sex worker rights. That's not my focus on the story I'm working on under contract. If I uncover anything to do with trafficking, I'll contact you. Maybe we can work together if possible?"

"As long as you don't step on my toes or burn me," he said. "I'm taking it on faith here that you respect Skip and Bud and wouldn't double-cross me."

"On my honor, Detective Wong."

He held out his hand. "Deal."

Echo left the precinct and headed to Courtney Bailey's home. There was something fishy about her agreement, and she was going to get to the bottom of it before spending another minute risking her neck.

SEVENTY-SEVEN

Bud handed a form to the Sergeant.

"I think it's all covered," he said. "Most of these places have reasonable business hours—"

"I can read, Detective Smith." It appeared to Bud that he was double-checking the list against a calendar. Eventually, he looked up from his desk and said, "Approved for three days. No more without meeting with me first. Understood?"

"Yes, Sergeant," Bud said. He knew the mayor and the city council were giving the department a lot of heat about their budget. The Sergeant had to answer to politicians, and that made his job more difficult. He said, "Thank you, sir," as he walked away. He didn't expect a "You're welcome", but he thought it would be nice if his boss was a little less gruff.

Bud took the signed sheet back to the war room.

"You get it?" Skip asked.

"Yeah," Bud replied. He handed him the sheet. "Three days' approval for the top dealers on the list. It's not foolproof, of course."

"No, it never is. I think if they're going to sell the gold in Fairview, it'll be in the next couple of days at most. Maybe today."

"Which means we'd better make some calls," Bud said.

They'd received approval to put stakeout teams on the several dealers that seemed most likely to be capable of buying a large amount of gold. This included staking out Ted's EZ-Pawn, but Skip and Bud agreed it was unlikely the two criminals they had on security footage would go back. Too much risk. Also, they'd had an officer call around to check prices, and there were two dealers with excellent reputations who paid more than Ted.

The chain-of-command rules required them to notify the department heads and the schedulers about the approved surveillance teams. And, of course, the officers involved. It took them over an hour to get everyone up to speed on the plan. Teams would scramble to cover each location for the rest of the day while Skip and Bud continued with the main investigation. Bud decided they needed to re-interview Heather Campbell and Gary Turner. They'd be ready to move on a location if the pair showed up later in the day. On the assignment sheet, they had a shift starting the next morning.

"So you think we can shake Heather or Gary?" Skip asked.

"One or both," Bud replied. "I'm sure of it. Teens talk. Criminals talk. You know how it is with people, they can't keep secrets."

"That's true. But this would be a big secret."

"It's obvious that May knew about the gold. She lied. That's a given. The question is, did she know something about the killers who stole it before they took it, or not until after?"

"That's a big question." Skip paced for a minute and looked at the corkboard. They'd covered it with pictures and clues, but so far, the puzzle was still unsolved. "If the information is accurate about May contacting a gang to go after the gold, that would mean she held back the identity of the thieves. Why would she do that?"

"Insurance fraud?" Bud suggested.

"It doesn't feel like that to me. It's possible, but I don't buy it. I think she was into something deeper."

"What if she hired the thieves to steal the gold and split it with her?"

"And the murders?"

"Unhappy accidents?"

"That would have made her an accessory. She'd be on the hook for a lot of years inside a prison."

"The alternative is that she planned to have them killed. But that's crazy," Bud said. "I can see an angry teen who feels cheated going after her parent's riches. I'll buy that. But having them killed seems…"

"Insane?"

"Yeah." Bud got up from the desk and moved to the board. He fiddled around with push pens and moved a few pictures. "The time between the first murders and May's death—you think these two guys were just hiding out trying to decide what to do? This whole thing seems better planned than that."

"Maybe the gold was unexpected."

"That would mean they were there to kill the parents."

"The fifty grand," they both said in unison.

Bud stepped back. "Could it really be she hired them to kill her folks, and the gold wasn't part of the deal?"

"Sure," Skip said. "If that's the case, then her going to organized crime figures she thinks she knows makes sense. In her mind, she could hire them to retrieve the gold."

"Maybe she was book smart, but she was naïve about how the street works."

"And that's probably what got her killed."

"So," Bud said, "that's why I think we should put some pressure on Heather and Gary. May must have said something to one of them. Could be they don't realize the importance of something they overheard or saw. Agreed?"

"Let's roll with that," Skip said. He made a fist and tapped the doorjamb as he walked out of the war room. "Knock on wood that one of the stakeout teams gets lucky."

"That's an aluminum frame," Bud pointed out.

"Don't be pedantic."

"That's a good, bad cop, partner."

"I'll stick to being nice," Skip said. "But we're running out of time. If the best friend or ex-boyfriend sounds even the littlest bit evasive, Bud, you hit 'em hard. Got it?"

"*Grrrr!* I'm already angry…"

SEVENTY-EIGHT

Echo waited at the door for ten minutes.

"I'm sorry," Courtney said when she opened the door. "I wasn't expecting you this quickly. I had to—"

"Never mind excuses," Echo said. "May I come in?"

The editor of *Soft Vanda* had good instincts, Echo saw. She knew something was wrong. It didn't matter. She would have to explain things to Echo's satisfaction, or it wouldn't matter if she talked or not. Echo would walk away.

"Yes, of course," Courtney answered. "My manners. Sorry. I've been distracted, and Chuck's still in Europe, and there's—oh, never mind. I won't bore you with more of my problems. Come in."

She led Echo down a different hallway than they'd used the last time. It led to an office on the ground floor on the opposite side of the house. The art in the office was modern, nothing like her husband's medieval pieces. Courtney noticed Echo gazing at a particular artwork.

"That's Dutch artist Hans van Dijk. He's a well-known abstract painter from the sixties. Died from a heroin overdose. Sad. But it made his art more collectible. Not that it matters, really. I bought that piece because it speaks to me, not as an investment."

"It's beautiful," Echo said. "And sad."

"Yes." Courtney walked behind her desk and sat. "Please, take a seat, Echo. What's on your mind?"

"I need to know why you lied to me," Echo said. "I met Detective Steve Wong this morning."

"That was bound to happen," Courtney said. She was still as a statue for a few beats and then smiled. "It's part of the job, you know? I didn't want to lead you in any particular direction. It was better for the story for you to follow your own gut instincts."

"Telling me you'd talked to him about sex trafficking wasn't leading me?"

"It was more like bait to get you excited about it," she said. "I regret that now, of course. It wasn't malicious, Echo. Just a little white lie."

"I don't like it when someone lies to me."

"That's understandable. But I think we can work past this thing. Just realize I was trying to convince you that there was a big story. And there is. That wasn't untrue. The story is huge. Tell me about what you've uncovered."

"Off the record?"

"Off the record."

"I have data. Lots of data. It's going to take a long time to—"

"Wait!" Courtney stood up. Her face turned red. "You have names?"

"Yes," Echo said. "Of course."

"Give them to me," Courtney demanded.

"No."

"No?"

"I owe you a story. Work product from the story is mine. Investigations I do produce evidence that I hold on to in case I need to defend myself. I'll give you the data and evidence necessary to verify facts in my article, of course. I'm not giving you, or anyone, a data dump. There are tons of privacy issues here. You know that."

"I demand to see the data." She sat and glared at Echo. "You can't keep this from me. You cannot do that. I trusted you. I have—"

"There is nothing unethical about me not handing over data recovered from a confidential source. There's a lot there. The bulk of it has nothing to do with my story. Names, customers, chats, messages—"

"You're not going to use this against me?"

Echo paused before answering. What had she meant?

"If you're looking for more money," Courtney said, "I can tell you to forget it right now. It's not going to happen. I won't be blackmailed."

"What?"

"Don't play naïve with me, Echo." Courtney stood again. "If you got the data and read it, which we both know you did, then you're here to pressure me about something. I'm not playing that game."

Echo hadn't read all the data. There was too much of it. She hadn't had the time to go through all the customer lists yet, but it was obvious that Courtney was hiding something. She played along. "Okay, I won't play with you. Tell me what you want me to do?"

"I want you to destroy that list," Courtney said. "You'll ruin me if that gets out."

"Even if I destroy everything I have," Echo explained, "hackers don't always play by the rules. You've been around long enough. You know what happens with this stuff. It gets out. It always does."

Courtney broke down crying. She sobbed without ceasing for six minutes. Echo timed it. When the crying stopped, Courtney took a handful of tissues and wiped her eyes and nose. "I'm screwed."

"This whole thing was personal? All along?" Echo asked.

"I'm sorry, Echo. Really, I'm truly sorry. I knew you could dig things up. I made some calls and came up with a plan to hire you for this job. That part was genuine. You're a brilliant journalist."

"And what part wasn't real? The part about you being in the Amanda's Secret data?"

Echo watched as she broke down in tears again. It was sad and ironic that Echo didn't know that Courtney Bailey was in the data breach. She wasn't interested in digging up dirt on cheaters. The reason she was interested in the story was to expose illegal activities, not immoral actions committed by self-loathing hypocrites.

Courtney regained her composure. "I'm in a terrible marriage, Echo. I won't bore you with the details, but I'm in a bad spot. Chuck was devious when he was dating me—he had a long story about being tricked by a woman. How he'd lost a lot of money in a divorce. And the alimony and child support and on and on. It was a moving story, I'll admit. I fell for it."

"He got you to sign a prenup that had a morality clause in it?" Echo asked.

"Yeah. Old-fashioned, I know," she answered. "It wasn't on my mind at the time, you know, the possibility of cheating. I never considered…"

"But it happened."

"Yes. It wasn't planned."

"Everyone says that, Courtney. It's so clichéd. It's almost embarrassing to hear you utter the words."

"I'm sorry," she said.

"So it sounds like this whole thing was just a play to find out if you were vulnerable—"

"No, Echo, that's not true. The job is real. I could use you. We—*Soft Vanda*—we could use you. The way you tackle stories is something that would give us an edge over the competition. I want to negotiate a contract. I think we'd find this a win-win."

"And the data?"

"I'm not going to press the issue. It's like you said. The hackers will do what they'd do. I can't help that. I didn't mean to cheat. I'm not a cheater. Chuck has been depressed for years. The art business is down. He's got money, mind you. Real estate. Stocks and other investments. He's rich, actually. I feel like a kept woman. I have this lifestyle, but even though I'm his wife, not a penny of this stuff is mine. There's not a bank account with a million dollars in it sitting there if he divorces me."

"I'm sorry, Courtney," Echo said. "I don't work for people I can't trust."

"But we have a—"

"We never had a permanent contract, just something for this single story."

"But—"

"There're no buts here, Courtney," Echo said. "I'll deliver you a story with a subject that meets my obligation per the freelancing deal, and then I'm done with you."

"But, Echo—"

"I've got nothing else to say," Echo said. She stood and moved towards the door. "I'll let myself out."

SEVENTY-NINE

Skip drove to Heather Campbell's house after calling her mother to approve the visit.

"You think she'll have something?" Bud asked.

"I'm not going to bet on it," Skip replied. "But I'm positive there's more known about what happened than people who were close to May are telling us."

"Why can't people be honest?"

"I think they believe telling the truth is just about not lying. But that's only a fraction of the truth. The whole truth is everything material they know. Withholding things is lying."

"My question was rhetorical, Skip."

"I'm practicing," he said. "For Heather."

"Oh. Good. I hope it works."

Not more than fifteen minutes later, Skip sat with Heather in the living room. Mrs. Campbell had agreed to allow them to speak semi-privately. They were bending the rules a little, but Skip and Bud had decided that Heather might have something embarrassing to admit. She'd be more comfortable talking if her mother wasn't hovering.

"We can sit just over here," Bud said to Mrs. Campbell. He led her to the other side of the room, close enough to hear Skip and Heather speaking, but too far to make out the exact words.

Skip smiled at Heather. He wanted her to feel safe. “Heather, I want to talk to you kind of off-the-record. I promise not to tell your mom or dad anything we talk about, as long as I know you’re not in danger, okay?”

“Okay,” she said. Heather’s face betrayed nervousness and anxiety, but those were often present in the innocent and the guilty. In fact, sometimes the guilty were more relaxed. “I’ll try to help you. Honest. I just don’t think there’s anything I haven’t already said.”

“Heather,” he said in a fatherly tone, “the truth isn’t just about telling facts. The truth isn’t just answering yes or no questions. The whole truth, the entirety of the truth, is telling everything. Everything that might matter. Anything that is potentially material to a case is important to me. Do you understand?”

“I think so,” she said. “I mean, I’m not totally sure I understand. I know the difference between truth and lies, if that’s what you mean.”

“Not exactly,” Skip said. “Of course, lying to the police is not good. In some cases, it could be a crime to do that. But I’m sure you’re an honest person, Heather. I’m not saying I think you’ve lied about something. I think, instead, that you might have forgotten to say something that you maybe thought wasn’t important. But right now, everything about this case can be important.”

Heather’s body tensed. “I remember a phone call.”

“Go ahead,” Skip said.

Before she started talking, her mother walked to the sofa and sat. “You need to tell them whatever you can, honey.”

"I know, mom," she said. "I can't believe she's dead." Heather cried, and her mother held her.

When she stopped, Bud, who'd silently moved to the sofa and sat, said, "It's not okay to allow your emotions to be the reason you aren't sharing things with Detective Malloy. He's sweet and kind. I'm not as patient, Heather. What did you hear? I know there's something you're not telling us."

Skip gave Bud the tinniest of nods. It was a signal to back off and let him take back control. He turned to Heather and said, "What my partner is trying to say, Heather, is that we know May was caught up in some things that were dangerous. She made some bad choices. You were her best friend, so certainly, you heard or saw something. Something, anything that helps bring this case to a close is important for us to hear."

Silence descended for a few moments. "Right now, Heather," Bud said to break the awkwardness of the moment. "What do you know?"

Skip nodded his head. He watched Heather's eyes drift to his and then lower. "Go on," he whispered.

"I have to go to the bathroom," she said.

"It can wait a couple more minutes, Heather," Bud said. "It's important to—"

Mrs. Campbell looked at Skip. "She's not under—"

"No, no, of course not," he said. "It's okay, Detective Smith. She can use the bathroom."

Heather returned minutes later. She set a gold coin on the coffee table. "That's called a panda," she said. "May gave it to me. I'm sorry I didn't say anything before, but I didn't think it was—I mean—it was a gift. I didn't think it was important to talk about it."

"Tell us when and where she gave that to you," Skip said.

"I—we—were in the game room. Downstairs. I think we were watching a movie about a treasure hunter or something, and May said, 'I have a bunch of gold'."

"Okay," Skip said when she didn't start talking again. "Go on."

"This was a long time ago. Well, not that long, but not recently. I guess. We went to the office, and she opened the safe and handed this to me. She said, 'You're my best friend, so I want you to have it,' and I said, 'Won't your parents get mad?' and she said, 'No.'"

"So it was a gift in your mind?" Skip asked. "She was giving you something that was hers to give?"

"Exactly," Heather answered. "I had no reason to think she was stealing it. We were in her house, and if she had the combination to the safe, I assumed it was okay."

"But now you realize something is wrong," Bud said. "Right?"

"Yeah. I know now she gave me something she didn't have the right to give me. Am I in trouble? I didn't know then. It seemed like a sweet gesture."

"Don't worry about being in trouble over this," Skip said, pointing at the coin. "But if you're withholding anything else about this case, that will get you in trouble. Think hard, Heather. There had to be something fishy you overheard. Something you saw. A person or persons who she met with that gave you a funny feeling. Anything that stands out, we want to hear about it."

"That night. Before she went to sleep," Heather said before hesitating. "I saw—on accident—a text message."

"The night of her parent's murders?"

"Yes. She was super agitated and upset. I assumed at first it was just because of how terrible everything was that night. My mom had given her a sleeping pill or something, and I was trying to give her space. But then she was messaging someone. It wasn't that surprising. I mean, she'd been on the phone a lot with family friends who wanted to know what happened and stuff. But this one was different."

"What did it say?" Bud asked.

"'Who gave you permission to open the safe'?"

"And anything else?"

Heather started crying. Between sobs, she said, "She wrote they were dead men if they didn't return the gold."

EIGHTY

Skip stood outside on the street and stared.

"You going to miss her?" Vivian asked.

"No. Yes. I suppose there're a lot of memories about to be bulldozed tomorrow."

"Memories aren't in things, Skip," she said, hugging him. "Memories live inside you."

The last of their belongings were in a box that Glenn Simmons carried. "Mr. Malloy," he asked, "where should I put this?"

Vivian reached over and took the box. "I'll get it, Glenn. Thank you." Skip was happy to see his daughter dating someone responsible and trustworthy. Glenn was also studying neuroscience at Amery University, and he'd been a good influence on Layla. They'd both come to help on the last day of moving.

"Where's Uncle Bud?" Lew Jr. asked. "He was supposed to bring the pizza."

"He's working on an important case," Skip replied. "I'll order pizza, don't worry."

"But when *he* does it," Lew Jr. continued, "we always get those cinnamon twisty things with sugar on them. You never order those."

"I will this time. If you behave until we get to the hotel."

"You're saying he can misbehave after you go back to work?" Vivian asked. "Thanks."

"I don't mean it like that," Skip said. "I mean…"

"Yeah, stumped."

"Layla, can you and Glenn stay for pizza?" Skip asked so he could change the subject.

"Yes, Dad," she said. "We were planning on it. As long as you order the cinnamon twisty things like Bud does."

Skip shook his head and got out his cell. "I'm ordering now. If anyone has anything else to suggest, you have about thirty seconds."

The pizza ordered, and the cars loaded with the last of their things, the Malloy family drove away. Demolition of the house would start first thing in the morning. The builder explained they'd carefully remove some items for recycling, but most of it would end up being crushed and then hauled away, leaving a space in the neighborhood until they completed the new house.

Skip and Vivian had taken pictures and talked about the ups and downs they'd experienced living there. "At the end of it all, a house isn't a home, Skip. A home is where family lives. You're my home."

"You're mine," he'd said. Driving away, he felt a little tug on his heart. The new house would become their home, he was sure of it. For now, however, they'd stay a few days in a hotel and then move into the house Robert had helped them rent from the bank.

He looked at Vivian. "You think it's going to be a year before we get back here?"

"I'm hoping for ten months," she replied.

"Is that based upon anything tangible?"

"Don't get all *detectivey* on me now, honey," she said. "It's an estimate."

"Okay. I guess ten months or a year, it's all about the same."

"We're not moving to Alaska, Skip. You're about the same distance to work. The kids will have to get up in the morning at the same time. Our routine won't change that much."

"But mom," Lew Jr. said from the backseat, "what about my—"

"None of that," Skip said. "If you nag your mom, I'm giving all your dessert to your sisters."

"Yes!" Lucy shouted. "He can't go five minutes without complaining."

"I can!"

"Can't!"

"That's it," Vivian said to Skip. "Call the Gypsies. I'll take half price."

"Okay, you—" Skip's cell interrupted him, and he saw it was Bud. "I got to take this."

Bud spoke without waiting for a greeting. "I got a hold of the ex-boyfriend. He'd had his phone off for a test. Anyway, he's agreed to meet, but it's got to be tonight because he's going out-of-town tomorrow."

"Alrighty, then. I'll see you in an hour. That fast enough?"

Yup.

Skip ended the call and looked over at Vivian. "I gotta run soon."

"I heard, Skip. Go get 'em."

"By your command, my Queen."

EIGHTY-ONE

Echo was frustrated with the turn of events caused by Courtney's deception.

She decided she'd complete the article in good faith. That didn't mean, however, that she'd use the full depth of her knowledge and skills on the piece. The series she was creating for *Above the Fold* was still in play. Frank had given her his support after she explained the situation she'd found herself in.

Echo used a contact to get on the phone with a lawyer who worked at the State Justice Department. Her inquiry about the bots used by Amanda's Secret was another brick wall. "If men want to pay money to talk to fake women," the lawyer had said, "that's their business."

Ultimately, she needed a connection in Little Shanghai that could talk to her about sex trafficking and prostitution. If there was a tie-in with Amanda's Secret, that would give her a basis for the article she owed *Soft Vanda*. If not, she'd need another angle. However, if any type of organized crime in Little Shanghai came across her radar, it would be fuel for her *Above the Fold* series.

She finished making phone calls and turned to her dark web connections.

ER43seer: *Hey, Bog, how are you?*

Bogdan87-DoR: *Good*

Have you considered my request?

Da.

And?

I'll get you a quote for my time and a scope of work.

Sounds very American.

I'm a good learner.

What time frame?

What you ask. Is dangerous. Maybe one week. Maybe two.

I understand. I'll wait to hear from you.

Echo's local hacker friend had recommended Bogdan. Whether he was a man or a woman, young or old, or really in Europe or Russia, Echo had no way to know. There wasn't really a need, she thought, other than the differences in time zones. But, with a project that would not happen immediately, instant answers weren't really necessary. She turned off her programs and thought about her next move.

That's when she realized she hadn't checked the Amanda's Secret apps on her burner phones. She pulled both phones out of a drawer and powered them on. The female profile had a ton of hits. Many men had sent likes, messages, and had tried to connect to her on the chat feature. She set the phone down. She might use some of that information in a story, but that wasn't her primary interest.

The male profile had a few hits as well. One stood out: SallyLin. Echo thumbed through the profile pictures that appeared to be professionally taken. Roulan Fang, if that was even the lawyer's real name, was stunning. She might have had a career as a model, had she chosen that instead of law school.

Thinking about universities and the bar, Echo opened up a web browser to search for Roulan Fang. If she was legit, Echo would find information about her online.

And sure enough, she was there. One of six partners in a Fairview law firm located just outside of the area known as Little Shanghai. Their website listed, in English, tax law, immigration, and financial concerns as their specialties. However, much of the website was in Chinese.

Echo used an online translator and discovered that the Chinese descriptions mostly matched the English ones. They had a partnership with a law firm in China that could help clients to deal with American laws as they related to immigration and cross-border financial issues.

Nothing looked or seemed fishy or strange to Echo, but obviously, if they were doing illegal activities under the board, they'd hardly advertise that openly.

The phone beeped.

Sally Lin had sent a message via the app's chat feature. She expressed interest in "David Green," the fake name Echo had used. She wanted to chat.

Echo wrote: *Hi! You're so pretty.* Immediately, she groaned. She thought, *How could I be so lame?* But Sally responded, so Echo forgot about it.

Sally: *I think you're handsome. You want to have some fun tonight?*

The question threw Echo off. Why was the other user being so aggressive? Why act so quickly? She wasn't sure what to write, but while she considered, Sally wrote again.

Sally: *I only meet at hotels the first time. But, if we like each other...*

The message was followed by a heart emoji.

Echo replied: *I'm a little confused. We haven't met yet. I'm not sure about this.*

Sally: *Oh! LOL. You're a first timer? Really?*

I guess so. I'm not sure how it works.

We have to switch to an encrypted messaging network. Then we can talk more. If we mention money here, we'll get banned. Are you interested?

Echo considered for a second and then typed in: *Sure!*

Sally, or whoever was on the other end of the conversation, gave Echo a number and an app's name. Echo recognized the messaging app: it was commonly used by millions of people around the world. Supposedly, totally secure. She entered Sally into her contacts and sent a quick *Hello*.

Once they connected, Sally got right to the point. She messaged a list of services and the prices. Echo pretended to think about it for a minute, then agreed to meet later that night.

They arranged a time.

Sally wrote: *Don't forget, it's cash only.*

Echo: *Okay, I understand.*

Sally: *And I appreciate tips! See you, honey! I promise to make you very happy!*

Echo sent a smiley face emoji. Then she called Conner to explain he had a "date" that evening in Little Shanghai. "I'm gonna need your help tonight," she said.

EIGHTY-TWO

Gary Turner sat in the corner of a worn-out sofa.

He glanced left to right and played with his hands. His roommates had agreed to leave the apartment for an hour. Skip had explained that while they could interview Gary at the station, they didn't intend to make it anything other than informal.

Skip noticed the same pizza boxes from the last trip. Nobody had taken them to the apartment building's dumpster, but at least the boxes had been stuffed into a garbage bag. *Progress*.

He hoped the interview would be the same. More progress figuring out what the truth was and wasn't. Skip sat directly across from Gary in a chair they'd grabbed from the kitchen. Bud sat at the opposite end of the sofa. The boxing-in of the interviewee was intentional. They knew he'd held back last time, and they wanted to put him under more pressure.

"So, as we said before," Skip explained, "you're not under arrest, and you're free to go—well, in this case, we're in your home—so you're free to ask for us to leave. We need to clear up a few things about our last interview. And we're hoping that you'd be cooperative and give us whatever things you know could be important material facts about our investigation into the murders of May and also her parents."

Gary's face turned a slight shade of pink. He fidgeted and then coughed.

"Skip's being nice, Gary," Bud said. "You were evasive last time. This time, if you aren't cooperative, we'll have to take you to the station for a more formal discussion."

"What my partner is trying to say," Skip added, "is that this is the easy way. The hard way is somewhere none of us want to go. Okay?"

"Yes," he answered firmly. "I want to cooperate. I was really nervous last time because I knew May had said some things that she didn't mean. She was just being emotional. May's confu—I mean, May was confused." He appeared embarrassed about his slip.

Gary Turner had solid alibis for both nights. May's murder and that of her parents. Skip never felt there was a reason to think he was involved—but he admitted to himself he'd also thought the same about May. He went back to cover some old ground.

"You told us last time that May had mentioned a life without her parents," Skip said.

"Yeah. I mean, she was just talking. I still can't believe she'd have anything to do with murder. That's just not possible. Maybe she had a feeling of relief after she realized she'd be free, but that doesn't mean she was happy about it."

"You had contact with her?"

"After the murders? No. Well, I'm still on her social media. I can see her posts and stuff, but no, we haven't seen each other for months."

"And how about messages or calls?"

"No calls. A couple of brief messages on social media, like I gave my condolences. But nothing beyond that. I didn't feel it would lead to anything positive, and I have a lot of studying to do in order to keep my grades acceptable."

"Tell us more about her posts or comments. Was there anything upsetting, or were there any statements she made that sounded strange?"

Gary shook his head at first. But, after a minute of silence, he began talking. Bud and Skip had a quick hand signal they used whenever they wanted each other to remain silent. The quiet would get uncomfortable, and invariably, a witness or suspect would begin talking. Sometimes, they'd ramble and give away more information than originally asked for. Gary began nervously but soon got into a stride. "May sounded unstable sometimes. Her posts would ramble and include music lyrics I often found disturbing. Things of a suicidal or dark nature. She would write cynical posts and things about leaving this world. The most troubling thing she'd posted was a news picture about a family that all died in a private plane crash. She fantasized, I think, about that happening to her family."

Gary continued with little prompting from Skip. He told them she took down the most disturbing posts, usually by the next day at most, but sometimes within minutes. "It was like she was calling for help, but then changed her mind."

Skip nodded his understanding but didn't speak.

"And then there was the gold. I forgot this last time. Remember, I told you about helping her sell a coin, but I forgot that she'd offered me one. It was after that—she said it was to thank me—I turned it down, of course."

"Why?" Bud asked.

"I'm from a wealthy family, Detective. I know it doesn't look like it from this apartment, but it's only because my trust money isn't released until I meet some conditions. Like, I have to graduate." He laughed, but awkwardly. "If I have a degree and hit twenty-five," he explained, "I get the money then. As long as I don't have a felony and I'm still single."

"That's in the trust?" Skip asked.

"My grandparents," Gary replied. "Super strict and religious. It's okay, I'm not planning to get married soon. And I'm definitely not going to prison." He laughed again.

"Let's hope not," Skip said. "Tell me, did May's murder completely shock you?" Gary hesitated for a fraction of a second, and Skip knew the answer. He stared into his eyes until he dropped them to the floor. "Okay, Gary, explain why you weren't shocked?"

"There were a few times May mentioned something about the Chinese gangs in Little Shanghai. Never any details. But I knew. I knew she was dating some guys she shouldn't have been dating. Connected guys. Gang members. It was a terrible decision on her part, and I knew it would lead to nothing good."

"You might have shared this with us last time," Bud said coldly.

"I didn't want to bring up stuff I couldn't substantiate. I didn't have any facts, just some things she said a long time ago. She'd posted a picture of a tough-looking Chinese guy a month back, but she took it down right away. It's not evidence of much, but I guess inside, I knew."

“So you never heard a name? Never?” Skip asked.

Gary shook his head. Skip knew he could be lying, but it was unlikely that simply knowing a name at this point would help. The task force knew the gang members. They’d need more to go on than a vague recollection of hearing May talk about dating someone. It was too easily denied.

And, of course, even if it was true, who’d testify about it?

Nobody.

Skip took Gary back through all the questions again. Bud got to play bad cop a little, but in the end, they were both convinced that Gary had nothing to break the case open. They got up to leave, and Gary stood as well.

Skip put his hand out and said, “Thank you for your cooperation, son. You let us know if anything else comes to mind. Bud, you ready?”

“One last question,” Bud said. “You ever hear anything about fifty grand in cash?”

Gary’s hand went to his mouth. “I would have sworn that was fake money.”

“Explain,” Bud said. He blocked Gary from moving further into the room. “What money do you think was fake?”

“She posted online,” Gary said. “I remember now. It was only up for an hour. It was a briefcase of cash. The caption said something about how fifty thousand dollars really looks or something like that. I don’t remember, really. It was a night I was studying really hard for a final.”

"Did she say what the money was for?" Skip asked.

"I don't remember. But it was to pay someone off for something. Like a crime is how she made it sound, but I took it as a joke. I'm sure she didn't really have that much money in cash. Why? Where would she get it? It had to be a joke, right?"

Skip didn't answer. He thought for a second and then asked Gary to look through his records and see if he could match the date of the exam he was studying for and the night of the post. It took him only five minutes of searching. He'd written the date in his school planner.

"Okay, Gary," Skip finally said, "thank you again for cooperation. We'll get in touch if we think of anything else, but I think we have all we need. You please call us if you think of anything else, okay?"

"Yes," he said. He walked to the door and opened it. "I promise."

On the drive back to the precinct, Skip asked Bud his opinion.

"Honestly, I don't think he's involved in anything illegal. Bad judgment, yes. But criminal? No."

"Rich white kid," Skip said.

"It's not that, partner. I just don't see him connected. I suppose we should check with the family and ask about the trust. Make sure. But I don't think he's good for any scheming or killing."

"So tomorrow, we pick one dealer and sit an old school stakeout in the morning."

"I'll bring coffee," Bud said. "You bring some doughnuts?"

"Yeah, sure."

"Cinnamon raisin?"

"You mean you want a cinnamon roll?"

"Yes," Bud said. "You know the ones I like. They're good luck."

"Cinnamon rolls are not doughnuts. They're Cinnamon rolls. Or maybe sticky buns or something."

"They sell them at the doughnut shop?"

"Yeah."

"Okay, then."

Skip shook his head. "No. Of course not. They also sell ham and cheese croissants there. And jelly rolls. Those aren't doughnuts."

"Don't get pedantic on me," Bud said. "And bring me two. We might get stuck there through lunchtime."

EIGHTY-THREE

Echo sat in the dark.

The hotel room wasn't a suite, but it was larger than a regular single room. It had a spectacular view of the city. She wasn't afraid, but she was anxious, thinking about all the things that could go wrong. Connor was in the hotel bar playing his role as David, a lonely husband, looking for adventure. Echo had given Sally a basic description of what "David" would be wearing. They agreed to meet at the bar and have a drink first.

Echo knew from prior stories that women in this line of work were cautious. She'd likely order sparkling water and watch to make sure the bartender opened it in her view. The drink wouldn't be left alone, and perhaps she'd only pretend to sip it.

She'd be mindful of the time, balancing that and her expectation of her new client's worth. If he seemed like a potential whale customer, someone who would call her often, she'd likely spend more time this evening and not rush. There would be lots of false compliments and flattery.

Time slowed to a glacier pace.

"Oh, you're so funny," a woman's voice said through the partially opened door. "And handsome."

"Thank you," Conner said. He allowed her to enter the room, and then he latched the door.

"It's so dark," she said.

"One second. I'll find a light switch."

Conner, still in his role as a John named David, turned on the light. “I need to tell you right now that I have a friend in the room.”

“Oh,” the woman said. It took her eyes a moment to adjust to the lights, but then she saw Echo. “You’re cute, but it’s still going to cost extra.”

“It’s not what you think,” Echo said. “I’m a journalist, and I’m doing a story.”

The woman turned to Conner. “You’re not getting a refund,” she said. “And if we’re not going to do anything, I’m leaving.”

“Hold tight,” he said. “I’ve paid you for an hour. Just because we’re not going to get in bed doesn’t mean I don’t want the hour.”

“All right,” she said, taking a seat in an upholstered chair by the window. “But I’m not talking. You two don’t realize what trouble I can get into.” She stared at Echo and added, “Or you, for that matter. I don’t think you realize the trouble—”

“I’m aware of General Zhang,” Echo said.

The woman broke into soft tears. “You’re going to get me killed.”

“No, no, we’re not,” Echo said. “I’m going to ask my friend to leave, okay? He’s going to wait outside, and we can talk in private. It’s just us girls. You don’t have to say anything, of course, but what you do say will be one hundred percent confidential.”

“I’m not talking. He can stay.”

“That’s not the plan,” Conner said. “I’m leaving. Echo, if you need me, just call. I’ll be close.”

Echo nodded.

“Your name is Echo?” the woman asked.

"Yes. Well, it's not my real name," Echo replied. "It's a nickname. I used to go home to a big empty house. I'd call for my parents, and it would just echo. That's how I got the name. What's yours? I know it's not Sally."

"I can't say," the woman said. "Please, call me Sally. I'd be more comfortable not discussing anything about my real life."

"That's fine. I met a woman the other day, Sally. Her name was Roulan Fang. She's an attorney."

Sally nodded her head. "I can't talk about it."

"Roulan is very beautiful."

"I know."

"You are, too," Echo said. But what she didn't say, even though they both knew it to be true, was that Sally wasn't anything like Roulan. There was little comparison, except they were both young Chinese women.

"Thank you," Sally said, but she blushed and looked at the floor when she spoke. "I know I'm not anything like Roulan. She could be on the covers of magazines."

"How did her picture get on your Amanda's Secret account?"

"I don't know. I didn't know that was the picture they were using this week. They change it around."

"Who's they?"

"My employers," she answered. Then she blushed again. "I can't say more. This money, it's important. I send most of it back to China, for my family. Please, understand. I need this job."

"Why do they change the pictures?"

"It's how they know what picture will work the best. Plus, the men, they like fresh faces."

"But don't the men complain? I mean, they think they're getting one woman to show up, but someone else comes."

"They're very ready," Sally said. Her face turned a deeper shade of red. "I'm sorry. Some American terms are still confusing to me. The men, they want a woman. Most of the time, they don't even say anything. They just accept it. Sometimes, if they ask me, I'll explain my friend got sick and asked me to come in her place. That almost always works. Sometimes, rarely, a man gets angry, but then I just call my driver. That ends it."

"Your driver?"

"Yes, we always get sent out with protection. It's policy," she replied. "If anything goes wrong, I can call him. If I'm not back within five minutes, he'll come looking. It's part of the reason I work for—you know, I can't talk about this anymore. I want to leave."

"Can you just answer a few more questions?" Echo asked. "I just want to know about Amanda's Secret and the—"

"I don't know anything about that," Sally said. "I go wherever they tell me to go. It wasn't me you were chatting with on the Amanda's Secret app. That was either Bobby or Fern. They're both—I really cannot talk another minute."

"Okay," Echo said. "You've been super helpful, and I promise this entire conversation is off the record. I'm investigating, but I won't use anything confidential you've told me. Nobody will ever know you talked to me. Can I get you a soda?" She pointed to the mini-fridge. "Or some nuts or something?"

The two women made small talk to finish the hour. Echo got a few more tidbits of helpful information, but she didn't want to press her luck too much. When Sally got up to leave, Echo asked her if it would be possible to see her again if she was willing to pay for the time. That way, it would remain a secret.

"I can't talk anymore," Sally said, but then she added, "If David makes a date with me, I'll have to come. As long as he pays, the office will never know. You sort of have me at a disadvantage. I can't tell them David's a fake if he's paying because then they'll want to know what I've already said. Please don't expose me."

"I promise," Echo said. She led her to the door.

As Sally left, Conner walked in. He took a beer from the mini-fridge and sat. "I hope this was worth the money."

"I can expense it. And, yes, it was. I understand part of what's going on now. With Amanda's Secret. I still don't know about trafficking. Sally said she was sending money back to China for her family. She didn't seem like a kidnapping victim. But it's impossible to know for sure as long as she won't talk. I tried to bring it up, but she clammed up. I think she's working under her own volition. But, you know, it's really impossible to know at this point. She was definitely scared."

"Be careful, Echo," he said.

"You know I am."

"What's next?"

"Tomorrow, my parents get back from Belize."

"You're taking a day off?"

"No, of course not. But I'm going to have a drink with them, and I'm going to get a date on the calendar so you guys can meet. Maybe next week."

"I'll be there."

EIGHTY-FOUR

Kurt wasn't happy waiting for another day.

Hank promised they'd leave in the morning. "Right after we cash out most of this gold."

"You trust the guy?" Kurt asked. He picked at his nails. "I think we're—"

"He needed to pull together the cash. I trust him. He's too vulnerable to screw around. If he called the cops or anything…"

"You sure?" Kurt trusted his older brother to make these big decisions, but sometimes he felt they were one minor mistake from going to prison. "It's a lot of gold. Temptation like that can be too much for some people."

"I asked around, bro," Hank said. "We're giving the guy twenty percent. That's no paperwork, no state reporting. The guy isn't calling the cops."

"I guess greed is something I can put my trust in."

"Exactly. Now get back to work. We need to know if we're going to New Mexico or not. It'll be a huge waste if we head south and have to turn around."

"I'm on it," Kurt said. He'd been chatting with a twenty-something who was desperate. He had student and credit card debt, but to make matters worse, he'd opened up an online trading account. The stupid kid had blown through a hundred grand and didn't want to tell his father.

The father was also a gambler—he was getting ready to put all the family wealth into a risky crypto play. The kid wanted him out of the picture before that happened. *It's crazy what desperate people will tell you*, Kurt thought, as he looked to see if there were new messages. Getting someone to talk about the idea of killing a parent—or both of them—wasn't difficult. It was getting them to commit and fork over the cash that was the hard part.

Hank usually worked on the logistics. Cars, weapons, fake fingerprints, and disguises. Kurt's job was working online. He hunted for clients, formed relationships, and then went for the sale after he'd gained some trust. Every potential client required Kurt to build a new online personality. There could be no connections for anyone to find, so each profile stood on its own. This meant dozens of burner phones and a spreadsheet to track them all.

"Maybe it was a mistake taking May as a client," Kurt mused as he searched. "There was that guy in New Jersey. Maybe I should have tried harder to sell him."

"No," Hank said. "If you have to push too hard, it's a bad sign. We don't want a client getting cold feet at the last minute."

"I understand," Kurt said, "but we also don't need a crazy woman threatening to expose us to the cops or Chinese gangs."

"May didn't know anyone in the Chinese mafia. That was just talk. She's a little—*was* a little girl. Nothing more. Of course, she was extremely pissed that we took her parent's gold. But maybe that was karma."

"You really think she said nothing to the cops or a reporter or a friend?"

"Even if she did, they'd still be in the dark. What would she have said, 'I hired Ying and Yang to murder my parents for-profit, and they double-crossed me and took my gold'?"

"Yeah, I guess it sounds stupid when you say it like that."

"She got what she had coming. If she'd just kept her mouth shut, she'd be spending the money from all the other stuff she inherited. I hate greedy people."

"You sure about the mafia?"

"Come on, Kurt, she was eighteen. Barely. You think mafia guys are hanging out with seventeen-year-old chicks?"

"Well, maybe."

"Maybe some gangbanger was dating the girl. Maybe. But that doesn't mean she gave him anything he could use to find us. We'll be gone tomorrow. Our appointment is in the morning. We'll eat some pancakes, load up the van, sell the gold, buy a new car, and get out of Fairview forever."

EIGHTY-FIVE

Echo opened her refrigerator and stared.

"I need to go shopping," she said.

Conner came back to Echo's apartment after their meeting with Sally. He sat in the living room. They'd carved out a few minutes for each other before diving back into their respective stories. "Tell me about it," he said. "I have mayo, mustard, and catsup at home, but I couldn't even make a sandwich if I wanted to. I hate to admit it, but when I'm deep in a story, I can't help but order something delivered."

"Modern life has gotten so easy it's hard."

"Don't sweat it," he said. He patted the sofa. "Come sit next to me. We can order Chinese while we discuss the Chinese."

"You think it'll help?"

"Sure, why not? If we were in New York researching the five families, we'd order pizza."

"Have you made any progress on the Lau case at all?"

"The PD is being tight-lipped about it, despite the mayor's call for transparency and a new era of helpfulness."

Echo left the kitchen and sat with Conner. She glanced over at his phone and said, "That one, please."

"You always order that."

"I know."

"Share a fried rice?" Conner asked, with his finger hovering over a button.

"Yes," she replied. "And get another order of wontons because I'll save the leftovers for breakfast."

Conner added the wontons and was about to hit the cart button when Echo grabbed his arm. She wanted an order of walnut shrimp as well. "Are you sure this is everything?"

"Yup."

"It's enough for five."

"I'm going to be up all night," Echo said. "I have to get this *Soft Vanda* thing off my plate, and I want to dig deeper into the organized crime story. And none of that even touches on the thing…"

"With your birth parents and the book," Conner said, finishing her sentence. He gave her a hug and then completed their dinner order. "Looks like an hour. You want to listen to some music or get back to our series?"

As Echo was deciding, her phone rang. It was Detective Malloy. "Hey Skip," she answered. "Anything breaking?"

"Not yet. I have an off-the-books favor to ask."

"Sure," she said. "Hold on a minute. I'm with Conner." Echo got up and walked to the office. Before she shared information with Conner about a potential lead in the Lau story—or any story—she'd have to clear it with Skip beforehand. They had an agreement built on mutual trust, and it only worked if they both kept their side of the bargain. Luckily for Echo, Conner totally understood the rules with sources. He mentioned nothing about her discussions with the detective unless she brought it up first. "Okay, I'm in my office," she said, closing the door. "Go ahead."

"We interviewed May's ex-boyfriend. He'd been holding back details. We think maybe he's playing straight with us now. The thing is, he said May had posted some strange things on her social media. Before and after her parent's murders. He said she'd often delete things within hours. We need someone—off the record—to do a little digging."

Echo thought about what he really meant. May's death, being very recent, would mean that her accounts would still, likely, be active. Messages, emails, posts, and comments. She decided to help. "I'll look into this. I'll be discrete. What can I pass along to Conner?"

"That's tricky. Why don't you see what you get, and then we'll talk, okay?"

"Fair enough," she said. "I'll message you."

The call over, she yelled down the hall to let Conner know she needed a minute. Conner yelled back. He understood. Echo figured she could do some social media hacking herself. It wasn't technically that hard, but Echo also knew a hacker. This woman was someone she'd once met in real life. Her specialty was hacking into social media and email accounts. They'd worked together before, and since most people had terrible security, the jobs were usually easy ones. Because there was so much work to do, and time was of the essence, Echo decided she'd share the workload.

She booted up her PC and sent a message.

MoonbeamGirlyGirl: *Hey! Long time no see.*

Echo spent a few minutes getting caught up, mostly using code and emojis. Then she gave MoonbeamGirlyGirl, whose real name was Ann, the gist of what she needed. She explained the sensitivity of the request and that there was a slight possibility Chinese gangsters could've been involved with May Lau before she was murdered.

That's terrible and sad. But, I'll be careful. Let's check with each other in a few hours?

Echo sent a thumb's up and a smiley emoji, then signed off. Before she stood to leave the desk, she felt a tug. An emotional pull. The way an old photograph can sometimes do. She opened a drawer and pulled out the book that once belonged to her father. She leafed through the pages, thinking that the codes appeared ordered and logical. But, she knew any well-designed code was impossible to decipher without the proper key. She was still absorbed in thought when Conner shouted from the living room. "Dinner's here!"

EIGHTY-SIX

At three in the morning, her apartment felt cold, lonely, and haunted.

Echo rubbed her eyes. She knew diminishing returns were setting in, and soon she'd need to sleep. She was successful in uncovering a few tidbits, but nothing earth-shattering—she'd also been distracted with her other projects. As she was considering how wonderful it would feel to put her head on a pillow, Ann messaged.

MoonbeamGirlyGirl: *Got it!*

She'd unlocked May's preferred email address. In one folder, there was a list of passwords for social media and her computers. May's PC, still in her bedroom, was online. Once Ann got access, she could control the PC remotely. She passed everything to Echo, who thanked her and made a crypto deposit to cover her time.

It didn't take long to find a thread of messages that shocked Echo more than she expected. Stunned, she read through them twice. The other party was obviously using a fake account. Yang was what he called himself. But Echo could see it wasn't because he was Chinese. He described himself as a slender Irish guy. He told May he'd meet her and he'd be with a guy he called Ying. The other guy, he wrote, was also Irish, bulky, and covered in tattoos.

The discussion was obviously a transaction for a murder-for-hire. Both parents. Fifty-thousand in cash. Echo nearly wept. She could understand being upset with her parents, maybe even distancing herself from them. But murder? Not in a million years. May had seemed like a sweet girl. Maybe a bit confused about life, but she hadn't stuck Echo as a sociopathic murderer.

The guy who called himself Yang wanted May to meet in an alley by a seedy bar in Little Shanghai. Echo had heard of the place but had never been there. May refused and asked that the meeting be at a Chinese restaurant on Fourth Street called The Golden Chopsticks. It catered to an upscale American crowd more than local Chinese, but Echo knew why May had picked it. The restaurant and bar were always crowded. The parking lot was large, well-lit, and had security.

Echo scrolled back to near the beginning of the messages, which started nearly four months before the murders and re-read them.

May: *I don't know if I can go through with this. I don't want to get caught.*

Yang: *You won't.*

Why do you have so much confidence?

We've done this before. Many times. We'll cover our tracks. Nobody will know.

I want to say yes.

Your parents won't stop controlling you. You know this. You've talked about it with me. You feel you'll never have a life with them around. And they're old. You're young. You deserve a life.

I know. But, I feel sort of bad.

But not totally bad?

Echo read more. The conversation jumped between May's doubts and fears and Yang's assurances that everything would be fine. They had experience, and they knew she'd get away with it. She'd get an inheritance, and she'd be able to move on. Live her life, finally, under her own terms.

Eventually, Yang put pressure on May to decide.

May: *Okay, I've really thought about it. I'm going to say yes.*

Yang: *We'll do a clean job. I promise.*

I don't want them to suffer.

That won't happen. It'll be swift and painless. Promise.

Okay.

Now, we need to discuss the upfront payment. Once we get that, there's no backing out.

I understand.

Echo created screenshots of everything and placed them into a file. The discovery was going to be tricky from law enforcement's perspective. It wasn't a legal search. Of course, one conspirator was already dead—the important thing would be to stop the two killers from striking again. Perhaps Skip could use her as a Confidential Informant and get a warrant for May's social media accounts.

It was half-past four in the morning when Echo quit. She messaged Skip and told him she had some news. *Call me after 8. I need some sleep.*

EIGHTY-SEVEN

Skip ate a second pork bun. “These are amazing,” he said.

“They are not cinnamon rolls,” Bud said as he picked up another bun.

“That’s your third one. Quit complaining.”

“I’m not complaining about the taste. It’s just that on morning stakeouts, it’s tradition to have doughnuts and coffee. We’re breaking the unspoken rules.”

“They’re not unspoken if you’re yapping about them.” Skip raised his binoculars to his face and said, “Well, look at that. We have company.”

“Whatcha got?”

“Grey Toyota two blocks north. Just pulled in a few minutes ago. Two Asian males. They’re sitting there.”

“Asian Task Force?”

“I don’t think so. But get on the horn and find out.”

It was nine-thirty. Mike Huang’s place didn’t open until ten. Huang’s Jewelry was on the Asian Task Force’s watch list as a possible fencing operation. Of the several places under surveillance, Skip and Bud had decided this Little Shanghai jewelry store that bought and sold gold, silver, and gemstones was the most likely spot for a couple of thieves to choose. They knew Mike could move large amounts of cash and product under the radar of authorities. At least, that was the belief of the Asian Task Force.

Earlier that morning, Skip had called Echo. She'd been excited about what she found and wanted to talk about how to help. Because the social media messages she'd discovered didn't use real names or talk about any plans, there wasn't actionable information at the moment. Skip told her he'd meet with her later in the day and come up with a plan.

Bud set down the radio. "Steve says it's not them. He said if we can forward a plate number or photos, he'll see if they've got a file on the players."

Skip put the binoculars up to his face again. "Plate's not visible. The guys are wearing sunglasses and hats. It's too far to get a clear picture."

"Should we ask for backup?"

Skip thought about it for a moment. If they called for backup now, the other teams might be left understaffed. There wasn't any action at the moment, and it would be another half an hour before Haung's Jewelry opened. "Let's wait and see."

"You got it, partner."

At five to ten, Mike Huang arrived. Skip watched him unlock the front door and step inside. A few minutes later, a neon sign that said "OPEN" lit up in red. Bud tapped him on the shoulder. "Action," he said, and Skip dropped the binoculars. A white van headed towards them. It passed the Toyota and parked in front of Huang's. Two men got out.

They were white guys, one buff, the other skinny. Both wore sunglasses, ski caps, and jackets. It was impossible for Skip to know if they were the two men from Ted's security video, but it seemed likely. The bigger one held a gym bag.

The next moment, time slowed.

As the two men approached Huang's, Skip watched as the pair of lookouts exited their car. They carried shotguns, and they'd covered their faces with black bandanas. The man carrying the gym bag rushed to open the door to Huang's, but apparently, it was locked. It likely had a buzzer system similar to the EZ-Pawn. A blast rang out.

Bud shouted into the radio's mic. "Shots fired! Shots fired! This is car four-nineteen. Officers need assistance."

Skip opened his door and drew his weapon. "Request an ambulance." He rushed across the street and took cover behind a cement bus stop. The bigger of the two men from the van had dropped the gym bag. He returned fire towards the two shotgun-wielding gang members. Bullets shattered car windows, and alarms blared. A shotgun blast tore apart the gym bag while the big man blindly fired his weapon. He dragged his skinny accomplice towards their van.

"Police!" Skip shouted. "Drop your weapons!"

He knew they couldn't hear him over the cacophony of car alarms. He watched as Bud moved down the other side of the street. It was apparent the two gang members saw him, but they didn't fire in their direction. Bud cautiously moved towards the scene, using cars as cover.

The tall man helped the skinny man into the passenger side of the van. It was clear he'd taken a hit to one of his legs—the injury was unlikely to be a life-threatening one, but Skip could see blood smeared behind him. The van pulled out. The gang members fired a single shot into the back window, then one of them moved towards the gym bag.

The skinny guy jumped from the car, apparently immune to the pain. He rushed toward the gym bag.

Skip shouted, but it was too loud for anyone to hear anything over the sound of the alarms.

The gang member nearest the gym bag stopped. He kicked the skinny man in the face—the criminal went down. Then the gang member fired at the van.

After the blast hit the passenger's door, the driver sped away.

The Asian criminal grabbed the bag and ran. A shower of yellow spilled on the sidewalk.

"Bud!" Skip yelled. He could see that Bud couldn't hear him, but he pointed at the van. Bud understood, he moved back to the car. He'd radio the description and likely give chase. Skip knew he and Bud shouldn't split up. The two Asian gang members were already running back to their car, so he moved towards the body on the sidewalk. Codes and ethics required that he try to save a life, even a criminal's life if he could do it without endangering himself or others.

The Toyota sped past him but slowed when it reached their stakeout vehicle. Skip felt the world stop because Bud was just getting on the radio. He was vulnerable. Although he could see everything happen, he was too far away to do anything. The Toyota slowed.

Two shotgun blasts echoed above the noise of car alarms. Skip's mind envisioned Bud's funeral. His breathing quickened, and he ran towards his partner.

Bud ducked, but it wasn't necessary. The gang members shot the car's tires. Obviously, they didn't want to be followed—fortunately, they also didn't want to kill any cops. They raced away in the van's direction.

Skip turned his attention back to the fallen criminal.

The skinny man appeared to be conscious. Skip ensured there were no weapons on his person and that he was breathing. Bud arrived. "Backup and EMTs are on the way." Skip could hear sirens.

"This one's gonna live, but he took a brutal kick to the face after getting shot in the leg."

"Live by the sword, die by the sword," Bud said.

"Shakespeare?"

"No," groaned the skinny criminal. "That's New Testament."

"You're under arrest," Skip said. "You've got the right to remain silent." He read the rest of the Miranda Rights from a laminated card. He looked at Bud after he finished. "Handcuffs?"

"Yeah, better safe than sorry," he said. "This is gonna hurt, buddy. But don't fight it."

He groaned but didn't struggle.

"So, Irish Catholic?" Skip asked.

"Huh?" the man said. He spat out some blood. "Oh, yeah. Bible school as a kid."

"I guess it didn't stick," Bud said. "The part about not stealing."

"No," he replied. "I want a lawyer, by the way. Is my brother okay?"

"Can't say," Skip said. "You're asking for a lawyer. We can't really talk to you."

Bud stood up. "Ambulance is in sight."

Twenty minutes later, the scene was crowded. Cops, EMTs, and the media. Little Shanghai had its share of crime, but gun battles in the street weren't common. Skip instructed a couple of rookie patrol cops to cordon off the area with yellow tape. "Keep the media out. Nobody touch that gold, as tempting as it might be to retire early. And somebody find Mike Huang. Tell him he's a material witness. He'd better stay put."

"I finally got ahold of Steve," Bud said. "He's sending over one of the ATF detectives, but he can't be seen down here."

The skinny guy wasn't carrying any identification. The only thing he kept saying was that he wanted a lawyer. Skip assigned a veteran cop to ride in the ambulance with him to the hospital. "He's under arrest. No phone calls unless it's to an attorney. That's it. Don't let him out of your sight. I don't want him trying to contact his accomplice."

"Ten-four, Malloy," the cop said. "I know the drill."

"Bud, we got our first break. Look at this shoe," Skip said. The skinny criminal was on a stretcher about to be loaded into the ambulance. The soles of his shoes were pointed right at him, and he remembered the shoe print. Whatever the guy had stepped in, it was still on the bottom of the shoe. It might as well have said "guilty" on it.

"Looks like a match to me," Bud said. "Give me a second. I'll need an extra-large evidence bag for this one."

Skip carefully removed both shoes, just to be safe, and put them into a plastic bag. He sealed it and wrote his badge number with a black marker. Looking up, he noticed the criminal staring at him. He gave him a crocodile smile. "Murder for hire, buddy. That's a life sentence twice over—and this'll tie you to May Lau. Once you contact your attorney, reconsider chatting with us. Maybe you can help yourself."

The man frowned.

"Then again," Skip said, "maybe not."

"He should have paid more attention in Sunday School," Bud added.

The crime scene tech shouted for Skip. "Detective Malloy! Looks like there are some perfect fingerprints on a few of these coins. I'll get a rush on processing them."

"Excellent," Skip said. "We'll be at the precinct waiting for your findings."

EIGHTY-EIGHT

Skip waited outside the Sergeant's office until he finished meeting with another detective.

"It's a busy day for criminals," the Sergeant said. "Where are you with your case?"

"Bud's at the hospital. The perp is in surgery."

"ID come through yet?"

Skip shook his head. "It's in the works. We have a suitable set of prints off the guy. The tech guys are going through the coins right now."

"Enough to retire, I heard." The Sergeant glared. "Better stay that way, or some heads are gonna roll."

Skip kept his opinions about the situation to himself. He had a general trust of his fellow officers, but he wasn't naïve. Sometimes things went missing when they shouldn't have. He, Bud, and one tech had photographed and cataloged the recovered coins. If anyone took even a single one, it wouldn't go unnoticed.

"Any luck with the white van?"

Skip hated to admit failure. "No luck. The two gangbangers with the shotguns followed him. He might be dead. None of the patrols rolling to the scene saw either vehicle. By the time we got a chopper in the air, some twenty minutes had gone by. They're in the wind for now."

"Once you ID the guy under the knife, maybe you'll get a lead. Okay, Detective Malloy, good work. Get out of here and wrap this case as soon as possible."

"You got it, Sergeant," he said. He turned and walked down the hallway towards the elevator. Then he took the stairs. *Might as well get some steps in*, he thought. As he entered the war room, a lab tech almost ran into him.

"Sorry, Detective," he said. "I just dropped the ID on your desk."

Skip picked up the file folder, removed the sheets, and read. The name in the hospital was Kurt Boyle. He'd done time, and one of his known associates was his brother, Hank Boyle. The techs knew it was likely the second man was the brother of the first, so they'd pulled records and photos on both. Skip was happy they'd done that without him having to ask. The job was easier when you worked with professionals who felt callings instead of those who just showed up for a paycheck.

He called Bud.

"What's shaking down there?" Skip said before Bud said hello. "How's our boy in surgery?"

"He's not under the knife but still in recovery."

"Okay, listen," Skip said. "I have an ID on him, Kurt Boyle. The getaway van driver is likely his older brother, Hank. Both have records going back."

"As expected."

"Yeah, as expected. Says in the files the father took a bullet in an armed robbery. The boys didn't fall far from the apple tree. Anyway, I'll start calling motels and lodges. Maybe we'll get lucky, and someone will remember two Irish brothers paying in cash and using fake names."

"Didn't Echo tell you they used some fake nicknames in the messages with May?"

“Yes,” Skip answered. “You’re correct.” He flipped through his notes. “Ying and Yang. That’s what she said they’d told May. I’ll call Echo and see if she can dig some more. Maybe there’s a clue in those messages about where they’d been hiding.”

EIGHTY-NINE

Hank turned onto a southbound highway and slammed his foot down on the accelerator.

"Damn thieves!" He shouted. "I'm going to..." He stopped talking when he realized Kurt wasn't sitting next to him. *Why did you jump, little bro?* It was the gold, he knew. Kurt just couldn't let it go, not after all they'd done to get it. And all the waiting they'd done to sell it.

He looked into the rearview mirror. One of the Chinese mafia guys was climbing out of the passenger's window. May wasn't joking, he realized. She really had had connections inside Little Shanghai. She got what she deserved, he believed, because she'd entered the game. If you play with the big boys, sometimes you get shot. Just like his little brother.

Hank accelerated to a hundred miles per hour. He slammed on the brakes. The van went into a skid, but he corrected it by turning into it. The Toyota, having closed the gap between the vehicles, slammed into the rear of the van. Hank jumped onto the highway before the two cars stopped moving. He shot the driver in the face.

The gang member who'd been halfway outside the car was sprawled on the highway. He appeared to be a broken and bloody mess, so Hank ignored him. He went for the gym bag instead.

It felt light.

"Damn thieves!" He shot the driver again, although he was obviously dead. Next, he walked to the passenger and shot him three times for good measure. The shotgun was lying on the asphalt, so he picked it up and tossed it into the passenger's seat of the van.

He looked at a passing car as the driver, in full panic, was yelling into her phone. She sped away. Traffic was light, but Hank knew it wouldn't be long before the cops showed up. He hopped into the driver's seat and sped to the next exit. The entire ordeal had lasted under three minutes. His heart was still pounding as he pulled into an alley. He parked in a partially obstructed spot.

He'd be safe for maybe an hour. Or maybe five minutes.

Discovering if his brother was alive was his priority. He turned on the radio and scanned for news but only heard the sports report and a few commercials before he got frustrated and turned it off. He'd call the hospitals later. His breathing sped up. He pounded on the dashboard.

"Dammit!"

He'd get his brother out of the hospital no matter what.

Patience, he told himself. The two thugs who'd found them trying to sell the gold had obviously gotten information from May. But she was dead now, too. The cops…

The cops probably didn't know who they were. How could they?

What mistakes have we made?

It didn't matter now, he realized. He had to rescue Kurt. That would be his mission. Get Kurt out of the hospital before processing at the police station took place. If that happened, he'd be sent to county. He'd be out of reach. Forever.

If they made a solid connection to the Lau murders, Kurt would be facing at least a life sentence. Maybe several. If he received consecutive life sentences, he'd never see the outside. He'd die in prison like a neglected pet.

That settled it for Hank. Either they'd both escape, or they'd both go down. *Brothers to the end.* He calmed himself, took several deep breaths, and formulated a plan.

NINETY

Echo had gone back to bed after talking in the morning with Skip about what she knew.

She was running on only a few hours of sleep. But by the afternoon, she was feeling more energized. In the kitchen, she reheated leftovers and made a cup of coffee. All-nighter food. It was good to feel excited about digging deeper into a story, but she also didn't want to cross boundaries with Conner. Skip had asked her to wait to tell him anything, and she'd agreed, but now anxiety crept up on her. It wouldn't be good for their relationship if the sharing didn't go both ways.

She was partway through a bowl of fried rice when she realized that she'd put her phone on silent. Retrieving her smartphone, she saw there were several missed calls and unread text messages from Skip and Connor.

She called Skip first. "Hello, Skip. More news?"

"Yes. We had a shootout in the streets."

"No!"

"Yes. It's all over the airwaves now, so no secret about it. There were two suspects from our case with May and a couple of gang members. Possibly Golden Dragons, but that's off the record for now."

"What can you tell me?"

"The suspects are brothers, Hank and Kurt Boyle. We have Kurt, the younger one, in custody. There's a description of Hank and his vehicle going out on all the news outlets. Nothing breaking there to give you, sorry."

Echo asked if there was anything she could get to Conner for an exclusive. Anything at all. Skip told her he'd try to find something to feed him, off-the-record, as a favor to Echo. The priority at the moment, however, was finding Hank. Which was why he'd called her.

"Can you get back into social media and look for anything that will give us a clue about where he might hide? A hotel, motel, lodge, or something? Maybe he gave May a clue. Anything that could help right now could save lives."

"Yes," Echo said. "Of course. I'll do whatever I can. I'm going to call Connor now and let him know he can call you later, okay?"

"Sure. I'll see what I can do. If you find anything at all, please call me."

"I'll do it," she said. Echo ended the call and hit speed dial for Connor. She told him what she knew and what Skip had said he'd try to do for him.

"That's great, Echo. But we could really use you down here."

"At *Above the Fold*?"

"Yes. Frank asked me to ask you. Didn't you read your messages?"

"I haven't opened them yet. I figured it was better just to call."

"Okay, fine. Get down here, okay? Frank has some possible stories he'd like to discuss with you."

"Sure. I'll get dressed and be there in thirty."

"Good, thank you. Have to run."

After Connor ended the call, Echo realized that she'd just promised Skip she'd dig for more information. There was a solution, she thought. She created a folder of screenshots; she could read them all again in the office. Then she sent a quick message to Ann and briefly explained the dilemma the police faced. Perhaps she could find a clue on May Lau's social media or emails. Echo ended the message with a promise that she'd pay extra if Ann could fit in the research immediately.

Echo drove towards the *Above the Fold* offices in a rush. A feeling of sadness hit her as she realized how desperate May Lau must have been to cause this chain of events to happen like a destructive earthquake.

Her cell phone rang through the car's stereo. "Hello, Mom." A smile broke across her face. It was as if fate understood it was a time she needed to hear her mother's voice. "I've missed you."

"Oh, honey, I've missed you too."

"Did you just land?"

"Yes, but we're still in the plane on the tarmac. And we're exhausted."

"I'm headed to the office. There's a huge story breaking, and I've got to help."

"Would you like to come to dinner?"

"Yes," Echo said. "Message me after you and Dad have taken naps."

Her mother laughed and said she would do just that. Echo felt a warmth in her heart. With all that had happened over the last week, it was good to feel that strong connection with her mom. She knew she'd get back to her search for her past. That wasn't over. She'd uncover the secrets that had died with her birth parents. But it could wait a few days.

Echo had time.

She thought of May Lau again, being so desperate for her "own life" that she was willing to kill the people who'd given her life. Even without the same DNA, Echo's parents, her mom and dad, were two of the most special people in the world to her. Hurting them, killing them, would never cross her mind. Echo realized she would never understand why May had taken that step. It was unfathomable and mysterious to her how someone could be driven to that point.

While she was thinking these thoughts, her phone rang again.

"Hello?"

"Are you the reporter Echo Rose?"

"Yes. Can I help you?" she asked, trying to place the voice. It belonged to a man—he sounded street-savvy and cold.

"I have information about the two killers and their connection to Little Shanghai."

That got Echo's attention. "Okay?"

"We need to meet."

"I don't know you," she said. "Where did you get this number? Who are you?"

"I got it from a friend. I'm not telling you my name. It's too dangerous."

"I'm not going to meet someone I don't know."

"Are you at the *Above the Fold* office?"

"I'm not telling you anything about my location," she said. A chill ran down her back. She was pulling into a parking space at the *Above the Fold* building and wasn't sure if she should end the call or ask for more. It could be a legitimate lead, she thought. "If you have something, talk to me now. If not, I'm hanging up."

"I have something to give you. A package. Can I bring it to you at the *Above the Fold* offices?"

"I'm not going to agree to meet someone who won't give me any information about himself."

"I'll drop it at the front desk. You are there, aren't you?"

She felt watched. Hunted. "I'm not giving out my location. But if you're a legitimate source with real information, sure, you can drop it at the office." Echo ended the call and stepped out of her car. She felt like a gazelle being chased by a lion as she hurried to get inside the building.

NINETY-ONE

Hank's plan had to work—he and his brother's freedom depended on it.

He cursed May Lau under his breath as he packed all their important belongings into one large suitcase and a carry-on-sized matching bag. Much of the clothes were unnecessary. He ditched them in a dumpster. *The homeless will find them soon enough*, he figured. Not that evidence identifying them was important at this point. They had Kurt. Through Kurt, they had him.

No matter.

He wiped down the shotgun as a matter of instinct and tossed it into a patch of weeds close to where he'd abandoned the van. He'd nearly wiped that down, too, until he reminded himself it was futile. The important items left were in the luggage. Laptops, disguises, burner cell phones, and the remaining gold. He estimated less than half had fallen out back in front of Mike Haung's Jewelry store.

What a waste...

All this was necessary because May Lau had lied to them. She'd tried to cheat them. It had cost her the remaining years of her life, which could have been good, Had she not been so greedy. May Lau had shown up the night of their meeting with nothing.

Not a penny.

Kurt had wanted to skip town, but May was convincing. She cried. And pleaded. Her parents had heard from an uncle, who'd heard from his wife, who'd heard from her daughter, that May Lau had posted a picture of fifty-thousand dollars on her social media. She'd removed the post showing the cash after only minutes, but the damage was done. Her dad had confronted her, May had told the brothers while crying her eyes out, and taken her money.

"He put the cash into his safe," May had said. "And he changed the combination."

Kurt still wanted to abort the plan and skip town. "It's too dangerous, Hank," he'd said. "She's obviously untrustworthy. We can get another job."

"I have another plan," Hank had said. "Trust me."

Hank and May agreed, against the better judgment of Kurt, that before they killed the Lau's, they'd simply force them to open the safe. "Don't take anything else," May had said naively. "Don't worry, honey," Hank had said with a smile. "We have a reputation to live up to. We'll only take the money you owe us for the job. That's it. You have my word." He'd stuck out his hand, and she'd taken it without hesitation.

Stupid, stupid girl.

The reason for their current dilemma was that May had been grossly misinformed.

Or she'd lied outright from the start. There was no money in the safe. Only gold. Perhaps her father had put it into a bank. That's where honest, tax-paying citizens kept their cash. It didn't matter to Hank, of course. He was always planning to take the gold. Had May not made threats, dumb threats, she'd still be alive. There was the house, the cars, the art, and probably a big life insurance policy on her parents. Maybe a trust fund. Certainly, there were business investments. If only she'd accepted the loss of the gold as payment for her own duplicity and lies, none of this insanity would have happened. But once she started making threats, Hank had agreed with Kurt. She needed to go away.

Not having the cash she'd promised became a problem for them. They had immediate expenses, and the foremost on that list had been a new vehicle. That was Hank's priority now—he needed to buy a car without drawing attention to himself. Or he needed to sell some gold first.

Either way was going to be tricky. He walked two blocks and entered a mini-mart. Pulling out his money clip, he counted. Two twenties, a ten, four fives, and six ones. They'd gotten down to seventy-six dollars. *Talk about cutting it close.* He bought chocolate milk and a bag of chips and asked for the bathroom key.

Fifteen minutes later, he looked like a completely different person. He'd trimmed his hair, military short. He put on a sports coat, one of those traveling salesman types that didn't wrinkle. With a tiny fake mustache and thick-rimmed glasses, he didn't even quite recognize himself. It was good enough, he thought.

“Where’s the nearest used car lot, partner?” he asked the clerk on the way out. All crappie neighborhoods like this had used cars for sale. He was certain of it.

“My cousin washes cars at one,” the clerk said. “It’s ten blocks from here. Near East and Union avenues, by the train crossing. They always got good deals. And if you tell them Joey Mack sent you, I’ll get a few bucks.”

Hank was silent. He stared like a shark.

“How about I call over there?” the clerk asked. “Maybe they send someone.”

“You do that, kid.”

Sure enough, forty minutes later, Hank was negotiating for a piece of crap car. He was overpaying, he knew. But he’d made a deal in trade for gold coins, and he’d emphasized the necessity of leaving the official paperwork sitting around for a week. Not that he’d used a real name, of course, but the less attention, the better.

The beater car had one thing going for it that Hank was happy about: it wasn’t noticeable. It was silver and looked like the automaker had mass-produced a million of them for car rental companies in the Florida Keys and people with no taste. Between the car and his new look, he had time.

He drove across town, parked, and watched a building for a girl. Hopefully, this one wasn’t stupid. He was counting on her to help him save his brother.

NINETY-TWO

Skip joined Bud at the county hospital.

"This coffee is horrible," he said. They'd been sitting for hours waiting to interview Kurt Boyle. Out on the street, no sign of his fugitive brother had surfaced.

Bud frowned. "You expected free coffee to be good?"

"Why not?"

"Free things are usually crappy," Bud said. "It's simple economics."

"I'm free, and I'm not crappy," said a man wearing a cheap suit and carrying a battered leather briefcase. "At least I'm free to my clients. Somebody always pays. Detectives, I'm Murry Goldman, attorney-at-law."

"Public Defender's office?" Skip said.

"No, but I'd imagine they'll be brought in at some point. Not sure right now. I'm on a certain judge's list. You know, the kind where you do penance for some slightly unorthodox courthouse maneuvering that wasn't especially appreciated."

"And you've got roped in to do some pro bono work?"

"You got it, Detective. Malloy, isn't it?"

"Yes, I'm Malloy. My partner, Detective Smith."

Bud nodded politely to the lawyer but didn't offer his hand. "So you're on the hook to defend Kurt Boyle?"

"I don't know about that, Detective Smith. Here's the deal. Because there's a huge manhunt going on for the alleged partner of Mr. Boyle, the mayor called a judge. A judge called me. They want you to have access. To lawfully interview my newest client. I'm told he asked for a lawyer while bleeding in the street. We'll get to potential law enforcement abuses later, Detectives, but for now, I'm going to speak to my client and verify with his doctor that he's capable of being interviewed without endangering his health. I'll let you know how all this works out just as soon as I know myself."

Skip walked to a gray steel chair. *Furniture you'd expect in a prison, not a hospital*, he thought as he sat. "Goldman, we've got a murderer running free. He left two bodies out on Highway Twenty-four. So, whatever you've got to do, do it."

Murry Goldman nodded his head and walked to the nearest nurse's station.

Bud looked at Skip and said, "He's not going to talk. Is he?"

"I guess we'll know in due time, partner."

An hour and twenty minutes later, Goldman approached the detectives. "We're ready for you, Detective Malloy. And your sidekick." He sneered at Bud.

"I don't think he likes you," Skip said.

"Don't care," Bud said as he sneered back at the lawyer. "He's going to like me less in a little while."

They entered a private room, walking past a cop who'd been posted at the door. Kurt Boyle's left hand was cuffed to the bed. An I.V. tube ran from his arm to a drip tube. A couple of machines blinked. He looked like a guy who'd just been shot and beaten. "Detectives," he mumbled. "I've really got nothing to say to you guys. Sorry."

"Your brother left a couple more bodies on the highway, Kurt. Those murders were part of your conspiracy, thus it's the same as if you'd pulled the trigger. We have five murders to pin on you. I'm sure your lawyer has made that clear."

"Alleged conspiracy, Detective," Goldman said. "He's not copping to any murder. I'll advise him to talk to you if we stop this nonsense about murder. He was simply walking into an establishment that buys and sells gold. They attacked him. Both of you witnessed that. Isn't that correct?"

"He had gold taken from a double murder for hire," Bud said. His face turned red. "I know you've got a job to do, Goldman. But come down to earth. We've got the gold, and we've got the prints. We've got enough physical evidence to throw your client behind bars for five lifetimes."

"So what do you guys want?" he asked.

"We're asking for cooperation. If Kurt helps us find his brother, especially before anyone else is hurt, we'd put in a good word with the DA's office. Maybe get some concessions. Avoid a lengthy trial. You know the deal, counselor."

"I'm not saying squat," Kurt said. "I've got a code. Even if you tortured me, I'd never give up my brother. It doesn't work that way."

"So, you're confirming that was, in fact, your brother who conspired with you to kill the Lau's and steal their gold?"

"Go to—"

"Hold it right there—"

"I'm talking now—"

The room echoed with the voices of three angry men. Skip folded his arms and watched. He knew nothing would come from the confrontation. He understood the code that Kurt spoke of—he didn't like the man's lifestyle, and he wanted him to go to prison—but he understood. Skip left the room and sat in the hallway. He listened to Bud and the lawyer argue back and forth for a few minutes and then tuned them out. It wouldn't go anywhere, but he knew Bud had to try.

Because they had eaten nothing since the stakeout, his stomach protested. He figured Bud would eventually tire of arguing with a practiced attorney and a stubborn criminal. Then they'd grab a quick dinner, debrief the Sergeant, and get home late. He called Vivian and explained his status. She understood. Accepting a cop's life was part of the bargain. Skip said, "I love you, too," and ended the call. He was about to put his cell into his pocket when it beeped.

A text message from Echo.

NINETY-THREE

Echo entered her parent's mansion and felt oddly at home.

The place was immense. Too much, really, even for three. For two, it was excessive. She entered the grand foyer and turned on the lights and the TV in the informal family room.

"Grace! Is that you?"

"Yes, mom," she answered. "It's me." She didn't like her mother calling her by her real name, but she also didn't want to argue about it. They'd been gone for a couple of weeks, and she missed them. Thoughts of May Lau passed through her mind, and she promised herself to make the evening nothing but pleasant.

Her mother's voice had come from the kitchen. She went there and asked her if she really had the energy to cook. "I could order something," Echo said.

"Nonsense," Didi said. "I'm back home and feel like having a homemade dinner."

Didi was petite, with short hair that had streaks of blonde highlights, and she wore a pastel-colored dress.

"Okay," Echo said. "I'll help. Where's Dad?"

"He'll be right down, darling. Hand me that spoon."

Echo fell into a rhythm and was helping her mother chop onions when her father, Edward, entered the kitchen. "I thought I heard some commotion."

Edward was tall, with trimmed salt and pepper hair, and he had on a light cardigan sweater.

He gave Echo a hug, and she said how happy she was to have them back home.

"Tell me more about the trip," Echo then added.

"First," Edward said, "I need a drink. Cocktail, Echo?"

"Okay," she said. "I guess one would be nice."

"I could use a glass of wine," Didi said.

Echo frowned but didn't speak. Her mother was known to drink a glass or two each night to unwind. It was on a night she'd had a few too many that she'd told Echo about her adoption. Didi had been depressed and let out her secrets in a drunken confession. "I thought you were quitting, Mom."

"I was good the entire trip, Grace. Really, I didn't even have a sip on the plane ride home. And I sure could have used one after we hit that turbulence."

"Sure, Mom. I understand. Let me go down to the wine cellar. I'll bring up a bottle."

"You're a dear," Didi said.

Upon her return to the kitchen, her father had made two cocktails. He handed one to her and said, "I'll trade you." Echo set the bottle on the marble counter and watched her father pull out the cork. She sipped her drink and wondered about the mystery of her birth. Then, realizing it wasn't a good time for thoughts to intrude, she asked again about their trip to Belize.

"You should have seen the fish, Grace," her mom said. "Such beauty. Come with us the next time. Please. I'll set up the diving school for you. You can get certified in Fairview if you don't want to drive out this way, but there's this really cute instructor—"

"I have a boyfriend," she said.

"Well, we haven't met him yet, have we?"

"I promised him we'd set a date on the calendar. We'll do that before I leave, and you'll meet him."

"I'm going to hold you to that."

"Of course, Mom. Now, put that into the oven and show me pictures."

Didi's face lit up. "You're not going to believe the places we went to."

NINETY-FOUR

Hank Boyle had sat for hours outside the *Above The Fold* offices listening to the news.

The radio in the car was junk, but it picked up a local A.M. talk radio channel well enough to get regular news reports. Hank knew the police would limit information, but he could confirm that his brother was alive. The reports said as much. There was a tip line set up by the police. Law enforcement had asked the public to call if anyone had information about him. He hoped the car reseller would remain quiet. He'd overpaid him, and hinted it would go extremely bad for him if he talked.

Echo Rose was easy to identify from various pictures he'd found online. When she finally left the newspaper offices, she drove to Camden. Hank followed cautiously. He needed her to help save his brother. When she pulled into the driveway of a mansion, he drove past and waited. Then, after he felt safe, he circled back and parked on the street where he could view the house.

He wanted to know if she was alone or not, but it was impossible to tell. The longer he waited, the higher the chance that a nosey neighbor would call nine-one-one. Rich people were like that. They also liked to install a lot of security, so he knew trying to break in the front wasn't going to fly. He left his car and made his way quickly to the side gate.

The lock to the gate wasn't sophisticated. He picked it in under two minutes. The backyard was filled with manicured plants, stone tiles, and the fancy patio furniture you'd expect at a resort in Hawaii. Or poolside in a five-star luxury resort in Las Vegas. A memory flashed across his mind, he and Kurt in Vegas. That was a glorious trip, he thought. They'd gambled, gone to shows, met some pretty women, and eaten at all the best buffets. The memory steeled his resolve to get to his brother.

As he approached the pool area, he stopped and listened for sound. There was nothing except the falling water in a sculpted fountain and the occasional bird. Funny, he thought, how leaving the city for the suburbs totally changed the noises. He crept to a window and looked inside.

The kitchen was massive and looked like it belonged in a restaurant. It was vacant, but the lights were on, and it appeared as if people had recently been preparing food. Wealthy people didn't leave messes on the counter. He was sure of it. That meant that Echo was likely with others. Friends? Parents? A boyfriend or lover? He realized it didn't matter. Nobody would get between him and saving Kurt.

He double-checked his surroundings. Once sure nobody else was present, nor that any neighbors had a view of him, he began picking a lockset in what he assumed was a service entrance door off the kitchen. It was windowless and solid.

Being more sophisticated than the gate lock, it took him ten minutes to pick. He put his tools into his back pocket and adjusted his gloves. He put a handgun in his left hand and slowly turned the doorknob with his right. Entering the room, he allowed his eyes to adjust. It was a storage room, as he thought. Shelves held pool supplies and gardening tools.

He crept to the interior door and gently opened it. Pausing, he heard the familiar sounds of laughter and chit-chat. Taking his time, he moved into the hallway, keeping the gun aimed in front of him. He judged there were three people. They were talking about a vacation.

Rich people, he silently scoffed. *I'm about to ruin your day.*

NINETY-FIVE

Echo listened as her father told her about the last dive they'd taken in Belize.

"It was a few days before we were scheduled to leave," he said.

"You can't fly right after a bunch of dives," Didi added. "It's got something to do with decompression. Oh, I don't understand it all. I just do what your father tells me."

"Anyway," he said, "before I was interrupted there. I was saying." He sipped his cocktail and then looked at Echo. "We'd signed up for a tour. A tame jungle hike. It looked fun, and it wasn't too long. However, it required sturdy footwear."

"Belize is infested with snakes," Didi said.

"I doubt 'infested' is the right word. But be that as it may, we needed jungle boots. So we went shopping and bought gear for the hike."

"There was a laminated card that helped identify which snakes were venomous and which were harmless," Didi explained. "I wanted to be extra careful, but—"

"But it's not like you were going to pick up a snake, regardless of whether or not it was a harmless one."

"That's true. I studied the card but ended up purchasing a pocket guidebook. You wouldn't believe the animals that live there in the jungle. Besides killer snakes, there are crocodiles, jaguars, and bats. Plus, some deadly spiders."

"So your mom was getting nervous by the time we got to the tour office. The guide assured her it was safe. They took tourists hiking every day, and nobody ever died."

"Like they'd admit it." Didi refilled her glass. "Nobody is going to tell you their tour might end up with you being eaten."

"To finish my story," Edward said, "your mother walks to the jeep they use to take hikers to the trailhead. She sees something on the ground. She screamed bloody murder and nearly fainted. It was a hose."

"I thought it looked exactly like a snake."

"It looked like a hose."

"Well, you hadn't studied the guidebook. There's a snake that looks like that hose. And it's deadly. One bite, and you've got ten minutes before you're dead unless they give you the antivenom."

"Sounds scary," Echo said. "I've been thinking of getting a pet."

"What?!" Her mom nearly spilled her wine.

"It always seems lonely when I go to my apartment."

"You're always welcome at home," Edward said. "You know that. The house is big enough."

"I know," Echo said. "But I need my own life. I love you both, but part of finding out who I am and what I want to be…" She stopped and reflected on her search. It was possible that her birth father had been a criminal. Maybe he'd turned. By providing state's evidence against a cartel, maybe he'd done the right thing after all. And it got him and Echo's birth mother killed.

Or maybe he was never involved in crime. Perhaps he was merely an innocent victim in the whole affair, and it was just bad luck that he discovered evidence that ended up costing him and his wife their lives. It was complicated. Echo didn't know yet if she was going to tell her parents about what she'd found. Her birth parents might not have been law-abiding citizens. Maybe she was the child of criminals? Would that change how her parents viewed her? There was too much to consider.

She decided to wait. After she knew more, at some point in the future, she'd have a talk with them and explain what she'd uncovered. It wasn't time yet.

"So what kind of pet, Grace?" her mother asked. "Please don't say a snake."

"I've considered a snake. Maybe a boa. They're pretty and not venomous," she replied. "But I don't know yet. Perhaps a lizard would be better. I'll definitely get some plants first. Maybe a fish tank."

"Well, if you get a fish tank," Edward said, "there's this lionfish. It's got these venomous spikes, but it's super beautiful. And it's not as if you'll be handling it."

"It's an invasive species there in Belize," Didi said. "So, it's damaging the—" Her face turned pale. White as a ghost. She dropped her wineglass, and it shattered on the floor. Her hand went to her mouth to stifle a scream.

Edward stood. He appeared angry and a little frightened.

Echo turned.

A tall man with a gun stood in the hallway. He walked into the room and pointed his weapon at them. He looked into Echo's eyes with malice and hatred. "Sit down," he said to Edward. He waved the gun. "Sit down, all of you. And keep your mouths shut."

NINETY-SIX

"You two stay quiet," Hank said to the couple. "I won't hesitate to shoot both of you."

"What do you want?" Echo asked.

"You're the reporter who interviewed May Lau," he said. It wasn't a question. "What did she tell you about me?"

"I don't know who you are," she said. "May never told me anything about her criminal involvement. She lied."

"That sounds like her. Cheating liar. This is all her fault. I wish she was still alive so I could kill her slowly."

"What do you want from me?"

"I need to know what hospital my brother is in," he replied. Hank realized if he killed the couple, Echo would be less inclined to help him. He needed a plan, and he needed one fast. If his brother got transferred, the gig would be up. There'd be no hope. That couldn't be allowed to happen. "I don't even know if he's still alive." He stood across from Echo but kept the gun aimed at the older woman.

"The news reports say he's alive," Echo said. "But I don't know more than that. I'm not a cop."

"You're a journalist. You're on the crime beat, so you can find out. Are these your parents?"

"I'm Echo's father," the older man said. "Edward Sanderson. You're trespassing in my home. Why are you here?"

"I'm here because my brother got shot. He's in custody, and I intend to save him. He's all I have in this world, so don't think for a second I won't hesitate to shoot all of you if I need to."

"Who shot your brother?" Echo asked. Apparently, she couldn't help but act like a journalist. Hank almost wanted to pull the trigger at that moment, but he knew killing her would be counterproductive. He considered his next move and realized that if he played along with her, allowed her to go into journalism mode, he'd be more likely to get the information he needed.

"A couple of Chinese mafia thugs attacked us this morning," he said. "I don't know who they were, but they're no longer breathing. You mess with an angry Irishman, you get what's coming to you, if you know what I mean."

"And how did the police get involved?"

"You know that black detective, don't you?" Hank asked. "Unlock your phone and hand it over." He pointed the gun at the couple again and waved it between them. "You two put your phones on the table. Right now. No sudden moves, or I'll put some holes in you." Hank laughed when he said that. "You know, Echo, I normally get paid to get rid of troublesome parents. But for you, I might do it for free. Phones! On the table. Now!"

They complied.

Hank picked up Echo's phone and considered his next move. He scrolled through the contacts and found an entry for Skip. There was a profile photo attached, and he realized it was the detective he'd seen on the news. "This is your cop buddy, right?" He turned the phone, so she could see the screen.

"That's him, yes," Echo said. "Detective Malloy."

"Skip," Hank said to himself. "Skip, Skip, Skip. How can I get you to help me save my brother?"

NINETY-SEVEN

Skip re-read the text message twice.

I have vital information about the Lau killings. Can't talk now. Come to my parent's house asap. It's sensitive. Come alone and quickly.

What in the world could she have discovered, he thought, *that she'd need me to go to her parent's house?* He looked at the address that she'd sent after the message. It was in Camden, and he figured he could be there in under an hour if he got lucky with traffic.

But what was she thinking?

Skip called her. It went straight to voicemail. Strange.

He walked to Kurt Boyle's room. Bud and Murray Goldman were still talking. It appeared as if Kurt had fallen asleep. "You guys come to any agreements?"

"Nope," Bud said. "Boyle isn't going to help himself here, and his fancy attorney isn't doing him any favors."

"Disagree, Detective," the lawyer said.

"I need to go talk to someone, Bud," Skip said. "Walk outside with me."

Bud followed Skip into the hall. "What's up?"

"Echo left me a strange message. I'm going to follow up on it. There's no news out there about where Hank Boyle might be holed up. They found his van, so he's changed vehicles. He could be anywhere."

"You think he'd leave town? Abandon his brother here?"

"Why not?" Skip asked. "What's he going to do? Storm the hospital?"

"We should ask the Sergeant to assign more security."

"I think you're right, even though I can't see it. His picture has gone up all over the news, and it's not like the hospital doesn't have good security as it stands."

"I'll call the Sergeant anyway. I'd like to make sure nothing unexpected catches us by surprise while Kurt's in here."

"The doctor give you any update?"

"He'll be transferred as early as tomorrow morning. That's all we know for now."

"Okay, you feel good about hanging tight? I'll head over to see Echo and let you know once I do what it's about."

Bud nodded. "Sounds good, partner. If Kurt changes his mind and talks, I'll call you."

"I wouldn't count on it."

"I'm not. Criminals aren't smart. If they were, they wouldn't get caught."

Skip thought about all those that got away. A lot of them never paid for their crimes. But he said nothing to his partner. He gave him a little wave and headed to the elevators.

What's going on, Echo?

He got into his car and turned on his mobile radio. He scanned the police frequencies for any chatter about the hunt for Hank Boyle. There was nothing but a lot of back-and-forths as officers checked in to relay that they'd gone through a certain neighborhood or talked to a potential witness with no luck. As he was about to pull onto the highway, he heard his name.

"Detective Malloy, are you monitoring this freq?"

"Ten-four," he answered. "Malloy here. Go ahead."

"This is Patrol Six. I'm at this mini-mart in the Oak Hills neighborhood. Apple street and William's Avenue. A guy, some local-yokel at the register, he thinks he might have sold a chocolate milk to your suspect."

Skip made a quick U-turn, nearly hitting a bus, and responded that he was en route. *Sorry, Echo, you're going to have to wait*, he thought. *Maybe we finally caught a break.*

NINETY-EIGHT

Echo had watched helplessly as the intruder scrolled through her phone's contacts and messages.

She felt powerless and violated. Because she'd been in dangerous situations before, she knew the best thing she could do would be to stay calm.

"I need to see a TV," he said. "Which way?"

Edward pointed towards the family room. "There's a big screen down that hallway in the family room."

"Okay. Everyone on their feet. Mom and Dad, you go first. No funny business, or I put a bullet into someone's back. Got it?"

"Yes," Echo said. "We understand." She walked up close to her mother and whispered that it would be okay. "Just do as he says. We'll get out of this."

"Shut up!" he yelled. "Follow my instructions, or else it's gonna be a problem."

"I'm sorry," Didi said. "I'm just nervous."

Edward turned and guided his wife to a seat in the family room. "The remote is on the coffee table."

"Everyone sit." He scrolled through the national cable news stations, but there wasn't anything about Fairview. He found a local station with news coming up in a little over an hour. "So we wait," he said.

"What are we waiting for?" Echo asked.

"Don't worry your little head about it," he replied, handing Echo her phone. "But I do have another idea."

She accepted her phone and gave him a puzzled look.

"Start calling your contacts. No cops. Don't do anything stupid, or I'll shoot your mom."

"Okay. What contacts? What are you trying to accomplish?"

"I want to know if my brother is alive. Then, I want to know what hospital he's in."

Echo knew the police would have a guard on their prisoner, even if he was seriously injured and in the hospital. Nothing this man could do was going to get his brother freed. So, she played along. Over the years, Echo had found herself in many perilous situations. For that reason, she carried a telescoping baton, pepper spray, and a knife. The first two weapons were in her glove compartment. It wasn't as if she'd ever expected to be in danger in her parent's home. However, she'd holstered the knife on her ankle. That was an old habit that had saved her life on a number of occasions.

If she could see an opening, she'd be able to pull up her pant leg and get the deadly blade. It would be a last resort, however, because the man had a gun aimed at her mother.

"No tricky business, Echo," he said. It was as if he could sense the danger she was projecting. "Make some calls. Now. And put it on speaker."

She complied. The first call, of course, was to Conner.

All four of them were frozen in anticipation as the call rang through to Conner's cell phone.

NINETY-NINE

Conner had left the offices of *Above The Fold* with anticipation that he'd get solid facts—and maybe a scoop—from Detective Smith.

"Can you tell me if the fugitive brother has been positively identified?" he asked.

"I can't say that," Bud answered. "We believe that the co-conspirator is Hank Boyle. There is an active search for him. I cannot comment about specific details of the investigation."

"Is Kurt Boyle facing charges in relation to the murders of Mister Lau and his wife?"

"No comment."

"What about May Lau?"

"Again, no comment. Formal charges are pending. The investigation is ongoing, and there's a fugitive at large."

"How about off the record?"

Bud frowned. Then he took Conner's arm and walked him away from the group of doctors, nurses, patients, and visitors that were coming and going to and from the nurse's station. He took a deep breath and exhaled. Then he spoke quietly, barely above a whisper. "I know you and Echo are close. Skip has deep gratitude towards her. He owes her a debt he'll never be able to repay. By extension, I want to offer you every courtesy I can here. Maybe we can help each other?"

Cops and reporters often shared information off-the-record to help each other's careers and to solve cases or get breaking stories. When a relationship was built on trust and mutual respect, it could end up being a win-win for many years into the future. But the trust couldn't be broken, not even once.

"I'm all ears, Detective," Conner said. "You know I'm a reliable source for information that can help in cases and advancement. Don't just take my word that I'm trustworthy. Ask around. As long as I'm never asked to break my ethics—my personal code—I'll do what I can to help you in exchange."

"Fair enough," Detective Smith said. "Call me Bud, then." He put out his hand, and they shook. "The first thing I'm going to ask you is that you keep our relationship off the record and secret. I mean, even from Echo and Skip. I trust them both, but I want something I can rely on that's just between us. Is that agreeable?"

"Deal," Conner said. "Okay, so anything off-the-record you can share with me?"

"Yes. It looks like we'll be formally charging Kurt with two murders for hire and one murder, May Lau, for personal gain. That's tricky. It might become a lying-in-wait case, but either way, it's going to be a lot of time once the DA figures it out. On top of that, there's two guys that were found on the highway shot dead. We're presuming that was Hank's work. If so, then those murders will also be tacked on to Kurt, as part of an overall conspiracy, etcetera. You know, if he was doing a felony and someone else pulls the trigger, he's still on the hook."

“And what’s the felony he’s charged with in regard to the shootout? The way it’s being reported, Kurt and Hank were victims of a holdup?”

“Yes, the two men who attacked them were likely gang members. We don’t know, but we’re assuming that they were there lying in wait because of something learned through May Lau. If she made a deal with a gang to retrieve her stolen gold, then it gets complicated. The defense will claim that Hank and Kurt were just innocent victims.”

“But of course, they stole the gold. Can you tie them to that?”

“Yes. That’s something you can’t report right now. We don’t know yet what, if any, evidence is still in Hank’s possession. Once he’s in custody, well, then we’ll move forward with all the charges. In the meantime, we can tie Kurt to the gold, which is connected to May. No matter what happens, Kurt is going away for a long time. We just don’t have all the ducks in a row to charge him with everything we think he did. Hopefully, Hank gets popped soon. That will clear up a lot.”

“What can you tell me about the connection between Little Shanghai and all this mess?”

“Not much. We think May Lau was in contact with a group called the Golden Dragons, but we haven’t nailed down any hard evidence of that fact as of now. We don’t believe that the original murders had anything to do with the Chinese organized crime groups. It’s apparently all at the feet of these two brothers.”

“Assuming the fugitive is Hank Boyle, correct?”

"Yes, that's where we stand. It's not a gigantic leap to make, but until he's caught, it's just the most likely conjecture we have." Bud pointed down the hallway. "I don't know when they're going to release him. Probably in the morning. There will need to be some formal charges drawn up to get the ball rolling, but not everything will be clear until we get the brother."

Conner looked at his phone. It was set to silent and was vibrating. "I've got to take this," he said to Bud. "It's Echo."

Bud nodded and walked away, giving Conner privacy. He answered the call.

"Hello, I was—"

Echo interrupted with a snappy question. She was on speaker; he could tell by the echoing in the background. She seemed tense and distant. "I'm calling to find out if you've heard from the police about a case involving a guy who was shot this morning. You know the case?"

"You're talking about Kurt Boyle?" he asked.

"Yes. That's the one."

"The police aren't saying much. The gunshot wound wasn't fatal. He's still in the hospital."

"What hospital?"

Conner hesitated. He could feel something was wrong, but he wasn't sure. He decided to test her. "I'm trying to find out what hospital. It's maybe Fairview General, but it might be County. I'm looking into it. I can call you. What's up? How are you?"

"I'm peachy."

Conner tensed. That was their code word for a situation that was fragile and dangerous. Echo couldn't talk. Someone was listening to the call. "I'm looking forward to that dinner you promised."

"I can't today. I'm visiting my parents. They just got back from Belize, so I need to spend some time with them. But maybe next week. You'll call me if you get an update on the brother, right?"

Conner tried to imagine all the possibilities about how Echo could have found herself in trouble. He said, "Yes, I'll make some calls and get back to you." Then he hung up and rushed to the stairwell. He needed to get to Echo, and he assumed her mention of being with her parents was the truth.

He also reflected on her use of the word "brother." Had she meant that as a clue?

As he raced to his car, he realized that in his rush, he'd said nothing to Detective Smith about where he was headed. They hadn't exchanged their cell numbers yet. Echo's call had interrupted their discussion. He pulled out of the hospital's parking lot and attempted to get a call through to the nurses' station.

Eventually, a nurse took his call and explained that the detective wasn't available at the moment. "I need to get him a message," he said. "Please, give him this number." Conner repeated his number twice and then ended the call. He hoped Bud would get the message and call, but he wasn't even sure yet what situation Echo was in. He briefly considered calling nine-one-one, but if Echo thought that was a dangerous play, he didn't want to second-guess her. Not yet, anyway.

Fortunately, traffic was light, and Conner knew he'd make good time getting to the residence of the Sandersons. He wondered what waited there for him. "I guess I'll find out soon enough," he muttered to himself.

ONE HUNDRED

Echo felt time slow, and she watched Kurt Boyle's face grow darker.

He was pacing like a trapped and wounded animal. His demeanor grew angrier. "I'm going to kill all of you if my brother dies."

"Hold on, Kurt," Echo pleaded. "Please give it more time. Conner will call back. We'll find out where your brother is being treated. Even the police can't take him out of the hospital until he's stable. I'll even drive you, if you'd like."

"Your friend better call. And he better have good news." He aimed his gun at Edward and Didi. "Our specialty. Parents. Rich parents who don't really love their children."

"We love Grace very much," Didi said. "Please, let her go. We'll give you money or whatever you need."

"That's right," Edward added. "We can give you the cash we have, and I can arrange a bank transfer. Whatever you want. As long as you don't hurt our daughter."

"You came for me," Echo said. "Leave them out of this. I'll help you find your brother." Tears welled in her eyes as she realized how much different her situation was to May Lau's. She and her parents were fighting to save each other. They were all willing to sacrifice themselves because of their love for their family. "I'm sorry I brought this on you, guys."

"It's not your fault, honey," Edward said. "This man is responsible. Not you. Whatever happens, we love you. It's my job to protect you, and I wish I'd done a better job of it."

"You have, Dad," she said. Echo had always assumed that her parents were too self-absorbed to truly care what happened to her, but she realized she was wrong. They did care, and they were both willing to put themselves in harm's way to save her. They were her parents in every sense of the word. She turned to look Hank in the eye. "You don't have to hurt my parents to achieve what you want. I'll help you save your brother. I have an idea, but I won't help you unless I'm assured that my parents are safe."

"And how do you propose that?" he asked. "I'm not just letting them walk out of here."

"No," she answered. "I understand that. There's always a way. Just give me a few minutes to think about it. I'll come up with a plan we can all live with."

"You have ten minutes," he said. Hank sat down again, but he kept the gun trained on Didi. "Any funny business and your mom dies first. I still have the gun. I'm still in charge. Now you have nine minutes."

Echo put her face in her hands and considered her options. She had the knife, and if she attacked, she had the element of surprise. But as long as Hank's handgun was aimed at her mother, she couldn't make any sudden moves. Even if she stopped Hank, he'd surely fire once. He was too close to miss.

She opened her eyes and scanned the room. There were no obvious weapons. As time ran out, Hank started a count-down.

"You've got one minute left," he said.

"I love you both," Edward said. "If this is the end of my life, I'm happy to have spent it with the both of you." He took his wife's hand. Didi was whimpering. "Together at the end."

"It's down to thirty seconds," Hank announced. "I'm going to have to kill all of you. Echo, you lied. You don't have any plan."

Echo looked him in the eye.

"Ten seconds."

A loud metallic crash echoed through the house. A car alarm blared. Echo's heart pounded. She looked for signs that Hank was distracted, but he appeared unfazed. Then a sound caught everyone's attention. There was someone inside the house.

Hank looked up as a brief shadow appeared in the hall.

Echo jumped in one smooth motion. She came up with her knife as Hank turned his head away from the distraction and back towards her. The gun's path moved across Edward and Didi without firing, but he pulled the trigger as it came in line with Echo.

Her ears rang with the explosion.

As her adrenaline surged, Echo wasn't sure if she'd been hit or not. She continued her forward movement and stabbed him with a forceable thrust into the abdomen. She used her powerful leg muscles to lunge forward, pushing the blade upward. The gun fired again, this time into the ceiling. Her hearing was all but gone. All she was aware of was a loud buzzing. The acrid smell of gunpowder filled her nose. If she'd been hit, she couldn't feel anything. She pushed.

Hank stumbled backward. He fell, and his head smashed into the marble fireplace mantel. Blood spilled from his wounds.

Echo rushed to the gun and kicked it out of his hand.

He appeared unconscious.

The next few seconds flashed in a blink. Her father rushed to her, and Conner did the same. He was the shadow that had tipped the advantage to Echo and had allowed her to attack.

Lip reading because she still couldn't hear much; it sounded to her as if Conner was asking if she was hurt. Edward picked up the gun. It sounded like he said something like, "I'll make sure he's covered."

"Are you hurt?" Conner asked again. This time, she could just make out the words.

"I don't think so," she answered. She ran her hands over her body, feeling for blood. Nothing. She turned to her mother, who sat stunned like a baby deer. "Mom!" She smiled and said, "I'm okay, Mom. It's okay. We're okay."

Didi broke down, crying uncontrollably.

"Echo," Conner said. "We need something to secure—"

"I'll get some zip-ties," she said.

ONE HUNDRED-ONE

After ensuring Hank Boyle was still breathing and adequately tied up, Echo sat next to her mother.

"Mom," she said, taking her hand. "This is Conner."

"I must look terrible," Didi said. She wiped her eyes. "I'm a mess, I know. But I'm pleased to meet you. I'm sorry for the circumstances."

"This is standard procedure when you date Echo Rose," he said. "Everyone knows it's true."

"I've never known a reporter to get into so much trouble," Skip said as he entered the room. "I hope you don't mind me letting myself inside. The front door was wide open, and I could smell that someone had fired a gun." He holstered his weapon. "I guess Echo did my job."

"Our job," Bud said. "It's our job. Well, we'll get credit for the collar in any case. You want to read the guy his rights? Or should *I* do it?"

"He's going to need an ambulance," Echo said. "I don't know that he's even conscious yet."

"Oh, he's conscious, all right," Skip said. "I just saw his eyes move. It's the same trick his brother made."

Hank rolled over and groaned. "I'm bleeding, and I want my lawyer."

"Yeah, yeah, yeah," Bud said in a mocking tone. "'I want my lawyer'. I get it. First, before the lawyer, you need medical attention. But I'm going to read you your rights anyway, just in case you decide you want to talk about anything."

"Is my brother—?"

"Uh-uh," Skip said, shaking his head. "No talking until we read your rights."

Bud pulled out his laminated card and read off the Miranda Rights one by one. "Okay, do you understand all the rights I've explained to you?"

"Yes," he said. "I'm not deaf or stupid. Now, tell me, how's my brother?"

"He's just fine," Bud said. "He's got an all-expenses-paid reservation in the Big House for about five lifetimes. Now, tell me, which one of you pulled the trigger when—"

"Nope," Hank said. "No talking without a lawyer. I want a lawyer. You guys all heard me. I want a lawyer."

The detectives secured him with handcuffs and removed the zip-ties that Echo had used. "Well, this was a crazy turn of events," Skip said. "Echo, you want to explain how Hank Boyle ended up at your parent's house?"

Echo explained that she'd received a call from a stranger who wanted to meet her at the *Above the Fold* offices. "It must have been him," she said, pointing at Hank. "He had my number from May's cell phone."

"How'd you know to come?" Bud asked Conner. "One second, you were talking to me in the hospital, and the next, you're gone."

"I tried to leave a message at the nurses' station."

"Yeah, I got it. That's how I put all this together. I called you back about six times."

Conner looked at his cell phone. "Wow, you did. Sorry. I was so worried about Echo I didn't even look at my phone. Instead of thinking about anything else, I sped here like I was driving in a NASCAR race. It's surprising I didn't get a ticket."

"Most of the force was out looking for Hank," Bud explained. "I'm going to check in with the Sergeant and get him updated. Skip, you want to see who's outside on patrol to help secure the scene?"

"I got it," Skip said. "No problem."

A moment later, a pair of EMTs came in with a stretcher. Skip warned them that the man on the floor was highly dangerous. "Don't turn your backs on him for a second. Either me or my partner will accompany you to the hospital. He must remain securely handcuffed at all times. No matter what."

"You got it, Detective Malloy," the lead EMT said. "We've dealt with this kind before." They got right to work ensuring the prisoner didn't bleed to death. While working on Hank, the EMT asked, "Is anyone else hurt?"

"I think we're all fine," Echo replied. "At least physically. Thank you."

"We're all *peachy*, aren't we?" Conner asked. He smiled. "I was hoping you knew I didn't forget our code."

"I'd never use 'peachy' in my normal life," Echo said. "You can be sure if I use that word, the sky is falling."

Three and a half hours later, the last of the crime scene techs left the house. Conner had stayed for two hours of that. He had eaten dinner with the Sandersons, although not in the circumstances he or Echo had been expecting. He'd kissed Echo goodbye and whispered that he knew she understood how much he cared about her and was glad she was unharmed. "I've got to get this story in, or Frank's going to kill me," he said.

"It's understood," she said. "I'm going to sit with my parents a little longer, but then I have things waiting for me, too. I don't even know where to start."

"You'll figure it out," he'd said. "You always do."

ONE HUNDRED-TWO

Skip and Bud were still at the precinct at two in the morning.

"I guess we should call it a night," Skip finally said. "I'm seeing double."

"We've got enough here to keep the DA's office busy all morning," Bud said. "It's enough. We can fill in all the blanks tomorrow. With the evidence from the used car, even a rookie prosecutor would have a slam dunk case."

"No, you're right," Skip agreed. "There's enough here to get them on five murders." The car Hank Boyle had left outside the Sanderson residence had the remaining gold. Other evidence included their clothes, computers, and material for disguises and creating fake fingerprints. The weapon he'd been carrying might not be the same one used on the Lau's and May, but it was the same caliber. It was probably a match, but even without it, there was an overwhelming amount of evidence. And now it was clear to Skip and Bud that Ming Lau had written the symbol for "daughter" before she died, a silent implication of May Lau.

"Knock-knock," Steve Wong said. "I heard you guys might have wrapped up the whole Lau case. Is that right? A couple of Irish thugs with long criminal records?"

"That's it," Skip said.

"Well, I got two Golden Dragons in the morgue," he said. "Which is why I'm still down here trying to get a handle on things in the middle of the night. I need access to your guys as soon as possible."

"Neither one's talking," Skip said. "But you're welcome to give it a shot."

"Yeah, I figured," Steve said. "Well, another day at the office for me. Dead gang members and a bunch of craziness. I guess if it turns out these two jokers did the killing, and it's not a rival gang, then things will quiet down."

Skip told Steve what he knew so far from the evidence they'd gathered and a few things Echo had discovered in her not-so-legal online searches of social media and email accounts. The Boyle brothers were not in any way connected to any gangs or organized crime. They were a team, but they worked only with each other.

"In their luggage and through a computer search of a laptop we found, the techs have identified a couple of other cases, maybe three or four, actually. It turns out the brothers had a profitable assassin for hire business going. They'd find unhappy children from wealthy families and do contract killings on one or both of the parents."

"That's pretty cold," Steve said. "I'm still shocked an educated Chinese girl from an upper-class family with all the opportunities she had going for her would stoop this low. It's almost unbelievable."

"Almost. But it's true," Bud said. "I found it hard to believe myself. I never would have guessed that first night we interviewed May that she was responsible."

"Some people are like chameleons," Steve said. "They hide their true colors behind deception and fraud. It's sad but true. You cannot trust anyone. Not a soul."

"I wish it wasn't true," Bud said. "But I guess I agree with you. To a point."

"So," Skip said, wanting to change the subject, "what's the connection, if any, from this to the visit that Echo Rose got from the General? Do you know anything? She's not in danger, is she?"

"It appears that General Zhang was telling Echo the truth. He wasn't involved in the Lau killings. Of course, that doesn't mean he's not a murdering criminal who runs a brutal organized crime operation. It just means he wasn't playing false with Echo. He wanted her to stop investigating the idea that the Golden Dragons were involved with the Lau deaths. But, of course, it turns out they were contacted by May to get their gold back. Which was very naïve of her. If they'd caught the Boyle brothers without you two sitting there on a stakeout, they'd have probably got the gold, and May never would have seen an ounce."

"She wasn't very smart for someone so educated," Bud said.

"Nope. It happens. There's a big difference between street knowledge and book knowledge. They're two domains that don't always overlap. Thinking you know what's up when you don't on the street can get you very dead. Sadly, that's what happened with May. She got in way over her head. If she'd just cut her losses and not threatened the Boyles, they would have left town."

"She'd still be alive."

“But we might have caught her,” Skip said. “Maybe she’d be going to prison instead of the grave.”

“I’m sure you two would have caught on,” Steve said. “She made too many mistakes. Well, I’d better get out of here. Tomorrow morning is coming like a freight train.”

“One thing,” Skip said, “before you go. Echo is working on this story about potential sex trafficking and prostitution as it might relate to Little Shanghai’s organized crime, and possibly with this app she mentioned, I forget the name… Amanda’s something?”

“Secret,” Steve said. “Yes, I’m aware of it. There’re some sting operations going on right now. If you talk to Echo, tell her to be careful. She could expose the wrong person and get herself hurt.”

“You don’t know Echo,” Skip said. “If I tell her that, it’ll be like waving red meat in front of a tiger.”

“Okay,” Steve said. “I’ll keep my eyes open and let you two know if I see or hear anything I think could be bad for her.”

“We appreciate that,” Skip said. “She’s not just an important journalist to me, she’s a friend.”

Steve nodded and left the two detectives alone. The building was quiet at this time of night, at least when nobody was moving a suspect to one of the interview rooms.

“I guess tomorrow we’ll need to notify other agencies about the evidence we’ve found,” Skip said. “We might help clear another five or six murders.”

“Not a terrible week for the good guys,” Bud said.

“Nope, not bad at all.”

ONE HUNDRED THREE

Skip sat down at the table and inhaled deeply.

"I love that smell," he said.

"I made the pancakes," Lew Junior said.

"I helped," Lucy said. She pointed at one of the pancakes. "The burned one wasn't my fault."

"Was to!"

"Was not!"

"Was!"

"Wassssnooooot!"

"Okay, enough," Vivian said. "Both of you. Your Dad has been working really hard catching bad guys, and I've been breaking my back trying to get settled in this house. So, either behave or go to your rooms without breakfast."

"Yes, Mom," they both said.

"You're not going to try to sell us again, are you?" Lucy asked.

"Not if you're good," Vivian said. "But you're on the edge. Skip, more orange juice?"

"Sit down, honey," Skip said. "You need a break, I can tell. I'll get the juice." He went to the refrigerator and returned to the table with a fresh bottle. "I'm glad Robert helped us, you know, Vivian? It's nice being here and not an apartment."

"I'm glad your friend Echo and her parents are alive after what happened."

"What happened, Mom?" Lew Junior asked.

"None of your business, Little Man," Skip said. "It was just some police business we can't talk about. But, just know that me and Uncle Bud were heroes again."

Vivian laughed. "Your dad is sooooo modest."

"Hey, when you're a star," Skip said, "you've got to let it shine."

"You want another serving of bacon, Mister Star?" Vivian asked.

"Of course," he replied. "Catching bad guys uses up a lot of energy."

"Apparently, not for Bud," Vivian said.

"Maybe he's more efficient with his calories." Skip smiled and ate a strip of bacon off of Lew Junior's plate.

"Dad!"

"It was just one piece, son," he said. "I'll replace it."

"Okay. Can you believe I took a long shower, and I didn't run out of hot water?" Lew Junior said.

"And there's no leaky roof, no creaky floors, and the lights go on and off every time you flip a switch," Lucy said. "I like this house.

"You're gonna like *my* new house even better," Skip said. "Wait and see."

"You mean *our* house, don't you, honey?" Vivian asked.

"Yes, I mean *our* house. When our house is built, you'll see. It's going to be great."

"I really want all my Legos," Lew Junior said.

"I need my blue dress, Mom," Lucy whined.

"There are some games in this box. I need to find my cards, too."

"And I forgot," Lucy added, "I need a folder that's in the box with my homework file."

"Okay, that's it. Skip, call the Gypsies."

Skip smiled and pretended to dial his cell phone. "Yes, is this the best place to get good prices for two partially rotten kids?" He nodded his head and pretended to be listening. "Yeah, they can work with their hands. They're both hard workers, and they hardly ever talk back."

"Dad!"

"He's only joking," Lucy said to her brother. "You talk back all the time."

"Mom!"

"Just eat your pancakes, Lew," she said. "Don't pay attention to either of them."

As Skip put down his phone, it rang.

"This is Malloy," he said. He listened for a bit and then said, "Understood. On my way."

"Sorry, family," he said. "Me and Bud are up on the board, and there's a fresh case. The bad guys never seem to want a vacation."

"But Dad..." Lew Junior pouted. "You promised to help me with my homework."

"Sorry, Son. I know. I'll make it up to you. And you know my promises to help are always conditioned on not getting a call out. I have to answer the call. It's my duty."

"I know..."

"Sorry, Viv," he said, kissing her on the cheek. "I'll check in once I can." He walked back to their new temporary bedroom and dressed in a work suit. He strapped on his weapon and took his wallet and badge off the dresser. Because the garage was full of moving boxes, he'd parked in the driveway.

He felt a slight drizzle as he walked onto the street.

Another case, another rainy day, he thought.

ONE HUNDRED-FOUR

Echo Rose had turned in a professionally written article to *Soft Vanda* several days before she'd completed her next crime series article for *Above the Fold.*

Her obligation to the magazine and Courtney Bailey was over for good. She had no intention of going public with the data breach—and so far, nobody else had leaked it to the public. It was apparent, however, that certain files had made it to government officials. The burner cell that she'd given as her cover with HR at Amanda's Secret, as well as with the tech, Mouse, was destroyed and untraceable.

She was confident she was in the clear.

After her piece in the newspaper appeared, there was a shakeup inside the organized crime group headed by General Zhang. Roulan Fang disappeared. Her name was removed from the partnership of lawyers where Echo had first found it. The number she'd used when calling Echo was no longer accepting calls.

They brought the prostitute who was using the name Sally Lin into the precinct. After Conner and Echo interviewed her twice in the field, pretending to be customers, she agreed to talk to Steve Wong. He convinced her he'd help her get someplace safe, and they reached an immunity deal with the District Attorney's office in exchange for information.

The State Attorney's office, in a joint operation with the FBI, raided Amanda's Secret's corporate offices. They'd been given insider information about how Amanda's Secret's corporate leadership had turned a blind eye to prostitution and possibly to sex trafficking. The investigation was ongoing.

Officer Figus and his wife, Judy, had invited Echo out for tea. He'd given her a file that contained information about her birth parents. "This didn't come from me," he'd said, winking. "I called in a few favors and hope it helps more than it hurts."

Echo promised she'd keep her source a secret. She waited until she'd returned home that evening to review the contents. There were accident and autopsy reports, but none of the documents mentioned a baby. One document was mysterious. Someone, or some agency, had redacted most of it. The issuing agency was WITSEC. The Federal Witness Protection Program.

All names and addresses were blacked out. However, there was a signature at the bottom of the form, along with a typed name. *Juan Pablo Alvarez, US Marshall.* Echo wondered if he'd be able to provide any clues about what happened to her parents or how she might decode the mysterious books she'd recovered.

Her cell phone rang. It was Willem Kuiper. "Hello, Willem," she answered. "How are you?"

"I'm good, Echo. Any recent developments?"

"Yes, some leads, but I haven't had the time yet to track them down. I had several projects and deadlines to deal with."

"I wanted to talk to you. In person."

"Okay," she said. They planned to meet. Echo wondered what surprise was in store for her next.

When she knocked on the door, after parking on Elm Street in front of the now-familiar house, she felt a strange premonition. Something about this place, where her parents used to live, where she lived as a baby for a short time, made her feel like the past wasn't completely done with her.

"Come in, Echo," Willem said, after opening the front door.

Daffodil, on cue, rubbed against her leg. In the foyer sat a cat transporter, the kind used to take a pet onto an airplane. Next to that, sat a cardboard box. Written in black ink on the box were the words, *Daffodil's things.*

"Are you going on a trip?" Echo asked.

"Yes, I am," he said. "Amsterdam, in fact. I'll be gone a few months."

"Has Daffodil flown before?"

"No," he replied. "She hasn't. And that's why I wanted to talk to you." He picked her up and scratched her head. The bell that Echo knew had come from her mother dangled from her neck and softly rang out. "I wanted to ask you if you'd take her home. I think, well, it's hard to say, but I had a dream, and I believe your mom wanted you to have her."

Echo felt a tear slide down her cheek. She took Daffodil into her arms. "Are you sure?"

"I'm sure," Willem said with a smile.

Visit the author's website:
www.finchambooks.com

Contact:
finchambooks@gmail.com

Join my Facebook page:
https://www.facebook.com/finchambooks/

ECHO ROSE SERIES

1) The Rose Garden
2) The Rose Tattoo
3) The Rose Thorn
4) The Rose Water
5) The Rose Grave

THOMAS FINCHAM holds a graduate degree in Economics. His travels throughout the world have given him an appreciation for other cultures and beliefs. He has lived in Africa, Asia, and North America. An avid reader of mysteries and thrillers, he decided to give writing a try. Several novels later, he can honestly say he has found his calling. He is married and lives in a hundred-year-old house. He is the author of the Lee Callaway Series, the Echo Rose Series, the Martin Rhodes Series, and the Hyder Ali Series.

Printed in Great Britain
by Amazon

78431268R00242